TOMORROW'S
TOO
LATE

Sniper 1  *Security*

NE LTD
BECAUSE NAUGHTY CAN BE OH SO NICE®

By Nicole Edwards

The Alluring Indulgence Series
Kaleb
Zane
Travis
Holidays with the Walker Brothers
Ethan
Braydon
Sawyer
Brendon

The Austin Arrows Series
Rush
Kaufman

The Bad Boys of Sports Series
Bad Reputation
Bad Business

The Caine Cousins Series
Hard to Hold
Hard to Handle

The Club Destiny Series
Conviction
Temptation
Addicted
Seduction
Infatuation
Captivated
Devotion
Perception
Entrusted
Adored
Distraction

The Coyote Ridge Series
Curtis
Jared

The Dead Heat Ranch Series
Boots Optional
Betting on Grace
Overnight Love

TOMORROW'S
TOO
LATE

Sniper 1 Security

Book Three

NICOLE EDWARDS

Nicole Edwards Limited
PO Box 806
Hutto, Texas 78634
NicoleEdwardsLimited.com

Cover Image: © stokkete (35824588) | 123rf.com - © Brandon Seidel
(736338) | 123rf.com
Interior Image: © vectora (30401106) | 123rf.com

Cover Design: © Nicole Edwards Limited
Editing: Blue Otter Editing | www.BlueOtterEditing.com

ISBN (ebook): 978-1-939786-89-0
ISBN (print): 978-1-939786-90-6

Ménage Romance/ Romantic Suspense
Mature Audience

Breakdown of the KOGANS AND TREXLERS

Below is an outline of the families within this series.

THE TREXLERS (from Sniper 1 Security)
Parents: Bryce and Emily
Children: Ryan/RT (35), Colby (33), Clay (30), Marissa (28), Austin (26)

THE KOGANS (from Sniper 1 Security)
Parents: Casper and Elizabeth
Children: Conner (35), Hunter (35), Trace (30), Courtney (28)
Grandchildren: Shelby (Conner's daughter)

BRYCE'S YOUNGER BROTHER'S FAMILY:

Parents: TJ (Bryce's younger brother) and Stephanie
Children: Tanner (27), Kira (26), Evan (25), Dominic (24)

THE ADORITES (from Southern Boy Mafia)
Parents: Samuel and Genevieve
Children: Maximillian (31), Brent (29), Ashlynn (28), Aidan (27), Victor (26), Madison (24)

PROLOGUE

Five years ago

"I NEED YOU TO BE absolutely sure, baby," Hunter Kogan insisted, staring intently at the woman before him. She was so beautiful, so sweet. And too damn innocent for the likes of him.

But that didn't stop him. He wanted her with every breath in his body.

Hell, Hunter wanted her with a hunger he couldn't explain. Not once in all of his twenty-nine years had he met a woman who reduced him to nothing more than a primal heartbeat, a selfish male, hell-bent on possessing her in the most primitive way possible. She was the only woman he wanted. Had been since the day she stumbled into his world almost two years ago.

Danielle Davidson had stolen his breath and his good sense at the same time. And she was it for him. Or rather, he wanted her to be. Up to this point, Dani had accepted him for who he was. The good, the bad, the ugly. She embraced his world—the danger, the intrigue, even his kinks and various eccentricities. And yes, all of his sexual needs.

Those she knew about, anyway.

Truth was, he had never expected to find a woman who could understand him on that deep of a level, much less crave those dark, erotic desires as much as he did. As they sat there now, Hunter prayed she was going to accept *all* of him.

"I'm sure." Her tone was ripe with conviction, although her gaze was hesitant as it slid across the room to the man sitting on the opposite couch.

"I don't think you understand," Hunter whispered roughly, needing her to be doubly certain about what she was committing to. He didn't want to ask a million times, but he would if it was necessary.

Based on the desire in her honey-gold eyes, Dani had some idea of where this was heading, but Hunter knew she didn't quite grasp the full extent of what he was asking of her. It didn't matter that she understood him, seemed to accept his kinks were darker than most, and was eager to give in to him. What he wanted was something she'd never experienced before.

And damn, did he want it.

He wanted to pluck that innocence from her, to show her things she'd never dreamed about, give her the sort of pleasure that not many people ever experienced.

"I understand, Hunter. I do." She sounded so resolute.

"Dani…"

She cut off his rebuttal with a kiss, her tongue forceful as it pushed past his lips. She wasn't shy, but she never had been. Hunter figured it was her way of pretending she was far more experienced than she really was. They'd been sleeping together for a year and a half, and during that time, the woman had rocked his world. But what he was asking of her now was going to defy most people's basic logic, their own needs having never crossed certain boundaries.

He knew Dani didn't truly grasp what he was asking of her, but he was beyond pulling back, in desperate need of what he had sitting right here in front of him. What Dani was agreeing to, even if she didn't truly understand.

Hunter kissed her back, jerking her closer, thrusting his hands in her hair as he held her tightly. He swallowed her brittle cry at the same time he loosened his grip. He didn't want to hurt her, but she drove him past the point of control. No one had ever stripped him so completely of his good sense and his restraint. No one but Dani.

"God, baby," he murmured against her mouth. "I want you so fucking bad I *hurt.*"

It had always been this way with her. A frantic, raging hunger that consumed him from the inside out. He knew he was rough with her at times, but he couldn't help himself. He could never seem to get enough of her.

She was pawing at him, seemingly as eager as he was to get closer.

"Shirt off," he insisted, needing her to make the move, needing her to maintain the control she was so easily willing to give up.

Dani sat up, then jerked her T-shirt over her head. But she didn't stop there. She then reached behind her back and unclasped her bra.

At that point, Hunter couldn't keep from touching her. He forced the thin straps off her shoulders while he grabbed at her, needing to feel her skin against his palms. She was fire and heat and so fucking soft.

"Dani," he growled roughly. "Fuck, baby. I need you."

He saw the way her eyes darted to Josh, to the man watching them with more than a little interest in his emerald-green eyes.

"I need you, too," she insisted.

"I need everything," Hunter clarified, once again grabbing her head, holding her still, forcing her to meet his eyes. "Do you understand what that means?"

She tried to nod, but he stopped her, knowing full well she was clueless when it came to this. He could see it in the slight uncertainty in her gaze.

He had to spell it out for her.

"I want to share you, baby," Hunter stated roughly. "I want to share you with Josh."

Josh moved and once again Dani's attention shifted to him.

Hunter held her face between his hands, forcing her to look at him while he searched those brilliant amber eyes. "Do you understand what that means?" Her eyes remained locked on his face, so he continued, "I want to feel your sweet pussy gripping my dick while Josh buries himself in your ass. Do you understand what I'm tellin' you, Dani?"

Josh Lee was his partner, the man he'd been paired with at Sniper 1 Security, the elite security company his father owned and operated with his business partner, Bryce Trexler. But Josh wasn't merely someone Hunter worked with, he was also a man he shared everything with. In every sense of the word.

His eyes slid to Josh briefly. He was ready, eager, but holding himself back as he waited for Hunter to give him the green light. Hunter turned back to Dani. She was watching him, curiosity and need making her golden eyes brighter.

He leaned forward, brushing his mouth against hers. "I want to feel his cock slide against mine while we're both inside you."

Her eyes widened, but Dani didn't try to pull away.

Sure, he was trying to scare her, attempting to force some sense into her. She might want him, but he knew she couldn't possibly want every part of him. Not this part.

"But that's not all," he told her. "I want Josh to fuck your pussy while I slide my cock deep in his ass, Dani. That's what I want. I want to share you with him. But I also want to share him with you. Maybe not tonight, but one day."

"Oh, God…" Her moan was so sexy, filled with need, hunger, and a wealth of desire.

He could see the indecision in her eyes, knew she was processing what he was trying to tell her.

"I won't hurt you," he promised.

That was the truth. He would die before he ever hurt her. From the moment he laid eyes on her, he'd been captivated, completely awestruck. Not only by her otherworldly beauty but by her brains, her sense of humor, her desire for life.

He would even go so far as to say he had fallen in love with her. Although he hadn't told her that. He knew he couldn't until she accepted him for who he truly was.

He briefly cut his eyes over to Josh and offered a small nod, signaling Josh to come closer, to join them. While Josh walked around the coffee table, taking a seat on the wooden top directly behind Dani and between Hunter's spread thighs, Hunter kissed Dani, molding his mouth to hers. Her sweet mewls made his dick throb, his balls ache.

And just as he'd expected, the second Josh's hands were on her naked back, Dani stiffened. Her tongue slid out of his mouth and she was once again staring into Hunter's soul. He didn't hide anything from her. He loved the idea of Josh touching her, bringing her the same sort of pleasure Hunter could.

Hunter released her head, cupping her breasts gently. He tried to relax, not wanting to rush this, giving Dani a chance to either accept all that Hunter wanted to show her or to go running from the room. Either way, he couldn't force her to want this. But this was a part of himself he refused to deny.

At twenty-one, Dani was far too innocent for what he had in mind. He suspected she knew what he was asking, even if she didn't quite understand the logistics. During the eighteen months they'd been seeing each other, he had shown her several facets, but not the complete makeup. They were at a turning point. He wanted to move to the next level. Hell, he wanted to ask her to marry him. Only, she had to know what she was getting into if she said yes.

While he hefted the weight of her perfect tits in his hands, he rolled her nipples between his index fingers and thumbs, gently at first, then a little more firmly. He could see Josh sitting behind her, his hands sliding over her back, slowly working their way down her hips, her thighs, then leisurely grazing her silk-covered pussy.

"Oh," Dani moaned, her eyes wide as she glanced down to see all four hands were on her.

Hunter never looked away, willing her to accept this, to accept him. Them.

"I won't lie to you, Dani," he told her. "I care about you. Fuck, I'd go so far as to say that I love you, but this is who I am. This is what I need. I long ago stopped trying to kid myself."

Dani's nipples hardened between his fingers and she sighed when Josh began kissing her shoulder, moving closer as his hand slipped beneath her panties.

"Josh." A long, soft moan escaped her. "Oh, God, that feels…" Her eyes closed. Her breath hitched.

Hunter glanced down, loving the sight of Josh touching her so intimately.

"More… I need…" To his surprise, Dani spread her knees wider, giving Josh better access as she swiveled her hips, attempting to force Josh's hand where she needed it.

"Oh, fuck, baby," Hunter groaned, pleased by her acquiescence. "This is everything I've ever fucking wanted."

In fact, *she* was everything he'd ever wanted.

And he was about to have her just the way he'd dreamed.

DANIELLE DAVIDSON KNEW THAT HUNTER—the man she loved with every ounce of her being—didn't believe her when she said she understood. Then again, she hadn't been telling the truth exactly, so she couldn't necessarily blame him. She didn't understand this. Not at all.

Two men, one woman. Touching, kissing, sharing. It didn't make sense. It defied her basic understanding of the intimate act of sex. It went against everything her mother had told her about how a man was supposed to love a woman.

That didn't stop her body from responding, craving what Josh was doing to her with his hands while Hunter touched her, too. It was surreal, almost as though it was happening to someone else. She wasn't sure where this would go from here, but she had heard what Hunter said.

He wanted to share her with Josh.

He wanted to share Josh with her.

That meant Hunter wanted to claim them both.

As simple as it sounded, Dani was having a hard time grasping the concept even though there was no denying the heat consuming her as they touched her so intimately. Based on everything she'd ever understood about sex and love, this defied the norm. It was erotic, hedonistic, lascivious.

It wasn't natural.

Or hell, maybe it was, and she still had a lot to learn.

But she knew that Hunter wasn't simply inviting Josh into their bed—or on the couch as was the case here. He was telling her that this thing with Josh was more than recreational sex. It was fueled by Hunter's deep desires.

But he'd told her that he loved her. Almost. It wasn't the most romantic way he could've said it, but she'd heard it in his voice. He wanted to love her, but he needed her acceptance.

Could she?

Was this something she wanted? Something she could come to crave the same way he did?

"Oh, God." Her body tensed as Josh's finger slipped through her slit, one finger delving inside her, her pussy gripping it, her body igniting into a firestorm of need and desire. Perhaps it wasn't natural, but it felt so damn good. She never wanted this to end.

It was true, Dani didn't have a lot of sexual experience. Every ounce of what she did have came from the time she'd spent with Hunter. He hadn't known she was a virgin when they made love the first time and she'd never had the guts to tell him. In truth, she didn't think it really mattered. But over the course of the last eighteen months, she had learned the true meaning of pleasure. Hunter was more than experienced, and he had shown her things she had never imagined.

Somehow, he'd caused her to crave everything he did to her. Whether he was rough or gentle, he was always so focused on her pleasure and she'd never known sex could be quite so amazing.

And now this…

Whatever was happening here, she wanted to say it didn't feel right, but God, that was a lie. It felt so freaking good. How could this not be okay? The way Josh's warm, smooth hands glided over her skin, his thick finger penetrating her, while Hunter continued to fondle her breasts, making her moan. It was intense, sensual. And she found her body responding in kind. She was greedy for their attention, desperate for them to quench the ache building inside her.

"Turn around, Dani," Hunter instructed, his heavy-lidded eyes meeting hers.

She nodded, knowing she would need his help. For one, she was straddling Hunter's legs while Josh sat behind her. She was practically crushed between them. If they wanted her to move, they would have to move first.

Josh seemed to understand, because his warmth disappeared from her back while Hunter shifted her so that she was still sitting on his lap, this time facing Josh.

Without words, Josh took each of her feet and planted them flat on the cushion, his big hands curling around her ankles, which effectively bent her knees and spread her legs wide. This time Hunter's fingers were the ones that slid down between her thighs, grazing her pussy, first over her panties, then under. The man had magical fingers and just the slightest graze of them had goose bumps forming on her skin.

"Kiss him," Hunter rumbled in her ear. "I want to watch you."

Josh leaned forward, but he didn't initiate the kiss. It was clear he was waiting for her, and if Dani wanted to kiss him, she was going to have to make the effort. She had no idea why, but she did. She wanted to feel his mouth on hers, his hands. Maybe she was going crazy. Or maybe she was so blinded by the feelings she had for Hunter that she was willing to do whatever he wanted.

Reaching up, Dani put her hand on the back of Josh's head and guided him closer. He came willingly, allowing her to kiss him before he took control, thrusting his tongue into her mouth. His lips were softer than Hunter's, his kiss different, not nearly as hungry, not quite as reckless, but still potent. She slid her fingers in his silky dark hair, and just like that, her body ignited. She wasn't sure she was supposed to want this, but it was clear her body did.

Hunter growled, something primitive and fierce, the vibration from his chest thrumming against her back. It made her pussy clench around his fingers.

"Oh, fuck, baby," Hunter whispered, thrusting two fingers deep inside her. "You like this, don't you?"

"Yes," she said honestly. She liked it a little too much.

"I want to watch you suck his cock," he said, his words wrapping around her. "I want you to suck his dick while I fuck your pussy. Can you give me that, Dani?"

He was grinding his erection against her ass, her pussy filled with two of his fingers. If he wasn't careful, she was going to come.

Josh pulled back, staring at her, heat in his emerald eyes. She could see the question there, knew he was waiting for her to give him the go-ahead.

"Yes," she whispered, reaching for the button on Josh's jeans.

Before she could get a grip on him, the two men took control, relieving her of her panties, shedding their own clothing. While Josh perched naked and waiting on the arm of the couch, Dani crawled forward, eager to take him in her mouth. She felt incredibly wanton. The gleam in his eyes spurred her on. The instant her lips wrapped around the thick crest, Hunter groaned from behind her. It was a wild sound, laced with approval and lust.

While she sucked Josh's cock, working him with her tongue, she felt Hunter behind her, the shift of the cushion, his legs brushing the insides of hers. In one slow thrust, he filled her. But it wasn't enough. Dani needed more. She needed everything, just like Hunter had asked for.

Hunter seemed to know what she craved, because he grabbed her hips, holding her still as he impaled her again and again. She could do nothing but offer her mouth to Josh while he drove his cock past her lips. They were in complete control and she didn't deny them. She didn't want to.

Dani tried to hold on. She tried desperately but it was too much. Her insides coiled tighter, warmth pooling deep in her core until it ignited an electric current that sparked every nerve ending.

"Hunter!" She cried out his name over and over as she came, her body racked with glorious, infinite pleasure that made her muscles weak, her breaths choppy.

She'd never been fucked liked that.

Josh pulled her head back down, his cock filling her mouth. She was sucking him furiously, desperate to give him the same intense feeling the two of them had given her.

"Fuck, yes!" Hunter slammed into her once more before she felt him pulsing inside her. "I'm coming, baby."

Josh's hand tightened in her hair as she felt him swell in her mouth seconds before he came. "Fuck, Dani," he groaned. "Your mouth is so damn sweet."

And then, as quickly as it had started, it was over.

She felt an odd tranquility wash over her as Hunter pulled her into his arms. They fell back onto the couch, Hunter spooning behind her. Dani didn't know where Josh disappeared to, but he didn't come back for several minutes. And when he did, he was dressed. To her surprise, he slipped out the front door and into the night.

"Dani?" Hunter whispered as his fingers trailed down her arm.

"Hmm?"

"You okay, baby?"

"Yeah." And surprisingly, it was the truth.

"You can't tell anyone. You know that right? People wouldn't understand."

No, they wouldn't. He was right about that.

"I won't say a word," she assured him.

Dani was good at keeping secrets.

After all, this wasn't the only one she was keeping.

Nor was it the biggest.

ONE

Five years later
Thanksgiving Day, 2016

DANIELLE COULDN'T BELIEVE SHE'D ALLOWED Max to strong-arm her into coming to this stupid dinner. She should've told him to go to hell, but that would've been rude. Not that she was opposed to being just that, but when it came to Max, she tried to refrain. So, rather than turn on the one person who had been keeping an eye on her since she'd returned to the States months ago, Dani had come up with a way to make this a win-win for her.

It also helped that she'd timed her arrival perfectly, avoiding the dreaded family dinner. Thankfully, it looked as though they'd already finished that portion of this evening's hellish activities.

Because Max had married Courtney Kogan, Dani had known there would be more than Adorites in attendance at this family get-together. More accurately, Courtney's brother Hunter would be there, and by showing up, Dani would appease her cousin, then, by approaching Hunter, she could, in essence, kill two birds with one stone.

Admittedly, now that she was here in Max's house, it seemed some of the nagging determination she'd harbored recently was waning.

Chin up, she mentally ordered. She could do this. She *would* do this. And once she'd spilled the beans to Hunter, she could get back to this life she'd just recently returned to, without all the guilt she'd been carrying around with her.

Despite her little pep talk, Dani was tempted to turn around and run out the same way she'd come in. With all the critical eyes tracking her as she moved across the room, the simple thing to do would be to disappear.

Again.

But … if she did that and caved to what would clearly be the easy way out, there would be no way to get her life back. It was bad enough that Samuel Adorite had been dead for a year now and Dani had yet to stop hiding completely. As far as she was concerned, she'd been on the run for long enough; it was time to stop and face the music. The threat to her was no longer, now that the old bastard was dead.

Okay, so that wasn't entirely true. However, if the horrific secret they'd been keeping was buried with him, then yes, she was finally free.

Well, almost. She still had to confess her reasons for hightailing it out of Dodge four years ago, but once that was done, she would be in the clear and able to move on. And this Thanksgiving meal was the perfect place to show the world that she was no longer putting miles on her Manolos. She'd picked this particular event for a reason. Namely because there were so many people. Here, she could confront Hunter Kogan and not risk having him go postal on her. She hoped.

Then again, Dani didn't even know if Hunter would speak to her after what she'd done to him all those years ago. And she couldn't blame him if he didn't.

Now that she thought about it, they'd been in a setting much like this one.

Only instead of a festive holiday dinner, it had been a wedding.

Hers.

And his.

Talk about coming full circle.

Since a wedding required vows, hers didn't quite qualify, because they'd never made it that far. Nope, that'd been the day she'd chickened out, running far and fast from the one and only man she'd ever loved.

It'd been easier than living a lie, or so she told herself.

"Dani?"

Turning at the sound of her name, Dani came face-to-face with Hunter's mother and father, Casper and Elizabeth Kogan. They were looking at her with wide-eyed wonder, as though she'd come back from the dead.

In a way, she kind of had.

"Mr. and Mrs. Kogan," she greeted politely, her voice trembling only slightly.

"We're so glad you could make it," Liz replied, but Dani could see it for the lie that it was.

They were more than likely trying to figure out why she was there. How she fit into this whole fiasco. They definitely weren't happy to see her, but she hadn't expected any less. She'd done the unthinkable, leaving the man she was supposed to marry—who happened to be their son—at the altar and not contacting him even one time since.

If only they knew who she really was, why she'd come into their lives in the first place … they certainly wouldn't be smiling at her now—fake or not.

"I'm glad I could, too," she lied.

Because Max had insisted—the man was probably unable to make a request—that she attend, Dani had known how things would turn out. And because of the guarantee that she would be face-to-face with the one man who probably never wanted to see her again, Dani had opted not to seek Hunter out earlier than now. This might've been the family's holiday celebration, but Dani was using it for her own agenda. As a way to see Hunter, to convince herself that what she thought had been the love to end all had only been a figment of her imagination. Plus, to free her conscience by admitting to him the truth. Or most of it, anyway.

"It's good to see you," Dani told Liz and Casper, desperately wanting to get away from her once-future in-laws. After all, Casper was the head of Sniper 1 Security, as well as a trained military sniper, and she didn't doubt that he could probably single-handedly take her out before she ever made it across the room to her intended target.

Not that he would.

Hopefully.

"You, too," Liz whispered, staring after her as Dani headed off to make her way around the perimeter of the room.

She scanned the crowd, noticing Hunter's brother Conner and Conner's daughter, Shelby, sitting together on one end of the oversized cream sofa, along with RT and Z on the opposite end. She took a moment to give the two men a cursory glance. Seeing them together brought back a memory of two different men and a very sexy night from so long ago. A night she would never forget for as long as she lived. It'd been the night she'd moved out of her comfort zone, trusted the man she'd fallen in love with, and experienced sensations she'd never even imagined possible.

A night that she would never have again.

Shaking off the thought, Dani took stock of the room. Others had started to move in, some seated on Max's furniture, several standing around, looking as uncomfortable to be there as Dani imagined them to be. These were two families who were on opposite sides of the law. Yet somehow they managed to coexist, or so it appeared, despite what Samuel Adorite had been up to all those years ago.

Dani caught sight of Courtney and Max, walking into the kitchen, hand in hand.

As good as it would've been to see some of her old friends again—if they would even talk to her—Dani hadn't come here for that. She wasn't looking for friends from her past. She was looking for one man in particular.

As though magnetized, her gaze swung to the far corner of the room, closest to the floor-to-ceiling windows near the back entrance.

And there he was.

Hunter Kogan.

Her heart did a strange little jump kick in her chest, but she ignored it.

God, he looked good.

Six foot one inch of prime alpha male sporting dark jeans that showcased his impressive ass and a crisp white shirt that accentuated his broad shoulders and wide back. As though he sensed her looking his way, Hunter turned. She could practically see his white-gray eyes glowing from where she stood. His light brown hair was a little longer than before, shaggier, his face a little more weathered, but he was just as ruggedly handsome as he'd always been.

Without stopping to chat with anyone else, Dani snaked her way through the people, glancing toward the kitchen briefly to ensure Max wasn't watching her. So far so good. He was the last person she wanted to run into at the moment, but only because their relation was supposed to be a secret. Only she knew that it was just another lie in a long list of them that'd been put in place over the years. Max might've believed that Dani was his first cousin, but she knew the truth.

However, she was only willing to divulge so much information.

Which she would do. Tonight.

But she needed it to be on her terms.

HUNTER KOGAN DIDN'T NEED TO be damn good at his job to know that the proverbial shit was about to hit the fan. He'd felt the prickling at the back of his neck for several minutes now, and though he'd scanned the room, searching for a threat, he'd already suspected what he would find.

And sure as shit, the threat was real, only this one was a woman—oftentimes far more dangerous than any top-secret mission he could be sent on by his family's security firm.

This particular woman decidedly so.

His cell phone buzzed in his pocket and he pulled it out.

Principal has arrived at the party. She had no issues walking right in.

The final confirmation of what he'd suspected. Danielle Davidson at Max Adorite's home. An invited guest, apparently.

Rather than respond to the agent he'd been using to follow Dani around since she'd miraculously reappeared in town several months ago, Hunter tucked his phone into his pocket. Although sneaking out the back door was ideal, he managed to remain motionless, pretending not to be affected by the determined chick who was making her way across the room toward him.

Truth time. He knew it. She knew it.

He hated it. Based on the extreme look of discomfort on her face, she did, too.

Good. At least they were on the same page.

Fuck.

But why did it have to be here? Now?

Even from across the room, he recognized that resolute gleam in her golden eyes. She was on a mission, and those sexy legs were carrying her right to her intended target.

Maybe he should run.

Though it was long overdue, Hunter suddenly didn't want to talk to her, didn't want her to share with him the reason she'd fucked his world beyond repair years ago. He didn't want to know the truth. Her version, that was. He didn't want to know anything at all. He simply wanted to continue pretending to be blissfully ignorant, drinking his Corona, talking to his brother, and acting as though he didn't know the sinfully beautiful woman whose attention seemed to be focused on him. The same sinfully beautiful woman who'd left him at the altar four goddamn years ago.

The same one who had crushed his heart into fucking dust.

Danielle Davidson. Max Adorite's fucking cousin.

Yeah. She thought no one knew that little secret, but he certainly did.

"You've got incoming, bro," Trace muttered in warning before turning away from Hunter and leaving him standing there, completely vulnerable.

Asshole.

"Hunter."

The sound of his name on her lips was very much as he remembered. For fuck's sake, he still heard that raspy tenor in his dreams.

Not by choice.

Opting for polite—this was his sister's home, after all—Hunter met her gaze. "Danielle," he replied, tipping his beer bottle to his lips as he peered down at her. "Surprised to see you here."

"No, you're not," she countered hotly, her eyes belying her frustrated tone.

What he saw in those glittering gold eyes wasn't animosity. If he didn't know better, Hunter would be inclined to believe she actually felt bad for what she'd done to him, leaving without ever looking back.

Too bad he did know better, and he wasn't falling for it again.

Setting his empty beer bottle on the tray of a passing waiter—a *waiter*, for chrissakes, at a family dinner—Hunter grabbed Dani's arm, pulling her deeper into the corner. Even with her in those five-inch heels, he towered over her and he needed that. Anything to give him the advantage. Bending down, he went nose to nose with her, refusing to inhale, not wanting to be reminded of how fucking good she used to smell.

"What the fuck are you doing here?"

Her eyes widened, but she didn't flinch. "We need to talk."

Hunter was tempted to laugh in her face, but he managed to refrain. "Talk? You're a few years too late for that, aren't ya, sweetheart?"

Dani frowned, and Hunter could feel that vise on his heart tighten.

She was the very reason he'd spent the last few months out of the country again, working any assignment that would keep him as far from here as possible. *Here* being anywhere she was. He'd known she was coming back, known she was planning to seek him out, and no matter how hard he tried, he hadn't been able to avoid the inevitable. Hence the reason he'd assigned Kye Sterling to keep an eye on her for the past few months. Hunter had been apprised of her whereabouts for three very long, very painful months.

And here she was, ready to chat.

He wasn't going to be her goddamn whipping boy this go-round. He didn't give a shit about her trying to get out from under the weight of her conscience, either. And damn it all to hell, seeing her now, he had anger boiling in his veins. But along with that, there was something else.

Longing.

Stupid fucking bastard.

Yep, he was, and arguing with that stupid-ass voice in his head wasn't going to make a damn bit of difference.

"Whatever you have to say," he began, keeping his tone hard, "I don't wanna hear it."

"I think you do," she said simply.

Hunter stood to his full height, glaring down at her as he studied her face. "Why here? Don't you know this is supposed to be a family event, Danielle?" A family she'd decided she didn't want to be part of. "Don't you have even a little respect for *my* family?"

Another frown creased her beautiful face, and he almost felt a measure of remorse. Almost.

"You're not an easy man to track down," she replied.

No, probably not. But that'd been on purpose. He didn't bother telling her as much; he assumed she already knew he'd spent the last couple of months avoiding this exact scenario.

"Get on with it," he urged. "But first, I need another beer."

Without worrying about social etiquette, Hunter walked away from Dani, making a beeline for the bar. No one other than Max Adorite would have a fucking bar in his house, complete with hired help to man it. After placing his order, Hunter stood there, resting his forearms on the sleek wooden top while he tried to calm his nerves. Part of him wished he'd simply invited Kye to be here with him tonight. It would've made this a little less painful.

Or maybe not.

After nodding to the bartender when he delivered his Corona, Hunter downed half of the beer, wondering just how many of them he'd need to make it through this conversation without wanting to put his fist through the wall.

A quick glance behind the bar and Hunter figured there wasn't enough liquor in the place to make this easy on him.

No matter how much he wished there was.

Casting a glance at Dani over his shoulder, he noticed she seemed deflated. As though she was lacking the bravado she'd had moments ago.

"What is it?" he questioned roughly, turning to face her.

"You know what?" Dani shook her head. "Never mind. This was a bad idea. A *really* bad idea. No matter what I say, you're still going to hate me."

He considered probing her for details, but she was right. He didn't need to hear them. It wouldn't change a thing, so he admitted as much. "You're right. Nothing you can do or say will ever change the way I feel about you. Nothing."

Her eyes widened, and this time Dani flinched, as though the heat of his words had been a physical blow. As with her excuses, he didn't care how he affected her. She'd earned his anger, his disdain, his … hatred.

Dani's mouth opened but then closed quickly. Hunter forced himself to stay rooted where he was, glaring back at her, daring her to say something.

With a nearly imperceptible nod, Dani squared her shoulders, spun around on her heel, and left the same way she'd come.

Hunter should've been relieved, only he wasn't. He had to remind himself that Danielle Davidson was his past, and he damn sure didn't have room for her in his future.

No matter how much … he really didn't hate her.

KYE STERLING WALKED IN HUNTER'S front door a little after midnight. He'd been surprised to see Hunter's Yamaha YZF-R1—one hell of a sports bike—out front. He figured the party would've lasted well into the morning hours. That was how family get-togethers at Kye's folks' place normally went, anyway. Back before his parents' world came crashing down when Kye's baby brother died. Toby Sterling's life had been taken far too soon at the age of nineteen. At that point, family functions had ceased and Kye and his four older sisters were left making their own way. Which they all seemed to have done. Separately.

Nope, the Sterling family didn't celebrate Thanksgiving or Christmas together much anymore. They chose to send cards and texts, but rarely did they try to meet up. As much as he wished it didn't bother him, it did. He very much missed his family, longed for that sense of normalcy he'd once known. Granted, without his brother, it wouldn't have been the same, so maybe it was for the best.

When he stepped into Hunter's living room, Kye noticed the house was dark, which likely meant Hunter was passed out. The guy slept like the dead. Since Kye had only come by to give the man a sit-rep on Danielle Davidson's progression after she'd left the party, waking him up wasn't necessary. Kye would simply grab a bottle of water, lock the door behind him, and catch up with the man in the morning.

Silently setting his keys on the side table by the door, he started for the kitchen. Maybe he could have a beer. Hang out here for a little while. Come morning, Hunter would never even know he'd been there.

From his left, a throat cleared, and instinct had Kye pulling his SIG Sauer .45 from the holster on his side. The pistol fit perfectly in his hand, an extension of himself. He peered into the darkness and made out the form of a man on the couch.

"Fuck, Hunter. Announce yourself, would ya?"

"Come here."

Oh, hell. Kye knew that tone. Hunter was in a mood—something Kye had long ago gotten used to.

And yes, maybe this was the real reason Kye had opted to do a face-to-face with Hunter tonight, instead of making a quick phone call. He'd had a feeling Hunter'd had a shit night and Kye wanted to be here to help him sort it out.

Kye set his SIG on the counter separating the kitchen from the living room, then headed toward the couch. Before he could even get there, Hunter was on his feet. Strong arms banded around him, firm lips crushing to his. The man tasted like beer and need and, yes, fury. Hunter was in rare form.

Although Kye had five inches on Hunter, it always seemed the man had all the control. Perhaps that was because Kye preferred it that way. He allowed Hunter to back him against the wall while warm hands wandered beneath his shirt.

"I need you naked," Hunter growled, his calloused hands sensually scraping Kye's chest. "Right fucking now."

Kye knew there would be time for talking later. He'd learned that trying to talk Hunter down from the proverbial ledge was the equivalent of interrupting a toddler during a temper tantrum. It usually only made things worse.

Hunter made quick work of removing Kye's shirt as well as his own. When their bare chests came together, Kye groaned, loving the feel of Hunter's skin on his. The man was getting bigger, more defined. His chest was cut to perfection, all hard angles. Clearly, he was spending time in the gym, likely trying to compensate for whatever was lacking in his life.

Rough hands tore at Kye's jeans. Instead of helping Hunter, he merely leaned back against the wall and waited. He knew he would be rewarded eventually and Hunter always liked things his way.

"You want to tell me what happened?" Kye figured it wouldn't hurt to *try* to talk.

"*She* fucking happened," Hunter barked, dropping to his knees in front of Kye.

"She— Aww, fuck." Hunter's lips circled the engorged head of his dick and Kye lost his train of thought. He reached for Hunter's head, twining his fingers into his thick, dark hair and holding him there. "Oh, fuck. Your mouth's so fucking hot."

Hunter wasn't gentle, but Kye was used to that, too. The man bobbed up and down on Kye's dick, sucking him hard enough to draw a long moan from deep within. Kye fumbled on the wall, searching for the light switch so he could see. When he finally found it, he flipped it on, bathing the room in bright white light.

Seeing Hunter on his knees in front of him... "Holy fuck."

But it wasn't merely the sight of his dick tunneling in and out of Hunter's lips that caught Kye's attention. It was the heat and anger that burned in Hunter's light gray eyes. The man was in rare form tonight, angrier than Kye had ever seen him.

Apparently, Hunter was done with the foreplay part of tonight's events, because he surged to his feet once again and slammed his mouth down on Kye's. He wasn't about to fight, because he craved Hunter. Any way he could have him. The man was moody on a good day, so this wasn't a surprise. Nor was his reasoning. There was only one woman who had the ability to push Hunter to his breaking point.

"How did it go with her?" Kye asked when Hunter began sucking on his neck. Not that he really cared to know. At least not right now.

Hunter pulled back and looked into his eyes. The molten silver was glowing hot and bright. The man looked downright lethal. Not to mention horny as hell.

Rather than answer, Hunter grabbed Kye's arm and pulled him toward the counter that separated the kitchen from the living room. Kye had enough warning to put his palms down on the granite top. Before he could turn around, Hunter was at his back.

"Take your jeans off," Hunter commanded.

Kye managed to shove them down and even toed one boot off, but that was as far as he got when Hunter's hand landed in the middle of his back, forcing his chest down onto the counter.

"I need your ass," Hunter growled. "So fucking bad."

Kye relaxed when Hunter forced two fingers inside his asshole. Thankfully the guy'd had the sense to have lube on hand. Evidently, he'd been planning this.

Those fingers didn't linger for long, but it didn't matter. Kye was ready for him, eager even. He enjoyed Hunter's meltdowns, especially when Hunter wanted to fuck him senseless. In the beginning—nearly three months they'd been doing this—he'd been stunned. Now, he expected it.

Hunter's cock breached his ass and Kye took a deep breath, pushing against the intrusion. The man was big and hard and not at all gentle as he withdrew before slamming in again.

But heaven help him, it felt so damn good. Better than any sex he'd ever had.

"Fuck, yes," Hunter hissed. "So fucking tight. So goddamn hot."

Hunter's palms gently ran up Kye's back and he knew the man was reining it in. He always did. Shifting so he could use the counter as leverage, Kye forced Hunter to take a step back. When he did, Kye thrust his ass against Hunter's hips, urging him deeper.

"Oh, yeah," Kye groaned, desperate for more.

"You like that?" Hunter's voice was coarse as his hand fisted in Kye's hair, pulling his head back. "You like when I'm rough with you?"

Fuck yes, he did. But this wasn't rough. Hunter was just getting started.

"Don't go easy, damn it," Kye hissed. "Fuck me…hard." The last word came out on a grunt when Hunter rammed his hips forward, impaling Kye on his cock.

Hunter obliged, hammering into him, one hand gripping Kye's hip firmly as he did, the other tugging on his hair, just the way Kye liked it. The only thing Kye could do was hold on. He allowed Hunter to use his body and he enjoyed every second of it.

"You're gonna make me come," Hunter announced.

Kye reached down and palmed his dick, stroking roughly while Hunter continued to plow into him over and over, harder, deeper. So fucking deep.

"Aww, damn. That's so good," Kye muttered, feeling his release building. It wouldn't take much to send him over, but he had to wait for Hunter.

"Goddamn," Hunter ground out. "Kye… Fuck…"

When Hunter roared his release, Kye let himself go. His breath slammed into his lungs, his heart beating a rapid tattoo in his chest. It took him a few seconds for the world to stop spinning and for his legs to steady.

As he stood upright, preparing to talk to Hunter about what had happened tonight, he noticed Hunter wouldn't look at him. He didn't make eye contact, which was the first clue that something was seriously off. More so than usual.

"Hey," Kye said softly.

Hunter still didn't look at him. Instead, he grabbed his clothes and walked right out of the room, mumbling, "Lock the door when you leave," as he did.

Okay, so he was apparently going to play it that way, huh?

And that part—the cold shoulder. Yeah, Kye damn sure didn't care much for it.

Not one fucking bit.

TWO

Fifteen months later, February
Present day

"I WON'T LIE TO YOU, Dani," Hunter told her. "I care about you. Fuck, I'd go so far to say that I love you, but this is who I am. This is what I need. I long ago stopped trying to kid myself."

Dani's nipples hardened between his fingers and she sighed when Kye began kissing her shoulder, moving closer as his hand slipped beneath her panties. Only it wasn't supposed to be Kye in his dream. It should've been Josh, he knew, but he couldn't seem to change it.

Hunter glanced down, loving the sight of Kye touching her so intimately.

To his surprise, Dani spread her knees wider, giving Kye better access.

"Oh, fuck, baby," Hunter groaned, pleased by her acquiescence. "This is everything I've ever fucking wanted."

The shrill sound of the phone ripped Hunter from his dream, bringing forth his stark reality. He was lying naked on his bed, covered in sweat, the blankets somewhere on the floor. His heart hammered against his ribs while his chest expanded, blessed air filling his lungs.

Hunter inhaled deeply, groaning on the exhale as he peered over at the nightstand and grabbed the offending object.

"Son of a bitch."

His hand clutched the phone, threatening to crack the case, but he refrained. Barely. He threw the damn thing across the room, none too gently, settling somewhat when it hit the wall and bounced to the floor. No way could he talk to RT right now. Hell, he couldn't talk to *anyone* right now.

His chest hurt from the pain of knowing he was awake, that the world he was living in was not the same as it once had been. This world, it was dark and gray. He spent his waking hours stumbling through, hating every second, most of the time wishing he didn't even exist.

All because of her.

Hunter had no fucking clue why this damn dream wouldn't release him from its brutal clutches. It had been more than a year since he'd seen Dani on Thanksgiving, definitely long enough for him to move on with his life. But no. It couldn't be that easy for him. For the past fifteen fucking months, he'd relived it over and over every time he closed his eyes.

The phone rang again, but Hunter pushed himself up and got to his feet. He dragged his sorry ass to the bathroom. He needed a shower and some coffee. Maybe then he'd be able to deal with whatever the hell RT—or anyone else, for that matter—wanted.

Until then, they could all go fuck themselves.

Something had to give. Hunter couldn't keep having this damn dream. It had started as Dani and Josh, a memory of that long-ago night when they'd started down the path that had ultimately changed his life. But Josh was dead, and Dani was gone. Their ghosts shouldn't still be haunting him. But they were.

Except, in recent months, the damn dream had morphed into something else entirely. As more days passed, the memory of Josh was fading from his mind, replaced by a man Hunter knew he had no business dreaming about.

A man, no matter how hard he tried, he couldn't seem to get out of his head.

The same man who was currently asleep in his bed.

*

"For fuck's sake, RT, I'm walkin' in the door now," Hunter hissed when he answered his phone, at the same time stabbing the button for the elevator.

"Good," RT stated firmly. "Because I think you'll wanna be here for this."

"Be here for—"

Hunter didn't even get the chance to ask what RT was talking about before the call ended.

"Asshole." He glared at the blank screen, then shoved his phone in his pocket as he stepped in the elevator. A minute later he was walking into the lavish lobby of Sniper 1 Security.

His mother had decorated this space, her goal to give it a masculine, professional feel. She'd succeeded with the rich wood-paneled walls and various paintings to go along with the dark furniture and plush carpeting. Hunter used to love walking into the office; now he dreaded it.

"Good morning, Hunter," Jayden Brooks, Sniper 1 Security's receptionist, greeted with a sweet smile. "I didn't realize you were back in town."

"Not for long," he said, keeping his eyes focused on the door that would lead to the back offices.

"Well, it's good to see you."

"Yeah, thanks. You, too," he grumbled back, then opened the door that would lead to the inner sanctum. He bypassed the few agents sitting in the bullpen but managed a nod when someone called out a good morning.

It wasn't a good morning. The look on his face should've told them that.

Hunter headed right for the conference room. When he turned the corner to step inside, he heard Ryan Trexler release a breath.

"What's so fuckin' urgent that you have to start callin' me so fuckin' early?" Hunter griped.

"Good to see you, too." RT's tone was polite, respectful, just as it always was.

For a fraction of a second, Hunter felt bad for being such an ass.

That passed quickly.

RT's attention dropped to his laptop. "In case someone didn't inform you, we don't hold regular office hours around here. Some of us have been here since before dawn."

"Some of us are idiots," he countered.

"That we are," Conner confirmed when he stepped into the room behind Hunter. "Glad you could grace us with your presence."

Hunter glared at his older brother, then glanced back at RT. "What's the urgency?"

"Have a seat," RT instructed. "We're waitin' on someone."

"Who?" They knew Hunter didn't like surprises.

"You headin' back out, Con?" RT asked Hunter's brother, his gaze never leaving his laptop screen.

Obviously they weren't going to bring Hunter up to speed.

Assholes.

Conner shook his head. "Wasn't plannin' on it. Gonna stick around the house for a while. Need to take care of some shit. Spend some time with my kiddo."

Hunter knew exactly what Conner meant. Being close to home was sometimes a necessity. Although his brother had just come off a short assignment in Florida, Hunter was finally getting used to being in one place for any length of time. As it was, Hunter had been focusing on out-of-country assignments, until a year and a half ago. It all started as a way to put off the inevitable encounter with Danielle, something he'd been trying to avoid if at all possible. Since that was no longer an issue thanks to their brief encounter the Thanksgiving before last, he had no reason to continue the escape-and-evade bit. He knew Dani was still in Dallas, but she seemed to be avoiding him as much as he was avoiding her.

Just the way he wanted it.

"I figured at sixteen, Shelby didn't want to have much to do with her old man," RT replied with a grin.

"Yeah, well. When I don't give her a choice, not much she can do about it," Conner told him with a chuckle.

"Regardless, I'm glad you're gonna stay put," RT muttered, grinning. "We could use some help around here." RT's head lifted, his eyes focusing on Hunter. "Now that you've got a permanent stateside address, I'm gonna have to give you some more responsibility."

"Do it and I'll be back on a plane." It was the same threat he made any time RT joked about giving Hunter something to do. It wouldn't have been an issue if RT wasn't referring to partnering up with him to run the family business. No thank you.

"Seriously, we're gonna need a few warm bodies."

Hunter knew that wasn't true. They had more than they could possibly want these days. If it wasn't for the fact that they'd recently acquired a relatively small, flailing security firm, Hunter might've believed it. As it was, they had a shit ton of new employees they were trying to place into new positions.

RT's gaze lifted, darting between the two of them. "Don't think I'm joking. All these toddlers need some serious training."

The toddlers being the new agents they'd acquired.

"I nominate Trace," Hunter and Conner said in unison.

"Where's Kye?" RT asked Hunter, obviously choosing to table this topic for later.

"I'm not his fuckin' babysitter," Hunter offered by way of answer. He had done his absolute best to avoid Kye as much as possible for the past year. Not that it was working since the man was still in his bed when he'd left a short while ago, a mistake Hunter continued to make about once every two or three weeks.

Considering the awkward tension between them, Hunter was still trying to figure out how to deal with that situation. Although Hunter had spent the past year and a half doing his best to push Kye away, to send the man running in the other direction, it didn't seem to be working. Kye just kept coming back for more. One of these days, Hunter was going to have to cut him loose, but he couldn't seem to bring himself to do it.

Truth was, Hunter was an emotional wreck and Kye was just what he needed. Simple, sexy, and so fucking eager. Hunter was still trying to set his world to rights, but he wasn't having much luck. It seemed the more he tried, the more he managed to fuck it all up.

The phone on the conference room table buzzed, drawing all of their attention. With a flick of his wrist, RT hit the button.

"What's up, Glue?"

"RT, your first appointment is here," Jayden Brooks, a.k.a. Glue, announced from the phone's speaker.

Hunter didn't move from his position against the wall, nor did his brother Conner, who was sitting in one of the high-back leather chairs.

"Send him back," RT instructed, obviously knowing who was dropping in on them.

"Who's here?" Conner asked, his dark brows making a V on his forehead.

"Max Adorite," RT replied easily.

Christ. Just what they all needed today. A run-in with Hunter's brother-in-law.

"What's goin' on?" Hunter asked because clearly RT wanted to make them squirm.

"I thought maybe you could tell me," RT countered.

"How the hell should I know?"

"Your sister's married to the guy," RT reminded him unnecessarily.

"She's *his* sister, too," Hunter argued, pointing at Conner. He couldn't help but smile as he said it.

"Maybe he wants to invite us over for Easter. Since, you know, Christmas was such a riot," Conner noted, propping his booted feet up on the table and leaning back in his chair. Why the hell was he getting comfortable?

The room went silent as they waited for the new arrival. The only sounds were the soft hum of the heater from the vents above, along with muted chatter going on outside the room.

"Max, you're being ridiculous. We really don't need to be here."

At the sound of the familiar voice, Hunter's ears perked up. He knew that voice. He knew it, and he loathed it. Never mind the fact that he still fucking *dreamed* about it, too.

He cast a quick glance at the windows in time to see Max, Leyton, and…

Fucking shit.

What the hell was she doing here?

40

"Well, *this* oughta be interesting," Conner mumbled, glancing at Hunter over his shoulder.

RT got to his feet when Max stepped into the room. Holding out his hand, he greeted the other man formally. "Good to see you, Max."

"Sorry to drop by on such short notice, but I really need to have a chat with you." Max's tone was firm, his eyes focused solely on RT.

"Not a problem." RT motioned toward the other chairs at the table. "Please, have a seat."

Hunter made no move to leave. He was too damn curious as to what the fuck was going on to even push off the wall. He could almost understand Max being there. After all, the guy was married to Hunter's sister, Courtney. He even understood why Leyton Matheson would be since the guy was Max's second-in-command.

But *her...*

Max took a seat, but Leyton opted to stand behind him while Dani took the chair beside Max. Hunter noticed she was doing her damnedest not to look at him.

"We really don't need to do this," Dani whispered to Max.

"We definitely do," Max countered, his attention once again returning to RT.

RT glanced between the two of them. "What can we help you with?"

Max cleared his throat. "As you might recall, we had some issues a couple of years back."

Issues? The guy's entire life was one big clusterfuck of issues. Ones he brought upon himself. That tended to happen when a man was in the fucking mafia.

RT raised his eyebrows in question.

"The incident with Ashlynn," Max added, not going into detail.

Incident?

Hunter barely managed to hold in a snort of derision. That's what the guy wanted to call his younger brother, Aiden, nearly getting beaten to death, his sister's house coming under fire, and two of her bodyguards getting a lethal dose of lead? Talk about understatement.

RT leaned back in his chair and studied Max. "I remember."

"Well, because of that, I've come to need your services."

RT nodded, obviously encouraging Max to continue.

"I'd like to acquire the services of Sniper 1 Security in an official capacity," Max clarified.

"Max," Dani scolded. "It's really not necessary. Not for me, anyway."

Max held his hand up to silence her.

"To do *what*, exactly?" Conner asked, still leaning back with his feet propped on the table. Hunter knew his brother was feeling anything but casual.

"For personal protection."

Hunter couldn't resist glancing over at Dani, wondering what role she played in all of this.

RT didn't miss a beat. "For whom?"

Max nodded toward Dani.

Silence settled over the room as though everyone was expecting some sort of bomb to go off.

And then it did.

"For my cousin, Danielle."

Hunter stood up straight, the pain in his hip shooting straight down his leg, but he ignored the fire that licked at his nerve endings. The news wasn't something that shocked him as much as hearing Max state it aloud. It was the first time they'd copped to the relation publicly.

Conner's feet dropped to the floor as he launched to his feet, his hands landing on the table with a resounding thud. "You wanna repeat that?"

Right. Conner wasn't privy to the information Hunter had. In fact, no one in his family was. Well, no one other than Hunter's father, Casper. But they'd agreed long ago that they wouldn't share the details unless it was necessary. Apparently, it was necessary.

Never looking away from Dani, Hunter felt the moment those caution-filled eyes lifted to meet his. As always, there was a hint of a challenge there, but he noticed something else … Regret, maybe?

"You're a fucking Adorite?" Conner blurted, his angry glare directed at Dani.

Hunter had some sympathy for his brother. He'd already gone through this rage-induced meltdown when he'd originally dug up the information. At that point, it all made sense. Dani showing up in their lives, the quick romance and easy acceptance of him, the rush to get to the altar… She'd been playing Hunter all along. The same way Hunter's father had used Courtney against the Adorites.

As though he hadn't just officially rocked the foundation of their entire fucking world, Max continued to speak to RT, ignoring Conner's outburst completely. "In recent weeks, we've come to learn of a new threat to my family."

Only one? Hunter knew better, but he kept his mouth shut.

"At this point, we've heightened security as best we can," Max continued. "I've got people watching my brothers and sisters as well as my mother. Unfortunately, there are only so many people I can trust within my circles right now, and I've come up short. I need your help to protect Dani."

"From who?" Conner asked.

RT was business as usual, ignoring Conner and focusing his attention on Max. "Are you referring to twenty-four-hour personal protection?"

"Of course."

"For how long?" RT inquired, tapping the keys on his laptop.

"That's undetermined at this time."

"Is there an actual threat or merely concern for one?" RT's ice-blue eyes lifted to meet Max's.

"It's real. And it's serious."

"Care to elaborate?" Conner inserted.

Max spared Conner a quick look. "No, I don't."

"I will," Dani offered.

"Oh, now you wanna have a conversation," Hunter muttered under his breath, glaring at the woman who had devastated him all those years ago.

Someone cleared their throat, but Hunter didn't pay attention to who it was.

He didn't give a shit.

WASN'T THIS LOVELY?

Hunter, Conner, and RT all together in one room. Just the guys she was hoping to *never* see again.

Damn it.

From the second Dani had stepped into the room to find three of the men who likely hated her most in the world, she knew this wasn't going to be pretty. She didn't want to be here as it was, but having to have this conversation while Hunter was trying to kill her with a look… Well, to be honest, she'd rather be anywhere else.

As a matter of fact, she'd rather face this so-called threat head on than have to deal with Hunter.

"Enlighten us, honey?" Conner snapped, his glare hot enough to set the smoke detectors off.

Dani decided to speak to RT because he seemed to be the only sensible one in the bunch.

"Max is being irrational," she explained, wishing she could've talked Max out of this long before they got to this point. Sure, she had tried, but Max was the most stubborn man she'd ever met. Well, aside from Hunter, of course.

"Irrational?" Max questioned, his tone as calm and cool as ever.

God, she hated that he could do that. Her nerves were fried, her palms were sweaty, and Max looked as though he'd just walked off the set of a magazine cover shoot. There was no doubt that Dani hadn't acquired the gene that gave her the ability to remain cool in the face of opposition like others in her family.

But she could do this. She *had* to do this.

She had finally settled back into a regular routine, working on getting her life on some level of normal, and here she was, once again being forced to address the fact that someone was likely trying to kill her.

"Yes, irrational," she confirmed. This was the second time in as many weeks that they'd had this conversation, and quite frankly, Dani was getting tired of having it. Only this time Max had gone too far. She had fallen for the ruse, though, agreeing to meet with him this morning to figure out what their next steps would be. The instant she realized they had pulled up to the Sniper 1 Security offices, she'd thought about running the other direction. "I don't need protection."

"The hell you don't," Max snapped. "Everyone in my family needs protection."

Okay, so she'd provoked a sliver of emotion that time. Enough that Dani turned her full attention on Max. She tried for reasonable. "It's over, Max. Marco Moroso is dead. He's no longer a threat to you or the family. I don't see why we have to assume otherwise."

"Moroso?" RT inquired. "The mobster?"

"Yes," she confirmed, never looking away from Max.

Max shook his head as though he couldn't believe what she was saying. It was true. Marco Moroso—loser that he was—had been taken out at Max's insistence after the man had put a hit out on Max's sister, Ashlynn. Max had gone so far as to kidnap Sabrina Moroso and her young son as a bargaining chip. And yes, Max had lived up to his word, releasing Marco's sister and her son once the guy was no longer a threat. But that was years ago and as far as she could tell…well, the threat had died with Marco.

Not that anyone in this room needed to know the minute details, but Dani knew that even if Dennis Moroso was out of prison and looking to take over the family business, he wasn't going to get very far. No one respected the man. No one.

However, Max seemed motivated to believe otherwise. He was convinced Dennis was a threat.

Hence the reason they were there, apparently.

"One of you can try to talk some sense into her if you'd like," Max muttered.

"We would if we knew what was goin' on," RT acknowledged, leaning back in his chair and regarding them casually. "Why don't you bring the rest of us into the loop?"

Dani had heard that RT had pretty much taken over the company in recent years, stepping up when his father, Bryce, and Bryce's partner, Casper, opted to retire. RT seemed to be doing rather well for himself. Plus, he knew how to command a room, because all eyes went to him.

"You heard about the judge who was murdered last week?" Max prompted, his attention still fixed on RT.

"Erik Roberts?"

Okay, so clearly RT was up to speed on local politics.

"One and the same. He was the Place Six judge for the Court of Criminal Appeals," Max clarified, his gaze darting her way before swinging back to RT. "He was on our payroll."

Payroll schmay-roll. More like Ashlynn was blackmailing the old goat because of his cocaine addiction, but whatever.

"And someone figured that out?" Conner grumbled, his disdain for the conversation apparent.

"Yes." Max glared at Conner. "And they took him out for it. Because of that, plus a large sum of money exchanging hands, Dennis Moroso, Marco's younger brother, was set free, his conviction overturned."

Which Dani knew, in their world, meant Dennis was taking control of the Moroso family and likely looking to establish the same territory Marco had been after. Unfortunately for them, the territory was spoken for. By the Adorites.

"And he's out for revenge," RT stated, clearly understanding.

Dani glanced down at her hands, which were clasped tightly in her lap. She fought the urge to pick nonexistent lint from her charcoal slacks. Although she wasn't looking at him, she knew Hunter's eyes were pinned on her. She could feel the heat from his gaze.

"Why the fuck should we protect her?" Conner asked, speaking directly to Max. "The woman lied about who she was. In fact, she led us to believe she had absolutely no family."

It was true, Dani had told them that. Back when Hunter's family had been planning their wedding, she'd had to lie and say she had no family, no one who would be there to witness the special occasion.

"Conner," RT said softly. "Leave the past in the past."

Dani continued to stare down at her lap.

"Fine," Conner conceded. "Then why is this Moroso brother a threat?"

Max snorted, as though the question was ridiculous. In a way, it was. These people had to know what Max was up to. There was no way they didn't. For the past year, Dani knew they'd been involved in some of the things going down with the Adorites. Even if they didn't want to be part of it, they were.

Not that they were happy about that, but everyone knew that family trumped all when it came to the Trexlers and the Kogans. And like it or not, the Adorites and the Kogans were now family. Ever since Courtney Kogan married Max Adorite.

RT cleared his throat and Dani peeked up at him from beneath her lashes. He was looking between her and Max, but for the life of her, she didn't know what was going through his head.

He obviously realized Max wasn't going to elaborate when he said, "I can assign someone to keep an eye on her. Although I'm a little light on agents at the moment."

Double damn it.

"I'll do it," Conner offered, shifting forward and setting his elbows on the table.

"The hell you will," Hunter countered hotly, causing Conner to lean back in his chair, swiveling around to glare at his brother.

Dani twisted in her chair to see the two men face off with one another. Hunter was a big guy, coming in at six one, but Conner was a little bigger. Not by much. Still, with Hunter standing, he seemed invincible.

"I didn't figure you wanted the job," Conner said softly, though it was loud enough for everyone in the room to hear.

"I don't." Hunter's white-gray eyes slid to her briefly. Dani saw the hatred.

"Like I said," Conner noted, "I'll do it."

"I don't care who does it," RT inserted, "however, I will need one of you to lead another job I've got coming up."

Both men glanced over at RT.

"You two decide who takes which job."

Hunter shook his head, then stared at Conner. "I'll take this one. You can pick up whatever else RT needs."

RT's voice was concerned when he said, "You sure about that?"

"Positive."

"I'm not sure that's a good idea." Dani figured she'd offer her two cents, although she doubted anyone would listen.

RT glanced at his computer. "Right now, Ms. Davidson, I don't have many options, unfortunately."

Dani knew she wasn't going to win this. Not right here with all the testosterone pulsing violently in the room. She needed to get Hunter alone so she could talk him out of this. Surely if she explained that Dennis Moroso wasn't a threat to her, he'd see things her way. Maybe then he'd tell them he was keeping an eye on her and then go about his business.

After all, she didn't believe Moroso was a threat. Not to her. However, there was something she had to do and an extra set of eyes on her wasn't going to make it any easier. Moroso might not be after her, but she feared someone was. Only she wasn't in a position to tell any of them about it. Not until she figured it out herself.

"Can I have a word with you?" Conner asked Hunter.

Hunter's eyes landed on her once more before he nodded to his brother and turned to leave the room.

Yep. Coming up with a compromise was a much better plan than to have Hunter pissed because he had to play babysitter.

Now, she just needed to get away from Max and, ultimately, away from all this nonsense.

KYE WANDERED INTO THE SNIPER 1 building with a smile on his face. "Good morning, Glue," he greeted the pretty receptionist.

"Good morning, Kye," she said sweetly, her strawberry-blonde curls scattering around her face when she pivoted to look at him. "I didn't expect to see you here today."

"Just came in to get another assignment," he admitted.

"Well, I can tell you they need someone to take control of the newbies," she told him. Her voice lowered to a conspiratorial whisper. "From what I heard, these guys and gals need some range time."

Kye knew she was referring to the men and women they'd acquired when they had absorbed CISS, a small security firm that had been going under financially. It had taken a while to get the logistics worked out, but they had finally managed to seal the deal. It hadn't been a huge surprise that S1S would want to expand. Considering CISS had specialized mostly in corporate security, it allowed Sniper 1 to expand its portfolio.

"How many?" he inquired, curious.

"All of them." Her huff was cute. "If I have to listen to RT moan and groan about them one more time…"

Kye laughed. "Well, I'm sure I can handle the task." He glanced at the door that led to the back offices. "Hunter here?"

Jayden nodded. "Yeah. He's in a meeting with RT and Conner."

That explained the early phone call that had woken Hunter and set him on a rampage this morning.

"You know who they're with?"

"Max Adorite," she whispered as though that was a bad word. "And Hunter's ex-fiancée."

Danielle Davidson was in the building?

Kye suddenly realized he needed to find a place to hide. As it was, Hunter had been having Kye keep tabs on her, and the last thing he needed was to blow his cover in the event Hunter wanted him to continue doing so.

"If we're lucky, the building'll still be standing when they're done," Jayden noted before turning her attention to the phone now ringing on her desk. "Good morning. Sniper 1 Security. How may I direct your call?"

While she was occupied, Kye slipped through the door and darted into the break room. Unfortunately, it wasn't empty.

Claire Donovan, Sniper 1's most experienced hacker, was adding sugar to her coffee. She gave him a quick glance and a smile. "Morning."

"Mornin'," he replied, peering out into the bullpen.

Claire turned toward him. "Hiding from someone?"

He laughed it off, hoping it didn't sound forced. "Nope. Not me."

"Right." She didn't sound convinced. "Don't worry. I'm sure Hunter's not going to chase you down right now." Claire nodded toward the door. "He's currently in a meeting with his ex. I'm sure he'll be preoccupied for a while."

That or on a homicidal mission. Although Kye wasn't privy to what had gone down between Hunter and Dani, he'd put a few things together on his own. One, the couple had been in love. Two, they'd been set to get married. And three, Dani had disappeared before that could happen.

Despite the gossip that ran through this office like a raging case of the flu, there wasn't much talk about Hunter and the woman he'd been set to marry all those years ago. Kye was a little fuzzy on the timeline. From what he gathered, Hunter met Dani eight years ago, started dating her roughly six months after that, which had led to him asking her to marry him six years ago. Roughly a year after that, she didn't show up for their blessed nuptials, disappearing off the face of the planet. Then, fifteen months ago, she reappeared, wanting to clear her conscience, but had chickened out at the last second.

Yep. That was what Kye had figured out on his own because no one else was forthcoming with information. In fact, he got the feeling no one talked about it for fear of enduring Hunter's wrath personally.

"You know why they're here?" he asked, trying to make casual conversation as he headed toward the coffeepot.

"Not a clue. But Max is in there with them."

Maximillian Adorite was Hunter's brother-in-law, and Kye was well aware that Hunter wasn't a member of the man's fan club. As a matter of fact, Kye would go so far as to say that Hunter despised the man who had married his sister.

As he took a sip of his coffee, his phone rang. He yanked it from his pocket and glanced down at the screen. He smiled.

"Hey, Mom," he greeted, moving closer to the door so he could peer out. "What's up?"

"Just checking in," she said sweetly. "I was thinking about you this morning."

"Yeah?"

"How did that assignment go? The one where you were keeping tabs on the cheating husband?"

Aw, shit. He hated that he had to lie to his mother about what he did, but the last thing he wanted was to have her worried about him. She spent so much of her time worried as it was, never having gotten over the fact that Toby had died. Which was the very reason Kye played down what he did, leading his mother to believe he only handled cheesy PI cases—scorned spouses, jealous husbands, that sort of thing.

"Yep. All done. Got some pictures and the wife's divorcing him."

"Well, that's good. I think."

The sound of a door slamming shut had Kye jerking his attention toward the bullpen. That was his cue to find someplace to disappear to. No way did he want to risk being seen by the elusive Danielle Davidson. Not if he expected to be assigned to follow her again.

And the truth was, he was really, really hoping for that chance.

"Hey, Mom. I'm gonna have to call you back."

MAXIMILLIAN ADORITE KNEW WALKING INTO this that he was going to have his hands full. Not only with his cousin Danielle, but also with the man she was in love with.

Oh, he wouldn't make that accusation to her face, because he knew Dani. She would go into immediate denial, claiming to hate Hunter with a passion that rivaled all. But Max wasn't an idiot. He could see it on her face. The woman was still in love with that man, even all these years later. No matter what she claimed.

Max knew that his crazy fuck of a father had enlisted Dani's help in spying on Casper Kogan. He'd planted her in the Kogans' world when she was still a teenager. As far as Max knew, Dani had never revealed any damaging information to Samuel, but he knew for a fact Dani had despised Max's father for putting her in that position. Especially since she'd fallen in love with Hunter.

Max didn't particularly like involving Sniper 1 Security in his personal business, but according to his wife, he didn't have a choice in the matter. Well, *technically* he did, but not if he wanted to keep her happy. And keeping Courtney happy was of the utmost importance to him, so here he was, seeking assistance from his in-laws.

Even acknowledging it left a bitter taste in his mouth.

It wouldn't have been necessary if Max had time to restructure his organization to handle Dennis Moroso, the most recent threat to his livelihood. It had actually been on Max's agenda to do just that, but it was no longer a possibility after what had transpired last night. Specifically, the gun fight that had taken place. Since a member of Max's security detail had been gunned down outside his own house, Max knew time was of the essence. Dennis was acting quickly, not sitting back and giving Max time to put anything in place. It was what Max would've done.

Since the Morosos were apt to make things personal, Max knew he had to step up his game. And quick. Which was the only reason Max was looking to his wife's family to assist. He honestly didn't think that Dani was in immediate danger from Dennis, considering Max had worked hard to keep her off everyone's radar. Thanks to her father sending her to France after her mother died, and the drastic efforts to keep her separated from the Adorite name for most of her life, the majority of Max's associates and enemies didn't know she was his cousin. Max wanted to keep it that way. She was a hell of a lot safer on the outside.

Unfortunately, it appeared someone had been doing some digging into Max's family as of late. He knew for a fact that Dani's relation to him had been leaked, but he didn't know who was responsible. Still, it meant he had to treat Dani as he would any of his brothers and sisters. He needed to know she was safe so he could come up with a plan to take down Moroso.

Max knew that with Hunter handling the situation—the guy wouldn't have let anyone else handle this, no matter how aloof he pretended to be—Dani would be protected. He had assumed—correctly—that Hunter's decision would not go over well with Max's little cousin, but at this point, he didn't really care. There was a tangible threat to him and his family and the most important thing was keeping them all safe. After the bullshit that had gone down with Marco Moroso two and a half years ago, Max wasn't willing to take any chances.

In all fairness, Max's goal was twofold. Not only would he know Dani was being protected but it would keep the Kogans and Trexlers looking the other way. Something that Max desperately needed at the moment.

When the two brothers stepped into the hallway, Max watched RT carefully. He'd known before he arrived that RT would agree to take the case because he was a good guy. There was a lot of tension between Max's family and the Kogans and Trexlers, but in the end, they would do whatever necessary to protect the innocent. And Dani was an innocent, even if she had been a pawn in Samuel Adorite's twisted game a time or two.

With a resigned sigh, RT got to his feet.

Max prepared himself to wait.

This would work out for the best if he remained patient. Not one of his strong suits, no. But he could do this.

For his wife.

THREE

"YOU SURE YOU WANT TO do this?" Conner asked after he dragged Hunter into the hall.

Hunter knew it was Conner's obvious attempt to have a side conversation, but it wasn't necessary. He appreciated his brother's concern, but Hunter was over Dani. This was business and if RT wanted to take Max's dirty money, there wasn't much he could do about it.

Hunter took a deep breath and nodded. "I'm fine. It's just a job."

It was the only answer he could give for several reasons. One, he had no intention of leaving Conner alone with Dani for an indefinite amount of time. Call him stupid, but he couldn't deny the underlying jealousy that had reared its ugly head when Conner made the offer. And two, if Dani's life *was* in danger, that was his job. Protect by any means necessary. That was their company motto, and Hunter was man enough to ignore their past if it meant keeping her safe.

That's what they were paid for.

The door opened, and RT stepped out into the hall. He looked at Hunter, then Conner, then back again. "Problem?"

"No. No problem," Hunter assured him. "I'll take the assignment. And I'm bringing Kye in as backup."

That earned him a curious look from both Conner and RT. Hunter shrugged it off. It didn't matter that Kye had been the only partner Hunter had taken on since Josh. For the past few years, Hunter had purposely avoided as many jobs as he could that would require him to work with anyone else. And he had his reasons for doing so. Mainly because he didn't want to chance getting close to someone. And also, because he didn't trust himself to watch someone else's back when he didn't even give a shit about his own.

However, this would allow Hunter the opportunity to set Kye straight and deal with his past at the same time. And when it was over in a few days, Hunter could move on with his life.

Plus, he and Kye both needed something to do, so this was a win-win.

And that much was actually true. After having spent the past few months sitting on his ass while RT attempted to convince Hunter that he needed to step up and help him take over the company, Hunter wasn't looking forward to twiddling his thumbs while he waited for someone to assign him a job. He had absolutely no intention of becoming a desk jockey, but he was having a hard time convincing RT of that.

This was the perfect chance to get back into the swing of things here on US soil and not have to deal with the concerned looks from his family.

RT frowned, but thankfully he kept his feelings to himself. Everyone knew how Dani's disappearance had affected Hunter, but in his defense, he was over her. Had been for years.

Or so he told himself.

Nodding toward the door, Hunter signaled for them to go back in. The sooner they got this over with, the faster he could get on with his life. Perhaps this was just what he needed. A few hours where he could get answers to the three dozen questions he wanted to ask Dani, starting with why the fuck she hadn't told him she was a goddamn Adorite all those years ago.

"Looks like it's settled," RT announced when they stepped back into the conference room. "I assume you want to implement this today?"

Max nodded as he got to his feet.

"Good, then we'll let you work out the logistics," RT stated, nodding toward Hunter.

"If you need anything or have any questions, let me know," Max said, his statement directed at Hunter.

"Will do." He doubted he would need anything more than Dani's address so he knew where he needed to be. Twenty-four-hour protection would require him to be at her house and her place of business.

It dawned on him that he didn't know what she did for a living. You know, besides lure in prey and pretend she wanted to marry them. Back when they'd been together, Dani had been good with computers. Maybe she worked in an office.

"If at all possible, you should get her out of town," Max noted.

"You could always take her to the beach house," Conner stated. "It's private and easy to keep an eye on. Plus, it's empty right now."

"I like that plan," Max said, as though he had any say in what Hunter chose to do.

"No," Dani stated adamantly. "I'm tired of running. If I have to have a babysitter, they can watch me at home."

Max didn't seem impressed with her argument, but the man held his tongue on the subject. "I'll take you home," he told Dani. "And I'll stay with you until Hunter arrives."

Hunter could tell Dani still wanted to argue, but she clamped her mouth shut and nodded, not making direct eye contact with anyone.

"I'll need an address," Hunter added. "You can leave it with RT, and I'll get it after I go home and pack a bag."

"Pack a bag?" Dani's eyes widened, her gaze cutting to his quickly. "Why do you need to pack a bag?"

"If I'm gonna keep an eye on you day and night, I can't do it from here, sweetheart."

Her eyes narrowed, and he knew she didn't appreciate the term of endearment, which was fine with him, since he'd meant it in a derogatory manner.

"I don't think it's necessary," she snapped.

"Oh, it's necessary." Rather than hash it out with her, Hunter said his goodbyes and turned for the door. When Dani called after him, he pretended not to hear.

Right now wasn't a good time for him to have a conversation with her.

He had promised to do a job, which he would. But she wasn't going to get any more than that. Not from him, at least.

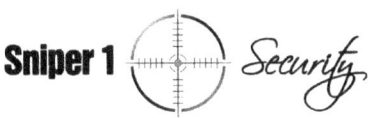

KYE ANSWERED THE PHONE AS soon as he saw Hunter's name come up on the screen. "What's up?"

"We've got a job," Hunter said, his tone hinting at his distaste for that fact.

"Fan-fucking-tastic." Kye hurried toward his truck in the parking garage, wanting to be a good distance from the building before Dani or Hunter came out and found him there. "So, no paperwork for me yet, right?"

"Not yet," Hunter confirmed.

Based on what he'd garnered from Hunter last night, Kye expected to have about a week of paper pushing before he got to head out again. Hence the reason he'd come into the office early this morning. Like most of the agents he knew, Kye didn't care much for the paper part of it. However, it was part of the job and he made a point not to bitch and complain about it. Knowing RT, he would've buried Kye underneath it if he knew how much he detested it.

"Long term?" he probed as he pulled out of the parking garage and headed out of downtown. Now that he was no longer having to babysit Danielle Davidson, he'd been assigned to a few one-off jobs—mostly local—and he was looking forward to something lengthier. "Wait." Kye just realized what Hunter had said. "You said *we*."

When it came to Hunter, the man worked solo. Ninety-nine percent of the time, anyway. Since Kye had been with Sniper 1 Security, he'd rarely seen Hunter work with anyone other than him. And damn sure not without a boatload of resistance. Sure, he'd heard rumors as to why, but he'd never confronted Hunter about it. They might've been fucking like rabbits for the past year, but they damn sure weren't doing much cuddling after. And certainly not sharing pillow talk.

"Yeah, *we*," Hunter confirmed. "But don't get too fucking excited. You're not gonna like this one."

That sounded interesting. "We gonna babysit another princess?"

"That's one way to put it."

Kye knew Hunter well enough to know he was purposely being vague. "Spill it, Hunter."

"Where're you at right now?"

"In my truck, headin' to the office," he lied smoothly. If need be, he could turn around and be back there in a few minutes.

"Meet me at my place. I'm on my way there now."

"Will do," Kye said, putting his foot on the gas and heading toward the Kogans' compound.

Before Kye could ask anything more, Hunter disconnected the call.

Since he wasn't going to get any answers from his iPhone, Kye turned up the radio and focused on putting some distance between him and Hunter, not wanting the man to catch up with him.

Admittedly, he was looking forward to seeing Hunter. He hadn't expected the man to slip out on him this morning. Then again, ever since the Thanksgiving before last, their interactions had been few and far between. Last night had been the first time Kye had spent the night with Hunter in two weeks. Oh, they were still having sex, but it was evident Hunter was using Kye to take the edge off.

And yes, he'd noticed that Hunter was purposely keeping his distance, not answering his phone the majority of the time, and only calling Kye late at night. The infamous booty call.

Kye figured Hunter was hiding out after the meltdown he'd had all those months ago. Not that Kye understood why. It certainly wasn't the first time Hunter had lost his cool and treated him like a third-rate whore after they'd fucked. Luckily, Hunter had kept himself in check since then. He wasn't exactly sweet and welcoming, but he wasn't shoving Kye out the door with his clothes afterward. Since Kye wasn't looking for a commitment, he'd learned to let it roll off. The sex was the best he'd ever had, so it was hard to say no, even if he'd wanted to.

Truth be told, Hunter wasn't all bad. The asshole in him was his most prominent feature, but that asshole wasn't there all the time. And there were plenty of other traits Kye admired in the guy. Sexy, smart, wickedly creative, especially when it came to sex.

However, Kye often found it amusing that Hunter liked to harp on the fact that his ex-fiancée—he never referred to Danielle by name—was the flighty one. From where Kye stood, Hunter wasn't much different. They both seemed intent on outrunning their demons.

Didn't look as though either of them was faring well in that.

In fact, Hunter seemed intent on pushing everyone away. Not only his family but also Kye, and he'd merely attempted to keep Hunter company when it seemed he needed a friend. Or a fuck buddy.

No, Kye wasn't naïve enough to think they had anything more than that. Although they'd logged quite a few naked hours together, he knew he was not an inch closer to the man than he had been when they first met. For one, Hunter wasn't out to his family, nor did it seem he ever would be. Kye also knew that Hunter had some serious skeletons in his closet. Things he wasn't willing to talk to anyone about and no one who knew him seemed to have any answers, either.

Not that Kye cared that Hunter was in the closet, nor did he care what was in there with him.

Okay, maybe he cared a little.

He hadn't in the beginning, but as time went on, he might've developed some feelings for the surly bastard. The biggest thing holding him back was the fact that Hunter clearly hadn't gotten over his past lover—quite possibly plural, since Kye suspected Dani had a lot to do with it, but he also believed Josh Lee did, too. Yeah, gossip was like the flu—highly contagious—and Kye had managed to get a few details even if no one liked to talk about it. If it hadn't been for those ghosts from Hunter's past, Kye figured they could've possibly had something more.

Sadly, that wasn't as easy as it sounded.

Mainly because Hunter had an ex-fiancée and a dead lover who still plagued his dreams, which meant Kye was the fourth wheel in this oddly unbalanced scenario.

However, Kye wasn't looking to balance things out. In fact, he'd been hoping for the triad thing himself. Sure, Kye was into men and he'd enjoyed the hell out of the time he'd spent with Hunter. However, he was also into women, but from what he could tell, Hunter had sworn off women indefinitely. Or he was pretending to, anyway. Kye had dreamed that one day he would find a man and a woman and live happily ever after. At twenty-nine, that dream was starting to fade around the edges. He'd found part of what he was looking for in Hunter, but...

He knew Hunter wasn't going to give him anything more than a little sex on the side. Certainly not pair up with him and a willing woman. And since neither of them seemed to be getting what they wanted, Kye figured they were going to be stuck in this crazy transition. Kye was simply trying to enjoy what he did have. Which, if he really thought about it, wasn't much.

Once he pulled into the Kogans' compound, Kye punched in the security code to open the gate. He then drove down the winding path that led to Hunter's cabin.

A few minutes later, he walked inside, not needing a key because he'd left the door unlocked when he left, per Hunter's instructions whenever Kye found himself waking up alone in Hunter's bed.

He grabbed a bottle of water and headed for the living room. He was about to plant his ass on the couch when he heard the distinct rumble of Hunter's motorcycle pulling up in front of the small house. Rather than get comfortable, he went to the door and waited.

The minute Hunter removed his helmet, Kye knew he wasn't going to like what the man was going to tell him. The frown that marred his forehead was deep enough to hold water.

Stepping back out of the way, he watched Hunter move past him, dumping his helmet into the recliner on his way to the kitchen.

"You wanna tell me what's goin' on?"

"Not really, no," Hunter grumbled, not making eye contact.

"Well, we can't take the job if I'm in the dark." Granted, he already had an idea what was going down, but he was hoping Hunter would go into detail.

He didn't. Instead, Hunter grabbed a bottle of water from the refrigerator, then slammed the door a little too hard.

Kye didn't say a word. He knew when to back off and now was definitely the time to do so.

"Just chill," Hunter ordered. "We're outta here in ten minutes."

Yeah.

This was going to be fun.

WAITING FOR MAX TO LEAVE was quickly becoming the most stressful part of her day.

And that was saying something considering Dani had been dealing with him for the better part of the morning. She knew he was trying to hold out until Hunter arrived, but she needed him to jet so she could do the same. Thankfully, she had a bag packed and ready, so it wouldn't take her any time at all once he did go.

Unfortunately, since they'd arrived back at her apartment, Max had busied himself by taking phone call after phone call. Any other time, Dani wouldn't have minded because it ensured Max didn't have the ability to ask a million questions. Which he would certainly have been doing if he weren't busy barking out orders to whomever he was talking to.

"You heard me. I want her and the boy picked up. I'm done playin' this fucking game. I'll end this shit once and for all." He lowered his voice as he continued, "Damn it, Leyton. That fucker killed Trey. I'm not gonna sit on my fucking thumbs waiting for him to gun someone else down. I need leverage and his sister and the boy'll work fine."

Dani pretended not to hear what Max was saying. She truly didn't want to know what he was up to. Her entire life had been spent pretending she wasn't part of the infamous Adorite family. Unlike Max, she had never embraced what they stood for. Didn't mean she hadn't been forced to do things she didn't want to do. She had. Too many times to count.

At twenty-seven, Dani was a regular veteran of this mafia crusade and it seemed no matter how hard she tried to distance herself, it never worked out in her favor.

"I don't give a good goddamn if she's boarded herself up in the fucking Alamo. Fucking get her. But watch your back."

Dani pulled back the sheer curtain that hung over her front window, overlooking the parking lot. She was expecting Hunter to arrive at any moment, and if he did, her plan to bolt would be thwarted. Fortunately, the only person she saw was Max's hired gun, the one who was supposedly guarding the parking lot while chain-smoking and talking on his phone. Good help was so hard to find these days.

"Danielle, get away from the goddamn window," Max barked from behind her.

Dani rolled her eyes but let the curtain fall as she turned to face him. For a brief second, she imagined spending an undetermined amount of time with this churlish man, and she figured Hunter probably was the lesser of two evils, although she preferred neither of them.

"I need you to go," she told him, keeping her tone as firm as possible.

Max's eyes jerked from his phone to her. "Why?"

"Because I have things to do, and since you insist that I have a babysitter, I'd like to take care of them before he gets here."

Max waved his hand as though she wouldn't be bothering him if she did whatever seemed so pressing.

"No, Max. You need to go."

He studied her for a brief moment. She fully expected him to argue, but to her shock, he didn't.

"You sure you'll be all right for a little while?"

Dani nodded. "I'm sure. Hunter's probably already on his way." God, she hoped not. "Plus, you've got Guido downstairs watching the building."

"His name's not Guido," Max noted with a grin.

A knock on her door had her head snapping in that direction.

No. Please don't be Hunter.

"It's Rock," Max informed her, regarding her curiously. "You seem a little jumpy. You sure you want me to leave?"

With a sigh of relief, she forced a smile. "Yes. I'm good. I just want a few minutes to myself."

Max opened the door, then turned to face her while the giant black man known as Rock stood behind him.

"Hi, Taye," she greeted him. Although everyone referred to him as Rock, Dani had always called Taye Smith by his real name. It seemed to amuse him, which was perhaps why she always did it. Well, that and she truly liked Taye. He was one of the good ones, even if he did have a devious streak. Proven by the fact that he was a bouncer turned mob hitman.

He shot her a brilliant white smile. "Dani. Good to see you."

"I'll be in touch," Max stated. "And lock the damn door behind me."

"I'm fine, Max. Really." She moved toward the door as both men stepped outside. Once they'd cleared the threshold, she shut the door and locked it, knowing Max would stand there until he heard the deadbolt engage.

She rushed over to the window and pulled back the curtain, peeking out to see Rock and Max heading down the stairs. They paused briefly to talk to the armed thug, then walked to Max's Escalade. As soon as they'd gotten into the SUV, backed out of the parking space, and she watched it turn the corner, Dani bolted to her bedroom, yanked open her closet door, and snatched her bag.

She was getting far too familiar with this method of exit, so she didn't waste time. Swinging her bag over her shoulder, she grabbed her purse and her keys, flipping the lights off as she went. She gave the room one more glance, mentally running through everything to ensure she had what she needed.

"Time to go," she whispered, then turned to the door.

She jerked it open, knowing time was of the essence. She hated that she was running again, but honestly, she didn't know any other way to do it. It was ingrained in her, something she'd learned from a very early age.

Dani blamed her family.

Two minutes later, after she snuck down the back stairs—heading in the opposite direction from Guido—she was pulling her little Nissan out of the apartment complex and heading due north. She had a safe house in Oklahoma that would offer a little solace until she figured out her next move.

God only knew what that would be.

She only hoped that the real threat wasn't tailing her, because she really was getting tired of this shit.

FOUR

HUNTER SHOULD'VE FUCKING KNOWN.

After going to Dani's apartment to find her gone, Hunter gave the two-bit thug who was supposed to be guarding the building a piece of his mind. Despite Max's incompetent bodyguard, Dani had slipped out sometime between Max's departure and Hunter's arrival.

After threatening the piece of shit's life, Hunter went straight to Sniper 1 Security, barging right into RT's office without bothering to knock.

"For fuck's sake, Hunter," RT barked, his head snapping over. He looked slightly shocked to see Hunter for the second time that day.

"She's gone," Hunter bit out.

RT leaned back in his chair regarding him like the crazy man he felt he'd become. He probably could've handled this with a phone call, but Hunter was all about the dramatics these days. For whatever reason, he was riled by the smallest things.

"A riddle," RT's husband Z said cheerfully. "Awesome. But I think we're gonna need a *little* more to go on."

Hunter held on to his frustration, not even bothering to look at the man.

RT sat up straight. "I assume you're referring to Dani?"

"Yep," Z said absently. "My man was always better at those riddle things than me."

Hunter nodded, again ignoring Z. "Went to her apartment and she's not there."

"Did you call Max?"

"Fuck no," he growled. "Do I look like an idiot?"

"Well, now that you mention it…" Z chuckled.

For the first time since Hunter walked into the room, RT glared at his husband.

Z chuckled sheepishly. "All right, all right, babe. I'll hold my tongue."

"I'm not playing this game with her, RT," Hunter declared. "She can pull the disappearing card on someone else. I'm done."

That seemed to catch RT's attention. "I thought Max was staying with her?"

"He left her there with some inept asshole standing guard outside."

"So, I'm not understanding," RT stated evenly. "Why are you here? You took this assignment, so she's now your responsibility. I specifically recall asking you to reconsider. You insisted. So find her."

Hunter had known RT would say that. It was part of the reason he'd come here.

"Did someone try calling *her*?" Z questioned, as though no one else had thought to do that.

This time Hunter did glare at the man. "Goes right to voice mail."

"You track it?"

"Working on it," he told Z.

"Where's Kye?" RT asked.

"I've got him watching her apartment," Hunter told him. "In the event she comes home."

"But you don't think she will." It wasn't a question.

"No, I don't. She's gotten good at this, and she was clear when she said she didn't want a bodyguard."

"I don't see how she's still our problem," Z offered. "Plus, if she's in hiding, there's no threat to her."

"Not necessarily true," RT said, leaning back in his chair again. "Max seemed pretty convinced that this Moroso brother was going to go after her."

Hunter was trying to play it cool, trying not to think that the asshole had already gotten his hands on her. He didn't want Dani to be his problem, but he knew there was no way he could look the other way. Not until they'd located her. Still, he wasn't going to do so without someone specifically instructing him to. It was a matter of pride.

"Grab Claire," RT instructed. "Give her all the information you've got on her. Let her work her magic, see if she can follow Dani's trail. Are there security cameras at her complex?"

Hunter nodded.

"Then I'm sure they caught her leaving. See if she left on her own and start a timeline from there." RT sighed. "In the meantime, I'll call Max."

"Keep him off my back," Hunter ordered. "I'm not his fucking lackey and I'm not gonna take his shit."

"Understood."

Knowing he wasn't going to get anything else accomplished, Hunter turned and left when RT picked up his phone. He'd come to get specific instructions from RT. Not because he needed them but because he didn't want to acknowledge the fact that he was going to go rogue to find this woman. This way, RT was giving him the go-ahead and Hunter was simply following instructions.

Hunter headed down the hall that led to the bullpen, where the analysts usually took up residence when the agents were out in the field. He found Claire sitting near the window, her attention focused on her laptop screen.

"Hey," he greeted, attempting to sound cool and unaffected.

Based on the way her gaze swung his way, Hunter didn't think he'd succeeded.

She smiled slowly. "What's up?"

"Need your help."

"Ah. Those are my three favorite words." It was obvious she was being a smartass.

"Need you to do some hacking."

Her grin widened, this time reaching her eyes. "Okay, you've got my attention."

He knew that was what Claire lived for, so he relayed as much information as he possibly could.

*

Twenty minutes later, Hunter called Kye as he walked into the parking garage. "Don't suppose you've got good news for me?"

"Sorry. No. No movement on her apartment. You find out anything?"

"I've got Claire digging into it. She'll pull up the security feeds, see if Dani was forced out of there, or if she left on her own."

"What does your gut tell you?" he asked.

"That she bolted so she doesn't have to deal with the situation," he said without thinking about it. That seemed to be Dani's MO. The girl was damn good at running from her problems.

"What do we do now?"

"I want you to stay there for a little while," Hunter instructed. "Keep an eye on her place. As soon as I find out more, I'll let you know."

"All right. And when that's done?"

"Meet me at the house," Hunter grumbled.

"Yeah…uh… No can do."

Hunter frowned. "Why the hell not?"

"Not a good idea right now."

For whatever reason, Hunter knew Kye's refusal had nothing to do with what happened with Dani today and everything to do with what would likely happen between them when they got back to the house.

As much as Hunter wanted to assure him that he'd keep his hands off, he couldn't. Simply seeing Kye revved Hunter up in ways no one else could. Unfortunately, when Hunter felt the anger and the rage come on, he tended to take it out on Kye. Sexually, of course.

He didn't blame Kye for not wanting to deal with him. Hunter had been a world-class asshole, getting more agitated and ornerier with every passing day. It was only fair that Kye pushed him away.

After all, it was nothing less than he deserved.

"Suit yourself," Hunter grumbled before disconnecting the call.

Tucking his phone into his pocket, Hunter pulled on his jacket and his helmet, then mounted his bike. He wasn't sure where he was going, but he couldn't just stand around doing nothing. He figured he'd start by cruising by Max's house, then maybe Devil's Playground, see if he could find Dani.

Although Max had said he would stay with her until Hunter arrived, the man wasn't known to be true to his word. He was a fucking mob boss, for fuck's sake. His word was shit.

More than likely, Max had left her alone with that weasel watching the parking lot. Dani probably wanted to talk to him, so she'd simply gone to find him. Obviously, she'd been unhappy about her cousin's high-handedness, so it made sense if she wanted to have words before she garnered a babysitter for the duration. She always did have a backbone—it was something Hunter had once admired about her—so she could easily be standing up to her cousin.

Then again, this was Dani. She was known for bolting without explanation. Maybe she got tired of dealing with it and decided it was time to move on. It wouldn't surprise him one bit. After all, she'd done it before.

However, Hunter couldn't make assumptions. And until he knew for sure that Dani was safe, no way was he going to be able to stop looking for her. It wasn't in his nature.

And it had nothing to do with the fact that he was once in love with her, either.

Or so he told himself.

*

An hour later, with absolutely no luck in tracking Dani down, Hunter made the decision to contact Max himself. He wished like hell he could put it off until tomorrow. Conversing with the grumpy bastard was the last damn thing Hunter wanted to deal with after this clusterfuck of a day.

"Max, you need to calm down," Hunter stated, pacing his living room while his brother-in-law used every curse word in his vocabulary.

"Fuck that," Max growled, clearly not open to taking his advice. "I hired you to do a fucking job and she disappeared? For fuck's sake, Hunter. What the hell kind of operation are you running?"

Hunter cast a quick glance at the windows, the inky darkness beyond reflecting his mood.

Fucking shit.

"Where the fuck is she?" Max growled. "I left her for five goddamn minutes."

"So, you talked to Weasel?" Hunter taunted.

"Yeah," Max replied with a snarl. "He said you threatened to shoot him in the head."

He had. Hunter didn't take kindly to people who couldn't do their fucking jobs.

"Why'd you leave?" Hunter inquired. "I thought you were staying until I got there."

Max sighed. "She said she needed a few minutes alone. I figured if she had to deal with you for an undetermined amount of time, she deserved that much."

"So she played you?" Hunter had no idea why Max would've believed Dani. She was prone to lying.

Max grunted, clearly not wanting to admit that she had.

"Do you know where she might've gone?" Hunter finally questioned. "Do you have a safe house somewhere?"

Max growled. "I've got plenty, but she doesn't know about them."

"Well, why the fuck not?" Hunter was surprised by his own anger. He knew that Max took care of his family, so why the fuck wouldn't he be keeping Dani in the loop, providing her with safe places to go?

"Because she has her own places," Max said gruffly. "You have to remember, Dani's mother kept her distance from my family. She didn't want Dani associated."

"And you blame her?"

"Jessica Davidson loved her daughter. I knew that much. However, she wasn't rational when it came to…everything. I could've kept Dani safe if she would've let me. Because of the shit her mother told her, Dani doesn't trust anyone. You should know that."

Oh, he did. Far too well.

"Hold on, I just got a text."

Hunter waited, his eyes scanning the darkness outside.

Max sighed when he returned. "That was a fucked-up text message from Dani. She said she's really sorry it has to be this way."

"Be *what* way?" Hunter snarled, pausing in the middle of the room.

"Fuck if I know. Shit. I'm as in the dark as you are. I thought you were handling this."

Yeah, well. Hunter knew Dani. Hell, he possibly knew her better than her own cousin. The woman was fiercely independent and if she did not want to be under Max's thumb, she would ensure that didn't happen. Apparently, running away was her method of choice.

"Do you think Moroso's on to her?" Hunter asked. He was grasping at straws, but he didn't know where else to turn.

"To be honest, Hunter, I don't know what Dennis is doing. I got word he's been asking questions and Dani's name came up. That put me on high alert considering we've managed to keep her relation to me a secret over the years. No one knows who she is."

"Bullshit," Hunter snapped. "If I figured it out, you can bet your ass someone else figured it out, too. And if this asshole can get to Dani so easily, what are you doing about my fucking sister? If you're keeping tabs on everyone else, who the fuck is protecting Courtney?"

Max's voice dropped several octaves and went cold when he said, "*I* protect my wife. No one else."

Hunter took a deep breath. He needed to calm down. It didn't help that Kye had refused to come over. It left him feeling out of sorts. He didn't have a fucking clue where Dani was, which just pissed him off even more.

Okay. He needed to start again.

"Do you think Dani's in danger? I mean, immediate danger?"

"Not likely," Max stated with a sigh. "But I think *she* believes she is."

"From Moroso?"

"No. She's been acting strange, even Courtney thinks so. I've tried talking to her, but she's keeping it to herself."

"Which is why she ran?"

"That's my guess."

Hunter wanted to put his fist through Max's face. If he were in the same room with him, he might've done it.

"As long as she keeps moving, she's safe," Max said, his voice back to that calm, cool, irritating tone.

"You don't know that." He did not like the fact that Dani had eluded him.

"If I hear anything else from her, I'll let you know, Hunter."

"Yeah. You do that." He hung up on his brother-in-law.

Hunter had no choice but to wait for something to happen. Until he could get more information from Claire, or attempt to find Dani himself, he was as dead in the water as the rest of these assholes.

BY THE TIME DANI MADE it to the safe house three hours later, she was having a hard time keeping her eyes open. The drive had been long and riddled with traffic, which had then required her to circle the area three times before she was comfortable that she wasn't being tailed. That was *after* she'd gone twenty miles out of her way to ditch her cell phone and pick up a burner.

At least she was confident no one was going to find her tonight. Who knew how long that would last though. In her experience, whoever was looking for her knew what she planned to do before she even did it.

Well, not this time. When she woke up that morning, Dani hadn't considered running. She had actually been rather content with the way her life was going. Of course, Max had to go and fuck it all up for her. The man was always meddling in other people's business when he should've had enough shit going on to keep him busy.

After pulling into the garage and closing the door, Dani dragged her bag and her purse into the house. She wasn't planning to unpack, but she did intend to shower and change clothes, so she needed her stuff. Tomorrow she would move on and find another place she could hide out for a couple of days. As long as she was on the move, she felt better.

Sort of.

*

Two hours later, it was painfully evident Dani wasn't going to get any sleep. Although it wasn't that late, she was exhausted, but no matter how hard she tried, she couldn't shut her brain down. Didn't help that every little creak and groan of the house made her jump.

"This was a good idea *why?*" she asked the woman staring back at her in the mirror.

Oh, right. Because if she hadn't run, she would've been sitting somewhere while Hunter tried to kill her with that death-ray glare of his. A few bumps in the night were nothing compared to having to deal with him face-to-face.

Frowning, Dani splashed cool water on her warm cheeks, then grabbed a hand towel. While she dried her face, she continued to stare at her appearance. Maybe she should dye her hair. No one would be looking for a blonde. As it was, her dark auburn strands stuck out like a sore thumb. Not only the color but also the length. However, the thought of putting any chemicals in her hair freaked her out. She'd never done it before. What happened if she burned all her hair off?

Okay, so maybe she wasn't cut out for life on the run. When she'd done it in the past, it had always been well-planned. She knew where she was going, how long she would be there, and she always knew she was far enough away that she was relatively safe. That wasn't the case anymore.

It wasn't that she was vain, but…okay, maybe a little. She knew she could've easily disappeared long ago if she would've simply altered her appearance somewhat. However, part of her had always expected she'd finally be able to go home. When Samuel died, that should've been the end of it.

Not that Dani truly had a home. The apartment she lived in was simply a place to eat and sleep until she needed to move again. That had been the story of her life for as long as she could remember.

Maybe she really should consider changing her hair color. And if it burned all her hair off…

"No one would be looking for a bald woman, either," she said aloud, grinning for the first time that night.

Then again, she could simply fake her death. Then she'd be free to do whatever the hell she wanted. No one would be looking for her, period. She could move to China or someplace exotic and it wouldn't matter that she would stick out like a sore thumb.

Shaking her head, she tossed the towel onto the sink and headed back to the living room. She glanced at her laptop but decided not to mess with it. If someone was trying to locate her, they'd have an opportunity to get a bead on her if she logged on. Dani knew she couldn't risk that tonight. Tomorrow, she'd stop in at an Internet café and log on using their free Wi-Fi. It would be a hell of a lot safer.

Plus, she'd be on the move again, so even if they did track her to Oklahoma, they wouldn't know where she went from there. Hell, Dani wasn't even sure where she was going from there.

Sighing, she reclined on the couch and pulled the blanket up to her neck, staring up at the ceiling. If she wasn't going to sleep, then she at least hoped morning would come soon. Otherwise, she was going to go crazy.

In fact, it was quite possible she was halfway there already. It didn't help that she couldn't stop thinking about Hunter. Ever since she'd seen him that morning, memories from her past continued to plague her.

Her overtaxed brain instantly conjured up images of the night he had proposed to her. She remembered it so clearly. Too clearly.

"You cooked," she said as soon as she walked through Hunter's front door to find him standing in the kitchen.

He smiled, and it warmed her insides. Hunter Kogan wasn't the smiling type. Not because he had anything to frown at, though. More because he was always so serious. According to him, his job had hardened him. She had never understood that, considering he told her he was mostly a glorified babysitter.

"Come," he said, motioning toward the small table. "Sit."

Dani set her purse on a barstool and moved into the kitchen. That was when she noticed the candles on the table and the bottle of wine chilling in an ice bucket.

He'd gone all out.

"Special occasion?" she asked, suddenly suspicious of his motives.

He smiled again, and her insides melted.

Hunter came over, pulled out a chair, and urged her into it. She went willingly, grinning like an idiot. This man wasn't usually sweet, but something was definitely up tonight.

"What's going on, Hunter?" she asked, reaching for his hand before he could turn away.

His eyes heated—God, she loved his eyes. Until she'd met him, Dani had never seen eyes like his. They were such a light gray, they were almost white. But when he was turned on like he was now, they were silver.

"I was going to wait," he said softly.

"For?"

"Until after dinner."

She smiled. He had purposely misunderstood her question.

"But I know how impatient you are," he said as he went to his knee in front of her.

Dani's heart kicked in her chest and she did her best to hide the fear that consumed her.

"What are you doing?"

The look he sent her was both wicked hot and oddly sweet.

"I'm asking you to marry me," he said simply.

She giggled. Hunter never was the type to mince words.

Hunter reached for her hand, pulling it toward his mouth. He kissed her gently, then met her gaze and held it. "Marry me, Danielle. I'm the luckiest bastard in the world. Marry me and make me the happiest."

Her heart lodged in her throat as pain rocketed through her entire body. Hunter had no idea who she was, why she'd come into his life. Yet somehow they'd fallen in love. She had never intended for that to happen.

"Hunter…" She needed to tell him the truth. He needed to know who she was. This wasn't supposed to happen.

"Say yes, Dani," he whispered, his eyes imploring her. "Please say yes."

She nodded, but the words wouldn't come. No matter how much she loved him, how much she wished this fairy tale could lead to a happily ever after, Dani knew it wouldn't.

After all, she wasn't who Hunter thought she was.

KYE STOMPED UP THE STEPS to Hunter's front porch. When he reached the front door, he grabbed the knob and shoved it open, letting it slam against the wall as he stepped inside.

"What the fuck?" Hunter bellowed, spinning around to stare at Kye as he reached for something on the counter.

His gun. Figured.

Kye slammed the door behind him, then made a beeline for the man in the kitchen. Hunter turned to face him, his facial expression proving he acknowledged Kye was a threat. Good. Kye fucking wanted him to. He was so damn pissed, there was a red haze clouding his vision.

"You're damn lucky I didn't shoot you," Hunter stated roughly, setting his weapon back on the counter.

"You're not that good a shot," Kye countered.

"Wanna bet?"

Kye narrowed his eyes, searching for all the words he'd rehearsed over the last couple of hours. All the things he wanted to say to this man.

"I thought I told you to stay at Dani's place," Hunter said, his shoulders squaring as Kye approached.

"Yeah? And how long would you have me do that, Hunter? Until you were finished punishing me?"

Hunter's eyes narrowed. "Punishing you? What the fuck am I punishing you for?"

Kye closed the distance between them, stopping only when he was toe-to-toe with Hunter. He stared into the man's eyes. "Until I showed up like you requested? Is that what I am to you? A quick fuck? And when I don't roll over, you think it's funny to keep me watching an empty apartment?"

Hunter didn't respond, which was Kye's first clue that he'd pegged the situation correctly.

Still holding his position, Kye jerked his jacket off and tossed it on the counter. "Well, I'm here. Isn't that what you wanted?"

Again, Hunter didn't say a word.

Kye continued to undress, reaching behind his head and pulling his T-shirt off. He tossed it onto the counter. Hunter's eyes immediately trailed to Kye's bare chest. The approval there heated Kye's blood, making it harder to hold on to his anger.

"Are you ready now?" Kye snapped.

"Ready for what?"

"For your routine orgasm," Kye ground out through clenched teeth. "If so, you've got too many fucking clothes on."

"Is that so?"

"Yeah. It's what you want, right? To fuck me out of your system? Well, two can play that game."

Just as he'd expected, Hunter didn't remain motionless for long. Kye had expected it to take a little longer, but he knew eventually Hunter would cave.

After all, Kye was only speaking the truth. He knew what Hunter was up to. Knew exactly why he wanted him there.

Hunter ripped his own shirt off, then gave Kye a shove, forcing him back.

Rather than give in to what the man wanted, Kye had other plans. He reached for Hunter, taking control of the situation instead of allowing Hunter to use him. It was time he turned the tables. He'd given in to Hunter too many times to count. It was high time he got what he needed.

"Not this time," Kye stated firmly, reaching behind Hunter's head and pulling him closer. He didn't crush their mouths together, choosing instead to hover mere centimeters away. "Tonight, I'm in charge. And if you can't handle that, you should tell me to leave right now."

Hunter didn't say a word, so Kye took that as his agreement and crushed their mouths together.

A firestorm ignited between them, emotional chaos ensuing just as it always did. Hunter would never admit he wanted Kye, but Kye knew different. The man couldn't stay away. No matter how hard he tried, as long as Kye continued to come back, Hunter would always let him in.

He had a surprise in store for Hunter. Tonight was the last night. Kye was tired of being this man's sexual punching bag. He was tired of being used. But he wasn't above taking what he wanted one more time before he walked away.

While their tongues dueled, Kye worked Hunter's jeans open, inching toward him until Hunter was pressed up against the kitchen counter. When he managed to free Hunter's cock, Kye dropped to his knees. He stared up at the man as he engulfed the thick shaft in his mouth, sucking and stroking, enjoying the way Hunter's eyes heated and his moans became louder.

"Fuck," Hunter growled, thrusting his hand into Kye's hair. "Suck me." He pumped his hips forward. "Suck me just like that."

He did, but not for long. No way was he allowing Hunter to finish in his mouth. Considering the situation, he wouldn't put it past Hunter to kick him to the curb before he ever got his. And Kye was going to get his tonight.

After jerking Hunter's jeans down to the floor, Kye stood as he freed his own cock. "Turn around."

Hunter glared at him for a few seconds but finally turned, placing his palms flat against the granite.

"Don't move."

Kye went to the bedroom to retrieve the lube. When he turned back around, he found Hunter standing in the bedroom doorway.

"I told you not to move," Kye grumbled.

"Fuck you," Hunter countered. "If you wanna fuck me, you can do it right here. Right now."

They stared at one another.

"That is your plan, right, Kye? You came over here to punish me the way you think I'm punishing you?"

Kye motioned toward the bed and Hunter walked over. He didn't lie down, instead planting his hands on the mattress. It was obvious he was going to push Kye to the breaking point. But that had always been Hunter's way. He never gave in, never gave up complete control.

"You want it like that? Fine."

In a rush, Kye discarded the rest of his clothes, then stepped up behind Hunter. The man didn't move, obviously waiting for Kye to fuck him.

Too bad.

Kye had other plans.

He dropped to his knees behind Hunter, gripping Hunter's ass cheeks before spreading him wide and thrusting his tongue into his ass.

Hunter moaned as he'd expected.

"Kye…" It sounded like a warning.

Hunter began pressing back against him while Kye rimmed his asshole, showing the man just how good it could be. It was always fast and dirty between the two of them. It wasn't often that they engaged in lengthy foreplay. Hunter never had enough patience for that.

Kye reached between Hunter's legs and cupped his balls, kneading them firmly while he tongue-fucked his ass. He didn't stop until Hunter was bucking against him, begging for him to fuck him.

It took tremendous effort to get to his feet, his body vibrating with urgency, but he managed. Seconds later, he had rolled on a condom and lubed his dick. The next thing he knew, he was impaling Hunter, pulling the man's hips back, thrusting in deep and hard.

Rarely did Hunter bottom for him, but Kye knew the man enjoyed it. Unfortunately, Hunter was usually all about control, but not tonight.

Not ever again.

Kye was tired of this game. He was tired of being Hunter's bitch. He might care for the asshole, but he was no longer going to only take what Hunter was willing to give.

"You like that?" Kye asked, his fingers digging into the flesh of Hunter's hips. "You like feeling my cock filling your ass?"

Hunter didn't speak, but he groaned his approval, rocking against Kye.

He wanted to punish Hunter for how he treated him, but Kye found it more difficult than he'd anticipated. He cared for this man. Much more than he would ever willingly admit. Walking away wasn't going to be easy, but it was necessary.

"You better come for me, Hunter," Kye demanded as he pounded his ass. "It's gonna be the last fucking time."

For a second, Hunter seemed to lose his rhythm, but Kye pretended not to notice. He'd obviously surprised the man with that revelation.

Reaching up, he wrapped his hand around Hunter's neck, holding him in place. He didn't choke him but applied enough pressure that Hunter knew exactly who was in charge. He pounded his ass, fucking in deep and hard, not holding back, even as his orgasm threatened to take his fucking head off.

"Fuck…" Hunter growled. "Kye…I'm…"

"Come for me," Kye insisted. "Then I'm gonna come in your ass."

That seemed to push Hunter over the edge, because he roared his release, his ass squeezing Kye's dick until he couldn't hold back. He came in a rush, swallowing the sound, not wanting to give Hunter the satisfaction of knowing just how much Kye needed this.

Several minutes later, after he'd cleaned up in the bathroom, Kye was once again dressed and walking out Hunter's front door.

He refused to look back.

Even when Hunter called out his name.

FIVE

Four months later, June

"SO, WHAT DO YOU THINK?" Conner asked when he joined Hunter behind the firing line.

Hunter had been standing there watching their new recruits, testing what he'd been drilling into them for the past four months.

"A few have some potential," he admitted, glancing over at his brother. "But not all of them."

Conner grinned. "Well, good news is that Claire's chomping at the bit to take a couple of them."

"Which ones?" he asked, turning his attention to the guy at the end. No matter how hard Hunter worked with him, the kid couldn't aim to save his life. Twice he'd shot the damn target to his left rather than his own. If they gave him a gun and sent him out into the field, someone was going to get killed. Probably one of the good guys.

"She mentioned Jake Davis and Nate Thomas."

Hunter looked at Conner. His brother was grinning from ear to ear.

"The two Alex insisted go out into the field?"

"Those'd be the ones."

"Not happenin'. Claire will have to find someone else." No way was he going to go back on the promise RT had made to Alex McDermott, the former owner of CISS. The man had been adamant that Nate and Jake were to be kept on as official agents, not relegated to some desk job manning home security monitors. Not to mention, Jake and Nate were the only two who actually showed any promise whatsoever.

"All right, fine," Conner conceded. "But I think we should split them up. Put 'em with experienced agents for a while."

"I agree." There was something going on between Nate and Jake. Hunter wasn't privy to their personal history, but he got the sense there had been a possible relationship there. Whatever it was didn't seem to be going on anymore from what he could tell. "You have suggestions on who?"

"Nah. Don't care enough."

Of course he didn't. "I was thinkin' we'd put Nate with Deck and Jake with Clay."

"Works. Both need a partner to keep 'em in line."

Plus, Hunter knew Decker Bromwell had been spending too much damn time in the office, sniffing around Kira Trexler, RT's cousin. It had actually been RT's suggestion to pair Deck with someone to get his ass out of the office for a while.

When Conner didn't sneak away, Hunter decided to ask a question of his own.

"You get any new information on that case I asked you to look into?"

"I've got a couple of leads." Conner peered over at him. "Not easy dredging up information about a decade-old cold case."

No, Hunter didn't figure it was. Hence the reason he'd asked Conner to look into it.

"Toby Sterling," Conner said. "That's Kye's brother, right?"

"Yeah."

Conner was quiet for a moment, but then his brother's mouth opened and stupid fell out.

"You heard from Kye?"

Hunter cut his eyes to his brother, curious as to why he'd asked that question. He hadn't heard from Kye in four months. Not since the night Kye came over and fucked him senseless. The next day, Hunter had learned that Kye turned in his notice and disappeared off the face of the earth. The same day RT had informed him that Max had located Dani and was keeping her in a secure location until they could get a handle on the threat to their family.

Finding out Dani was safe had been a relief. He couldn't say the same for knowing Kye had left.
It had bothered him at first, but he'd managed to forget about him in the past few months.

Okay, that was a big fucking lie. He was trying his damnedest to forget about Kye, but it wasn't working. Still, he was glad Kye had been the one to walk away. They had both known that what they had wouldn't last. Hunter wasn't the type to settle down. He'd tried that once, but it hadn't worked out. No sense in trying again.

In an effort to clear his own conscience, Hunter had decided to look into Kye's brother's murder. He figured if he could bring justice to the Sterling family, perhaps he could ease his own guilt. Whether it would work was yet to be seen.

"Why would I hear from him?"

Conner shrugged. "Just thought I'd ask. I'm headin' back to the office. Need anything before I go?"

"Nope." Hunter didn't need anything from anyone. He was content to stand right here and watch these toddlers try to learn how to shoot.

Yeah. That was another fucking lie.

Seemed he was getting pretty damn good at them these days.

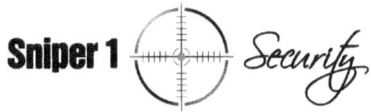

DANI FINGERED THE GUN RESTING in her lap beneath the table. It had become an extension of her over these past few months, and right now, it was the only thing that offered her a relative sense of comfort. She had never been fond of firearms, but she wasn't naïve enough to believe it wouldn't come in handy in a pinch.

Keep your head down; don't look at him.

Him being the blond Adonis currently doing push-ups not twenty yards from where she sat on the balcony of the tiny, in-need-of-updating condo she'd come to call home these past four days.

Now that she thought about it, four seemed to be her magic number. Four days she'd been there. Fourth time she'd seen the same guy, doing the same thing, in the exact same spot.

She pretended to be interested in the paperback sitting in front of her. Truth was, she couldn't recall a single thing about the book and she'd been attempting to read it for…you guessed it. Four days.

Keeping her head tilted downward, she lifted her eyes to see what the blond guy was doing.

Still doing push-ups and clearly showing off those super-sized arms of his.

The first time she'd noticed Adonis and his arms, she would've sworn he'd been looking right at her. Not that it surprised her. He'd taken up residence on the long, wooden walkway that jutted out from the parking level of the two condos—hers and his. The larger deck that extended from it seemed like the perfect place for him to do his daily exercise, which he was doing right now. And it just happened to be in her sight line to the ocean.

Look away, girl. Just look away.

Yeah. She had a hard time doing that.

It seemed a relatively normal thing for a handsome, well-built guy to do. Not totally out of the norm, she figured. Except, at three o'clock in the afternoon in the middle of June, when the temps were hovering in the third-level-of-hell range, Dani wasn't sure how he could stand it. Despite the clouds that had moved in, it was still hot. And the strong breeze blowing over the Gulf of Mexico wasn't doing a damn thing to cool things off, either.

Which was likely the reason all the red flags were snapping in the breeze every time she noticed him.

On the plus side, the guy was wearing a pair of shorts and nothing else, which offered her a perfect view of every delectable plane and angle of his upper body. He looked good enough to eat, yes, but he had to be sweating his balls off.

Dani knew she shouldn't care what he was doing, but for some unknown reason, she couldn't stop watching him. The view from her first-floor balcony was perfect for watching the sunrise over the ocean in the mornings and that was why she enjoyed sitting out here so much. Or so she tried to tell herself.

She was trying not to stare. Really. It wasn't like she hadn't been laid in almost six freaking years.

Oh, wait. Yes, it was.

Okay, so she could blame her need to stare on her hormones. However, she knew that self-preservation was a more valid reason *not* to ogle him from head to toe. It didn't even matter that he was built like a Greek god with all of those sleek, rippling muscles and she was currently riding a six-year dry spell because she should've been slipping the safety off and taking up a defensive position inside, where it was far safer for her to be. Or better yet, hopping in her car and hitting the open road.

Because someone was stalking her, of that she had no doubt.

You should call Max, her subconscious told her for the umpteenth time.

Yep. She should.

Dani should simply break down and give Max a call, tell him everything that was going on, and let him shelter her from the storm. She'd spent the past four months effectively evading everyone who might've been looking for her—Sniper 1 Security, her entire family, even the psycho she knew was attempting to track her down and kill her—but for some reason she felt as though she was running out of time.

If she had, in fact, been found by this blond Adonis, someone really needed to know. As much as she didn't want to, Dani knew she had to eventually tell Max—and the rest of her family—the truth. It was going to come out sooner or later. She honestly would rather be alive to see it than to have them hear the news when they were burying her.

Shit.

The blond sun god stood tall, his eyes scanning the horizon, then coming to land on her. And there was no doubt about it, the guy was tall. Likely six and a half feet if she'd had to guess. Built like a brick shithouse, as Ashlynn liked to say.

What if this blond sun god wasn't actually working out? What if he'd been hired to find her and she was now looking at the man who could ultimately lead whomever wanted her dead right to her doorstep?

Or worse. What if he was the guy who was going to snuff her out?

In all fairness, he probably would've done that by now.

Of course, her irrational brain wondered if he was one of those psycho hitmen who liked to draw the cat-and-mouse game out because he preyed on his target's fear. Which made far more sense considering the game she'd been trapped in for the past four months. Whoever was after her certainly wanted her to keep running scared. And they'd succeeded because that was about all she seemed to be doing these days.

YOU CAN RUN BUT YOU CAN'T HIDE.

Damn. She could still see the words written in blood on the safe house wall. Whose blood, she wasn't sure, and truthfully, she didn't want to know.

THE CHILD SHALL PAY FOR THE SINS OF THE FATHER.

That was the message she'd received at the last safe house she'd stayed in. Hence the reason she ran.

And the need to hide, to collect her thoughts and come up with a plan, was the reason she was here in this one-bedroom condo on South Padre Island in the first place. This was her safe haven, or it was supposed to be, anyway. At least until she could decide what to do next.

Although her cousin Max—at least the family believed he was her cousin—had attempted to bring her back into the fold when she returned home two years ago—after Samuel Adorite met his demise—Dani should've known that it wasn't possible to put down roots.

There was a reason someone wanted her dead and she hadn't gotten lucky enough that her secret had died with Samuel Adorite. The bastard. She wished she could dig him up, resuscitate him, just so she could have the pleasure of killing him herself.

And fine. Perhaps that wasn't the best idea in the world, since there was no way in hell she'd last a minute in jail. Not because she was a wuss, either. Someone would put her lights out permanently before Dani could eat her first behind-bars meal. She was, after all, an Adorite.

So, it was a good thing she hadn't killed the son of a bitch. But to her dismay, the secret she and her mother had tried so hard to keep was out and that meant Dani was as good as dead if they found her. And someone *was* looking for her. Although everyone seemed to assume it was Dennis Moroso, Dani knew it wasn't the mobster hell-bent on seeking revenge on Max for killing Moroso's lunatic brother.

Nope, that would've been too easy. Dani might not be able to survive prison, but she wasn't a lightweight. She could handle her own, thank you very much.

Whoever the crazy guy was who'd been trailing her across the country and back again was definitely not the dead, wannabe mob boss's vengeful brother. This guy was good. He was trained, he was lethal, and above all else, he was batshit crazy. On top of that, the asshole was usually one step ahead of her.

But so far, Dani had proven to be better.

However, she knew she would eventually reach the end of the line.

Her eyes tracked Adonis as he grabbed his towel and scrubbed the sweat from his face.

Yeah. Running was about the only thing she had left to do.

Except, the money she had left wasn't going to go far. Especially not after she'd paid cash for the run-down little Honda Civic that'd brought her from the safe house she'd been staying at in Florida to Corpus Christi. That'd set her back nine hundred dollars. Another six hundred in gas and cheap motel rooms along the way had pretty much run her dry. She had plenty of money in the bank, but cash was her only option. The second she used a credit card or withdrew money from any of her accounts, he'd be on her in a heartbeat. As would Max, and until Dani was ready, she didn't want anyone knowing where she was. Not even her family.

Which meant, the two weeks she'd paid—with her dwindling stash—on this beachfront rental, hoping for some time to figure out what she was going to do next, had pretty much been the end of the line for her.

Unless she went to Max for help.

Didn't really make sense to go back, though. Not unless she had the guts to tell him what was really going on. As it was, she felt sort of like the girl who cried wolf. Constantly running in circles, never accomplishing anything, and appearing crazy in the process.

Her attention returned to the ridiculously sexy buff guy finishing up his afternoon workout. She didn't think this was a coincidence that he seemed to be watching her. However, there wasn't that itch at the back of her neck like she'd felt before when she was in danger. Still, she needed to be careful.

No, she needed to do more than be careful. She needed to change her identity, relocate to another country, and start a whole new life. She hated permanently leaving what little family she had, but if she wanted to stay alive—which she most definitely did—she didn't think she had a choice any longer. These past four months had proven that she wasn't capable of doing this on her own. She didn't stand a chance against this guy—whoever he was.

Movement out of the corner of her eye had Dani looking up in time to see the blond Adonis walking back toward the building beside hers. She remembered the brief conversation she'd had with him when she had originally encountered him on her first trip down to the water.

"Hey, neighbor," he greeted.

His voice—laced with a rich Texas drawl—was deeper than she'd anticipated.

"Hi." Dani glanced around, instinctively looking for an escape route. The subcompact .45 she had tucked in her towel was within easy reach. At this range, it would do what it was intended to do. That made her feel marginally better.

"I saw you moved into building one. Vacation?"

Dani nodded, trying to hide her nervousness.

"It's a nice place to be," he said, his eyes roaming over her face. It was as though he could sense her tension. "I'm Joe."

Joe? He did not look like a Joe. Then again, why would he lie to her?

He held out his hand, but she simply stared at him. She didn't question him or his motives; instead, Dani forced a smile. "Nice to meet you, Joe."

His gas-flame-blue eyes lit with amusement. He obviously realized she wasn't going to shake his hand or tell him her name.

That was the first conversation they'd had. It seemed every evening when she headed down for a swim, he was always there. She would see him when she was heading back to shore because he always set up a chair right beside hers.

At first, she'd been freaked, but then Joe had started to chat. Nothing too deep, but enough to keep her company. He wasn't intrusive with his questions, which was why she hadn't told him to take a hike. Truth was, Dani was tired of being alone and a little conversation with Joe didn't seem to be hurting anything.

Yesterday, they'd talked endlessly about his hearing aids. Dani had noticed them right off and she had initially thought he was some sort of agent. They tended to wear those things, she knew. However, Joe had informed her he wasn't some clandestine undercover agent getting intel fed to him through his earpiece. He was, in fact, hearing impaired. Had been since birth. He'd gone so far as to take one out and let her listen. Sure enough, he'd been telling the truth.

She knew she was being stupid, taking a risk she shouldn't, but Dani couldn't help but like the guy. She didn't have any friends and she was latching on to the man, hoping like hell he was what he claimed to be.

Regardless of their daily conversations, Dani continued to see him out on that deck, religiously going through his workout routine. He glanced her way every time and he caught her looking back at him, which was only slightly embarrassing. He was nice to look at; she would admit that.

And okay, fine. Maybe she had done a little flirting. She figured it wouldn't hurt to be nice. She knew how to handle herself. It wasn't like she was going to be alone with him or anything. The beach was overly crowded as it was.

Dani glanced between the wooden slats on the railing in time to see Joe disappear below her, but not before their eyes connected once more.

He smiled and winked, and she felt a strange flutter in her belly.

Shit.

She could feel her heart pounding in her chest. It was the same anxiety that'd been coursing through her for the past few days. Ever since she arrived here. Unable to run anymore, she'd had to do something. Staying off the grid always proved futile. Ever since she first bolted nearly six years ago—evading Hunter and her own family, not wanting to answer their questions—she hadn't been able to stay in one place for long.

Although Dani had put thousands of miles between herself and her old life, it still didn't feel like enough. And here she was again, not nearly as far away, but in just as much danger as before. Every creak she heard at night made her jump. She couldn't sleep, hardly ate, desperate to be alert, to be ready for an attack.

And that was the one thing she absolutely could not let happen.

Because no matter what, she was not going to let Samuel Adorite win. She couldn't. She no longer believed Max when he told her that things would get better, that he could protect her. That tomorrow was a new day.

As far as she was concerned, tomorrow was too late.

KYE GRABBED HIS CELL PHONE after wiping the sweat off his face with a towel. He punched in the familiar number, then let it ring through the Bluetooth linking his hearing aids to his phone.

He'd come to depend on the technology that Austin Trexler had come up with. The day Austin had presented Kye with a receiver that attached to his shirt, allowing him to maintain a communication link between himself and whomever was on the other end, Kye had realized he was finally part of the team. It also worked to merely Bluetooth his phone, which allowed him to use his hearing aids as both earphones for music and to answer and make calls.

He particularly liked it because most people never would've thought anything about it since Kye did wear hearing aids because of his hearing loss. Now they were merely multifunctional and discreet.

A deep voice sounded in his ear. "Yeah?"

"She's still here," Kye explained, making his way to the refrigerator. He snatched a bottle of Gatorade. "But she's seriously spooked this time. You find anything out about what happened in that last safe house?"

"No," Ryan Trexler said with a sigh. "We tried to recover what the writing on the wall said, but she did a good job of cleaning it."

Damn. He'd been hoping to get a clue as to why she was running.

"You sure Moroso isn't watching her? Or someone else? Someone who's *not* us?"

"Not that I can tell," RT stated firmly. "I've had Claire looking into it, but we can't trace anything. She's definitely running, but I have no idea who it is coming for her."

Well, Kye got the feeling someone was, and he was starting to doubt it was Moroso. Although he didn't know why.

"Any news on Moroso?" Kye asked.

Kye made a point to call in several times a day, keeping RT abreast of the situation, which up to this point had proven to be not much of a situation at all. Although Hunter and everyone else believed Kye had left Sniper 1 Security, he was actually on an undercover assignment for RT. Watching none other than the elusive Danielle Davidson. Kye had become a glorified babysitter ghost, had been since he attempted to resign, only to be ordered to tail the twenty-seven-year-old beauty four months ago, not long after she had high-tailed it out of town. According to RT, everyone believed Max was keeping Dani in one of his many safe houses. But Kye knew the mob boss had no idea where his cousin was.

"Not yet. I talked to Max. He seems to think Dennis is in the process of getting all his ducks in a row."

Kye had no idea what that meant when it came to illegal guns and drugs, but he wasn't going to question it.

"Well, I'll check back in with you later. And if you hear anything in the meantime, let me know."

"Will do."

With that, the call disconnected and Kye was left staring at the ugly blue walls of the desperately-in-need-of-some-updating condo he was staying in. Not that he gave a shit about the décor. Sniper 1 Security was paying for the digs, and Kye was not in a position to complain. When the assignments were handed out, he took them, no questions asked.

Well, to be fair, he had asked a few questions regarding this particular assignment, only he'd gotten exactly zero answers. After his last meltdown with Hunter—which he wasn't proud of—Kye had gone into the office the following morning and handed in his resignation. RT had refused to accept it but took advantage of the situation. Only two people knew he was still on Sniper 1's payroll. RT and whoever paid him on a monthly basis.

Kye had been ordered to keep it that way.

Not too difficult considering he'd spent the past four months tracking Dani across the country and then back again. It wasn't until she had settled in here that he'd decided to get a little closer to her. Not only had he stuck his neck out and managed to get cameras set up inside her condo, Kye had taken it upon himself to officially introduce himself to the incredibly hot Danielle Davidson.

He shouldn't have done it, but after months of tracking her, he was starting to go stir-crazy. Up until now, he had remained in the shadows, ensuring she didn't see him. It hadn't been all that difficult to do, but that was because Kye was good at his job. Having done a short stint as a private investigator prior to coming to work for Sniper 1 Security, he'd gotten rather good at being discreet and keeping a low profile.

However, his patience had finally run out.

Since no one was willing to divulge the details of Hunter's past relationship with Danielle, Kye figured he'd make a move, attempt to get to know her a little. At first it didn't help. She had kept him at a distance.

Of course, persistence was key and now Kye was getting to spend every evening by her side, down by the water. It was quickly becoming the highlight of his day.

Granted, she wasn't much of a talker. Most of what he knew about the woman, he'd garnered from the hidden cameras he'd planted outside the houses she'd been staying in. This was the first time he'd managed to get inside, though.

During their chats, the only thing she'd copped to was that she was an only child, and her parents were dead, but other than that, she hadn't gone into detail, nor did he think she was going to.

Not that he was going to stop trying.

So, Kye spent most of his time waiting, coming up with all the questions he wanted to ask the woman. Questions that wouldn't tip her off to who he was or why he'd joined her on this little stretch of beach in South Padre. Since his only job was to keep an eye on her, to follow her if and when she bolted—which she was certainly prone to do—he damn sure didn't have much to bitch about.

Thankfully, she'd paid two weeks' rent on the condo she was staying in, which allowed Kye to relax a little. It was unlike her, but he figured she felt safe here. The beach was busy this time of year, which probably helped. She could easily blend in with the other beachgoers. However, her decision to dig her heels in for the short term meant Kye was going to have to find something to keep his attention. As it was, other than their brief evening conversations, he was fucking bored to tears.

As he made his way to the bathroom, he tossed his cell phone on the bed, then swiped his finger over the track pad on his laptop. He typed in his password, and a second later, the screen came to life. Several different camera angles filled the screen. He focused on the one in the kitchen of Dani's condo. She'd obviously gone inside to eat. Peanut butter and jelly, from what he could tell.

"Great." Kye admired her for a moment, then took a deep breath. He needed a shower. Time to wash off the sand so he could spend the rest of the evening with his thumb up his ass while he waited for Dani to do something.

Several minutes later, Kye stood in the shower, allowing the hot water to rain down on him. He couldn't stop thinking about her for some fucking reason.

He knew she was running from someone and he was relatively certain it wasn't the sleazy mob boss's brother. Originally, he'd thought she was trying to evade Hunter, but that didn't make sense, either. Kye didn't believe she was on to him. If she was, she obviously didn't consider him a threat.

No, he was fairly certain she was running from someone or something only she could see. What or whom, he had yet to determine. The way her eyes were constantly darting around as though she expected danger to be lurking in the flora covering the dunes... It brought out a protective instinct in him, something he'd been born with. Not to mention the gun that was practically glued to her hand. Oh, yeah. He'd noticed.

All in all, he couldn't complain. He had a beautiful woman to keep him company in the evenings and endless days to spend doing whatever he wanted. Well, as long as he kept an eye on her, that was.

Ever since he started working for Sniper 1 Security two years ago, Kye had finally found some peace with himself. At the ripe young age of thirty, he had now found his calling. At first, he had considered Hunter to be a bonus, although *that* had died four months ago.

Of course, Kye still spent plenty of time thinking about Hunter.

Add Dani into the mix and Kye could spend hours lost in a ridiculous fantasy. Hell, the mere thought of that beautiful woman there with them while Hunter fucked him into oblivion made his dick twitch. The image of the woman next door flashed in his mind. She was naked, Hunter's dick tunneling in and out of her mouth while Kye ate her pussy. Writhing, moaning.

Fuck.

It wouldn't do him any good to start fantasizing about a woman he might never see again. Every day he went to work out, he expected her balcony to be empty. One day it would be, and she'd be nothing more than a fantasy. One that might fuel some pleasurable encounters while he was alone, sure. But that wasn't enough. Not anymore.

Shaking off the reverie, Kye shut off the water and reached for a towel.

Seriously, something had to give because it'd been too many damn months that Kye had been following the auburn-haired beauty, and up to this point, the only thing he'd done was log a shit ton of miles following her. He could only hope that she was getting ready to pack it up and head home since she'd worked her way back to Texas.

Maybe once she did that, someone would tell him what the hell was going on.

Then again, if that someone was supposed to be Hunter … probably not.

*

Kye waited exactly twenty minutes after Dani left her condo to head down to the water. He knew she would spend some time in the ocean before returning to the beach to sit and watch the last rays of the sun disappear behind her. Kye had made it a point to spend those few minutes by her side.

When he reached the sand, he realized she had moved from her normal spot and she hadn't brought a chair with her this time. It made him smile, but it didn't deter him in the least. He stuck his chair near the walkway back to the condos and then trekked over to her spot, laying his towel out beside hers.

This was the best part of his day and no way did he intend to let it pass him by.

Sure as shit, a few minutes later, Dani emerged from the ocean, water dripping from her body, the sun highlighting all that smooth, luscious skin.

Christ Almighty. He needed to mentally lock this image down so he never forgot it.

"I'm starting to think you're stalking me," she said when she joined him.

"Who me?" He gave her a brilliant smile, keeping his eyes on her face rather than trailing over all those delicious curves. "Now, why would I be stalking a beautiful woman?"

One dark eyebrow quirked upward, but surprisingly, Dani smiled back at him.

"I don't know, Joe. Why would you?"

He peered out at the water. The sun was setting behind them, making the sky dark, even as the water glittered from the last rays.

"I think this is my favorite part of the day," he admitted, releasing a breath when she finally sat down.

Kye noticed she pulled her clothes closer. He had learned that was where she kept her gun.

"Watching the sun set?" she asked as she reached for the familiar purple and blue water bottle she had brought with her. It was how he'd learned where she was sitting.

"No," he told her, looking her way. "Talking to you."

"Now why do I find that hard to believe?"

"You think I'd lie about that?"

"You're a man, aren't you?"

Oh, he was definitely a man, all right.

Rather than give her reason to criticize him, Kye smiled as he reclined on his towel and stared up at the sky. "It's surprisingly peaceful out here."

He turned his head to the side, watching as several families were packing things up for the evening. On the weekend, there were plenty of people who camped along the shoreline, but during the week, he had learned it was relatively scarce. Especially on a Monday, when most people had gone back to work.

"Except for the chatterbox," Dani teased.

Kye turned his head to look at her. He noticed she was lying down as well. His eyes trailed over her body, cataloging every curve that was revealed by that teeny-tiny bikini. The woman made his mouth water.

For a brief moment, he thought about Hunter, thought about how angry the man would be if he knew Kye was putting the moves on this particular woman. No matter what Hunter said, Kye knew the man still had feelings for her.

Not that Kye cared anymore. He was doing his job, which did not involve worrying about what Hunter would and would not approve of.

"You get any reading done?" Kye finally asked when Dani was quiet for a while.

Her head snapped his way and he recognized the suspicious gleam in her eyes. "How did you know I was reading?"

"Um…because you're always sitting on the balcony with a book in your hand?"

She smiled but turned away quickly. "You're spying on me, Joe."

If she only knew. "I'd rather use the word *admiring*. It doesn't sound quite so devious."

"Speaking of spying," she continued, "what is it that you do for a living?"

"I manage a chain of sporting goods stores," he lied. If Dani decided to do any research, she would find it to be true. RT had worked his magic to give Kye a solid cover should that happen. Joe Davis did, in fact, manage a chain of sporting goods stores out of Kansas. Never married, no kids, Joe was an uninteresting suburbanite who spent his spare time reading. In a word, he was boring.

"Really?" She didn't sound convinced.

"Yeah." He sighed heavily. "I'd originally intended to go into the military, but my hearing impairment eliminated that option."

Dani frowned at him. "Really? They'll keep you out for that?"

"Unfortunately, yes. With only thirty percent of my hearing, I couldn't pass the physical." That much was true. "Same with becoming a cop." He forced a smile. "So, I ended up with a business degree."

"Hmm. You don't look like the business degree type."

Yeah, well.

More minutes passed as they lay there beneath the darkening sky, watching the stars come out. The beach was practically deserted by the time Dani spoke again. He thought for sure she was going to head back in, but she surprised him by turning toward him and propping her head on her hand.

"Tell me about your brother."

Kye hid his surprise by staring up at the sky. He was shocked that Dani had decided to pick up the conversation where they'd left off two days ago. For whatever reason, Kye had started talking about his family and he'd mentioned his brother had died, but he hadn't elaborated on the subject.

"What about him?" he asked, keeping his tone level.

"How did he die?"

"He was murdered," he admitted, still not looking at her.

Dani's soft hand touched his arm and he felt the smoothness of her skin. He couldn't keep from looking her way. Kye knew what she would see in his eyes. Regret, remorse, even anger.

"What happened, Joe?"

Sighing, he decided to give her some of the details. Considering it had been a public case, he knew he couldn't give her too much. Should she choose to research, she would easily find out he was not who he claimed to be.

"He got in with the wrong crowd."

"How old was he?"

"Nineteen." He still remembered that day like it was yesterday. Two detectives had showed up at his parents' door to inform them that their youngest child would not be coming home ever again.

It had hit Kye hard considering he'd been close to Toby. With only ten months separating them, they'd been practically twins, spending most of their time together.

"Gang related?" she asked.

Kye shook his head.

"Drugs?"

"No."

He wanted to tell her everything, wanted to get it off his chest, but he knew he couldn't. The death of Toby Sterling had made the front page of the *Dallas Morning News*. His brother was gay, and according to the police reports, he'd been murdered because of it. Kye had spent months trying to find out who had brutally tortured and killed his brother, never coming up with any answers. Whoever did it had gotten away. It was now a cold case and he doubted anyone would ever be brought to justice.

And that was part of the reason he'd ended up at Sniper 1 Security. He knew if anyone could find who was responsible for his brother's death, it would be them. Which was the very reason he'd shared those details with Hunter back when he first started. He'd seen the sympathy in his eyes, knew he wouldn't be able to let it go. One day, Kye would learn the identity of the people responsible. And he would put them down like the dogs they were.

"I'm sorry," she said softly.

Kye turned and realized Dani was close, her face only inches from his. If he wanted to, he could've easily kissed her, fused his lips to hers and explored the sweetness of her mouth. And oh, how he wanted to. Unfortunately, that wasn't an option. His goal was to gain her trust, and getting his hands on her probably wouldn't help him achieve his goal.

For several long seconds, their eyes remained locked and he wished like hell she would close that gap, but she never did.

Dani was the first to look away and she must've realized they were practically alone on the long stretch of beach, because she shifted until she was sitting up. "I should go."

Kye didn't try to talk her out of it. He wanted to get this woman to feel comfortable with him and he knew pushing her wasn't going to help.

"Tomorrow night then?" he asked, keeping his tone teasing. "Same time, same place?"

Dani smiled as she looked down at him. "Maybe if you're lucky."

Kye could've told her he'd never been lucky in his entire life.

But for some reason, he was hoping Dani was going to be the one to change that.

SIX

"GOIN' SOMEWHERE, SWEETHEART?" Hunter asked when Dani nearly face-planted into his chest as she was running out of her apartment.

She figured he already knew the answer to that by the bag thrown over her shoulder.

"I'm… No," she stated adamantly.

He didn't look convinced.

Hunter motioned her back into the apartment. "Does Max know you're headin' out so soon?"

"Hunter, I can—"

"I don't need to hear it," he interrupted, closing the door behind them, taking a deep breath as he did.

Dani knew he didn't want to hear it. He never did. No matter how badly she wanted to tell him the truth, she knew Hunter would never listen. He hated her, and she feared he would always feel that way.

She glanced around her apartment, feeling his presence overwhelming her. This was the first time they'd been alone since before their failed nuptials. She wasn't sure she liked it. Not only was she uncomfortable, it brought back painful memories of all that she'd lost.

While he stood there, Dani could tell he tried not to look around, but she wasn't sure why. He seemed intent on staring at her, keeping a watchful eye as though he expected her to disappear into thin air. God, she wished that was a talent she had learned long ago. It would've made this so much easier.

"Hunter…"

He didn't look at her.

"I really think this is a bad idea," she finally said.

"Bad? Or ironic?" He smirked, glancing at her over his shoulder. "Never thought you'd be the job, did you?"

She sighed. "You weren't a job."

"Right." He turned away from her. "But that's the past and right now, I'm here to keep your ass safe. So, if you'll be a good little girl and go…" He motioned toward the couch.

"You're such a jerk."

"You ain't seen nothin' yet, sweetheart."

"Come on, Hunter. You know you want to be here even less than I want you here," she said, desperate for him to hear her out. "So, what'd'ya say we pretend today never happened and you go about your business so I can go about mine."

This time he turned to face her. "Sweetheart, I've been pretendin' a lot of things never happened. But your family hired me to do a job; therefore, I'm gonna do my job."

"I'll tell Max that you're keeping an eye on me," she said in a rush. "He doesn't have to know. If he talks to you, just say… I don't know. Say whatever you need to say to keep him happy. I don't need a babysitter, Hunter."

The man remained silent.

"I'm serious, Hunter. You don't want to be here, and I don't want you here, so why can't we pretend that you're doing what you said you'd do? Max will still pay. I won't say a word."

"Sit," he commanded, his hand snapping out as he pointed toward the couch. "I don't want to hear another word outta your mouth."

"Hunt—"

"I said shut it," he ground out, "and sit down. I need to have a look around."

He started toward the kitchen but then suddenly turned.

"Better yet," he said, motioning her toward him, "show me around."

"I seriously doubt you need an escort," she grumbled, not moving from her spot.

"No, but I'm not willin' to risk you high-tailin' it while I'm checkin' out the bedroom." He snapped his fingers and pointed to the floor in front of him.

Dani flipped him off.

Dani bolted up in her bed, her eyes bouncing around the room.

The beach.

She wasn't in her apartment and Hunter wasn't there.

Dani fought to catch her breath. She'd been having that stupid dream for a while now. She figured it was her subconscious's way of doing what she felt she should've done the last time she'd left. If she had, where would she be now? Still locked in her apartment with Hunter there watching over her? Or would they have caught the bastard who was threatening her?

When her heart finally resumed a normal beat, Dani forced her legs over the side of the bed. She grabbed her gun and headed for the kitchen. There was no sense living the what-ifs. No matter what she wanted, she couldn't turn back time.

*

Dani hated that she was looking forward to spending time with Joe down by the water. She knew it was only due to the fact that he was the first human interaction she'd had in so long. Someone who actually wanted to spend time with her.

Honestly, Dani was tired of being alone. For so long, she'd been depending only on herself, trying to come up with a way to save herself from whatever danger was lurking. No matter how hard she tried, she failed over and over again. Whoever was after her never failed to find her. She knew this time would be no different. It was only a matter of time before he showed up on her doorstep and she was forced to flee again.

It was a pathetic life she was living. Alone and afraid all the time.

And here she was, once again sitting on the balcony, the warm breeze blowing over her while Joe went through his exercise routine out on the deck. She wanted to join him, to force him to go down to the water with her. Maybe spend some time frolicking in the surf.

"You're an idiot," she mumbled to herself. "And you do not frolic."

Her thoughts drifted back to her dream of Hunter. Her heart constricted, the pain stealing her breath. Hunter Kogan was the only man she'd ever loved, and she missed him. She missed what they'd shared, how he'd made her feel. Safe, cherished. But it had all been a lie, one Dani couldn't live with, so she had run away, leaving him behind.

She didn't blame him for hating her. She deserved it.

"Hey, gorgeous."

Dani's gaze flew down to the walkway and she noticed Joe standing there, staring up at her. She forced a smile and caressed the gun hidden in her lap.

"You wanna catch some sun today?"

Her eyes darted out to the water, then back to him. Could she? Could she really spend an afternoon not hiding, not thinking about who was trying to kill her? Maybe laugh a little?

"I…uh…"

"Come on," he said, motioning his head toward the ocean. "Just a little while."

Once again, she peered out at the water.

"Yeah. Okay." Feeling lighter, Dani forced herself out of her chair. "I'll meet you down there."

The smile on Joe's face warmed her from the inside out. She wasn't sure what it was about this man, but she enjoyed his company. Oddly enough, she felt safe with him. As for whether or not she believed he was a sports store manager, she wasn't sure, but there was something about him that called to her.

Of course, that could've been her libido trying to pull one over on her. It had been six years since she'd had sex. And Joe was hot. So freaking hot.

Even as she ran inside to change into her swimsuit, Dani tried to talk herself out of going down there. Getting close to this man was stupid. She could be gone tomorrow, and she would never see him again. What would she do then?

What if she developed feelings for this hunky guy and she had to run? Where would that leave her? With another broken heart?

"Don't be silly," she muttered to herself. "You're not gonna fall in love with the guy."

She wouldn't. She knew she wouldn't because there was only one man she would ever love.

By the time she made it down to the water a few minutes later, Dani was second-guessing herself. She was an idiot who was looking to get herself killed.

No. No, she wasn't. She was simply tired of being alone. That was all it was. She was only looking for a little company.

"Hey," Joe greeted with a grin. "I figured you'd go inside and hide on me."

"I thought about it," she told him honestly.

He studied her face for a few seconds and Dani fought the urge to look away. She worried he could see too much. What if he figured out she was on the run?

"Are you finally gonna tell me your name?" he asked.

"Dani," she blurted before she could think better of it. Crap.

"Is it short for something?" he asked, still staring into her eyes.

"Danielle," she admitted. She was already in too deep. Might as well jump all the way in the hole she'd dug.

"It's a beautiful name."

She smiled shyly and glanced at the ground.

"You wanna take a walk? Or get in the water?"

Dani peered down the beach. There were only a few people out, but enough that she would be able to get someone's attention if necessary.

"A walk would be nice."

They fell into step together, though Dani could tell Joe was pacing himself. Considering how long his legs were, he would likely get wherever they were going twice as fast as she could.

"Where are you from, Joe?"

"Kansas," he said without missing a beat.

"Really?" She glanced over at him. "I didn't think anyone was really from Kansas."

He chuckled. "Well, I am. What about you?"

"Texas," she admitted.

"Ah. So not far from home?"

Oh, she was a long way from home. She always was. Even if she was in the same zip code as her family, she was still a long, long way away. Or at least that was what it felt like these days.

"Not too far," she answered.

When Joe reached for her hand, Dani paused briefly but then allowed him to link their fingers together as they continued to walk. Her stomach did a flip at the contact. She couldn't remember the last time anyone had held her hand. Hunter had never been the type to hold her hand. Sure, he would usually have his hands on her, but handholding was never his thing.

"When are you going back to Kansas?" Dani asked, trying to make conversation.

Joe shrugged. "Supposed to leave on Friday." His eyes dropped to their hands. "But I'm not sure I'll be ready to go at that point."

She knew how he felt. It hadn't taken long, but for whatever reason, Dani was relaxing around this man. Getting comfortable. She didn't want him to leave, because then she wouldn't have anyone to talk to, to walk on the beach with. To hold her hand.

Her eyes strayed to the water once more.

Perhaps it was time for her to move on. Getting comfortable meant getting killed.

And no matter how much she liked this man, Dani knew her life wasn't worth the risk.

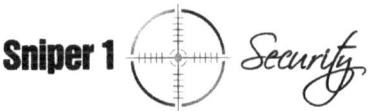

"WHERE IS HE?" HUNTER DEMANDED when he stepped into RT's office.

RT slowly turned to look at him, obviously disturbed by Hunter's outburst. Not that Hunter gave a shit. Something was up; he could feel it. There was an itch at the back of his neck letting him know he was missing something crucial. He got the feeling RT knew exactly what was going on, which was what had led him here. He was tired of questioning it. He needed some fucking answers.

"Where is *who*?" RT questioned with a frown.

"Kye."

That frown only deepened. "What are you talking about? Kye gave his notice back in February, remember? He left."

"Yeah?" Hunter wasn't buying it. "Did he really? Or is that what you want me to believe?"

"He really did," RT stated firmly, his hand going to the top drawer of his desk. "Why would I lie about that?"

Hunter watched as RT retrieved a sheet of paper, then passed it over.

To whom it may concern,

Thank you for the opportunity, however, I am no longer able to fulfill my obligation as an agent with Sniper 1 Security due to personal reasons. Please accept this as my resignation. Unfortunately, I cannot give two weeks for you to find my replacement, but I figure with the overwhelming abundance of new employees, this will not be a problem.

It appeared legit and was even signed by Kye, but Hunter still had his doubts. Or was that merely wishful thinking?

"Why would you accept that?" he questioned.

RT frowned. "Why wouldn't I? He insisted he could no longer work here. I'm not in the business of keeping people against their will, Hunter."

"He was one of the best fucking agents we had."

"Maybe so, but clearly he had an issue. He said it was personal. I wasn't going to invade his privacy." RT's gaze never wavered from his face. "Was there some reason you think I should've forced his hand?"

Hunter didn't have an answer for that. If he said what he was thinking, he would give too much away. Although RT had come out to his family long ago, Hunter wasn't about to reveal his own secrets. It was no one's business what Hunter did behind closed doors.

RT's expression turned inquisitive. "Why do you ask, anyway? He's been gone for months. Are you just now noticing?"

Hunter continued to glare at RT, hating himself for having been weak and coming in here in the first place. He should've kept his mouth shut.

"Hunter?"

"Forget it," Hunter barked, pivoting toward the door.

"Stay," RT demanded.

Reluctantly, Hunter turned back to face the man he'd come to respect not only as a friend but also as his boss. With Casper and Bryce having retired, RT was the only one who had stepped up to take over the company their fathers had worked so hard to build. Although Conner should've been working alongside RT to run the family business, everyone knew Conner's past wouldn't allow him to do that. That made Hunter next in line, but he would rather die than sit behind a desk, drowning in political bullshit and paperwork.

"Have a seat." RT motioned toward the chair across from his desk.

Hunter shook his head. "I'd rather stand."

"Your hip still bothering you?"

"It's fine." It wasn't, but he wasn't the sort to bitch and moan about his pain. Although the doctors had managed to remove the bullet from his body, the pain had never completely dissipated.

"Did something happen between you and Kye?"

"That's none of your business," he grunted.

"Is it the reason he left? I've always wondered."

"Probably." Hunter hated admitting that, but it was the truth. Although he wasn't about to divulge their personal relationship, it was no secret that Hunter was a difficult man to work with.

"Have you tried calling him?" RT questioned.

"No."

"Are you going to?"

Hunter grimaced. "Of course not. He left on his own. If he wanted to talk to me, he would've called me."

RT was silent for a few minutes and Hunter was gearing up to bolt when the man finally spoke.

"I know about you and Josh," RT revealed.

Now Hunter was getting defensive. "What *about* me and Josh?"

"The two of you were more than partners."

"The fuck we were," he countered, lying through his teeth.

RT sighed as he leaned back in his chair. "Look. I don't care what my agents do on their personal time, Hunter. And you can deny it all day long, but I knew you had a personal relationship with Josh."

"I was with Dani," Hunter argued.

"*And* Josh."

Hunter narrowed his eyes, trying to read his friend's mind. Did he really know about him and Josh and Dani? Or was RT simply digging, trying to get Hunter to admit it?

"The three of you were together," RT said. "I saw you."

"You were fucking spying on me?"

RT barked a laugh. "Fuck no. Trust me, that's something I wish I could unsee."

Yeah. Hunter knew no one would understand.

"The last thing I want is the image of your naked ass in my head. But don't for a second think that I'm judging you. I don't give a shit who you're with. You're more than welcome to love whoever you want."

"Even if it's two people?"

RT shrugged. "The heart wants what the heart wants, man. And if all parties are on board, whose decision is it anyway as to what's appropriate and what's not? I certainly don't give a shit."

Hunter wasn't sure how they'd gotten on this topic, but he suddenly felt incredibly uncomfortable.

"As for Kye…" RT sighed heavily. "The day he handed in his notice, he was upset. I could see it in his eyes. He didn't say why, and I didn't ask. But if you're worried about him, call him. See where he is."

Hunter shook his head as he turned toward the door. "I'm not worried. Sorry I bothered you."

The last thing he heard was, "Goddamn it, Hunter," right as he was walking out RT's door.

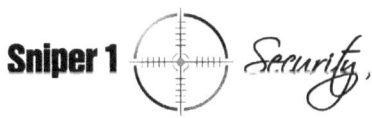

"FUCK," KYE WHISPERED AS HE pressed his lips to Dani's.

He honestly had no idea how they'd ended up back at her condo, much less rolling around in her bed.

Okay, he did know because that had been his intention all along. He had spent the day with her, flirting and laughing, offering casual touches, doing his level best to get close to the woman. And it had worked, much to his relief.

"Joe," she murmured against his mouth. "Please."

"Please, what, baby?" he asked softly, sliding his hands over her smooth, soft skin. She was practically naked beneath him, her bikini bottoms the only article of clothing still covering her. He wanted those gone so he could bury himself inside her heat, get as close as two people could.

"I need you," she whispered.

Fuck. Kye knew he should push away, walk right out of her bedroom and out of her life. He wasn't who she thought he was. He was lying through his teeth with every breath he took. Well, except for this. He wanted the woman with a passion. He hadn't intended to let it go this far, but he couldn't seem to turn back. Touching her felt so damn good. Being with her the only thing he could think about.

"What do you need, baby?" Kye trailed his lips down her neck, over her collarbone, then lower. He stopped when his tongue grazed her nipple.

Dani's hands curled around his head, holding him to her. She was so hot, practically melting beneath him. He had to wonder how long it had been for her, because she seemed to be coming apart at the seams.

When he sucked her nipple into his mouth, his cock throbbed as she moaned.

"Joe…oh, God. Don't stop doing that."

He hated that she didn't know his name. Hated that he was someone else entirely when he was with her. Kye wanted to hear Dani scream *his* name, to beg and plead as he slid into the warm depths of her body. He didn't want to be Joe, the sports store manager. He wanted to be Kye, her lover, the man who wanted to keep her safe no matter what.

Dani's hips shifted as she ground against him. His cock was pressed against her thigh, hard and aching, desperate for her touch.

As though summoned by his mental request, Dani's hand slipped down, caressing him through his shorts. He groaned, tweaking her nipple with his teeth.

She cried out, her hand curling around his cock as she writhed beneath him.

"Please...Joe..." Her eyes opened, and she looked right at him. "I need to feel you inside me."

For fuck's sake.

Kye knew deep down that he shouldn't be here. He was taking advantage of this woman, but he couldn't help himself. He wanted her with a passion he'd never felt before.

When Dani shoved his shorts down his hips, Kye knew he was a goner. Before he pushed them down his legs, he retrieved the condom he had tucked in his pocket before he went out for his afternoon workout. He hadn't expected anything, but he'd been hopeful.

Dani smiled up at him when he went to his knees, ripping the condom open with his teeth while she deftly removed her bikini bottoms.

And then she was naked. So fucking hot. And naked.

"You were a Boy Scout, weren't you?" she teased.

He laughed. "No."

"That's surprising."

Kye rolled the condom on, then moved over Dani once more. Tucking his hand behind her head, he pressed his lips to hers. She kissed him, their bodies molding together as his cock slid against her pussy. He was dying here, and Dani had no idea. Kye knew without a doubt he wouldn't be able to walk away from this woman when this was over. Sure, she would likely hate him when she figured out who he was, but no way could Kye walk away.

"Inside me," she demanded, her lips brushing his.

Reaching between their bodies, Kye guided his cock to her entrance, pushing in slowly.

Dani's eyes closed, her head tipping back as a soft moan escaped her.

She was so fucking tight, her pussy clasping his cock like a velvet vice.

"Aww, fuck," he moaned. "You feel so good."

Too good. Kye wasn't sure he would last. He shook off the thought. He damn sure didn't want this to be over before it even started.

Taking control of his body, Kye began rocking into her, pushing in deep, retreating slowly. He kept his eyes locked on her face as he made love to the sexiest woman he'd ever met. She would hate him for this, he knew. But he didn't want to think about that. Not now. Not when he had her in his arms, so pliant, so fucking sweet.

"More…please…" Dani's hands gripped his hips, jerking him closer.

Okay, maybe not sweet. Dani was a wildcat, taking what she wanted from him.

He thrust his hips forward, driving into her as deep as he could.

"Yes…" Dani's eyes closed. "Harder. Please."

Unable to refuse her request, Kye slammed into her over and over, watching as the need consuming her contorted her beautiful face. She was in the throes of pleasure as he fucked her ruthlessly, driving them both closer and closer to their inevitable release.

"Don't stop…oh, God. I'm so close…"

"Look at me, Dani," he insisted. Kye wanted her to be looking at him when she came, to know exactly who was inside her, who was giving her this much pleasure.

Her eyes opened.

"I want to see your pretty eyes when you come," he whispered.

Kye continued the brutal momentum, slamming into her, loving the way her body twisted, trying to get closer, her hands sliding over him as she held out. Her pussy fluttered over his cock numerous times and he knew she was close. Was she holding out for him? Did she never want this to end, the same way he did?

"Joe! Oh, God!"

Dani's body went still, her pussy gripping him tightly as her orgasm rocked her. She was so fucking beautiful. He never closed his eyes, even when his climax ripped through him, driving the sanity right out of him. Dani was everything he'd ever hoped for, everything he'd ever needed besides the one man who had refused to accept him.

She was also the very thing that would keep Kye from ever truly being happy.

Unfortunately, that was his own fucking fault.

*

Two days later, Kye was in his condo. Alone.

He couldn't sleep, so he decided to entertain himself by watching the cameras set up in Dani's condo. Granted, there wasn't a damn thing going on over there. All the lights were off, the doors were locked up tight—he'd watched her check them three times—and she was curled beneath the blankets in the big king bed.

God, he wished he was still there with her, wrapped tightly around her as she slept in his arms. They'd spent the past two days fucking each other senseless. Rather than spend their evenings down by the water, they spent them naked in her bed with Kye lodged deep inside her.

Each night, he would leave her, hating himself all the more for doing so. It was obvious she didn't want him to stay the night, but Kye couldn't have even if she had wanted him to. He had to stay alert, and being with Dani…it would've been too much to sleep in the same bed with her. As it was, he could already feel himself falling for her.

His thoughts drifted to Hunter. Although he was overwhelmed with desire when it came to Dani, he couldn't stop thinking about Hunter. About how the man would hate him for what he was doing. Then again, so would Dani. The two people he'd come to care about would likely shun him from their lives as soon as they realized what he'd done.

He sipped the water bottle and flipped to one of the outdoor cameras. Leaning forward, he kept his eye on the black Maxima pulling into the parking garage. One o'clock in the morning wasn't all that late for someone to be strolling in. At least not in the real world. Out here in the sticks, the only people around were the elderly folks who lived in the beachfront condos full-time and the families of four who were enjoying their summer vacation right on the water.

This person qualified as neither.

Reaching down, he grabbed his SIG, checking the clip and the chamber, then ensuring the safety was on before tucking it into the holster on his side.

"What're you up to, you sneaky bastard?" Kye mumbled to himself as a man exited the vehicle.

Squinting, he tried to get a look at the guy's face, but the man was keeping his head down, the ball cap he wore effectively shielding his identity.

"Damn it."

Kye got to his feet but didn't leave the computer. He had no idea who this guy was or where he was going, but whatever his motives, they weren't good. He knew that much. Most guys around there didn't dress all in black and slink up the stairs in the middle of the damn night.

"Fucker. Why'd you have to stop on the first floor?"

Kye flipped to the camera he'd put in place to monitor the first-floor walkway. He watched as the mystery man moved toward Dani's front door. Kye wouldn't have a bead on him from this point on, but the least he could do was tip her off. With the punch of a button, he caused the alarm clock on the nightstand to go off.

In the other camera angle, he saw Dani bolt out of bed, grabbing her gun. He could tell her attention was now on the front door.

"Good girl," he whispered, then took off at a run out of his condo, not even bothering with shoes.

Unfortunately, he was in the building next to hers, on the third floor to boot, so it took him some time to make it down the stairs. He stayed as silent as possible, not wanting to alert the other tenants. The last thing he needed was for the cops to be called.

He eliminated the distance between the buildings, then darted up the stairs. As he was nearing the end where Dani's condo was, he heard a car engine start up. He ran to the railing and glanced over just in time to see Dani lay on the gas, tires squealing as she hauled ass out of the parking garage.

Good thing was, she wasn't in danger.

Bad thing was, Kye needed to figure out who this asshole was.

Kye moved with as much stealth as he could, keeping to the shadows as he neared the condo. So far, so good. No one had come out to check on the noise, so he considered that a good thing.

Knowing he was going to have to confront this asshole at some point, he took a deep breath. If he was lucky, the bad guy hadn't gone out the way Dani had, which Kye assumed was via the patio. No doubt, she'd selected the condo that was on the first floor for a reason. Although there was a parking garage beneath, she could've easily scaled the balcony railing and dropped down to the grass below without injury.

With his back to the wall, he inched closer to Dani's door.

"Please be unlocked," he muttered softly.

He gripped the knob and turned it slowly.

Well, someone upstairs was listening tonight.

It turned, and he pushed it in an inch. The interior was completely dark except for the muted light from the cheap bulb over the stove. It was enough to see that no one was in the entry hall.

Stepping inside, Kye closed the door, his eyes easily adjusting to the shadowy interior. Without moving, he strained to hear what was going on in the other room. The hearing aids did wonders to amplify the sound, but he wouldn't hear as well as someone without a hearing impairment. Not that he gave it a second thought. He didn't know any different.

Keeping to the inside wall, he moved toward the kitchen. With his gun at the ready, he peered around the corner. The small area was empty. Two feet more and he could see the entire living room. Nope. No one there, either.

That meant the person was either in the bedroom or the bathroom, nowhere else for them to go.

The question now was whether or not he waited them out. At this point, Kye had the element of surprise on his side.

Darting to the opposite side of the room, Kye pressed his back to the wall, inching closer to the bedroom door. Taking a deep breath, he opted to wait. Mystery man wouldn't find much if he was hoping to search the condo now that Dani had bolted. Kye had already done a cursory look several days ago when Dani had been down at the beach. During his exploration, he'd found only the bare necessities. Whatever was personal and important, Dani wouldn't be carrying with her and, if she was smart, she kept secured in a safety deposit box somewhere. He figured that was likely the case since the woman was obviously prepared to run whenever she needed to.

What sounded like footsteps made Kye's body go rigid. He lifted his right hand close to his chest, the gun securely in his grip, safety off, finger hovering beside the trigger. As soon as the intruder took one step past him, Kye put his gun to the man's head.

"Who are you and why're you visiting my girlfriend?" Kye asked, his tone menacing.

If he thought this was going to be easy, he should've known better.

Before an answer could come, the man in black's elbow reared back, catching Kye in the side, his forearm catching Kye's and knocking his gun to the floor. Instinct had Kye kicking out, trying to take his attacker out at the knees. It worked, but the guy was on his feet once more, and he wasn't pulling any punches.

Well … technically he was.

They collided, the impact jarring. Fists, knees, elbows. They all connected, but this guy was good.

Kye knew better than to underestimate the nameless, faceless intruder. It didn't matter that Kye had extensive hand-to-hand combat training thanks to Sniper 1's agent boot camp. He soon learned they were evenly matched, despite the fact Kye had significant bulk and height on the guy.

He took a fist to the jaw, which rattled his brain a little, but Kye landed one to the guy's gut, causing him to double over. He aimed his fist for the man's head, but Speedy jumped back at the last second, causing Kye to follow the momentum of his swing. Before he could turn around, the fight was over as the guy darted out of the condo, leaving the door open wide behind him. Kye grabbed his gun, then went after him on foot. By the time he reached the bottom of the stairs, the black Maxima was heading for the main road.

He reached for his phone, but it wasn't in his pocket, which meant it had been knocked out during the scuffle.

"Son of a bitch," he grumbled, wiping the blood from his lip with the back of his hand as he ascended the stairs one more time. "Teach me to complain about being bored."

SEVEN

"DAMN, YOU'RE UP EARLY," RT greeted when Hunter stepped into the conference room on Friday morning.

It was early. Considering Hunter rarely strolled into the building before eight, he figured he deserved RT's harassment.

"Couldn't sleep." It was a lie. Partially.

He wasn't sleeping all that much these days. And whenever he did, he found himself caught up in a fucking dream that made the last one feel like rainbows and unicorns. This one left him pissed off and looking for revenge. Because in this damn dream, Danielle and Kye ended up dead rather than embracing the pleasure Hunter could offer them. Every time he woke up, he was covered in sweat, his heart racing, and he was looking for the threat that wasn't there.

He knew why he was having the damn dream. He'd pushed them both away when he could've held them close. But in his defense, Kye deserved a hell of a lot better than him, and Dani…well, Dani didn't want him in the first fucking place.

"Well, I'm glad you're here," RT admitted.

At least someone was. "Yeah?"

Conner stepped into the room behind him, followed closely by RT's husband, Z.

"Oh, good, we've got support," Conner declared.

"Support for what?" Hunter glanced at his brother, waiting for someone to elaborate.

"I brought donuts!" Trace offered, grinning like a loon when he joined them.

"Shouldn't you be taking those to your pregnant wife?" Conner questioned their younger brother.

"Trust me, I already took care of her. No way were y'all gettin' donuts before she did."

Hunter smiled. His sister-in-law was four and a half months pregnant with their second child and doing well. Not that you'd know it based on the way Trace followed her around like a puppy. He was there to cater to her every whim while still managing to work full-time and help her take care of their ten-month-old son, Gabriel. It would've been cute if, you know, it wasn't.

"So, what's the low-down?" Z asked, taking the chair beside RT.

"I'll fill you in once everyone gets settled." RT peered over at Hunter. "You hear from Decker yet?"

"Not since he threw a fit when I told him he had a new partner."

Deck had been downright pissed, which had surprised the shit out of Hunter. Not that he cared, but he could admit he was curious as to the other man's reaction to gaining a tagalong.

"You hear from Kye lately?" Trace asked.

The question took Hunter off guard. Why did it seem everyone was asking about him these days?

His gaze cut over to RT, who immediately turned his attention to his laptop.

"No. Should I?"

Trace shrugged.

Hunter hadn't talked to Kye since that last night they were together. He'd thought about him a million times, but he hadn't tried to contact him. He knew better. If Kye was ten feet away from him, Hunter would've ensured they were still a million miles apart because that was the way he operated. Hunter couldn't blame Kye for not wanting to deal with him anymore.

Although he thought about him often and wished the man would simply stumble in his front door from time to time, Hunter knew it was better this way. As it was, before Kye left Sniper 1, Hunter had been meaning to sit him down to let him know that the thing between them—which really wasn't much of a thing—couldn't continue. For the months prior, Hunter had given in to his cravings—using Kye and allowing Kye to use him—trying to fight his past, desperate to stop the ache in his chest whenever he thought about all he'd lost.

First Dani, then Josh.

Granted, Dani was still alive, but Josh was dead. Hunter's partner had been taken by a madman who'd been out to kill RT's sister, Marissa. It had happened in Oklahoma, at a safe house that turned out to be anything but safe. The bastard got to Marissa by going through two of their agents. First Ian, then Josh. Ian had sustained a serious bullet wound that had broken his clavicle, but Josh had taken a fatal one. In the end, Trace had managed to save Marissa's ass, and ultimately save the day. At least she was out of danger now, but Josh was gone forever.

Sometimes it felt like so long ago, other times…

Nope, he wasn't going to go there.

Not that his refusal to deal with it had helped any. Hunter's dreams were plagued with Kye, Josh, and Dani. Every single time he closed his fucking eyes, there they were, in brilliant Technicolor, haunting him in the worst way possible. With every passing day, Josh seemed to be fading more and more from his memory, replaced by Kye.

One day, they would all fade away and Hunter would be left alone. He refused to let himself get attached to anyone else, so putting space between them had been his only option. It had worked. All too well. Maybe he wasn't willing to divulge his deepest, darkest fantasies, but he couldn't deny that he still cared about Kye and Dani. Despite his better judgement.

Just as everyone got situated, Jayden stuck her head into the room. "Hey, RT. I've got Kye on line one."

RT's gaze instantly darted to Hunter before he grabbed the receiver to take the call.

"What the fuck?" Hunter roared, moving closer to RT.

"What's up, Kye?"

Hunter reached down and stabbed the speaker button.

"I…uh…" RT glared up at him. "Kye, I've got you on speaker. Most of the team—"

"She's gone," Kye interrupted, his tone rough.

"Who's gone?" RT continued to stare at Hunter and the guilt on his face spoke volumes.

"Danielle Davidson. She's fucking gone."

Fuck.

"You had him fucking following her?" Hunter accused, his voice far too loud for the confines of the small room.

RT ignored Hunter. "What do you mean gone, Kye?"

"I mean, she's not fucking there, RT. At the condo."

"Where'd she go?"

"Fuck if I know. I guess when that asshole showed up at one o'clock this morning she decided to haul ass again."

"What asshole?" Hunter bellowed. It took everything in him not to reach across the table and rip RT right out of his fucking chair.

"If RT would've answered his fucking phone this morning, he'd already have the fucking answer to that."

Hunter tried to incinerate RT with a look.

"Just tell us what's going on, Kye," RT said, his voice as calm as ever.

"Guy showed up in the middle of the damn night," Kye explained. "I alerted her and she high-tailed it. I went a couple rounds with the asshole, but he got away from me."

A couple rounds? What the fuck was going on?

"Are you hurt?" RT asked, ever the calm one.

"No."

Well, thank God for that.

As for Dani, Hunter wasn't surprised she'd run. The woman had bolted more times than they could count, but she'd always left everything in pristine condition upon her exit, and usually not in the middle of the damn night. Whatever had happened, it had to have been serious.

Hunter figured that could only mean one thing. Whomever she was running from had finally caught up to her.

Hunter felt several eyes on him, but he kept his attention on RT.

"Get your ass back here," Hunter rumbled roughly. "As fast as you fucking can."

"Yeah. I came up with that plan at one thirty. I'm ten minutes from the office now. See you in a few."

With that, Kye hung up.

"You want to tell me what the fuck is going on?" Hunter said, his voice deadly calm. "Why everyone believed Kye resigned, yet he's somehow on a top-secret mission for you?"

"I need to talk to Max," RT said firmly.

"You told me Max had her safely stashed away." Hunter rolled his eyes. "Another fucking lie?"

Conner stood beside Hunter, his full attention on RT. "What the fuck is goin' on? You're havin' Dani followed? What the hell's wrong with you?"

RT frowned his way. "It's none of your business, Conner."

"But it is mine. Start talkin'," Hunter demanded.

"I'll explain after the meeting."

"Bullshit!" Hunter stood tall. "Are these orders from Max?"

"Yes," RT said, his eyes leveled on Hunter's face.

"You're an asshole, Trexler. A fucking asshole." Hunter shook his head, turning toward the door, but Conner stopped him with a rough hand on his arm. Spinning back around, Hunter shoved Conner back, feeling that all familiar anger surge in his bloodstream. "Leave me the fuck alone."

Conner's forehead creased, his eyes narrowed. "Where're you goin?"

"To talk to Max myself."

"RT…" Conner sounded violent.

"Look, Hunter," RT called from behind him. "I know I went behind your back on this one, but I had to."

"Had to?" Hunter stared at the man who had betrayed him.

"Yeah. You're too close to this one."

"I thought you were passing Dani back over to her cousin?" he questioned. "You *told* me he was keeping her safe."

"That was my intention back when Dani left four months ago. At the time, I thought it was better left alone, but something told me Dani was in serious trouble."

"Something? Or someone?" Namely Max. If Hunter had to guess, Max had paid RT to keep this from Hunter.

"Max wanted me to keep an eye on her. This was the best way to handle it. I won't apologize for my decision."

Hunter was so fucking furious. He still remembered the conversation he'd had with RT right after Kye turned in his notice. Or faked it, anyway. Hunter had gone to RT, concerned about Dani's safety. After Claire had tracked Dani a couple of hours north in Oklahoma, RT had told him to back off. Said he needed to relay the information to Max so he could take care of it, but to back off.

In an attempt to take the high road, Hunter had done as RT requested, sharing what intel he had with Max. That was when his brother-in-law had not-so-kindly informed him that Dani would be Dani and Hunter needed to forget she even existed. They had followed it up with a fictitious story of how Max had tracked Dani and she was safely holed up somewhere.

"You're an asshole," Hunter repeated. "A lying bastard."

"Hey," Z said defensively. "That's enough. You want to have a conversation with him, do it in private."

"Did you know about this?" Hunter asked Z.

The remorseful look on his face said he did.

Hunter had never felt more betrayed than he did at that moment. He spun around to leave.

"Where're you goin'?" Conner asked.

"I'm goin' to talk to Max." That was as much as he was willing to divulge. He damn sure didn't intend to explain himself. And the details of what he was doing with Dani from this point forward were on a need-to-know basis. No one needed to know as far as Hunter was concerned.

Desperate to get out of there, he grabbed the doorknob and jerked it open.

"Hunter, wait," RT stated firmly.

Pausing, Hunter gripped the edge of the door and started silently counting down from ten.

"If you're gonna go at Max, at least take someone with you."

He shook his head. "I don't need anyone with me. I've got this."

"You're not thinkin' straight," Conner noted. "This chick has you fucked up, man. Still. She's not your problem anymore, goddammit. You need to let it go. Max can keep an eye on her."

Hunter pivoted once more, staring at his brother. "Yeah? Then why the fuck did someone break into her condo? Why the fuck did she feel the need to run?" He cut his eyes over to RT. "If she was so fucking safe, why did Kye lose her, huh? And where's Max now? If he was so fucking worried about her, then why isn't he up in your shit about this?"

"Maybe he doesn't know," RT mused. "Or maybe he's got it handled."

Z popped off at the mouth. "Maybe he doesn't think it's any of our business."

Hunter frowned. "Oh, he fucking knows all right," he told RT, ignoring Z's jab. "I guarantee he knows."

Conner glanced at RT, and Hunter noted the worried look on his brother's face. Hunter shrugged it off. He didn't have time for this.

"I'm goin' with you," Conner demanded.

"No, you're not. I don't want or need your help," Hunter drawled, pulling open the door.

He needed to talk to Max, find out where the hell Dani was, and once that was cleared up, he would confront Kye one last time. He was done with this shit. For real this time.

In fact, he was done with all of them. As far as he was concerned, RT could take the fucking job and shove it up his fucking ass.

DANI FELT AS THOUGH SHE'D been driving for days.

Perhaps that was because she was still in her car, having stopped only for gas, a bite to eat when she had started to feel light-headed, and to change clothes. Granted, what should've been a six-hour drive had taken her eight thanks to all the detours she'd taken in an effort to ensure no one was following her.

Finally, she was in Dallas, ready to have a sit-down with Max. It was time she did something drastic and there was only one person who could help her with that.

Her mind drifted back to Joe. Ever since she hopped in her car in the middle of the night, she'd thought about him endlessly. Hell, she'd contemplated finding him to let him know she had to leave. Of course, she hadn't put too much thought into that because it hadn't been an option. If she'd gone searching for the man, she would've been risking her life. And his.

But shit, it hurt knowing she would never see him again. She hadn't meant to get close to him, but she had. Now, she would never know if it could've been something more.

Dani really was tired of this.

Honestly, she thought she'd put all the running behind her when Samuel died. The bastard had been wreaking havoc on her life for long enough; it wasn't fair that he could do it from the grave, too. Unfortunately, it looked as though that was what he was doing.

The man who publicly claimed her as his niece had started his attempt to ruin her life when she was only nineteen years old. He began by blackmailing her, insisting that she do his dirty work, and by twenty, he had positioned her in the Kogans' life in order to get inside dirt on the family. She never understood why Samuel hated Casper Kogan so much, and it wasn't until Samuel's death that Max had told her the long, sordid story. It had been a shock. Casper and Samuel had been on the outs because of a girl. Specifically, Max's mother, Genevieve, who had become Samuel Adorite's bride at the age of thirteen. Apparently, Casper hadn't taken kindly to a monster like Samuel pulling Genevieve down into hell with him.

It was no secret that Samuel Adorite had never been in his right mind. In fact, the bastard had been stone-cold crazy. And no one was off-limits to him. No one.

Dani had known early on to steer clear of the man, but evading him hadn't been possible because Samuel didn't do a damn thing without having a backup plan. At first, Dani had refused to be a pawn in his game, but then he'd always known her weak spot—her mother—and he had fully intended to exploit it. It didn't take long before Samuel had trapped Dani in his web of blackmail and deceit. He'd threatened to kill her mother if she didn't do what he wanted. Dani knew he wasn't bluffing.

She was well aware of what he was capable of because her mother had warned her. Jessica Davidson had shared a multitude of horror stories, all painting Samuel as the monster he truly was. The crazy fuck hadn't even cared that Dani's mother had been married to Nick Adorite, Samuel's younger brother. It should've meant that Jessica was off-limits, but their nuptials hadn't stopped Samuel from brutally raping Jessica from the very beginning. Repeatedly.

Until, yes, the son of a bitch finally knocked her up.

Nine months later, Dani had been born.

Which meant her cousin Max wasn't really her cousin. He was her half brother.

No doubt about it, Samuel and his brothers had all been crazy, but Samuel was the craziest. Dani's father, Nick—the man who had claimed her—had merely been a liar, a cheater, and a drunk. Oh, and a coward. Not once had the man ever tried to protect his wife from Samuel's brutal attacks.

However, when you looked at the three of them as a whole, Nick was the least of anyone's worries. Their other brother, Patrick, was a disgusting, pathetic excuse for a human being. She'd never thought there could be anything worse than a rapist, but there was. Patrick had been a pedophile. The sick fuck had preyed on children. Dani honestly hadn't been sad when Max had killed him after Max found good ol' Uncle Patrick attempting to rape Max's sister, Ashlynn. She'd been fifteen at the time.

The only person Dani had ever depended on was her mother. Hence the reason she'd given in to Samuel, doing his dirty work in an effort to keep him away from Jessica. Unfortunately, cancer had been what stole her mother from her just a few short weeks before Dani was set to marry Hunter. At that point, Samuel no longer had anything to hold over her. That was when Dani decided to cut and run. Nick had been a man for once in his life, sending Dani across the world, trying to keep her as safe as he could.

It should've worked, only someone had figured out their secret.

Someone out there knew that Dani was Samuel Adorite's illegitimate daughter. And it appeared they were out to exact their revenge through her.

She just didn't know who it was.

And she didn't know their reasons.

But knowing what Samuel was capable of, knowing all the things he'd done, Dani knew she would never be safe until she disappeared forever, or she was dead.

Taking her secret with her.

KYE PULLED UP TO THE Sniper 1 Security parking garage at the same time Hunter was walking out of the building. He slammed on the brakes, tires squealing as he stopped his truck directly in front of the man and rolled down the window.

"Where're you goin'?" Kye demanded, watching as Hunter stopped, his gaze intense as he peered into the truck.

"None of your goddamn business," Hunter growled.

"The hell it ain't," Kye countered, leaning forward to maintain eye contact with the unruly asshole glaring back at him.

Hunter's eyes narrowed, but at least he had the decency to stop walking and face Kye through the passenger-door window.

"Do you know where she is?" Kye tried to read Hunter's expression, desperate for an answer to that question. Although this was a sort of homecoming for him, Kye was anxious to find out if Dani was all right.

On the flip side, it was damn good to see Hunter. It was all he could do to keep from eyeing Hunter up and down. He hadn't seen the man in four painfully long months and…well, he was trying to fight back the strange sensations that had erupted in his gut the instant their eyes had met. Although it had been easy to stay away when he had a job, being front and center with Hunter now was anything but.

"Not that it's any of your business, but I'm goin' to talk to Max," Hunter finally said, his eyes scanning their surroundings.

"About Dani? I'll go with you."

Hunter's gaze slammed into his and he frowned. "No, you won't. I don't want you anywhere near that shit."

Ah. So Hunter felt the need to protect him? Sweet.

Not.

"I don't think I'm the one you need to protect," Kye countered hotly. "Get in the truck, Hunter."

"Go inside," Hunter hissed. "This assignment's over. Go talk to your boss. I'm sure RT'll give you another job. This is no longer your problem."

Okay. Enough was enough.

Kye threw the truck in Park and jumped out, coming around to cut Hunter off before he could get to his motorcycle.

"What the fuck is goin' on?" Kye insisted. "I've spent the past four months tailing your fucking ex-girlfriend and I'm no closer to knowing what's going on than I was when I started. Either you start talkin'…or I walk."

"Like you did the last time?" Hunter goaded. "Good one."

"Fuck you, Hunter. You don't give two shits about me, much less what I do."

"You're right. I don't."

Damn, but that hurt. Kye hoped like hell he concealed the pain from his expression, but he felt it through his entire body.

Still, he couldn't back down. "I'm serious this time, Hunter. You bring me in or I walk. For good. I'm sick and tired of gettin' the runaround from you. I want some fucking answers. Now get in the goddamn truck!"

For a brief second, Kye thought Hunter would tell him to go to hell.

"It's best if you stay out of it," Hunter argued, his tone a little calmer than before.

"A little late for that, don't you think?" For the love of Christ. Hunter Kogan was the most stubborn man Kye had ever met. "Get. In. The. Truck," Kye snarled.

Only when Hunter stomped toward the passenger door did Kye release the breath he'd been holding. Although he would make good on his threat, Kye didn't want to leave Sniper 1. And he certainly didn't want to cut ties with Hunter. Or Dani.

Not completely.

These past four months had taught him that he couldn't harden his heart simply because it was the easiest thing to do. He cared about Hunter and Dani. He couldn't fight it anymore.

Running his hand down his shirt, Kye inhaled deeply and headed for the driver's door. He climbed in, buckled his seat belt, put the truck in drive, then glanced over at Hunter. "Where to?"

"Devil's Playground," Hunter grumbled.

Kye mentally mapped out the directions to the downtown Dallas club as he started out of the garage.

"You think Dani's going to see Max?" Although Hunter had been extremely vague about his interactions with Dani, Kye did know a few things about her.

Such as Danielle Davidson—she had never legally taken the Adorite name, instead using her mother's maiden name—was Maximillian Adorite's cousin. It wasn't something that a lot of people knew, though, which had made it extremely difficult for Kye to seek answers. Even most of Hunter's family didn't know, so he'd kept that tidbit of information to himself.

Plus, Dani and Hunter had been, at one point in their lives, in love. They'd even been slated to get married, only Dani had bolted on their wedding day. On top of that soap opera, Dani was prone to running for her life. At first, Kye had thought the girl was nuts, but it hadn't taken long to realize she was aware of a threat the rest of them weren't.

Yep. That was the extent of Kye's knowledge.

Well, that and how fucking amazing it was to have her beneath him, her hands roaming over his skin.

He shook off the thought. This was not the time or place for him to relive those intimate moments he'd shared with her.

"My plan is to let Max know she's gone and to tell him to keep a better eye on her."

"You don't think he's gonna want to know why she ran again?"

Hunter groaned. "I don't fucking care. It's done. We're through babysitting her. Max can find someone else to do it. Sniper 1 is no longer available."

Right.

"You know, you're never gonna get over this if you hang on to that denial." As soon as the words were out of his mouth, Kye instantly regretted saying them aloud.

"Fuck you," Hunter snarled. "You don't know the first goddamn thing about me."

Oh, he knew, all right. He knew that Hunter was hung up on the past, unable to let go of Dani or Josh. It was obvious Hunter wanted to, but something kept him tethered to those memories, making it impossible for him to ever be happy. And in turn, Hunter managed to hurt everyone who tried to get close to him. Kye's name was at the top of that list.

"You're right," Kye said on a sigh. "I don't. But not for lack of trying."

"Just get me to the fucking club, will ya? You can save all this feeling bullshit for someone who gives a damn."

Kye tried not to let Hunter's anger spur his own, but it wasn't easy. He considered himself a laid-back kind of guy. He usually let most shit roll right off him. Which was one of the reasons he and Hunter had meshed in the beginning. Kye hadn't asked for anything more than Hunter was willing to give. Hunter had still managed to insert a wedge between them. On purpose.

Yet here they were once again. Acting as though nothing had ever happened between them, as though the months they'd spent together meant absolutely nothing.

Maybe it really was time for Kye to move on. He could find another place to work. There were plenty of security services out there. He could start over.

"Quit drivin' like my grandmother," Hunter snarled.

Yes.

It was definitely something to consider.

EIGHT

FIFTEEN MINUTES LATER, HUNTER WAS ready to launch himself out of the truck. He didn't give a shit how fast Kye was going. He simply needed to move and the thought of diving headfirst into asphalt wasn't a bad one.

Then, finally, Kye pulled his truck into the parking lot across the street from Dallas's nightly hot spot, Devil's Playground.

"What's the plan, Hunter?" Kye questioned as he put the truck in park.

Hunter didn't bother to answer as he forcefully opened the door.

"Damn it, Hunter. I'm your backup."

"Stay here," Hunter commanded, slamming the door shut. He hadn't invited Kye, so the man could sit his happy ass in the truck while Hunter took care of this shit once and for all.

Without looking back, Hunter made a beeline across the street, directly to the nightclub. Devil's Playground was closed during daytime hours, but it was no secret that Max spent a significant amount of time there during the day.

Not that Hunter had known where Max was, but he'd suspected. However, he did know for a fact now because he'd called his sister, inquiring as much. With a less-than-kind warning to be nice, Courtney had given him her husband's whereabouts.

Hunter pounded on the main door, then stepped back.

When the armed bodyguard pulled it open, glaring at him, Hunter pushed past him without waiting for a verbal invitation. If the guy thought to intimidate Hunter with his holstered gun, he had another thing coming.

"Where is he?" Hunter bellowed, stepping out of the sunlight and into the dimly lit entrance.

Surprisingly, the man didn't try to stop him. Then again, Max had cameras all over the damn place, so he probably knew Hunter was there.

"Hunter, I'm serious," Courtney declared when she greeted him near the door. Apparently, she had been watching for him, as well. "Whatever this is about, you need to be civil."

Civil? Hunter wasn't sure he knew the meaning of that word anymore. And yes, Hunter wouldn't deny that, back when Max married Courtney, he and his brothers had been rather *un*civil when it came to finding out how Max intended to keep their sister safe from his life of crime. But that was a long damn time ago and he wasn't here to keep his temper in check.

Hunter waited for Courtney to move closer. If he had to guess, she'd just come from the penthouse apartment she and Max had, which was in the office building adjacent to the club. Hunter had learned sometime last year about the underground tunnel that connected the two buildings.

"Where's your husband?"

"I'm right here."

Hunter pivoted around at the sound of Max's deep voice echoing across the open room. He squinted into the dimly lit club to see the mob boss standing by the bar on the far wall, backlit by the glowing blue LEDs that showcased the top shelf.

"What's goin' on, Hunter?" Courtney inquired, sounding more worried than before.

Hunter ignored her, heading right for Max. He managed to make it all the way across the space before several of Max's bodyguards, strategically placed around the room, stepped toward him. The sound of weapons being cocked and loaded were loud in the otherwise silent room. Max didn't bother coming out from behind the bar.

"Put them away," Max stated, his tone as calm and cool as ever. "You want my wife to kick your collective ass?"

Hunter didn't look at the other men. He no longer gave a shit if someone wanted to take him out. He'd surpassed that several years ago when his life went to shit.

"Where the fuck is she?" Hunter snarled the words, the anger inside him boiling. Something about his brother-in-law pissed him off. Always had, probably always would.

Sure, some of the family had begun to tolerate Max, but Hunter wasn't one of them. The man was a lowlife, a thief, a murderer. He was the exact opposite of everything Hunter's family valued, yet his sister had fallen in love with the bastard.

Didn't mean Hunter had to like him.

"Where is *who*?" Max sounded far too calm.

Christ. They were going to play this game?

Hunter growled. "Dani. Where the fuck is she?"

"Why do you care, Hunter?" Max inquired, seemingly genuinely curious.

"Because someone broke into her condo last night," he stated, although he honestly *didn't* care. He simply needed to know where she'd gone so… Fuck. He didn't even know why he needed to know. Rather than let that tidbit of obvious insanity out, Hunter rephrased so Max would understand. "Where. The. Fuck. Is. She?"

"What do you mean someone broke in?" Courtney questioned, her concern evident.

"Exactly how it sounded." Hunter wasn't interested in playing Twenty Questions.

Max sighed when Courtney came around the bar to stand beside him. He then motioned for the men with weapons to back off. Max cocked his head. "Your guy's been trackin' her," he said calmly. "Why don't *you* tell *me*?"

"My guy?" Hunter's hands balled into fists at his side. "I didn't even fucking know about this goddamn assignment. It was something you concocted with RT. Not me."

"Semantics," Max said dismissively.

"Tell me what happened," Courtney demanded.

Hunter felt fire burning in his veins. "I don't know. I wasn't there. I only know someone broke in and she bolted."

That did seem to get Max's attention. "What do you mean?"

"She's fucking gone," Hunter snarled. "Someone broke into her place last night. Kye managed to warn her and she disappeared."

"Where's Kye?" Courtney asked.

"Outside."

"Why don't you—" Max's head turned to the man stepping into the room.

"Sir?"

"What?"

"We've got incoming," Dane warned. "Ms. Davidson just pulled in across the street."

Hunter took a deep breath, standing tall.

"Well, I think you have your answer," Max said, his tone still calm, but Hunter would've sworn he saw a hint of concern in the man's eyes.

"Yes. I do. And just so we're clear, she's your problem now. Keep a better eye on her because the assignment's over. Sniper 1 is no longer at your disposal."

"And that's your call to make?" Max countered with a smirk.

"It is now."

It was time Hunter stopped kidding himself. Dani wasn't his problem anymore. Nor his family's. If Max was worried about her, he could lock her in the fucking basement for all he cared. Hunter didn't give a shit what Dani did, who she did it with, or whether or not she was safe.

Maybe if he repeated that a few billion times, it might actually sink in.

Sniper 1 Security

KYE HUNCHED DOWN IN HIS seat as soon as he saw Dani pulling into the parking lot. She wasn't fifteen feet away from him. If she glanced to her left, she would see him sitting there.

Although it was a relief to see her, to know she was all right, he couldn't blow his cover. Dani would be suspicious if she saw him, which would likely have her bolting again. At least she'd had some sense to come home. Her cousin might be a lowlife, but he would keep her safe. If she would let him, that was.

Kye watched as she muttered to herself behind the wheel before squaring her shoulders and opening her door.

His eyes instantly scanned the area, making sure there were no visible threats. He even retrieved his SIG. After a brief pause to wait for traffic to pass, the woman walked straight for the club, her head held high as though she had nothing in the world to worry about.

Kye knew that if he was ever in a real relationship with Dani, she would make him absolutely crazy. She didn't seem at all concerned that someone could have a bead on her right then. With one twitch of a finger, they could take her out, leaving her bleeding in the street.

His gut churned at the thought even as his eyes scanned the surrounding buildings.

It wasn't until she made it inside that he took a breath.

Of course, now he had nothing to do but sit on his thumbs and wait for Hunter to return.

He didn't know what was worse, watching Dani walk away—possibly forever—or waiting for Hunter to walk toward him.

Sniper 1 Security

SHE WAS TIRED, SHE WAS hungry and most importantly, Dani wanted a hot bath and a glass of wine.

Unfortunately, she wasn't going to be able to do a damn thing about any one of those things until she had this conversation with Max.

"No one asked you to follow her, Hunter," Max was saying when she stepped into the club. "RT's been handling the case, so I'm not sure how this is any of your business."

"Because it's *my* company," the deep, grumbling voice retorted.

Clearly the universe was out to get her again, because when Dani walked into the room, she realized Max wasn't the only one in the broad expanse of real estate known as Devil's Playground. The club was closed, and without all the lights and techno music thumping through the speakers, it was dark and far too quiet. Well, except for the two men shouting at one another.

"Fine. You want to play it that way, you worry about your family, I'll worry about—" Max's counter argument was halted when she stepped into view.

From the moment her gaze settled on Hunter, Dani knew this wasn't going to be pretty. It took everything in her to keep from giving him an excessive glance. As it was, she managed to take him in from head to toe. From the giant boots on his feet, the well-faded blue jeans, the black T-shirt molded to his exquisite torso beneath the leather jacket, all the way up to his recently cut hair and the sexy stubble on his chin. The man looked good, not to mention extremely dangerous.

For a brief moment, Dani felt a hint of guilt trickle through her. She had slept with another man. Not that she was ashamed of what she'd done. Joe…well, Joe had come to mean something to her in such a brief amount of time. But as she looked at Hunter, Dani realized she still wasn't over him. She wasn't sure she ever would be.

But that wasn't relevant. Dani didn't want to be here as it was, but having to have this conversation while Hunter was glaring at her, his anger apparent… Story of her fucking life. No matter how hard she tried, she couldn't seem to put enough distance between them. If it weren't for this stupid threat on her life, she wanted to believe she would have.

Threat.

Right.

The reason she was here.

The very reason she had bolted from the condo in the middle of the damn night, running scared.

She'd known it was only a matter of time. It sucked, but what could she do? Something had spooked her—a premonition, perhaps—which she had learned wasn't necessarily a bad thing. Being scared meant she was staying alert. For that very reason, she had packed up the few important things she'd had with her and loaded them into the trunk of her car last night before she'd attempted to get some sleep. At one, when she'd been awoken by the sound of her alarm clock blaring, followed by the sound of someone jimmying open the front door, Dani had slipped out the sliding glass door, easily hopped over the railing on the patio, and hauled ass out of there.

"Why are you here?" Max questioned, his tone hard.

Rather than explain all of that, Dani went with, "Good to see you, too."

Trying to keep her cool, Dani focused on the sound of her heels clicking across the concrete floor as she headed toward the bar. She had made a detour to a truck stop before she hit the city limits, needing some sort of armor to get her through this meeting. She'd felt significantly better once she changed out of her yoga pants and T-shirt and into what she liked to consider her mood-affecting clothes. She felt far more powerful when she was dressed up rather than slumming it.

She did her best not to look at Hunter, which wasn't an easy feat. The man was a large, looming presence. Not only in size but also in attitude. The anger coming off him was palpable, but she wasn't sure if it was aimed at her or Max. Or both. Probably both. Everyone knew that Hunter didn't belong to either of their fan clubs.

"Goddammit, Dani," Max huffed. "You walked right in the front fucking door. What are you thinkin'?"

Dani frowned. "I'm *thinkin'* that I need to talk to you. To let you know there's a problem. How else did you want me to get inside?"

"The back door?" Courtney suggested. She didn't sound the least bit impressed.

Dani knew Courtney didn't like her. Her once almost-sister-in-law didn't try to hide that fact, either. Not that Dani blamed her since Dani had been the one to leave Courtney's brother on their wedding day. There might be tension between Courtney and her own family since Courtney was in bed with the enemy—literally—but Dani knew the woman was a bulldog when it came to protecting them.

"A problem?" Max sounded indignant. "Honey, there's a shit ton of problems. One of which is you walkin' in the front fucking door."

Okay, so he clearly had an issue with that. Dani wasn't quite sure why. It was broad daylight on a Friday afternoon and they were in the middle of downtown Dallas. What did he think was going to happen?

"You need to leave," Max demanded. "And *you*"— Max glared at Hunter—"need to take her somewhere safe. Right fucking now."

"No can do," Hunter stated, his tone laced with hatred. "She ain't my problem anymore."

"Then why'd you barge into my fucking club demanding to know where she was?"

Dani swung her head in Hunter's direction, waiting for him to answer that question. He'd come here? For her? But how? Why?

"Because she was missin'. Now she's not. That means she's your problem."

What did he mean she was missing? From where?

"Hunter?" Courtney called out. "We could use your help with this, seriously."

"No. RT's working on another case and I've got better things to do."

"Someone's trying to kill me," Dani stated, not quite sure who she was talking to. Didn't matter, since those five words had captured the attention of everyone in the room, including Leyton, Max's second-in-command.

"Same song, different verse." Hunter stared at her, disbelief practically dripping from his pores. "Is this one real, Dani? Or are you still haunted by ghosts?"

"Fuck you," she hissed, sparing him a quick glance.

She understood that Hunter was pissed, but she didn't have to answer to him anymore. She was here to make a deal with Max, so she turned her attention to him. "I ditched the condo when someone tried to break in." Dani kept her eyes locked on Max's face. "I didn't stick around to ask them *why* they wanted to kill me."

"What the fuck is goin' on?" Hunter asked, but this time it seemed he was also talking to Max. "I thought you were handling the Moroso issue."

"Fuck." Max slammed his glass against the bar.

Okay then.

"It's not Moroso," Dani insisted.

"You need to hide her," Max demanded, his attention on Hunter.

Unlike last time, Hunter didn't seem to have a response to that, so Dani filled in for him.

"I don't need him watchin' me. More importantly, I don't *want* him watchin' me."

"The feeling's mutual, sweetheart. Trust me."

Dani ignored him again. "I'm not plannin' to stay, but I do need to do something more … permanent."

"It wasn't a request," Max snapped, obviously not listening to a word she said. "You can't fuckin' be here, Dani."

"Well, too late. I'm here. And once I tell you what I came to say, I'll be out of your hair for good."

All eyes seemed to still be looking at her.

She had come back so she could let Max know that she was disappearing forever. She couldn't keep running and it was time that she started over. Considering she was low on funds, she needed his help in that regard. And in an effort to keep him from searching for her, Dani had wanted to give him a heads-up. Not to mention, she knew Max had ways of making people disappear. Permanently. If he could do that with others, he could certainly assist her. Starting over, far, far away from anyone she knew, was her only option.

"We need to talk," she told him softly. It was pointless to have her death staged if so many people knew she was doing it. "The sooner we do, the faster I'll be out of here." That was obviously what he wanted.

"You're not goin' anywhere, Dani," Max bit out. "In case you haven't fucking noticed, I've got people gunnin' for me and my family."

She tried for reasonable. "Exactly. Which is what I came to talk to you about."

"Who's gunnin' for you now?" Hunter asked her directly. He seemed to be the only one who'd heard her earlier declaration. "Moroso? The mobster's brother?"

"No. Well, maybe. But if he is, he's not the only one," Dani confirmed, never looking away from Max.

"You don't know the half of it, Dani," Max said with a heavy sigh.

"Why don't you enlighten me then?"

"I'm not gonna have this argument with you again. You defied me last time. It's time you go underground, let us take care of you," Max stated firmly, glancing over at Hunter, then to Leyton. "If someone other than Moroso really is after her—"

"Someone *is*," Dani interrupted. "Hence the reason I've been running, Max. Damn it. You think I want to do this?" Okay, so she hadn't meant to get angry, but she couldn't help it. She was pissed. And scared.

"Is the Moroso brother still a threat?" Hunter asked again, clearly oblivious to her little meltdown.

Dani sighed.

"More so now than ever," Courtney confirmed. "From the information we've gathered, he's stabilizing his organization," Courtney supplied, obviously in the loop. "Which is the only reason he hasn't made a move yet."

"And he's proving to be a *real* threat?" Hunter questioned.

Max snorted, as though the question was ridiculous. In a way, it was. These people had to know what Max was up to, what he'd done. That after Marco Moroso put out a hit on Ashlynn, Max had the man taken out. It had taken some time, and a couple of people had died—including two of Ashlynn's bodyguards, one of which was the brother of one of her lovers. In the end, Marco had said good night. Permanently.

Dani doubted that Hunter didn't know this. Then again, maybe he didn't. Maybe Max and Courtney really did keep the details on a need-to-know basis. However, that was hard to believe since, for the past couple of years, Dani knew Hunter's family had been involved in some of the things going down with the Adorites.

Then again, she wasn't sure of Hunter's part in all of it. From what she'd figured out, he spent a lot of time out of the country. Or he had, anyway. She wasn't sure what he was up to these days.

Hunter cleared his throat and Dani peeked up at him from beneath her lashes. He was looking between her and Max, but for the life of her, she didn't know what was going through his head.

"I need someone to keep an eye on her," Max stated firmly. "I'm not askin'. I'm tellin'. This went sideways once. I don't want that happenin' again, Hunter."

"Good luck with that," Hunter grumbled as he turned toward the door.

"Hunter!" Courtney called after him. "Seriously. We need your help. This isn't a joke. She's Max's cousin. We need—"

"Not my problem," he called back, his gaze sliding to Dani once more.

As he walked past her, there was no mistaking the hatred in his white-gray eyes.

While staring Hunter down, Dani decided it was time to deliver the bomb. "I'm not Max's cousin."

Hunter stopped immediately, but he wasn't the one to speak.

"What?" Max asked. "What the fuck are you talkin' about?"

Dani tore her gaze from Hunter and turned her attention to Max. "I'm not your cousin."

"I heard you the first time. What the fuck does that mean?"

She swallowed hard, hating that she'd reached her breaking point. This information was better kept buried, but unfortunately, as she'd learned recently, that was no longer an option.

"Nick isn't my father," she told him. "Samuel is."

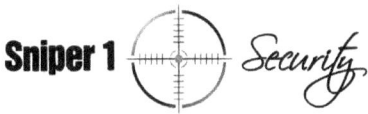

"THE COUSIN'S BACK," THE GRAVELLY voice rumbled into the phone. "So is the old boyfriend."

Dennis Moroso was pleased with the information, but the last comment had his brain scurrying to tie it all together. Then it hit him. "Ah. The wife's brother?"

"That's the one." There was a strange tension in the man's tone.

"You have a problem with him, Dmitry?"

Dennis was met with a few seconds of silence before the Russian assassin said, "It's a personal matter."

"Will it compromise the job?" Dennis didn't give a fuck what personal issues the man was having, but he did need to know the man was capable of completing the mission.

"No."

"Good. Then deal with that however you need to," Dennis told him. "But don't let it interfere with my plan. It's time to herd them like cattle. I've waited long enough. Make sure you don't take Max out, though. Injure him all you want, but that bastard is mine. When it's time to take him out, I will do it myself. Slowly. Painfully."

"Of course."

"Make sure no one sees you."

The man snorted. "Like ghost."

With that, the phone disconnected, and Dennis turned his attention to the food on his plate. He wasn't particularly hungry, but he had ventured out so that he would be seen. This had been his brother's favorite restaurant, so he'd come here on purpose. While the eggs benedict was divine, it wasn't what would sate the hunger that was burning in Dennis's gut. The only way to do that was with revenge.

And he would have his.

The Adorites were directly responsible for the downfall of his entire family. His brother was dead and Dennis had every intention of paying back the bastard who had taken his life. Business was business, and sure, Dennis understood Max Adorite's reasons for killing Marcus. Dennis's brother hadn't been right for a while. He never should've put a hit out on Max's sister. If he wanted to take her out, he should've done it himself.

However, family was family and Dennis had every right to avenge his brother's death. He would start by taking out Max's family members. One by one. He knew exactly how he wanted it to go down. A little at a time. Dennis had spent the better part of the last year learning everything there was to know about Max Adorite and his family. It had taken some time, but he'd come up with a plan to hurt Max the same way Max had hurt his family.

First, he'd start with the cousin, Danielle. She didn't seem to be all that close to Max, but she was still family. From there, Dennis would go down the line, one after the other. The mother, the uncle, all the brothers and sisters would go, and then, while Max watched, Dennis would kill the man's wife.

Of course, Max's life wouldn't be quite over at that point.

But he would certainly wish that it was.

NINE

"I NEED YOU TO LISTEN to me," Dani said from somewhere behind Hunter. "Just let Hunter leave. Once you hear me out, you'll see I know how to solve this."

Hunter refused to turn around, refused to ask her what the hell that meant. In fact, he wasn't sure he could because he was still trying to process what she'd said.

She wasn't Max's cousin? She was his fucking sister? And no one knew this?

"I'm not here to stay," Dani continued. "I just need your help."

She wasn't staying? Where the hell was she going to go now?

Not that it fucking mattered. He needed to walk right out of this goddamn club and never look back. The sooner she was gone, the better off he'd be.

"What do you mean Samuel's your father?" Max asked, his tone ridiculously calm. "I need you to start from—"

Before Max could finish his thought, the room exploded with sound.

Rat-tat-tat. Rat-tat-tat.

Glass shattered. Bullets slammed into concrete and wood, sending debris flying. Chaos ensued. Screaming, grunting, yelling. One of the bodyguards only a few feet to Dani's right took several hits to the chest, his entire body jerking as he hit the wall.

Rat-tat-tat. Rat-tat-tat.

It felt like slow motion as Hunter lunged, taking Dani to the ground in an effort to keep her from being next. She screamed when their bodies collided, but Hunter couldn't worry whether or not he'd hurt her. With a single-minded purpose, he threw himself on top of her and slid right into the small alcove beneath the stairs, protected by the steel beams that lined the wall.

Leyton was instantly spitting out orders while everyone scattered, attempting to take cover, waiting for the next volley of gunfire.

Son of a bitch.

"Oh, my God! Oh, my God!" Dani screamed louder, even when the gunshots ceased, her voice echoing in the cavernous space. "Oh, my God! Oh, my—"

Hunter slammed his hand over her mouth, forcing her to be quiet. "Stop." Hunter met her terror-filled gaze. "Dani. Stop."

Her eyes were glassy and far too wide as she stared up at him. Hunter could see the fear shining back at him.

Leyton was calling out to someone, likely the guy manning the door.

Footsteps sounded as people started moving. Leyton darted over to the guy bleeding on the floor, just a few feet away from where Hunter remained motionless, keeping Dani protected beneath his own body.

While he took stock of his surroundings, a voice rang out in Hunter's head.

"Fuck. Hunter," Kye's words sounded in his earpiece. "What the fuck was that? Goddamn it! Answer me!"

"Give me a chance and I will," he told Kye. "Where are you?" Hunter kept his tone as low and as even as he possibly could.

Dani's eyes widened as though she wanted to answer him. He simply shook his head, keeping his hand firmly over her mouth.

"Right where you left me. Across the street."

"Did you see where the shots came from?"

"Looked to be coming from directly across the street from you. Third floor of the bank building. Are you hit? Is everyone else okay? Is…Dani all right? And why the fuck doesn't Adorite have bulletproof glass?"

Hunter relayed the information about the shooter to Leyton, then glanced across the dark room toward the bar. "Max? Courtney?"

"We're good," his brother-in-law shot back. "We've got to get the fuck outta here."

"You might want to invest in bulletproof glass," Hunter offered, knowing it wouldn't do a damn bit of good now, but hey, a mob boss should be ready for an attack.

"It's on my to-do list, Kogan," Max growled back.

"You're bleeding, Max! Where were you shot?" Courtney screamed.

Fuck.

"It's okay, baby," Max crooned, clearly trying to calm his wife. "It grazed me. But we are gettin' the hell outta here. Right fucking now."

"We need an ambulance," Courtney insisted, her tone oddly calm. Then again, Hunter knew his sister was relatively good under pressure.

"No ambulance," Max refuted. "No hospitals. Let's get to safety and someone'll patch me up."

"Gonna be hard to do," Courtney countered hotly, "since Moroso took out the good doctor last night."

"We'll find someone," he assured her.

Hunter knew that Max wouldn't dare take the chance of going to a hospital. Gunshot wounds would attract police. Everyone knew that Max and the police didn't mesh. If the man could walk out of here, he would do so without a police escort.

Hunter took a moment to move his hands over Dani, ensuring there was no blood oozing from her body. He pretended not to notice the way his hands were trembling, and he hoped like fuck she didn't notice.

"Were you hit?"

Dani shrugged.

Oh, damn. He tried to keep his touch impersonal, but the instant he felt her curves beneath his fingers, memories of long ago came back full force. He pushed them back, mentally locking them in a fucking box that he never intended to open again for as long as he lived.

"Hunter, stop. I'm—I'm not hit," she said insistently, running her hands over her own body as though she didn't quite believe it. "I'm…f-fine. Are you okay?"

Hunter nodded curtly, then began speaking so that Kye could hear him. "Kye, Max took a bullet, but it's superficial. Or so he says." Not that Hunter was going to stick around to find out if Max lived or died. The man had a fucking army. He could take care of himself. On the contrary, Hunter was on his own.

"Hunter," Courtney yelled. "Take her. Get her out of here. Don't be an asshole right now. Just do this for me."

He shook his head in disbelief. Of all the favors Courtney could ask of him, why did she have to do this now?

"Did you hear me?" she shouted.

"Yes, goddammit," he grumbled. "I fucking heard you." He glared at Dani, hoping she saw the anger he felt pulsing inside him. "Kye, I've gotta get Dani outta here."

"Roger that. There's an underground garage. I'm pulling around there now."

"Is there another way to the garage from here?" Hunter asked Leyton, keeping his voice low.

"Two feet to your left," Leyton informed him, crouching beside where Hunter was still lying on top of Dani. "Follow the hall. It'll lead right outside through the mechanical room."

"You get that, Kye?" he asked the man on the other end of his earpiece.

"Ten-four," Kye replied. "Give me two minutes, then be ready to come out."

Hunter took a deep breath, forced his heartbeat to slow. He tried to blame his rapid pulse on the adrenaline, but he knew it was more than that. Seeing Dani lying there, practically beneath him, her eyes wide. Someone had tried to kill her. He wasn't sure what he would've done if they'd succeeded. As much as he wanted to believe that he didn't fucking care, Hunter knew better. He hated it, but he still knew better.

"I'm sending Max and Courtney through the penthouse," Leyton informed him. "Dane will keep them safe. And I'll get ahold of Rock. Have him find someone to patch Max up when we get the boss to him. Take Dani with you and we'll be in touch."

Hunter resigned himself to dealing with the situation. He simply needed to get Dani out, keep her alive, and then he could pass her off to Kye. The man would protect her, Hunter knew that much. Hell, he'd been doing it for the past four months.

Dani's eyes were wide, and he could feel her heart slamming against her ribs. Hunter hadn't bothered to move off of her since they hit the floor and he was having a difficult time doing so now. If the gunman was still out there, they were all sitting ducks.

"Hunter!" Courtney yelled. "Take her now."

"Looks like we're gonna jet, sweetheart. I'm gonna move offa you, but you have to stay right where you are. And don't scream, for chrissakes. Got it?"

She nodded.

"Max," Hunter called out. "I'm takin' her with me. You want me to take Courtney?"

"Not goin' anywhere," his sister snarled. "Not without Max."

"She's a stubborn one," Max said, peering over at Hunter from his perch behind the bar. "We're good. Take her and call me later. Leyton, you're with us. Have Darius deal with the police, and make sure he takes care of Felix's body. We were never here."

A string of curse words followed when Max took a good long look at the dead man Hunter assumed was Felix.

The second Hunter moved off of Dani, her mouth opened. Before she could get a single word out, he silenced her again. "No talking. We're gonna get the fuck outta here before whoever it is that wants your family dead comes to ensure they accomplished their goal. There'll be plenty of time to ask questions later." Not that he intended to answer them.

Hunter could hear sirens in the distance. Any minute now, the police would be rolling up to the club and it wouldn't take a genius to figure out who had been the target.

"Hunter?" Kye sounded in his ear.

"Yeah."

"We've got three minutes tops before the cops roll up. It's now or never, man."

Now or never.

The fucking story of his life.

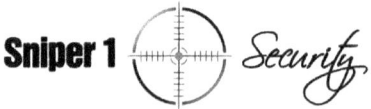

ONE MINUTE DANI WAS PLEADING her case as to why she had come back to talk to Max, and the next, she was running out a hidden hallway in Max's club after someone tried to kill her.

They'd freaking tried to kill her!

Twice in one day.

This was getting ridiculous.

It took everything in her not to panic, not to break down, not to give in to the urge to cry. How could this be happening? She'd spent too much time on the run. Was it ever going to end? Would she ever be able to have a normal life?

Truth was, she continued to hold out hope that one day she would be able to come home, settle down, do something mundane like work in an office. She hated this shit and it seemed that trouble continued to follow her. The last thing she wanted to do was be on the run all over again. She simply wanted to pack up her crap, secure a fake ID, stage her own death, and start a new life. Alone. Without the people she cared about. Max's world was dangerous enough. He definitely didn't need the problems she brought to the table.

Trying to keep up with Hunter, Dani ran alongside him. Not easy in four-inch heels, but she was up for the challenge. She knew he was purposely running faster, forcing her to keep up, but Dani pretended not to notice. She didn't complain, but her lungs were burning from the exertion. Teach her to avoid the treadmill, now wouldn't it?

Without giving her a chance to say anything, Hunter ushered her right through the outer door and into the parking garage, where a big, black, four-door truck sat idling. Hunter grabbed the back-door handle, yanked it open, and shoved her inside. He then hopped in the front.

Before anyone could say anything, the blond-haired man in the driver's seat put his foot to the floor, tires squealing on concrete as he headed toward the exit. He peered over his shoulder at her and their eyes locked.

Dani's breath hitched in her chest. There in the front seat was…

"Kye Sterling. Nice to officially meet you," the man said, his gaze darting between her and the road in front of him. "We'll make formal introductions later. In the meantime, I want you to get your ass in the floorboard, and don't get up for any reason. No matter what, Dani. Understand?"

No, she didn't understand. Kye Sterling? His name was Kye fucking Sterling? Not Joe? Her god-like neighbor who liked to work out on the beach every day at three o'clock, the man she'd gotten closed to, allowed into her bed? What the hell was he doing here?

"I thought your name was Joe," she hissed, glancing from him to Hunter, then back.

He was a liar.

That earned her a remorseful smile from Kye Sterling and she knew right then that he had played her. His name obviously wasn't Joe and he damn sure wasn't a sports store manager.

Dani realized that his name wasn't the important part of his statement.

"Down, Dani. Goddammit," Hunter thundered.

She dropped onto the floor, crouching low enough that she couldn't be seen from the window.

What the fuck was going on? Why was Hunter helping her to escape what looked to be an assassination attempt? Did they really call it assassination? Sure, if she were royalty, or a president, maybe they would. She didn't know. It sounded funny, though. Not *ha-ha* funny, because there was nothing funny about this. Then again, she didn't know for sure that those bullets had been meant for her. Max had been there, too. To be fair, however, no one had tried to kill Max for quite some time now. Not that she knew of, anyway.

Shit. This was surreal.

"Dani? You with me?" Kye asked, his tone calm, although he was still driving like a madman.

"Fuck you," she ground out, still trying to catch her breath. "Don't talk to me."

"Take me to the office," Hunter demanded. "I'll get my bike. I want you to disappear with her. I'll catch up with you later."

"Roger that," Kye answered, obviously used to taking orders from the man. "Dani? Stay down, beautiful," Kye said. "We don't need anyone seein' your pretty face."

Hunter growled.

It was only then that she realized she'd been trying to peek out the window. Not wanting to endure Hunter's wrath, she dropped back down, putting her forehead on her knees and closing her eyes while she braced her arms against the back of the seat to keep from being thrown to the other side of the truck.

She wanted to ask why they couldn't trust the police to take care of this. It seemed like a fairly simple solution. Then again, Max didn't trust the police, and if they dug deep enough, she knew they'd find out who she really was. Probably not a good thing, considering.

Dani remained crouched on the floor for what felt like an eternity. She couldn't see a damn thing out the window other than the brilliant, cloudless blue sky. Once the sirens faded in the distance, she figured she was safe. Still, she didn't get up from where she was, afraid Hunter would yell at her. The only thing she cared about was getting away from Hunter and Kye Sterling—the lying snake—as fast as she could.

Oh, and staying alive. She *really* cared about that.

"Drop me here," Hunter mumbled.

The truck came to a stop. Dani heard the door open, then slam closed. A motorcycle rumbled to a start as Kye was pulling away.

"Can I sit up now?"

"Hop on up here, doll," Kye answered, a smile in his voice.

"Don't you dare call me that," she demanded as she unfolded herself from the floorboard, then slid over the console into the front seat. Good thing she'd opted for pants today. She pulled on her seat belt as Kye was pulling out of yet another parking garage. "Where're we going?"

"Vacation time," he said with a quick smile, although it appeared somewhat sad.

Did he feel bad that he'd used her?

Asshole.

"I don't need a vacation," she told him. "And I damn sure don't want to be alone with you."

"Dani…"

"No!" she shrieked. "You don't get to talk to me."

He sighed heavily. "I'll explain everything when we get to our destination."

She didn't bother to tell him she didn't want to hear it. "What about Hunter? Where's he going?"

"Trust me, he's not far behind us."

"How do you know?"

"Because he's Hunter. He's never that far behind me."

Dani got the sense he was joking, but she was out of the loop.

"Relax," he said, his voice soft as he reached over and squeezed her hand. She jerked out of his reach. "Seriously, Hunter's fine. He'll probably get there before we do."

God, she hoped so. Right now, she feared for Kye's safety.

Because she wanted to kill him.

WHEN THOSE BULLETS HAD STARTED flying, Kye's entire life flashed before his eyes.

He'd nearly hyperventilated waiting for confirmation from Hunter that they were both all right. The thought of something happening to either of them…Kye couldn't even think about it now. It made his chest hurt.

As he drove, he cut his eyes over to Dani briefly. He needed to assure himself that she really was all right. Even if she was angry, even if she wanted to kill him—which he suspected she did—Kye merely needed to know that she wasn't hurt.

"Are you okay? Really okay?" he asked softly.

She glared at him momentarily, then turned her attention to the passenger window.

He would take that as a yes, but he still couldn't stop stealing glances her way.

Dani looked a little rumpled as she was staring out the window. Her long, auburn hair had slipped out of the ponytail, causing some of the strands to trail down her back. She had the longest hair he'd ever seen, all the way to her ass. But even disheveled, it was sleek and shiny, and he remembered how silky it felt against his skin.

Unlike at the beach, when she'd sported mostly shorts or bikinis, Dani was wearing a pair of black slacks, custom fit to cling to her curves nicely. She had on an off-white silk blouse that showcased her impressive rack.

To his shock, she hadn't said anything since they hit the highway. He figured for sure she would lay into him, making accusations, insisting that he explain why he had been at the beach with her. Nope, she'd kept to herself, watching their surroundings almost as diligently as he was.

She didn't ask him who he was or why he'd been stalking her or why he'd given her a fake name. Since she'd seen him with Hunter, she had probably figured that one out. She didn't ask why someone had been shooting at her—she probably knew the answer to that already, too.

But it was a good thing she wasn't asking a lot of questions, because Kye wasn't sure he was ready to give her any answers. Certainly not about where they were going. Hell, Hunter had given him the bare minimum as far as details of this op went. He hadn't verbally told him where to take her; instead, Hunter had pulled up the GPS coordinates on the truck's navigation system while Kye drove. Hell, he was lucky Hunter had thought to jot down the alarm code for the safe house before he got out of the truck.

As usual, Kye felt a little left out. Especially regarding why someone would be gunning for the woman. Hunter hadn't seemed to be surprised. Kye found it hard to believe that for the four months he'd followed her, never once had someone opened fire. In fact, he didn't remember seeing a gun on the intruder last night.

Yet she was in Max's presence for less than ten minutes and someone was using her as target practice? Nah. He wasn't buying it. Kye got the sense this had nothing to do with the guy he'd encountered at her condo. This was something else entirely, something aimed at Max.

"Did Hunter assign you to follow me? Is that why you were at the beach?"

Kye glanced over at Dani. She was trying to fix her ponytail, pulling the elastic band out and clenching it between her teeth while she ran her hands over her hair.

"Actually, no," he told her. "Hunter didn't know about it."

"What?" She frowned his way. "What do you mean he didn't know?"

Kye kept his eyes on the road. "Hunter thought I left Sniper 1."

"Why?"

"Because I turned in my resignation."

"You're not making any sense," she accused.

"I know."

Rather than pelt him with more questions, she glanced out the window again.

So, there they were, driving in silence to a private cabin in some small town on the Texas-Oklahoma border while Hunter was going to do a little digging of his own. It would've been easy enough for him to disappear with them, but Kye knew Hunter. The man wasn't going to leave this up to the police. He would do some investigating first and try to get some answers.

"Who are you?" Dani questioned, her voice raspy yet smooth.

"Kye Sterling," he told her again.

"Yeah, I got that," she snapped. "I want to know who you are. Why you told me your name was Joe. And *why* you were…at the beach."

"I promise, I'll give you all the answers I can," he told her honestly. "But not right now."

Dani snorted. "Right. Like I'm gonna believe anything you say. I'd have a better chance getting the truth out of Hunter."

Kye glanced over at her. "Maybe."

Dani snorted. "I was being facetious. Do you not know Hunter? I'm probably number one on his worst-enemies list. I'm the last person he'd be honest with."

Kye fought the urge to grin. Yeah, Hunter wanted everyone to believe that Dani was on his shit list, but Kye knew a few things about Hunter that others would never have a chance to know. For one, Hunter talked in his sleep. And two, Hunter talked about Dani in his sleep. Based on what Kye had heard, Hunter didn't consider her an enemy. Not by a long shot.

"Are you hungry?" he asked, hoping to change the subject.

"No. Hard to have an appetite when someone tried to kill you."

True. He'd been there a few times himself.

"Do you think this was the same guy from my condo?" she asked.

"I have no idea."

She glanced his way and nodded toward his busted lip. "I take it you're the one who tipped me off?"

Kye didn't respond. He'd purposely set up the alarm clock so he would have a way to tip her off if necessary. Damn good thing, too.

"That was kinda smart," she said, her voice low. "Did you get a look at him?"

"Not really, no. It was dark. And he wasn't in a chatty mood."

"Was it one guy? Or more?"

"Only one." Which was surprising. Had it been Kye attempting to surprise Dani, he would've had someone covering the other exit. However, Kye figured whoever it was had hoped for the element of surprise.

She didn't say anything more, so they drove in silence for a few minutes.

"Once we get closer to the cabin," he finally said, "we'll stop and grab some stuff. Food, drinks."

"I'm gonna need some clothes," she told him, not bothering to look his way.

"I'll add it to my mental list."

Dani sighed and Kye knew this wasn't easy for her. He was impressed, actually. Plenty of women would've broken down at this point. Erupted into a slobbering, snotty mess of tears.

Not Danielle Davidson.

He hadn't thought he'd be able to like the woman any more than he already had.

He'd been wrong.

TEN

AFTER CIRCLING BACK TO DEVIL'S Playground, Hunter realized he wouldn't be able to check things out for himself. The place was surrounded by cops.

Not surprising considering the bullets.

He figured they would linger longer than normal due to the fact that this had to do with an Adorite. In fact, he wouldn't be surprised if the FBI showed up, looking for a way to inch their way into the fold. They'd been trying to take down the Southern Boy Mafia for some time now. How he managed, Hunter didn't know, but Max Adorite was proving to be untouchable just like his father.

No way did Hunter want to be associated with the mess, so he had parked a couple of blocks over and attempted to get into the bank building to check out the shooter's nest. No luck on that front, either. Cops had been crawling all over the place, obviously figuring out where the bullets had come from.

So, rather than risk it, Hunter had headed back to his house to grab a bag, then hit the road, roughly three hours behind Kye and Dani. For some godforsaken reason, he was desperate to get there.

He tried to tell himself it was because he needed to see for himself that Dani was all right. Or, which he really wished was the case, he was eager to get settled because the near-death experience had him so worked up.

The truth was, Hunter didn't want Dani to be alone with Kye. The minute he'd learned that Kye had been assigned to watch Dani, he'd nearly lost his shit.

What had they done in the four months they were together?

It was clear by Dani's reaction that Kye hadn't remained in the shadows while he was with her. And for some stupid fucking reason, Hunter was feeling territorial. If something had happened between them, Hunter wanted an explanation. He wanted to know what, when, how, and why. And he wanted to know if it was serious.

And wasn't that just a fucked-up mess?

Hunter had absolutely no claim on either of them, yet he couldn't seem to grasp that.

He could still hear Kye's voice in his head.

Dani? Stay down, beautiful. We don't need anyone seein' your pretty face.

Those few words had conjured up a wicked fantasy. One that involved the three of them naked, writhing together on the bed…

Except, his timing couldn't have been worse. Dani had been shot at. Hunter was now in charge of keeping her bullet free, which meant there was no time for his ridiculous fantasies. Not to mention, Hunter had effectively put a rift between himself and Kye. He had to be delusional to think either of them would give him the time of day.

For fuck's sake. Dani was Max's sister.

Holy shit.

His teeth clenched as he realized he'd almost married Max Adorite's fucking sister.

Of all the people in all the world. Perhaps it was a good thing Dani had bolted on him.

Nope. He wasn't going to think about that. It didn't matter. Just like it didn't matter what Kye and Dani did while they'd been shacking up at the beach.

Hunter shook it off. He wasn't going to think about Kye or Dani or how Kye had looked at Dani.

Shit.

No, Hunter didn't have a way with women when it came to sweet words and romantic bullshit. He knew how to seduce a woman, sure. Getting her naked was never the problem. But not with compliments and sweet words the way Kye could.

Was that what had happened? Had Kye wined and dined Dani? Had they slept together?

His muscles tightened as anger surged in his veins.

Whatever the reason for his need to get to them, Hunter simply wanted to make tracks as fast as possible. When he saw with his own eyes that Dani and Kye were in one piece, he'd relax and stop thinking crazy shit.

Unfortunately, two hours on the motorcycle left him too much time for his brain to wander. He constantly thought about his time with Josh and Dani, all those years ago. The way the three of them had come together. It'd been incredible.

But it was not meant to be. Dani had left a whole in Hunter's heart, and when Josh died, the rest of it had died with him.

He still remembered the day he had found out about Josh's death. When his brother Trace had called to let him know that Josh was no longer in the land of the living … Hunter swallowed hard, even now. God, that call had changed his fucking life. He hadn't been in love with Josh, but he had cared for the man. And he'd died.

Fucking died.

Of course, Hunter hadn't been able to show the emotion that had tangled him up inside, because no one other than Dani and Josh had known about his relationship with the man.

Or so he'd thought.

He remembered RT's confession about seeing them together.

But Hunter hadn't known anyone was on to them, so he'd been forced to be stoic during the funeral, pretending he was simply there to pay his respects to a fallen teammate.

The second those bullets started flying today, Hunter thought he'd lost Dani, too. He hadn't been able to save Josh, hadn't even been anywhere close when it happened, but heaven help him, he was not going to let Dani die, too.

After that initial incident, a piece of Hunter had ceased to exist. Josh's death had compounded the fact that Dani had left him, and Hunter had been lost. He'd gone off the rails, started acting stupid. It was the very reason he'd gotten himself shot. Without Dani and Josh … Hunter thought he hadn't had anything to live for. Turned out, he wasn't bulletproof.

As though God knew Hunter's plan, one day Kye had appeared, looking for a job. Hunter still remembered meeting him at the Sniper 1 office. The attraction had been instantaneous. But Hunter refused to get close to anyone again. Which was the very reason he kept sex between them impersonal. As impersonal as an intimate act could be kept, anyway.

Hunter had known from an early age that he was bisexual. It was something he'd always hidden from everyone—with the exception of the one woman he'd thought he would marry. And, of course, Josh.

He'd never suspected anyone else knew. In fact, it wasn't until Josh and Dani that Hunter had taken the risk with anyone who knew his family. And before Kye, his trysts had been with married couples looking for a third to play out their fantasies. It'd given Hunter what he needed, allowed him to escape the hellish memories of the two people he'd thought were it for him, and allowed him the anonymity to ensure his family wouldn't find out.

He'd done a damn good job hiding it, until Kye. When it came to the man, Hunter found it nearly impossible to hide what he was thinking. Kye could read him. It was as though he had a hotline into his brain and could tell all the dirty things racing around in there.

Perhaps it was the fact that Kye was bisexual, too. One night, after an especially rough assignment, the two of them had gotten shit-faced drunk. Nothing had happened that night, but Hunter had wanted it. Desperately. And for the first time in four fucking years, Hunter had been looking forward to waking up in the morning.

From the first day Hunter met Kye, he hadn't bothered hiding who he really was from the man. He'd instantly recognized Kye's interest, the way he eyed him as though he was mentally undressing him. In the beginning, he'd attempted to push Kye away, to make him uncomfortable.

But there was something about Kye. Hunter had suspected from the very beginning that they had something major in common. And yeah, thanks to a few conversations over drinks, Hunter had learned that they definitely did. Mainly the fact that they were both bisexual. Not that Hunter had come out and admitted as much. That was his secret to keep, but Kye had been rather chatty after a few glasses of whiskey.

Rather than pursue him, Hunter had held back. Instead, they'd worked together on a few short assignments, talked often, but never moved past that.

Ever since Dani had walked out on him, Hunter hadn't been right in the head. She had fucked his world nine ways to Sunday, and for the longest time he'd been confused about what he wanted. It wasn't until he'd been shot—a bullet had caught him in his right hip nearly two years before—that he'd decided to stop pretending to be someone he wasn't.

Mostly.

He hadn't been ready to break the news to his family just yet—he wasn't sure they would understand—but he'd been more than happy to let Kye in on the action, so to speak.

The guy did it for him in ways he'd never expected.

Hunter remembered the first time he'd made a move on Kye. They'd been on an assignment, the two of them holed up in a private suite while the actress they'd been hired to protect slept soundly in her bedroom a few rooms down.

"You're back early," Hunter called out when Kye walked into the room.

"Princess decided to go to bed. I didn't feel like waiting around," Kye muttered as he passed Hunter on his way to the hall that led to the two bedrooms in their fancy hotel suite. "It's fucking cold in here. It's gotta be like fifty fucking degrees. You're gonna make my nuts shrivel up."

Hunter watched Kye closely, admiring the man as he moved gracefully past him. He was hot and sweaty from his workout, so apparently the cold air was getting to him. Good thing Hunter could help with that.

"I know a way to warm you up."

Kye stopped in his tracks, casting a curious glance over his shoulder.

Hunter met his stare, held it, but didn't say a word.

"Keep looking at me like that and my shorts are gonna disintegrate," Kye quipped.

Yeah, they might.

Hunter let the words hang between them, wanting to keep the man waiting. It was a game he'd come to enjoy playing. It kept his mind off ... other things.

"I know that look," Hunter said when Kye's gaze slid to the balcony doors.

"What look?" Kye asked, pretending as he always did not to know what Hunter was talking about.

But he knew. "She's not the type."

Kye simply stared, again acting as though he was oblivious.

"No, that snooty princess would keel over if she had any idea what was going on in that head of yours," Hunter continued. "But that's not stopping you from thinking about it." He lowered his voice another octave. "You're imagining her naked between us."

Hunter noticed Kye's erection tenting his shorts. It happened quite frequently. Only, Hunter had never acted on it before. He'd been tempted, sure, but he was waiting for a signal from Kye.

Tonight, he was taking the hard-on as a sign.

"She'd never be willing to take us both at the same time," Hunter said, keeping his voice low. "But it's a nice fantasy."

"What are you doing?" Kye asked when Hunter got to his feet.

"Something you don't think I should, based on the way you're looking at me," Hunter replied with a smirk.

"I didn't say that," Kye mumbled as Hunter stalked him.

Tonight, Hunter fully intended to change that.

Hunter noticed Kye slowly walking backward, attempting to put space between them.

"Are you gonna run from me?" Hunter teased, his voice rough.

Kye didn't say anything. His blue eyes glowed with heat.

"I'm thinkin' you're stuck where you are because your dick is causing major interference with your brain. Am I right?"

Kye shrugged.
Fuck, the guy was hot.

Blond hair, blue eyes, features so stark it was as though they were chiseled to perfection. All sun-bronzed skin and rippling muscle. Hunter found it damn hard to resist him.

When Kye didn't try to move away again, Hunter took that as an invitation. "Turn around."

Kye did as instructed, pivoting around until he was facing the balcony doors overlooking the ocean just a few yards away.

Moving up behind him, Hunter allowed his rough hands to slide over the smooth muscle of Kye's back. He stopped at his shoulders and kneaded the tense muscles he encountered. Stepping closer, Hunter pressed his bare chest against Kye's bare back. Kye's skin was hot and slick with sweat, and it made Hunter want him all the more. To ensure Kye knew what he was after, Hunter ground the hard ridge of his dick against Kye's tight ass.

"I watched you while you worked out earlier," Hunter told him, his voice low. Princess had insisted she get some cardio in, and Kye had willingly obliged her while Hunter came up with an excuse. He'd stuck around for a little while, though, just because he could. "Was she watching you, too?"

Kye nodded.

"She was wearing those short shorts and the sports bra?" Hunter murmured, continuing to massage Kye with his fingertips. "Did you picture her naked?" He allowed the stubble on his jaw to scrape sensually against Kye's neck. "Riding your dick?"

A growl rumbled up from Kye's chest, making Hunter's dick jump in his shorts.

Sliding his hands around to Kye's chest, he enjoyed the smooth skin beneath his palms as he brushed his lips against Kye's ear. "Or did you think about my dick in your ass while you sink deep inside her sweet, wet pussy?"

Kye reached for his dick, but Hunter stopped him. He was enjoying this far too much to let Kye touch himself right now.

"Put your hands on the glass," Hunter ordered him.

Kye hesitated only briefly before flattening his palms on the glass as he stared out at the ocean.

Hunter inched his right hand into the waistband of Kye's shorts, seeking his rigid erection.

"Fuck," Kye groaned, his entire body jerking when Hunter's fist circled the thick shaft.

"Oh, yeah. That makes you hard, doesn't it? Thinking about me fucking your ass while you plow her pussy."

"Keep talking like that and I'm gonna come in your hand," Kye stated.

Then Kye was in luck, because Hunter got off on it, too.

He tightened his grip on Kye's dick. "I can imagine her sassy little mouth wrapped around the head of my dick while I watch you lick her cunt."

"You're gonna make me come, Hunter."

That was the plan. Eventually.

Hunter continued to stroke Kye, his mind conjuring up images of Dani and Kye ... God, he'd had so many fantasies about the two of them. He knew it was wrong, but he couldn't help himself.

"Faster," Kye whispered, his hips driving forward.

"Take your shorts off," Hunter insisted.

Kye quickly removed his hands from the glass and pushed his shorts down, letting them fall to the floor before once again resuming the position. Hunter never released him, continuing to stroke his hand up and down Kye's shaft.

"One of these days, you'll find a willing woman. Then you'll have to make nice with her," Hunter stated, nibbling Kye's earlobe. "That way we can get to know her, talk her out of her clothes and into bed."

Whoever they found wouldn't be the woman Hunter wanted, but Hunter knew that ship had long ago sailed. No matter how much he wished Dani were still in his life, he knew it would never be.

And it wasn't as though Kye was going to be able to walk right up to any woman and invite her into their bed. You didn't meet women every day who were interested in being with two men. They might claim to fantasize about it, but there was a mile-wide gap between fantasy and reality. Hunter had been around long enough to know that. Sure, there were plenty of wild women who wanted to experience two men for one night, but when the woman realized they were into each other as much as they were into her, it usually made things a little awkward.

Not that they could change who they were.

That was one of the things Hunter liked about Kye. He didn't pretend to be anyone other than who he was. Although Hunter hadn't come out to his family—nor did he have any plans to—the idea of being with Kye worked for him. They were honest with one another about what they wanted, and they didn't make excuses for it.

"Do you know how bad I want to fuck you right now?" Hunter growled, gritting his teeth as lust surged through his bloodstream. "I want to walk you right out there on the balcony, bend you over, and drive my dick into your ass. I want to hear you beg me to fuck you harder ... deeper ... faster."

He would, too. And based on what he knew of Kye, the man would not say no. In fact, he probably got off on having an audience.

Kye released the glass and leaned back against him, reaching around and holding Hunter's head while Hunter continued to jack Kye off. The curtains were open and if those people walking down the beach were to look close enough, they'd see them.

Hunter pressed his lips to Kye's shoulder, sucking his warm skin into his mouth. Kye responded by thrusting into Hunter's hand.

"When I get back here, I want to find you in my bed, naked," Hunter rumbled. "I'm going to watch you suck my dick, then I'm going to fuck you until you scream my name."

Kye's dick pulsed and Hunter knew he was close. So damn close.

"That's it. Come in my hand." He watched the scene play out in the reflection of the glass. He lowered his voice one more time, using the gruff tone that would make Kye come. "Come all over my fucking hand."

Kye's hips jerked wildly, his dick pulsing as he came, spurting all over his stomach and Hunter's hand.

Hunter could watch that a million times and never get tired of it.

Although, in the back of his mind, he was also imagining one particular woman watching them.

A woman he had no business thinking about at all.

That had been one hell of a night. The following night had been incredible, too. But then the assignment was over, and Hunter had come back to reality. He couldn't have Kye. Not permanently. No way was he going to get in over his head again. He'd learned his lesson already. He couldn't handle losing anyone else.

Of course, he had dragged it out for more than a year, but it was over now. Kye had walked away. Just like Dani had.

Now, as the miles passed beneath his tires, Hunter started thinking other things. His memories of him and Dani and Josh were now warped, twisted. This time, it was him, Dani, and Kye. He couldn't help but wonder what it would feel like to pull Dani into his arms, to slide her between him and Kye…

Soft skin, warm lips…

It was a fucking fantasy he had no business partaking in. He couldn't let himself get carried away. Sure, he knew what he wanted out of life. Unfortunately, he had to settle for less than what he wanted because he damn sure didn't deserve anything more. For him, sex was sex. No strings, simply pleasure.

And if the day ever came when he found the two people who understood the score, then so be it. Regardless, there would never be a happily ever after. Not with Hunter, anyway.

Still, he saw an image of Kye and Dani in his mind's eye…

Lord help him, his dick was getting intimately familiar with the fucking gas tank on his motorcycle and that was not helping one fucking bit. Hunter took a deep breath and focused on the road. He was only forty-five minutes out and he needed to get his shit together.

Goddamn. He still remembered the look in Dani's eyes when he'd tackled her to the ground. The instant those fucking bullets started flying…

Once again, his heart was pounding a million miles a second. Dani could've died this afternoon. Snuffed out before his very eyes. The hatred he'd felt for her right up to that very minute had yet to return. It was hard to hate someone who could've been easily yanked out of his life forever.

Then again, she'd yanked herself out of his life already.

But that was different.

Death was irreversible. It was one thing to know Dani was alive and kicking somewhere. Even if he didn't get to see her for himself. Although Hunter didn't know why she'd left him, and he'd hated her for that, he'd felt better believing she was alive and safe.

Now someone wanted her dead.

Looked as though Max should've taken matters into his own hands before now. Hunter still needed to put in a call to RT to let him know the status of what had gone down.

All in all, today had been full of unending luck. No one dead. No one following.

Then again, no one in custody, either. Which meant the threat was still there and getting closer. More importantly, that meant Hunter couldn't let down his guard for a second.

He only hoped the temptation he would face wasn't going to test his willpower.

Sniper 1 *Security*

"WHAT'RE YOU DOING?" DANI ASKED as Kye led her through the racks of clothing.

From the moment they'd stepped foot in the door, Kye had grabbed a cart, then her hand, and began pulling Dani down one aisle after another. They'd stopped at Walmart to stock up on food and get Dani a few things because her attempted assassination had made it impossible for her to get her car, much less grab her clothes.

"You need panties, don't you?" His ocean-blue eyes were locked on her face. "Or do you go commando? If you do, that's ... *totally* cool."

"No. I don't go commando, thank you very much."

"Then we came to the right place." Kye turned and surveyed the row of brightly colored underwear. "What size?"

Dani glared at him.

He simply cocked an eyebrow. "I can't help you pick 'em out if I don't know your size."

"You're not gonna help me pick them out," she told him, praying he didn't see the blush that was heating her face. It didn't matter how angry she was at him, there was still something between them, something she could feel like a physical caress.

"I really think you'll look good in red."

Again, she tried to kill him with her glare. That got her nowhere because the man simply grinned. A full-fledged, panty-melting smile. Straight white teeth were starkly perfect against his tanned face. He really was obscenely attractive, in a very not Hunter sort of way. And she suspected he knew it, too.

"Go away," she told him now.

"Sorry, sweetheart. I'm not leavin' your side. And you've got thirty seconds before we move on to the next department. As much as I enjoy looking at lingerie that you'll possibly be wearing later, we have to move."

"Do you think they followed us?" Dani glanced around to see who might be watching them. She saw a white-haired woman looking through a clearance rack, a lady pushing a small kid in a cart, another going through a bin of what looked like socks. No one was paying them any attention.

"I'm not willin' to stick around to find out, are you?"

Okay, he had her there.

Dani exhaled sharply and grabbed… "How many do I need? How long will we be there?"

Kye shrugged. "Could be a few days, could be a month. Don't know. But there's a washer and a dryer. Which reminds me, we should probably pick up laundry detergent."

Dani snatched five pairs of panties and tossed them into the cart Kye was pushing.

Kye reached over and grabbed a pair of polka-dotted ones, in her size.

Great.

He tossed them into the cart, then checked out another section.

"Bras?"

She rolled her eyes but turned to the bras and grabbed five of those, too.

"Those are matching, right?"

"I'm tempted to hit you," she told him now, trying to keep her voice down.

"How about shorts? Shirts? Pajamas?" He cocked his head slightly to the side. "Of course, you're welcome to just sleep naked. That's totally cool with me, too."

Dani couldn't believe he was blatantly flirting with her. Even knowing he'd been lying to her, using her. She reminded herself that she hated him.

"I don't sleep naked," she told him, allowing him to lead her through the women's clothing section, where she grabbed several pairs of shorts, shirts, and yes, even a couple pairs of pajamas.

"Too bad there's not a pool." He peered over at her with a sinful smirk. "I'd give my left nut to see you in a bikini again."

She didn't respond. If he was lucky, he would remain fully intact during their time together. If he pushed her too hard, Dani would gladly relieve him of that left nut.

Kye simply chuckled, then took her hand and continued to lead her through the store. He was moving with purpose, clearly not wanting to waste too much time. After he helped her pick out a pair of reasonable footwear—his words—Kye filled the cart with everything from flashlights to donuts—apparently, he had a sweet tooth. He also didn't mind cooking, doing laundry, or cleaning bathrooms, which, now that Dani thought about it, meant he quite possibly could be the perfect man.

Well, aside from the lying, conniving asshole part.

As he briskly walked through the store, he talked, informing her that he had four older sisters and he'd learned from a very early age that they would be much nicer to him if he helped out. So, he had.

Dani tried to picture him with four sisters. She couldn't.

Then again, she tried to tie this guy back to the one she'd met at the beach. She wondered if anything he'd told her had been true.

"Was your brother really murdered?" she blurted. "Or was that just a lie to garner my sympathy?"

Kye stopped, then turned to face her slowly. His eyes were hard, the joking, teasing man disappearing altogether. "I wouldn't lie about that."

Dani studied his face momentarily. She finally nodded.

When he turned away, he cleared his throat and picked up his conversation again. "We've got wine, milk, eggs, clothes, Tylenol—which comes in handy when dealing with Hunter, as you probably know."

That made her laugh, but she covered it with a cough.

"I think we've got enough crap to feed us for a few days. What else, baby cakes?"

God, could he be any more annoying?

He leaned in, lowering his voice. "Feminine stuff?"

If he meant to embarrass her, it didn't work. "Yes," she said very clearly, also a little louder than she probably should have. "I need tampons," she noted as they walked. "I should also get pads. Both regular and overnight because, you know. Sometimes…"

"Got it. Oh, and don't forget condoms," he announced in a singsong voice.

Dani nearly swallowed her tongue when a woman stopped to look between the two of them.

"Like I said," he added with a chuckle, "four older sisters, doll face. You can't make me blush."

Okay, if she'd meant to embarrass him, it hadn't worked, either. And for some reason, that made her like this man even though she really, really hated him for lying to her.

Which was a reminder that they weren't a couple out for a vacation. She was on the run from someone who was trying to kill her. Multiple someones, possibly.

She needed Kye to start talking.

And she fully intended to insist that he did, just as soon as they got to where they were going.

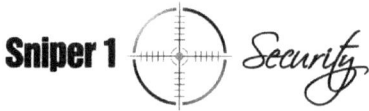

KYE COULD DEFINITELY UNDERSTAND WHAT Hunter saw in this girl. Well, technically, Dani wasn't much of a girl. She was a full-fledged woman with a body that just wouldn't quit. It really was too bad she was going to spend the rest of her life hating him for what he'd done. Although he understood it, Kye desperately wanted to go back to that place when she'd welcomed him into her bed, into her body. He couldn't stop thinking about it, about her.

And yes, he owed her some explanations. Maybe once he told her the truth, Dani would forgive him, maybe even let him get close to her again.

But then he'd had to think about how that would work out. He didn't see Hunter being too happy about the fact that Kye had nailed this chick to the mattress. In fact, Kye would probably get his ass kicked for even thinking it, much less admitting it had happened or that he wanted it to happen again. And he was certainly thinking about it, all right. At least twenty times since they'd pulled out of the Walmart parking lot, in fact. Only ten times since they'd turned off the main road and onto a dirt path that led far up into the trees. And it wasn't a long road, so that was saying something.

However, now that they were walking into the cabin, he wasn't thinking about anything except checking the place out, ensuring they had no surprise visitors. The alarm was beeping its warning countdown, so he quickly entered the code to turn it off. Once they had everything inside, he'd reset it, minus the motion sensor.

"Wow. This…looks nothing like I expected," Dani said with a slow whistle.

Kye grinned to himself. On the outside, it appeared to be a dilapidated mess of a cabin. On the inside, completely the opposite. It wasn't huge, but it was big enough to keep the three of them for a few days or even weeks. Although it had a slightly musty smell, it was clean.

After going through the house with Dani right on his heels—at his insistence—making sure the rooms were empty, including under the beds and in the closets, showers, dresser—one could never be too careful. Maybe the guy who was looking to kill Dani could contort himself into a rectangle, neatly fitting in the drawer. Kye made a point to never underestimate anyone.

"All clear," he announced, walking Dani back to the kitchen. "Why don't you start unloading, and I'll get the rest of the stuff."

He was out the door in a flash. A quick perimeter search proved that no one was hiding under the deck—front or back—or in the barbecue grill, the dilapidated shed, or even in the air conditioner, for that matter.

Once he was back inside with the rest of their purchases, Kye closed and locked the door, then coded the alarm for stay, and took the bags to the kitchen, where Dani was still unpacking, putting things into the refrigerator and freezer.

"Do you really eat this stuff?" Dani asked, holding up the box of Toaster Strudel.

"Well, yeah. Doesn't everyone?" He smiled. "Or are you more of a Pop-Tart kinda girl? I can totally get down with that. I mean, opposites attract, right?"

Dani glared at him, probably reminded of the fact that they'd slept together before she knew that he was not a Pop-Tart kinda guy.

Still, even with the death glare, Dani was so damn sexy Kye had to focus on not thinking about nailing her to the nearest soft surface. Or the wall. He didn't discriminate. Hell, the counter would be nice. He was just the right height for her to hop right up there and…

"Where do these go?"

Kye glanced over to see her holding up the box of condoms. Never hurt to be prepared.

He grinned, pretending to be sheepish. "I'll take 'em."

"You really think you're going to get a chance to use those?" she asked, her eyes studying his face.

"If I'm lucky."

Dani glanced around, as though looking for something. "Well, I for one do not see any willing women here right now." Her eyes darted to the glass door that overlooked the back deck and the miles of trees that surrounded the place. "But you might have better luck finding one out there."

"What makes you think I only want a woman?"

Her eyes flared for a moment, her cheeks turned a pretty shade of pink, but then she looked away quickly. "Oh, my God."

He watched as she processed what he was saying.

She glanced over at him once more. "Are you and Hunter…?"

Kye didn't answer that. He cleared his expression and stared at her blankly.

"It's just…"

Funny, she was still blushing.

"I know about Hunter's … you know … needs. I know he isn't just with women; he also likes men."

Kye desperately wanted to ask her how she felt about that, if she'd be willing to be with him and Hunter at the same time, but he knew he couldn't. Knowing Dani, she would rather shoot him than ever sleep with him again.

But the thought of…

Holy fuck.

That was why Hunter had his dick in a knot when it came to Dani. He wasn't merely running from ghosts from his past, he was running from the two people he'd… How had he not seen it? At one point, Hunter had shared this woman. With Josh. And she'd agreed to marry him.

Only, she hadn't. Married him. She had run.

Which begged the question…why? Was she running from someone trying to kill her? Or had Danielle run away from Hunter because she realized she didn't want what he had to offer?

Son of a bitch.

Kye hoped that wasn't the case, but he didn't really know why that was.

Okay, yes, he did. He hoped it wasn't so because he now had super hi-def visions of this sexy chick with the rocking body crushed between him and Hunter.

Holy fucking fuck.

Now Kye had to turn away again. No way could he hide the hard-on he was sporting at that thought.

ELEVEN

"I'M A PATIENT MAN," DENNIS told the Russian. "But I don't have an infinite supply. Understand?"

"Da. I find them and take care of girl."

"I want them *all* taken care of. The old boyfriend and whoever else is with them. Just get it done." Dennis didn't have time for this shit. He had much more important things to deal with, and getting to Max was his ultimate end goal. He didn't want to waste time.

When the call disconnected, Dennis pocketed his phone, then turned toward the window overlooking the seemingly never-ending rows of corn. He hated this fucking house. Hated everything about it. Yet here he was, walking in his brother's shoes in an effort to take down the very family that had disrupted his.

Although killing Max Adorite was high on his priority list, it wasn't the only thing he was thinking about. He had a business to run, one that had taken a severe hit after his brother's death. The Adorites had a hell of a lot to atone for, and Dennis intended to pay them back by acquiring most, if not all, of their business. No way in hell was Dennis going to allow the Adorites to not feel the impact. One way or the other, he was going to get his revenge.

Of course, once his plans were carried out, there would be no more Adorites to get in his way.

Retrieving his phone, he pulled up his contacts and then hit the button to make the call.

"Yo."

Dennis pulled the phone back and stared down at it. Had he really answered with *yo*?

Good help was so fucking hard to find.

Putting the phone back to his ear, Dennis said, "Brian, I need you to find Sabrina. I want them taken to ground until this is over. I'm not willing to risk Max getting his hands on her again. She's too much of a bargaining chip." Dennis knew his sister wouldn't be happy, but he didn't give a shit. He wanted her safe, and once he upped the ante, Sabrina's life would hang in the balance once again. As it was, there had been rumors that Max was going to grab her. No one seemed to know when, though. And this time, he seriously doubted Max was going to do the noble thing twice in his life. He damn sure wouldn't once Dennis started offing his family.

Hell, he'd taken out three of Max's bodyguards already, as well as their devoted doctor. Dennis wanted to ensure that any damage that occurred could not be repaired. He already had someone looking into some of Max's other minions, too.

At some point, he would push Max to his breaking point, forcing the man's hand. When that happened, Dennis would be ready for him.

"Understood," the lackey on the phone replied. "I'll have her secured within the hour and let you know when it's done."

Dennis disconnected the call, continuing to stare out the window.

This was all about to end. It might take a few days, but he was going to take down the fucking Adorites. And he damn sure wasn't going to let anyone stand in his way.

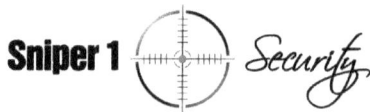

BY THE TIME HUNTER MADE it to the safe house, Dani had already claimed one of the bedrooms and had locked herself in. Initially, he'd been pissed, but Kye had not so kindly pointed out that, first, he didn't have the right to be pissed, and second, he needed to scrounge up a little compassion because someone had tried to kill her today. Twice. A lot for a girl to deal with, Kye had pointedly informed him with that irritating smirk that usually had Hunter wanting to strip the man and fuck him into oblivion.

There would be no fucking going on now, though. Hunter had nailed that coffin shut a long damn time ago simply by being an asshole.

So, rather than get worked up about it, Hunter had retreated to the other bedroom, dumped his bag, then gone to take a shower while Kye insisted on cooking dinner. He'd picked up the makings for fajitas—which for Kye meant tortillas, pre-cooked chicken, refried beans, cheddar cheese, and guacamole. He wasn't trying to go the from-scratch route, that was for sure.

Not that Hunter minded. His stomach was threatening to eat itself, he was so fucking hungry. Shit, breakfast had been hours ago, and he'd chosen to skip it, going only for coffee. He should've known better. The day he chose to skip a meal, the shit was always prone to hit the fan.

After a quick hosing down in the ridiculously small shower, Hunter had dressed in a pair of cargo shorts and a T-shirt. He preferred to go without a shirt—it was too damn hot—but he'd tried to be presentable in the event Dani did appear once she smelled the fantastic aroma coming from the kitchen.

"Perfect timing," Kye told him, grabbing plates from the cabinet and setting them on the small table near the back window. "You get a chance to talk to RT?"

Hunter wondered if Kye was referring to the obvious or if he meant had Hunter had the conversation as to why RT thought it was a good idea to send Kye undercover without telling Hunter about it?

He opted to believe he was referring to the first because thinking about the latter only pissed him off more. He fucking hated being lied to.

"Yeah." Evidently, RT had called Kye after he'd tried Hunter and gotten voice mail. "As I said, Max's wound was superficial." The bullet got him in the fleshy part of his shoulder.

"You sound like that's a bad thing," Kye noted.

"It's the equivalent of poking the bear. Max is on edge, and I'm sure he's plotting someone's murder right about now." The bastard would never get caught; Hunter knew that much. How the guy managed to do what he did and evade the police and FBI still left Hunter baffled.

The guy was into everything from running guns and drugs to prostitution and racketeering. He had his hand in a number of bad-guy pies. So many, Hunter had to pretend he didn't even know the guy.

Not that he was going to turn his brother-in-law in. Hunter had learned long ago not to stick his nose where it didn't belong. And if the bad guys wanted to take out the bad guys … well, there were worse things in the world. As long as innocents didn't get caught in the crossfire, he didn't really give a shit.

He immediately thought about Dani.

How innocent was she in all of this? She was Max's fucking sister, for God's sake. Sister. Not cousin like Hunter had believed. Then again, Max had seemed quite shocked by that revelation as well.

Her entire life was a lie. He had to wonder why she'd taken the Davidson name rather than Adorite. What had been her plan there? Hunter figured it had something to do with him or his family. How else had she ended up in his life?

He should've known it was too good to be true. She was a phenomenally beautiful woman. And he meant that in a very serious way. It should've dawned on him that she was an Adorite. Hunter had seen Max's sisters. They were all runway-model beautiful, but Dani was world class in every way. Long legs, hips that he could grab on to, thick, shiny hair, chiseled cheekbones, eyes that were more gold than brown, a nose that fit perfectly on her face, and her lips…

God, he didn't want to get started on her lips.

Sure, Hunter had met his fair share of beautiful women over the years. He didn't consider himself conventionally handsome. Not like Kye was. Not by any means. But he did have a certain look that attracted the ladies. The eyes helped. People were generally captivated by his nearly colorless eyes. Some found them odd, but women generally found them appealing. Other than that, Hunter was in excellent shape, but that was mostly due to genetics. In fact, he'd earned his six-pack abs when he was in high school, with very little effort. He attempted to eat right and work out, although he was laxer than he probably should be considering he was in his thirties.

Hunter grabbed a glass from the cabinet, filled it with ice and water, then leaned against the counter while Kye filled his plate.

Anger surged in his veins, but he'd long ago learned to ignore it. He wanted nothing more than to find out what Kye had been thinking going undercover for RT. Why he hadn't bothered to share those details with Hunter.

He already knew the answer, so perhaps that was why he didn't bother to ask. He and Kye hadn't been on good terms when Kye stormed out of his house that night. To the point Hunter hadn't expected to ever see Kye again. Maybe he should be grateful to RT for keeping Kye around.

He did his best not to admire the man. It wasn't easy, considering. Hell, Hunter hadn't had sex since the night Kye stormed out of his fucking house. Although he could've found a way to get some, it really hadn't been important to him. Someone probably needed to remind his dick that he still wasn't interested in sex. Didn't matter that Dani and Kye were under the same roof for an undetermined amount of time. Hunter had to keep his hands off. Both of them.

Of course, thinking about staying away brought his thoughts back around to Dani and how he'd allowed her to waltz right into his life and turn it upside-fucking-down. He should've been suspicious when she just appeared out of the blue. They'd met at a coffee shop of all places. Right place, right time, or so he'd thought. While he had been waiting for a phone call, ready to be sent on another job, Dani had walked in. His eyes had followed her from the moment she stepped through the door until she asked if she could use his extra chair because the table beside him had been robbed of seating. Rather than nod, he'd suggested she sit with him.

The rest had been history. They'd shared plenty of laughs and some apocalyptically good sex. Amazing sex. The kind that threatened to blow the top of a man's head off when he came. She hadn't batted an eye when he'd told her what he wanted from her, how he'd wanted to share her with Josh. Or how he'd wanted to share Josh with her.

Yep. He'd been a dumb ass. Blinded by lust.

He'd been her mark, and Hunter had welcomed her with open arms. Then he'd gone and fallen in love with her and asked her to marry him. It was no wonder she never showed at the church. She'd apparently gotten what she needed from him. That or he'd thwarted her plan by pushing for something more serious.

Thinking about it made his stomach cramp and his chest hurt. He'd thought his world had ended when he lost Dani. And as though God hadn't finished punishing him for whatever sins he'd committed, Hunter had lost Josh, too.

No way could he ever forgive Dani for what she'd done to him.

No fucking way.

And unfortunately, that meant sex was completely off the table.

For the time being.

DANI SQUEEZED HER EYES SHUT, trying to block out the memory. It had been at the forefront of her mind since Hunter shoved her into the backseat of the truck and she'd laid her eyes on…the man in the front seat.

"Bastard," she whispered.

"Joe…" Dani felt as though she was going to die if he didn't hurry up and do something. *"Please."*

"Please, what, baby?"

"I need you."

"What do you need, baby?"

Kye's delectable mouth glided over her neck, her collarbone. He continued lower until his tongue rasped over her nipple. She curled her hands around his head, trying to get him closer. Needing more than he was giving her.

When he finally closed his lips around her nipple and sucked, Dani's entire body drew tight, a desperate moan escaping. "Joe…oh, God. Don't stop doing that."

She ground her hips against him, needing friction on her clit. She could feel the rock-hard length of him against her thigh, knew he was as eager as she was. But he was taking his time, not going fast enough. She needed more, and she wasn't too embarrassed to let him know it. Sliding her hand between their bodies, she found his cock, fisting it tightly.

"Please … Joe … I need to feel you inside me."

Joe.

Dani had spent those nights with a man who didn't even exist. She had allowed him to kiss her, to slide inside her body. In fact, she had allowed herself to get carried away on hopes and dreams that should've been left alone. She had thought for a brief moment that Joe could somehow be important to her.

"Ugghh," she growled, anger making her head hurt.

Dani smelled something cooking and her stomach rumbled, reminding her that she hadn't eaten since dinner last night. Still, she refused to go out of the bedroom, not wanting to run into Kye. As a matter of fact, she never wanted to see him again. Him or Hunter. She knew Hunter was back because she'd heard the deep rumble of his voice. He had one of those voices that was pitched ridiculously low. A sexy, gravelly tenor that made her think of erotically dark sex.

She snorted.

Thinking about sex and Hunter was not a good combination. It was bad enough she sometimes remembered the moments they'd spent together. All the things she'd given up by walking away. The man had pulled her sexual fantasies—even some she hadn't realized she had—right out of her, made her crave the eroticism only he could provide. Well, he and Josh.

It brought back the memory of that first night Hunter had shown her a world she hadn't even known existed. A pleasure unlike any other. That night had resulted in several more with the three of them getting quite cozy. Oddly enough, she'd never gotten close to Josh—outside of the bedroom, so to speak. But she had spent plenty of time naked with him. Without even meaning to, she'd developed feelings for the man.

Pulling herself out of the past, Dani took a deep breath. She wondered what had happened to Josh. Did he still work for Sniper 1 Security? She had to assume Hunter was no longer with Josh. She got the sneaking suspicion something was going on with Hunter and Kye. They had a history at the very least, she was almost positive. Was Kye the reason Hunter and Josh had broken up?

Truth was, when she'd gone off the grid, attempting to hide from the sins of her past, Dani had refused to follow up on Hunter or any of his family and friends. She told herself it was to protect them. Dani knew what Samuel was capable of. Hell, the bastard had looked the other way when Samuel's own crazy, fucked-up brother had tried to take his share of the family business from Samuel's fifteen-year-old daughter. And though Samuel hadn't had anything to hold over her at the time, Dani knew he would still exact his revenge given the opportunity.

Not that any of it mattered anymore. Samuel was dead; Max had taken over the family. Yet Samuel's legacy still lived on, and clearly someone wanted to kill her because they'd figured out who she was. Dani didn't pretend to understand what it was all about, but that didn't mean she was willing to sit back and wait for her death sentence.

She needed a plan.

Dani glanced at the bedroom door and sighed.

It looked as though she was going to have to face Hunter and Kye after all.

Sniper 1 *Security*

THE INSTANT DANI JOINED THEM in the kitchen, Kye felt the tension in the room rocket up to thirty on a scale of one to ten. Four months ago, he could've blamed all of it on Hunter and Dani. Now…well, now Kye knew Dani had a bone to pick with him as well. And he had every intention of explaining himself, but he wanted the opportunity to do so in private.

Which meant he had to focus their attention elsewhere. These two had some serious issues to deal with, yet it was obvious neither of them had any intention of doing so. Unprovoked, that was.

Fortunately for them, Kye was there to help move things along.

"So…" Kye reached for his beer. "Tell me how the two of you know each other."

Hunter pierced him with a ball-shriveling glare, but Kye didn't back down. He took a long pull on the bottle and glanced between the two of them. No, he'd never been the kind to nose his way into Hunter's business. But that was before. Before Hunter put this rift between them, before Hunter forced Kye to play his hand.

Not that it had worked. He'd hoped that by walking away, Hunter would realize what they had going on between them. Perhaps track him down so they could find a way to work through it. Hunter Kogan was as stubborn as they came, though. Not once in the four months since Kye left had Hunter ever tried to contact him.

Lifting an eyebrow, Kye glanced between the two of them, waiting for someone to answer.

Dani was the first to show any sign of acknowledgment. She put her napkin on the table and grabbed the glass of iced tea. "We met at a coffee shop."

Hunter didn't stop eating. He didn't even look at them.

"Yeah?" Kye grinned, glancing down at his plate. "Hunter always did like coffee shops."

"How did the two of you meet?" Dani asked, her question directed more at Kye than Hunter.

"I applied for a job."

"Interesting."

That caught his attention. Kye peered up at Dani. "How so?"

"Is that how you came to be following me?" she asked Kye, her face a stony mask. She wasn't going to give anything away.

"Actually, no," Hunter answered. "That was all RT's doing."

Kye stared at Hunter, feeling the full extent of his hatred. Yeah, they'd be talking later, too.

"Not that I believe that," Dani said as she took a drink of her iced tea.

"I'm not the liar in this game, sweetheart," Hunter growled, pointing his fork at Dani.

"Nope. Never. You're the martyr, Hunter. Always have been, probably always will be."

Kye couldn't help but watch the two of them. There was a wealth of anger surging in the air, but there was something else, too.

"What the fuck does that mean?" Hunter asked, his eyes narrowed.

"Oh, nothing." Dani focused on her food, but now Hunter was staring at her.

Well, it was more of a glare actually.

"Don't act like you know a fucking thing about me," Hunter grumbled, his voice so deep, so rough, Kye couldn't look away. His protective instincts reared, ready and willing to stand in front of Dani if Hunter wanted to go at it.

"Oh, trust me," she said flippantly, "I would never do that."

Kye knew this was going to get ugly, but like a badly mangled car on the front end of a Mack truck, he couldn't seem to look away as the pair stared one another down.

"So, what's with the tone?" Hunter demanded.

Dani shrugged. "It's just..." She glanced at Kye, then back to Hunter. "I thought you already had a partner. Seems they're replaceable, depending on—"

Before Dani could finish her statement, Hunter was on his feet. He slammed his fists onto the table and got right up in her face. "Josh fucking died, Dani. Have a little bit of a heart, would you?"

As Hunter stormed out of the room, Dani's eyes widened and Kye was fairly certain he saw tears building. He swallowed hard, unsure what to say. Should he comfort her? There was no way she could've known about Josh.

Well, that wasn't entirely true. Had she not bailed on Hunter all those years ago, she would've known.

Still, Kye wasn't sure she deserved that.

"You okay?"

Dani's head snapped over, her eyes slamming into him. It was as though she didn't realize he was still sitting there. She cleared her throat as she got to her feet.

Without another word, she walked right out of the room.

Leaving Kye alone with his beer.

"This is going to be fun," he muttered to himself.

*

Two hours later, after he'd cleaned up the kitchen and done another perimeter search, Kye decided to call it a night. Neither Hunter nor Dani had emerged from their respective rooms and he didn't figure they intended to. Since there were only two bedrooms, Kye was going to get to sleep on the couch. Yay. Six feet six inches crowded on a five-foot couch. So much fucking fun.

Sure, there was a pull-out bed, but he couldn't imagine it was all that comfortable. He'd just as soon sleep on the floor. Probably have less body aches in the morning if he did. Then again, maybe he would just stay up, keep an eye on things.

He yawned.

Or maybe not.

He'd been up for thirty hours and it was catching up to him quickly.

Kye glanced at the door to Hunter's room. He really needed to check in before he tried to get some sleep. Someone had to keep an eye out and he knew Hunter would be awake. The man didn't look like he slept all that much these days.

With a resigned sigh, Kye walked over to the door and rapped his knuckles lightly on the wood. Hunter grumbled something, but Kye couldn't quite make it out. Choosing to take it as permission to enter, Kye opened the door.

He didn't get the damn thing open all that much when he found a very naked, very hard Hunter lying on his bed, jacking off roughly.

"Shut the goddamn door," Hunter snarled, his eyes never leaving Kye's face. He didn't try to hide what he was doing.

Kye could see the heat simmering in his eyes. The man might've been pissed off after what happened at dinner, but there was no denying he was horny as hell.

Instead of doing as instructed, Kye stood there, leaning his shoulder against the frame, his eyes glued to the way Hunter's hand moved crudely over his dick. His own dick stirred. A natural response to something so…hot.

"You gonna stand there and watch?" Hunter didn't sound bothered by the idea.

"Yeah," Kye exhaled roughly. "I think I will."

"Fine by me." Hunter continued to fist his cock, his eyes closing as he did.

"You thinkin' about me?" Kye asked. There was no teasing in his tone. He wanted to fucking know. It'd been a long damn time since he and Hunter had been together, but that didn't mean Kye had stopped thinking about him.

"No."

"Liar," Kye retorted.

Hunter's eyes flew open. "Is that what you want? For me to think about you when I jack off? If I said I was, would it bother you?"

"Not at all."

Kye's dick was swelling, but he fought the urge to give in. He wasn't about to let himself get carried away. He knew it would take nothing more than a strong wind for him to give in to Hunter.

And everyone knew that was the last damn thing he needed.

TWELVE

HUNTER KNEW HE SHOULD'VE ORDERED Kye out of the room. The man would've listened if Hunter had put some real effort into it. Instead, Kye was standing in the doorway watching Hunter jack off while Hunter secretly wished that Dani would come out of her room, too.

It was a stupid wish, he couldn't deny that. But having both of them there in the same house … Fuck. He was having a difficult time focusing on anything other than them. He hated himself for it, but try as he might, he couldn't stop the fucking fantasies from overwhelming him.

Forcing his eyes open, Hunter trained his gaze on Kye. He saw the heat, the desire, the pure need reflecting back at him, but he also noticed sheer determination in Kye's blue eyes. The man wasn't going to give in. And Hunter didn't blame him.

"How long's it been?" Hunter asked him.

Kye didn't respond, but Hunter knew he understood what he was asking. Had he fucked Dani? Did the two of them get together in the dark of night to work off a little restless energy?

Ah, fuck. The thought should've angered him, but it didn't. Simply thinking about the two of them together made his dick so fucking hard it hurt.

"Since you've suddenly lost your voice, why don't you put that smartass mouth to good use," Hunter growled, gripping his dick firmly.

"Give me two good reasons why I should, and I'm on it," Kye taunted.

Yeah. They both knew Hunter didn't have *one* good reason, much less two.

Once again stroking his dick, Hunter gave himself over to the fantasy. If he could have nothing else, he could have that. And if he had to be plagued by it, no reason Kye shouldn't be as well.

"I think about it all the time. Your mouth on my cock. Hot, wet…" Hunter groaned as the mental image took root. He couldn't block it out. "The way you look at me when you deep throat my dick." Another groan ripped through him and his hand slowed momentarily. "And I think about plowing into your ass, the hot depths of your body squeezing the fucking life out of me."

He damn sure wouldn't admit it to anyone but he fucking missed Kye. He missed everything about the man. Not merely the sex, although that was likely what he missed most.

"What about Dani?" Kye asked.

The words surprised him, forcing Hunter to open his eyes. He noticed Kye had stepped into the room, but the door was still open. He obviously didn't intend to stay.

"Do you think about her, too?"

"Yeah," Hunter groaned. "I fucking do. Why?" He hated admitting that, but it was the truth. Like it or not.

Kye shrugged. "It took me a while, but I finally put two and two together. You shared her with Josh."

"Yeah. So?" He squeezed his cock, the topic not doing a damn thing to stave off his orgasm.

"Do you think about me and Dani?" Kye inquired. "Together?"

Hunter met Kye's eyes, but he didn't respond. He held his gaze, continuing to jack off, wishing like hell he could come and get this over with. At the same time, he wanted to prolong the exquisite torture. This was as close as he'd been to Kye in months and having him right there, so close…

"Tell me what you think about," Kye commanded, his tone firm.

"Sliding into her wet pussy," Hunter bit out roughly. "While you're fucking her mouth." He sounded as though he was strangling, trying to hold on to the last vestiges of his control. "Coming inside her, hearing her tell me she lov—"

He snapped his mouth shut, realizing what he almost revealed.

"Don't stop," Kye commanded, his tone rough with his apparent lust.

Hunter wasn't used to Kye being the demanding one, but he couldn't deny that he liked it. He fucking craved it. Like that night Kye had barged into Hunter's house and fucked him. Kye had never done that before, never been quite so demanding. And just like that night, Hunter wanted to let go of his control, to let someone else take the reins. No doubt, Kye was good at it. He would shatter Hunter's control given the chance.

Rather than say as much, Hunter stroked himself, his balls tightening, his insides coiling as his orgasm neared. It was as much from his hand as it was from the heat he saw in Kye's eyes as the man watched intently.

"Come for me, Hunter," Kye demanded. "Let me watch. Just this one time."

It was clear Kye had caught his blunder, but the man wasn't going to let Hunter get lost in his own head this time.

"Think about what it'd be like to sink into my ass while I'm lodged balls deep in her pussy."

Yeah. That did it.

Hunter didn't take his eyes off Kye as he came, his dick jerking in his hand.

Before either of them could acknowledge what happened, Kye turned and walked out of the room, gently closing the door behind him.

Funny. The guy never did tell him what he needed.

It took a long time for Hunter to catch his breath, and when he did, he managed to relax. He needed to get up, to clean himself. Then, perhaps he'd be able to sleep.

Then again, probably not.

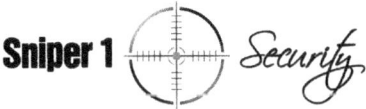

DANI DIDN'T BUDGE FROM WHERE she stood, her bedroom door slightly ajar as she stared out into the hallway. She didn't even move when Kye came out of Hunter's room, his eyes sliding right over to her.

Think about what it'd be like to sink into my ass while I'm lodged balls deep in her pussy.

She could still hear Kye's words in her head. Hell, she could feel them in her entire body. Warmth had instantly radiated out from her core when she heard him talking to Hunter. He obviously knew she was there. Which made her wonder if his questions to Hunter had been for her benefit. It kind of sounded like it.

Dani knew who Hunter was. She knew what he enjoyed. Obviously, he'd enjoyed Kye a time or two. For all she knew, they could still be lovers, but she didn't think so. There was something off between them. As though things hadn't ended well, whatever those things might have been.

Which made her wonder why Kye had seduced her. To get back at Hunter? Had he fucked her so he could rub it in Hunter's face?

Mortification flooded her, making her face hot.

Had she played right into his trap?

Dani sighed and peered out into the hallway.

Whatever had happened in that bedroom tonight was definitely of the intimate nature and not once had Kye mentioned sleeping with her, so maybe that hadn't been his intention. From the second she heard the two men talking, Dani's curiosity had gotten the best of her and she'd gone to the door, too chicken to do anything more than peek out.

Good thing, too. She wasn't sure she could've handled seeing Hunter like that. She had a fairly good idea what he'd been doing. And the fact that Kye had been watching…

There was an ache between her legs that caused her to clench her thighs together. No way was any of this doing them any good. Yet as though someone was intent on punishing them, they were all confined to this house for the foreseeable future. How in the world were they going to get through the endless days and never-ending nights?

Her thoughts drifted back to dinner, to the way Hunter had told her Josh was dead. It had taken everything in her not to sob uncontrollably at that revelation. She had wanted to accuse him of lying, but she'd seen the pain in his eyes.

Josh was dead.

She didn't know how or why or even when, but it was clear from Hunter's expression that it was still haunting him. First, she had walked out and then Josh had died. At some point, Hunter had been completely alone.

Although she knew she shouldn't care, Dani's heart ached for him. He'd lost her and Josh. And she suspected that was what had transformed him from the cold, calculating man he'd once been into this heartless asshole.

No, Hunter had never been the hearts-and-flowers type. He'd told her she was beautiful a million times, but other than that, he hadn't been the sort to shower her with kind words. But she'd felt his love when they were together. The way he'd protected her, always making sure she was all right.

But she'd blown any chance she could have with him when she walked out, leaving him at the altar without so much as a goodbye.

Because she had convinced him that she had no family, Hunter would've had no way of locating her. She wondered if he had even tried.

Dani walked back over to the bed and sat on the edge of the mattress. A tear dripped down her face, but she didn't attempt to hold it back. For so long, she'd had to be the strong one, always on guard, always looking out for the danger that lurked. Oddly enough, she felt safe with Hunter and Kye. Regardless of their feelings for her, she knew they wouldn't allow anything to happen to her.

Another tear fell, then another. The next thing she knew, Dani was crying uncontrollably as all those emotions flooded to the surface. She was so caught up in it she didn't hear the door open, didn't realize someone was there until Kye was sitting on the bed beside her, his warm arm coming around her shoulders as he pulled her close.

"It's all right, baby," he whispered, tugging her closer to his chest. "You're safe now."

Her first thought was to push him away, but she didn't. She welcomed the safe haven of his embrace, needed it even. Although he had lied to her, she had come to trust him.

And she wanted to believe that everything would be all right, but it was only a platitude. Until they figured out who was gunning for her, she would never be safe. The only thing she knew for certain was that she was not running anymore. She would figure this out if it killed her.

She only hoped it didn't come to that.

For the longest time, she sat there, relishing the warmth of Kye's arms holding her. She probably should've turned him away, but she hadn't felt anyone's touch in so long. Not until him. When he pressed a kiss to her forehead, the tears fell even harder.

"I hate this," she admitted, leaning into him. "I hate running. I hate hiding. I've been doing it my whole life and…" And she wanted to go home.

No, she wanted to go back in time and make her way into that church, to walk down the aisle to say her vows to Hunter, to accept his ring. Perhaps they would've had a happy ever after if she had. Maybe Josh wouldn't be dead.

But then she wouldn't have met Kye. And though she was angry with him for what he'd done, she didn't want to think about a life without him in it.

"You don't have to run anymore," Kye assured her. "We won't let anything happen to you. I swear it."

Pulling back, she stared up into his eyes. She didn't know what she was looking for, but what she found appeared to be a promise. He wasn't merely talking to console her. He was serious.

"Why'd you do it?" she asked, needing to know. "Why'd you sleep with me?"

"Because…" Kye sighed. "Because I wanted to be close to you."

He sounded sincere, but could she believe him?

"I was with you, Dani, because I couldn't stay away from you. I hated that I had to lie to you, but…"

"It was your job," she told him, suddenly realizing that what he had done was no different than what she'd done to Hunter.

"Not that part," he said softly. "Never that part. I made love to you because I needed you, Dani." His voice dropped again. "I still do. I want to take care of you, to keep you safe."

"I don't deserve it," she told him. "I don't deserve anyone's help."

"You do," he said, his hand curling around her neck as his thumb brushed the tears from her cheek.

Dani shook her head. "No. I don't. Hunter hates me, and I don't blame him. I fucked up his life. But I had my reasons." He would know because he'd done the same to her.

"Maybe you should tell him the reasons," Kye whispered. "Maybe there's a chance to salvage what you once had."

No. There was no chance of that. Hunter deserved far better than what she could give him. And it had nothing to do with her past or her family. What she'd done was unforgiveable. She had allowed Samuel to blackmail her, to convince her to infiltrate the Kogans' world. It didn't matter that she'd fallen in love with Hunter. He would never forgive her for that.

"I'm so tired," she admitted.

"I know, baby." He leaned forward and kissed her forehead once more. "Lie down."

When Kye nudged her back onto the bed, Dani didn't try to stop him. She wasn't sure she even could. She was exhausted, her mind and body wrung out from the stress of running for so long.

When her head hit the pillow, Kye got to his feet. He pulled the blanket from the end of the bed and draped it over her.

"Sleep, Dani. It'll all be here in the morning."

When she didn't try to fight it, Dani felt herself drifting off, tears still leaking from her eyes.

KYE WAITED UNTIL DANI'S BREATHING had evened out before he slipped out of her bedroom and into the hall. He found Hunter standing there, leaning against the wall, his arms crossed over his chest.

"Care to tell me what happened between the two of you on that op?"

Kye shook his head as he pulled the door closed. "No. I don't."

"You fucked her," Hunter accused.

Kye glared at him.

"She'll manipulate you if you let her," he said roughly.

"She's not manipulating anyone," Kye told him as he walked right past Hunter on the way to the living room.

"No? And you think you know her because you've spent a few hours with her?"

Kye spun around and glared at Hunter. "This chip on your shoulder…it's going to get someone killed, Hunter. I don't intend to die, and I don't intend to let anything happen to Dani. So, if you have an issue protecting her, I suggest you take your ass on back to Dallas."

Hunter's eyes narrowed. "Chip on my shoulder?" He snorted. "Is that what you call it when the fucking woman I loved left me at the altar? A fucking *chip* on my shoulder? She lied to me, Kye. She lied about who she was."

"Did you ever ask her why?" Kye questioned.

Hunter barked a laugh. "She didn't give me the chance."

"Well," he motioned toward the bedroom door, "it looks like you've got the chance now."

Hunter dropped his arms and walked into the kitchen. Kye didn't feel the need to follow him. For so long, he had allowed Hunter to get the best of him. To use him the way he needed. Kye wasn't about to go back to that place. He'd put months and miles between them and he intended to stand his ground. As much as he'd missed Hunter—something he damn sure wouldn't admit to—Kye wasn't a glutton for punishment.

As he was taking a seat on the couch, Hunter reappeared, a beer in his hand. He leaned his shoulder against the wall and stared Kye down.

"She's not Max's cousin," Hunter said.

"Okay." Kye wasn't sure where he was going with this.

"She's Max's sister."

He couldn't hide his shock that time. "What? When did you find that out?"

"Today. She dropped that little bomb on Max."

"Max didn't know?"

Hunter shook his head. "Didn't look like it. Then again, that was about the time the bullets started flyin'."

Kye glanced down the hallway. "His sister?"

"Yep. Good ol' Samuel Adorite is her daddy."

Kye considered this for a minute, trying to tie it all together. He leaned back on the couch and stared at the wall. "So, her mother and Max's dad had an affair?"

"Probably. Can't trust an Adorite to save your life," Hunter said with a grunt. He took a long pull on his beer.

Kye's head snapped toward Hunter. "What? Are you saying Dani's mother willingly jumped into bed with that psychopath?"

Kye hadn't known Samuel Adorite, but he'd done some research on the man. It had all been in an effort to understand Hunter better. The way the man treated his brother-in-law wasn't typical family drama. There was something about Max that Hunter didn't like. Probably had a lot to do with the fact the guy was into some illegal shit. That went against Hunter's nature, so it made sense.

What Kye had learned about Samuel Adorite had made his stomach turn.

"How else would you explain it?" Hunter countered, his tone dripping with sarcasm.

"My mother was raped," the soft voice said.

Kye's head jerked over to see Dani standing in the mouth of the hallway, staring at them both. Her eyes were still puffy from crying and probably from exhaustion. He'd hoped she would sleep, but clearly that wasn't in her plan. He glanced back at Hunter, noticing the way the man's entire body had gone rigid.

"Raped?" Kye questioned, motioning toward the couch, hoping Dani would at least sit down.

She slowly moved toward them, her arms wrapped around herself as though she was cold. Or perhaps trying to hold herself together.

"Yes. No one was off-limits to Samuel," she said, not speaking to anyone specifically. When she sat, she stared off into space. "He used everyone for his own personal gain. And he was batshit crazy. My mother never willingly slept with him," she stated adamantly, glancing up at Hunter. "And I doubt Genevieve did, either."

Kye knew Genevieve was Max's mother, the woman Samuel had married when she was merely a child herself. The guy truly was despicable.

Kye expected Hunter to say something spiteful, but surprisingly he kept his mouth shut.

"Why didn't you take Samuel's name?" Kye asked.

Dani glared up at him. "I didn't take the Adorite name for my own protection." Her gaze dropped. "Or rather that's why my mother chose to give me her maiden name. She said I was safer not being part of the family."

"That makes sense," Hunter mumbled.

"Well, it didn't protect me completely," she bit out. "Samuel still got his hooks into me."

"Did he know?" Kye asked. "That you were his daughter?"

She nodded. "Oh, yeah. That bastard knew. And he used it against my mother all the time."

"Against her?" Hunter moved into the room. "He threatened to tell her husband?"

Dani laughed, but there wasn't any humor behind it. "Oh, no. Nick knew. He knew about every single time Samuel had forced himself on my mother." The words came out as though they were bitter in her mouth. Dani shook her head. "No, my mother didn't want word getting out that I was Samuel's illegitimate daughter for my own protection. The man has some serious enemies."

"You mean had," Hunter countered.

Her gaze lifted to him once more. "There are still people out to get him, Hunter. Doesn't matter that he's dead."

"I'm lost," Kye said, mainly hoping she would elaborate.

Dani sighed heavily, clasping her hands together tightly. "My mother protected me as best she could while she was alive. However, Samuel still managed to get me to do his bidding. He…" She swallowed hard but didn't look up. "He started blackmailing me when I was nineteen years old. Said if I didn't do what he wanted, he would kill my mother."

Kye shifted his legs when Hunter came and sat on the coffee table in front of Dani. She continued to stare down at her hands.

"He insisted that I dig up as much dirt on your father as I could," she told Hunter without looking at him. "That was the reason I came into your life."

"And did it work?" Hunter asked, his voice lower than before.

Dani shook her head. "I never actually tried. I simply told him a bunch of crap when he asked for updates. Nothing he didn't already know. I would've done anything to protect my mother."

"What happened to her?" Kye asked.

"She died." Her fingers clasped together tightly. "Lung cancer. It stole her from me three weeks before I was set to marry…" Dani nudged her shoulder toward Hunter.

Holy shit. It all made sense to Kye. Dani hadn't run out on Hunter because she didn't love him. She had left because she did.

Kye peered up at Hunter, wondering if the man understood that. Or if he was going to need Dani to spell it out for him.

THIRTEEN

HUNTER WAS TRYING TO PROCESS everything Dani had told him. It was all there, so many explanations he'd never received, and it made perfect sense.

Only it didn't.

"Once she died, Samuel no longer had anything to hold over your head," he stated bluntly. "So, you no longer needed me. Is that what you're telling me?"

Dani's eyes flew up to his face and he could see pure anger there. "Really? Is that what you think of me? You think I was only with you because—"

"Because your biological father threatened to kill your mother." He smiled coldly. "I'm not the one who told the story, Dani."

Dani shot to her feet. "Fuck you, Hunter."

When she stormed out of the room, he didn't bother trying to stop her. And when she slammed her bedroom door, he didn't even flinch.

"You're a fucking idiot," Kye muttered as he pushed up off the couch and headed for the kitchen.

Hunter was on his feet then, grabbing Kye's arm and spinning him around. "I'm an idiot? It sounds fairly logical to me. When her mother died, the threat was gone, was it not? She had no reason to be in my life, so she bolted."

Kye's smile said he felt sorry for Hunter. "If that's what you think of her, then I guess it would make sense to you."

"And you see it differently?"

Kye shrugged and jerked out of his hold. "She's not the villain you make her out to be."

Hunter laughed mirthlessly. "No? Are you saying this because you *know* her? Or because you're hoping to get in her pants?"

Kye spun around, moving with purpose until they were damn near toe-to-toe. "You might not have any respect for her, but I do."

"Oh, right. So, you don't want to fuck her? You'd rather make love to her? Is that the form of respect you feel?"

Those blue eyes were steely as they stared back at Hunter.

And it confirmed exactly what Hunter had suspected.

"You *did* fuck her," he snarled. "You fucking bastard."

"Me? Why am I the bastard here, Hunter?" Kye taunted. "You threw her away. You didn't want anything to do with her."

"You fucked her to get back at me."

The next thing Hunter knew, Kye's fist reared back, then flew forward, catching him in the jaw. Hunter stumbled backward, glaring at the other man.

"Whether you like it or not, it's not always about you," Kye growled. "I'll take the first shift. Outside."

Hunter didn't retaliate, because he deserved that punch. In fact, he deserved both of their wrath. He was being an asshole of the first order.

Unfortunately, that was his only option.

Well, that or admit that he'd lost out on the best fucking thing that had ever happened to him because he'd allowed her to run away without trying to stop her. Without getting the answers he'd so desperately needed.

More than five fucking years he'd wasted.

"Fuck," he hissed as he made his way to the bedroom.

He paused in the hallway, staring at Dani's door. He should go in there and apologize. Hell, he should go in there and beg her forgiveness. All this time, he'd thought she disappeared because she didn't give a shit about him. He wasn't so dense that he didn't realize she'd left in order to save him from her, from her deception.

Hunter merely didn't want to believe it because it meant he was at fault.

It was all on him.

Everything.

Losing Dani. Losing Kye.

He'd fucked it all up himself.

Taking a deep breath, he opened his bedroom door and stepped inside. He couldn't talk to Dani yet. He'd already pissed her off enough for one night. He could wait until everyone had calmed down. Maybe tomorrow he could have a civilized conversation with her. Maybe even apologize.

After closing the door, he flopped down on his bed and stared up at the ceiling. He knew he should be thinking about the job, thinking about ways to find the bastard who was trying to kill the woman he loved. Not lying around feeling sorry for himself.

"For fuck's sake," he groused.

After all this time, Hunter found it difficult to believe he still loved Dani. But he knew deep down that it was true. He'd never stopped loving her. Sure, he'd hated her, but he'd never stopped loving her.

Only to find out that if he had put his pride aside for five goddamn minutes, the years wouldn't have passed him by. If he would've just gone after Dani that day…

His mind drifted back to his wedding day.

"Lookin' sharp, bro," Trace said with a smirk. "Never thought you'd put on a monkey suit."

"It's my wedding day," Hunter countered as he adjusted his tie, staring at the man in the mirror. The smile on his face seemed to be a permanent fixture these days. In just a few hours, Danielle Davidson would be his bride.

The door to his dressing area opened and Conner walked in, followed by Casper. Behind his father was Bryce, Tanner, Hunter's grandfather Frank, along with RT and a handful of the agents he worked with. Including Josh.

His eyes met and held Josh's for the longest time. The two of them had spent last night together. Not merely because Hunter wanted to be close to the man but also because he needed to know Josh was good with this. From what Josh had told him, he truly was happy that Hunter was marrying Dani.

"Looks like we're about ready to start," Casper announced. "You've got a full house out there."

Hunter glanced at the group. "Out there? Or in here?"

Casper chuckled. "We thought we'd do a toast before you said your vows."

"Well, I won't turn it down," he told his father.

Frank produced a bottle of whiskey and Conner handed over a stack of clear plastic cups. They were passed around, then filled before everyone came together as a group.

"Here's to today and all the happiness that it'll bring," his father stated, holding up his cup.

Everyone toasted, then tossed back their drink. Hunter was then patted on the back as they all filtered back out to the chapel.

"You ready for this?" Conner asked, staying back.

"Of course I am," he admitted, staring at his older brother.

Conner smiled, but it was sad. Hunter hated seeing his brother suffer. After Conner's wife had been gunned down last year, he hadn't been the same man. Not that Hunter had expected anything different. He couldn't imagine what the man was going through. The thought of losing Dani…he couldn't even fathom it.

"Well, be good to her, man."

"I intend to."

Conner nodded, then slapped him on the shoulder. "See you in a few."

When Conner left, and the door clicked behind him, Hunter turned back to stare at his reflection. Today was by far the happiest day of his life. He gave himself another full-length glance. That was when he noticed Josh standing behind him.

Hunter turned around to see Josh smiling at him. "You look good."

"You do, too," Hunter admitted. He was tempted to reach out and touch him, but he refrained. Barely.

"I wanted to reassure you that this is a good thing," Josh told him. "I know you've been questioning it."

He had, and Josh knew him well enough to see it.

"It only makes sense that one of us would eventually fall in love with someone."

Because they weren't in love with each other. They both knew that.

Oh, Hunter had wanted to be in love with Josh, but it hadn't happened, and he knew he could never force something like that. He cared for him, but it wasn't love.

"Marry her, man. Have tons of babies. Live happily ever after."

"You know I'm not done with you yet," he told his lover.

Josh smirked. "Oh, I know. And I'll be there. As long as Dani wants me around."

Only, it hadn't ended that way. There hadn't been a wedding or a happily ever after for anyone.

Just a short time later, Dani hadn't shown up and Hunter had been left reeling, trying to understand why the woman would've disappeared. And she had. Without a trace. Since Dani had told him she didn't have any family—no one he could track down to get her whereabouts—he'd been forced to let her go, to move on.

Unfortunately, Hunter had never been able to move on.

He wasn't sure it was even possible.

Even now. All these years later.

THE FOLLOWING MORNING, DANI WOKE groggy and irritable.

Probably had a lot to do with the fact that she had cried herself to sleep and then endured dreams of Hunter. In every one of them, he was telling her how horrible she was, how much he hated her.

So, not too far from reality.

She still couldn't believe that he thought she had disappeared because she hadn't needed him. The man clearly had never loved her the way she had loved him. Sometimes she wondered if she should've married him, should've simply gone through with it and begged for Hunter's forgiveness once the truth finally did come out.

But she knew Hunter. It wouldn't have mattered. The man was so hard, so cold. He would've kicked her to the curb, accusing her of some other heinous crime against him. No matter what, her heart would've been broken.

And now, as she stared up at the ceiling, she wondered how she was going to face him. Personally, she didn't want to, but she knew she didn't have much of a choice. Until the man who was attempting to kill her made another move, or Kye and Hunter decided to go after him, they were pretty much stuck.

Perhaps that was what she needed to do. Convince them to go after the man before he could get to her first. The last thing she wanted was for anything to happen to Hunter or Kye. And it was always better to be one step ahead of the enemy. Or so she'd heard.

Stretching, Dani decided it was time to get up. Light was already filtering through the window shade, but she had no clue what time it was. She could take a shower, have some coffee, and figure out a way to get herself out of this mess once and for all.

When she stepped into the hallway a short time later, she heard the rumbling of voices coming from the far side of the house. Kye and Hunter were both awake. Dani glanced at the bathroom door, then back down the hallway. Should she have coffee first? Or shower?

Touching the tangled mess that was her hair, she realized a shower was definitely in order, so she slipped back into her bedroom, grabbed a few things from the pile of new clothing they'd purchased yesterday, then darted into the bathroom and closed the door. The lock on the doorknob was broken.

"Of course it is," she muttered to herself.

Figuring she needed to hurry, Dani turned on the water to heat, then stripped out of her pajamas. When she was finally under the spray, she closed her eyes and let the warm water soothe some of the aches in her muscles. The bed had been perfectly comfortable, but it had done little to alleviate the tension in her body. She was stressed, and she knew it wouldn't get any better until she was finally home.

Wherever home ended up being.

Her apartment was gone. She hadn't been able to pay the rent because she didn't want to possibly alert the man who was after her of her whereabouts. And since she refused to send cash in the mail, she'd had to let it go.

Yep. Technically, she was homeless.

But that was the way it'd always been for her.

Dani still remembered the very first time she'd left the only home she'd ever known, when Nick, her father for all intents and purposes, sent her to France of all places. It'd been her wedding day. The day she should've married Hunter Kogan, the man who had stolen her heart. Before they could take their vows, Dani's conscience had caught up with her.

At the ripe young age of nineteen, Samuel had fixed his sights on her. At twenty, she'd officially become a plant in the Kogans' world. At twenty-two, she'd found herself engaged to the greatest man she'd ever met, and at that point, she'd realized she couldn't go on living a lie. She wasn't supposed to fall in love with Hunter, but she had. Then her mother had died, and her world had been turned upside down. So, she had left him, not wanting Hunter to find out who she really was, hating herself for what she'd done to him, the lies she'd told.

Rather than slip into her dress and make her way down the aisle, Dani had ducked out unnoticed and called a cab. She was fairly certain the taxi driver thought she had escaped from the mental hospital, based on the way he'd been eyeing her. When she told him to take her to the hotel near the airport, only a few miles down the road, she'd seen his hesitation, but when she offered two hundred dollars for what should've been a thirty-dollar fare, his interest in her had faded, just as she'd hoped it would.

Dani washed her hair using the travel items she had bought yesterday, then scrubbed her body. She thought about not shaving but figured that was a stupid idea. She had to feel her best and the only way to do that was to look her best. With a resigned sigh, she went to work prettying herself up.

*

An hour later, Dani emerged from the bathroom. Her hair was dry, her face scrubbed clean of makeup, and she felt significantly better. Some of the puffiness under her eyes had diminished, which she was grateful for.

Knowing she had wasted enough time, she headed for the kitchen. She glanced around, realizing Hunter was the only one in the room.

"Mornin'," he greeted.

For the first time since she'd run into him again, the man's tone wasn't tinged with irritation or hatred. It caused her to snap her head in his direction.

"Good...morning," she replied, confused.

"Can I get you some coffee?"

Dani peered over at the coffeepot. She considered getting it herself but figured it would be better to allow Hunter to do the honors. If he was offering, that meant he was willing. Since he wasn't shooting death rays from his eyeballs, she wanted to keep it that way.

"That would be great, thank you," she said kindly.

He pushed up from his chair, then pulled another one out for her. "Have a seat."

Dani moved to the chair with purpose, eased down into it, and stared at the man moving around the kitchen. This morning he was wearing a pair of jeans and a charcoal T-shirt, his boots on his feet. He looked as though he had been up for a while.

"Where's Kye?"

He nodded toward the back door. "He's checking things out there."

"Is there a problem?"

"Not that we can see, no." Hunter picked up the coffee carafe and poured the dark liquid into a mug he had retrieved from the cabinet. "Still take it with sugar and milk?"

"Yes, please."

He smiled down at the mug as he grabbed the glass sugar container. "Just a little coffee with your sweetener?"

"Yes," she admitted, feeling her cheeks warm from embarrassment. Hunter always had given her shit about the fact that her coffee was more sugar than caffeine.

When he finished preparing it, he carried it over to her, then set it on the table. She watched him closely, trying to figure out what was on his mind. He seemed different this morning. Despite the fact that he'd been so hateful last night.

Wrapping her hands around the warm mug, she stared at him as he took a seat.

"Look, Hunter—"

"Dani—"

They both smiled. "I'm sorry. You go first," she told him.

"No, go ahead."

Dani nodded, then took a sip of her coffee. "I just wanted to apologize."

"For?"

She swallowed hard. "For leaving you on our wedding day." Dani kept her gaze pinned on the table. "I know you probably won't ever believe me, but I did it because I didn't want to hurt you anymore. Samuel blackmailed me to get me into your life and I didn't think it was fair to you, so I ran."

His warm hand covered hers and her eyes flew up to his face. "Did you love me, Dani?"

She hadn't expected that question, but she decided to be truthful. "More than I've ever loved anyone."

Hunter stared at her for the longest time, as though he was searching her face for the truth. She understood why. After all, she had spent most of their relationship lying to him, pretending to be someone she wasn't, and she refused to do that to him again.

"Then apology accepted," he finally said, his voice rough.

Dani frowned as she studied his face. "Really?"

Hunter nodded solemnly, releasing her hand. "Yeah. I've spent a long time wondering why you left."

"And you believe me?" She couldn't believe it was that easy. Nothing was easy when it came to Hunter.

"I knew Samuel, Dani. And I've heard plenty of horror stories about the asshole." He shook his head. "I probably should've figured it out myself."

Yeah, well. He might have if he hadn't been so angry with her. She couldn't blame him.

"Now that I know, I figure it's best to put it all in the past."

Right. The past.

What they had once shared would forever be relegated to the past.

Dani hated knowing that. Perhaps not having closure had been easier for her because it always meant there was still a chance for her and Hunter to pick up where they'd left off. She'd been naïve to think that way. Regardless of her reasons, Dani had still left him. She hadn't given him the explanation that he rightfully deserved before disappearing from his life.

"I truly am sorry," she said, letting her gaze settle on her coffee mug once more.

"So am I, baby," he whispered softly.

When Dani looked up again, she could see the residual pain in Hunter's eyes. It was evident he was haunted by his past and she hated that she was part of the reason for it.

"And I'm so sorry about Josh," she said softly. "I honestly had no idea. I've thought about him over the years, but I never knew he…"

"Died," Hunter added. "Yeah. My life completely unraveled at that point."

"You loved him," she concluded aloud.

"No. But I cared about him." He swallowed hard. "I loved *you.*"

A tear slipped from her eye and trailed down her cheek. Another followed quickly behind, but she didn't look away from Hunter. She'd spent years missing him, aching for him in a way she knew no one could ever ease.

"Don't," he said roughly, his hand moving up to cup her face, his thumb brushing over her cheek. "Don't cry."

More tears fell. She couldn't stop them. It seemed the dam had been broken last night and she wondered if she would ever stop.

"Ah, fuck, Dani. Don't cry." His words were raspy with emotion.

Hunter moved closer, his chair coming with him. Their legs brushed as they continued to stare at one another.

"I am so sorry," she whispered. "So sorry, Hunter."

When Hunter leaned closer, she thought for a second that he was going to kiss her. She was disappointed when he didn't, but his forehead pressed against hers and she found herself content with that. He was touching her, and for the first time since she'd left him, she felt as though she wasn't completely out of control.

Sniper 1  *Security*

AS HE MADE HIS THIRD pass over the back deck, Kye glanced into the house.

He stopped instantly when he saw Hunter and Dani at the kitchen table. Neither of them were moving but their foreheads were touching. It was an intimate scene, one he probably should've turned away from, but he couldn't help himself. Right there in that moment, he knew exactly what they meant to one another. There was no way either of them could hide their vulnerability, even if they wanted to.

Guilt and jealousy had his chest constricting. He cared as much for them as he could care for anyone. Kye would go so far as to say he had fallen in love with Hunter. And in the short time he'd known Dani, he had come to care for her deeply. Although, he seriously doubted either of them would ever feel for him what they did for each other. They had too much history for that to happen.

He'd spent most of the night thinking about the two of them. Wondering how in the hell either of them could've walked away. For Hunter to have carried all that anger and hurt with him for so long, Kye knew Dani had meant more to him than he had ever let on.

And of course, Kye had spent part of the night wondering how he fit into all of this. Not that he did, but he certainly wanted to. Never in his wildest dreams could he have imagined finding someone who would understand him. Not only did Hunter get him, he shared the same desires, accepted his lifestyle.

And they'd had some serious fun back in the beginning. Based on their conversations, Kye knew that most people—including the man's family—weren't aware of Hunter's bisexuality. That had made it a little more risqué. And hot as fuck. Especially those times when they'd fantasized about bringing a woman into their bed. Granted, Kye knew it would take a special woman to be able to commit to something like that long term, but he'd actually started thinking about it again recently.

He'd actually started thinking about it with Hunter, although he knew that was a waste of time. For one, Kye had successfully put an end to their sexual encounters because he knew that was what Hunter wanted. The man knew exactly what buttons to push to keep everyone at a distance. Since the night Kye had walked away, he'd ensured he didn't come face-to-face with Hunter. Whatever they'd had together hadn't been working, so it shouldn't have mattered.

Unfortunately, Hunter still mattered to Kye.

And so did Dani.

A noise in the trees alerted him and Kye spun around, pulling his gun from the holster at his back. He silently slipped down the stairs, moving along the edge of the house. He didn't see anyone, but that didn't mean they weren't there.

Come on, you bastard, show your face.

Kye did his best not to step on the dried leaves that had fallen from the trees in the previous months. It was probably safe to assume a squirrel was trekking through the brush, but he wasn't the type to assume anything. Plus, he'd been out there for the better part of the morning and had yet to hear any of the forest critters moving about.

The noise sounded again as he moved closer to the tree line. He paused as he scanned the area. He didn't see anyone, but he sensed they were there. Since Dani and Hunter were in a vulnerable position in front of that window, he knew he had to signal his partner.

He tapped his watch, engaging the mic. "We might have company, Hunter."

"Ten-four," came the reply. "Location?"

"Back. But that doesn't mean someone's not out front."

Since Dani's intruder had failed the last time, Kye wouldn't put it past him to bring backup. That was what Kye would've done.

Suddenly, someone shouted and Kye glanced back at the house. The next thing he knew, several guys were stepping out of the trees, all dressed in black.

Oh, shit. They were so fucked. No way could they defend themselves against all of these guys. No fucking way.

Kye lined up his sight on the one closest to him. He tried to run through a scenario that might have him breathing at the end of this. There were too damn many of them. They would have to surrender and fucking hope for the best.

Hunter's voice sounded in his ear. "Stand down, Sterling. It's Dani's…*brother*."

"Yeah. I'm not buying that," he replied. These guys were military, he was almost certain of it. He had witnessed Max's bodyguards. They were hired guns, not assassins. Whoever these guys were…

"Wasn't about to let him crash the party all by himself," a familiar voice said as another black-clad figure stepped forward.

"Son of a bitch," Kye grumbled. "You know, Conner, we do have a front door."

"Yeah, well, I figured I'd let Max use that entrance."

Kye glanced away from Hunter's brother long enough to take a mental count of at least half a dozen other men guarding the perimeter.

"Kye," Hunter's voice sounded in his hearing aid. "I need you inside. Let my brother keep an eye out there."

Great.

Kye peered back at Conner.

"We were keeping tabs on Max," Conner explained. "We expected he would seek her out after the bomb she dropped yesterday." Conner glared up at the house.

"How'd he figure out where she was?" Kye didn't like the fact that they'd found them so easily.

"No idea. But that's why we're here. I've got people surrounding the place. I'll alert you if there's anyone who isn't welcome to the party."

Kye sighed. He wanted to tell Conner that Max wasn't welcome to the party, but it wasn't his place. Holstering his weapon, Kye turned toward the house. He traipsed through the leaves, not bothering to be silent. When he reached the porch, he could hear loud voices coming from inside. He made his way through the back door.

"I don't give a fuck," Hunter snarled. "You're going to get her killed. Whoever's after her is likely watching you."

"I'm sure they are," Max noted.

Courtney was standing beside her husband. The glare she shot Dani said she wasn't happy about any of this.

"So, why'd you come?" Hunter asked.

Max smiled, but it wasn't a happy one. "You think I could let my sister disappear without figuring out what the hell was going on?"

"When she was your cousin, it didn't seem to matter that much to you," Hunter bit out.

Max snarled but didn't say anything. Kye figured the man knew it was the truth.

"We're not gonna get anywhere if the two of you are at each other's throats," Courtney said. "You've got ten minutes, Max. Then we have to leave."

That seemed to settle the man somewhat.

"I'd like to talk to Dani alone," Max said, peering up at Hunter.

Hunter looked at Dani and she nodded her agreement. Hunter sighed heavily, then moved toward Kye.

"The fucker's gonna get her killed," Hunter grumbled as he headed over to the kitchen counter.

"Conner brought an army," Kye informed him.

"Thank fuck for that. Max isn't thinking straight."

Was anyone? Tempers seemed to be high all around.

Doing his best not to eavesdrop, Kye stood in the kitchen and watched as Dani and Max walked down the hall to the bedroom she had taken as her own. He couldn't necessarily blame Max for wanting to get more information. It sounded as though no one knew about Dani's secret. How she'd managed to spend her entire life pretending to be someone else, he wasn't sure.

"When they leave, we move out," Hunter stated.

"Where to?"

"Back to Dallas. You'll take the scenic route, come in under the cover of darkness. We'll stay at the compound. No way anyone can get to her there."

Yeah. That was probably true. Yet... "Why didn't we go there in the first place?"

Hunter cut a quick look his way. "Because I was hoping to keep Max from finding her." He nodded toward the bedroom. "As much as he wants to protect her from his enemies, the idiot just leads them right to her."

"Good point." Kye could be ready to leave in thirty seconds. The only thing he needed was his go bag, which was currently packed and ready.

Oh, and that box of condoms.

He would certainly be grabbing those.

You know, wishful thinking and all that.

FOURTEEN

BY THE TIME DANI AND Kye made it back to his house, Hunter was going stir-crazy. He'd headed back as soon as Max left, while Kye and Dani had taken a three-hour detour with an armed escort that consisted of Conner and the men Conner had pulled together to track Max to the Oklahoma safe house.

To pass some of the time, Hunter had gone into the office, hoping to get a chance to talk to RT. Unfortunately, being that it was Saturday, RT had opted to spend time with his husband, so Hunter had bailed, far too wired to be cooped up in that office for an extended period of time. He had ridden around for a while, but then headed home.

It wasn't until Dani and Kye walked inside that Hunter released a breath he hadn't realized he'd been holding. He had worried about both of them endlessly while they'd been out of his sight.

Dani looked tired, but he couldn't very well blame her. It had been a trying day for them all. After she had given Max the sordid details of Samuel's lies and deceit where she was concerned, she had turned in on herself. It hadn't been easy leaving her behind, but Hunter knew it was the best thing. His concern was for her safety and he knew without a doubt that Kye would protect her with his life.

Now that she was here, his concern was something else entirely.

"Are you hungry?" he asked as she peered around his house.

It probably didn't look much different to her than it had before. In fact, it was possibly the exact same as when she'd been there all those years ago. He hadn't changed a damn thing.

"We grabbed burgers," Kye informed him, holding up a white paper sack. "Well, technically, one of the other agents stopped to pick them up and delivered them to us. We ate ours on the road, but there's one for you. If it's wrong, take it up with them."

Hunter smiled as he took the food from Kye. "Thanks."

He set it on the counter and moved toward Dani. She looked lost and exhausted. Hunter knew exactly how she felt. After their brief conversation that morning, he had felt the same. Spending hours on his motorcycle had given him plenty of time to think. And he had come to one conclusion.

Hunter was tired of wasting time. Hell, wasting his life. He'd spent the past five years living with the bottled-up rage and anger over things he couldn't control. He had blamed Dani for so much, although he was far guiltier than she was. If he had honestly wanted to find her, he could have. Sniper 1 Security could've tracked her down for him. Of that, he had no doubt.

Instead, Hunter had played the martyr, exactly as Dani had accused. Rather than suffer in silence, though, Hunter had taken his anger out on anyone who got in his way. He was tired of being angry and he was tired of lying to himself. Kye and Dani were what he wanted most in the world and he'd spent so much time fighting that, he was ready to give in.

Granted, he wasn't sure either of them would be on board with his plan, but he was hoping they would warm up to it. After all, he'd been fighting them both for so long now, he was ready to beg for their forgiveness.

"I'm gonna shower," Kye stated as he glanced between the two of them.

"Sure," Hunter said, never looking away from Dani.

She moved through the living room, touching the few photos he had of his family, then running her fingers over the furniture. When she turned to look at him, he could see pain in her eyes.

"What's wrong?"

Dani offered a partial shrug. "I'm sorry Max is so stubborn. I didn't expect him to track me down."

"I did."

She offered a partial smile. "Well, thank you for letting me stay here."

He frowned as he closed the distance between them. "I'm glad you're here," he admitted.

"Are you really?" She didn't sound convinced, her golden eyes sliding up to his face.

Hunter moved even closer.

"Or are you looking for a little payback?"

"For what?"

Dani cocked one dark eyebrow. "Oh, I don't know. Me leaving you on our wedding day." Her eyes dropped to the floor. "Or me sleeping with Kye."

So, it had happened. He'd assumed as much, but he hadn't sat Kye down to seriously discuss it. Sure, Hunter had accused him, but he'd been angry at the time. Truth was, Kye was right. Hunter had no claim on Dani, and he damn sure didn't have the right to come between them.

"Is this payback?" Dani sounded uncertain.

Yesterday, he might've said yes. Today, that wasn't the case. "No." Hunter couldn't resist touching her. He cupped her face between both of his hands. "I'm not looking to hurt you, Dani. I understand why you walked away."

She smiled sadly. "I'm glad one of us does. I'm always questioning why I didn't stay. Why I didn't trust you."

"It wouldn't've mattered." He leaned in closer. "I would've been angry and we both know I'm prone to knee-jerk reactions."

Dani chuckled softly. "That you are."

He held her stare. "What's happening here, Dani?"

"I have no idea."

"Is this just about me keeping you safe?"

She stared back at him as though she didn't understand what he was getting at.

"I want you." He couldn't keep that to himself anymore. "I still want you. The same way I did back then."

"What about Kye?"

"What about him?" Hunter wasn't sure what she was getting at.

"Do you want him?"

He didn't look away. "I do."

"The same way you wanted Josh?"

"No," he admitted. "Not the same way."

She frowned, and Hunter could tell she wasn't happy with his revelation. "What's different?"

"I…" He knew he had to throw this out there. If he didn't, it was going to eat him up inside. "I feel something more for Kye than I felt for Josh."

He hated himself for acknowledging that, but it was the truth. He had cared about Josh, but he had never loved him. With Kye…it was different. Hunter felt something deeper, stronger. Even though they'd been apart for months, Hunter still felt it. He still wanted that man with a desperation he had never known before.

And he knew this because he felt for Kye the same way he felt about Dani. Love wasn't a rational thing. People didn't get to choose who they loved. It merely happened. Would he admit to anyone else that he never loved Josh? No. He couldn't. Hunter wasn't going to tarnish his memories of Josh by psychoanalyzing it.

But he could admit the truth about how he felt for the two of them now.

Dani's gaze dropped to his mouth and Hunter couldn't resist leaning in closer, allowing her breath to fan against his lips. He tilted his head, angling to claim her mouth the way he'd dreamed about for so long.

"Is this a good idea?" she asked, her voice strained, as though she feared he was leading her on.

"It's the only idea I have."

When Dani's palms flattened against his chest, Hunter thought she would push him away. Instead, she fisted his shirt and pulled him closer, effectively eliminating the scant few inches that had separated their lips.

He pressed his mouth to hers, all the old feelings slamming into him. He remembered her kiss, remembered the way her hands felt on him. The soft moans she made. Dani was a drug Hunter couldn't resist. Although he'd abstained for years, he couldn't hold back any longer.

Attempting to take things slow, he didn't deepen the kiss, didn't thrust his tongue into her mouth. He remained lip-locked with her, breathing through his nose as the emotions within him rioted, anxious to find the balm that could soothe his soul after all this time.

Dani was the first to pull back, but Hunter didn't let her get far.

"Aww, Christ," he growled, sliding his hand around to cradle the back of her head as he crushed his mouth to hers. He thrust his tongue past her lips, inhaling her soft mewl as she kissed him back with equal passion.

The woman had always done this to him. Reduced him to nothing more than a barely restrained animal desperate to claim her.

When her arms wreathed his neck, Hunter dropped one hand to her ass, jerking her closer. He needed to feel her, all of her against him. He feared he would go crazy if he didn't have her.

He only prayed he could keep from unleashing on her.

The last thing he wanted was to scare her away just when he'd gotten her back.

Sniper 1 *Security*

DANI KNEW SHE SHOULD TELL Hunter that she was conflicted.

Back when they'd been together the first time … when Hunter had brought Josh into their relationship … Dani had been with Josh to appease Hunter. However, with Kye … she felt different about Kye. She cared about him, but she also wanted him. In a way she'd never wanted Josh.

Although they'd only had a short time together at the beach, Dani had fallen for the man. And though she understood why he had lied to her about his name and occupation, she knew he hadn't lied about himself. She had felt it when they made love. He had been honest with her then.

During their trip back from the safe house, they had talked as much as they could with two agents sitting in the backseat. They hadn't gone deep into the conversation the way she'd wanted to, but Kye had admitted enough. Unlike Hunter, Kye opened up to her, shared his past, his feelings. And he had held her hand the entire way, making her feel safe and protected. It had done something to her, made her worry that what she wanted couldn't possibly be allowed.

Because Dani wanted both of them.

"What is it?" Hunter asked when he pulled his mouth from hers.

She was panting, hating that he broke the kiss, knowing she had to tell him the truth. Dani refused to lie to him ever again. Although she had no idea what tomorrow might bring, she knew she would not go forward without being completely honest with Hunter. He deserved at least that much from her.

"Kye," she said softly.

"What about him?"

She stared into Hunter's beautiful eyes. "I want him."

Dani expected to see confusion, but instead, she saw nothing but pure passion.

"You want me to share you with him?"

Dani shook her head because it was far more complicated than that. "No. I want to share *him* with *you*. I want to share *you* with *him*."

She couldn't explain what had happened, how she'd come to feel so strongly about Kye in such a short amount of time. Perhaps it was like that movie *Speed*. The one with Sandra Bullock. She had fallen in love with the man who saved her.

It could be that, but Dani didn't think so. She wasn't prone to falling in love. And she couldn't say what she felt for Kye was love for certain, but it was something.

"You care about him?" Hunter asked.

"Yes. And before you ask, I can't explain it. Nor do I want to. But I'm torn."

Dani inhaled sharply when a warm body pressed up against her back. Rough stubble grazed her cheek.

"Don't be," Kye whispered. "We're both right here."

Her stomach flipped as the two men sandwiched her between them.

Kye's lips trailed over her neck as Hunter stared back at them. She couldn't tell what he was thinking, and she nearly panicked when he took a single step back. However, she didn't have time, because Kye turned her so that she was in his arms. And suddenly, his mouth was on hers.

She moaned softly as she gave in to her desires. His kiss was so different than Hunter's, but equally enthralling. Dani threw her arms around him, holding him as close as she could while she stood on her tiptoes, trying to get closer. His hair was wet from his shower but just as soft as she remembered.

When Hunter's warm body pressed up against her back, she felt whole once more. She dropped one arm from around Kye's neck and curled it around Hunter's when he leaned down and pressed his lips to her neck.

Damn, this felt good. The two of them holding her, kissing her, touching her.

She almost let herself get lost in them, but she knew she had to clarify one more thing before she could allow this to continue. After relishing the moment for a few seconds longer, Dani finally managed to pull her mouth from Kye's.

"I won't move forward unless the two of you are willing," she told them. "I know you've got issues between you…" She didn't know what they were, but she knew something had happened, and the two of them had to get back on solid ground or this would never work.

The absolute last thing she wanted was to be played by both of them.

Kye stood to his full height, staring at Hunter over her head. Dani shifted, moving out from between them, never looking away. They remained like that for several seconds, staring but not speaking.

Kye was the first to break the awkward silence. "First of all, I won't apologize for what happened between me and Dani. That wasn't about you."

Hunter nodded. "I know."

"Secondly, I won't let you use me anymore."

Well, that seemed to sum up what their issues were.

Dani glanced at Hunter.

"I never used you," Hunter said, his voice pitched low.

Kye shook his head, looking slightly disappointed. "Keep lying to yourself, Hunter. But until you can be honest with me"—Kye glanced over at Dani, then back to Hunter—"I can't do this."

When he turned to walk away, Dani wanted to reach for him, but Hunter beat her to it. Kye paused, facing away from Hunter.

"Fine. You're right," Hunter stated gruffly. "I used you. The same as you used me."

Kye didn't turn around, nor did he deny Hunter's accusation.

"In the beginning," Hunter added. "But when you walked away, I wasn't using you then. I was…scared."

Dani watched as Kye's shoulders tensed. Her heart constricted at the honesty she heard in Hunter's voice.

"I care about you, Kye."

Dani could tell it had taken a tremendous amount of effort for Hunter to admit that.

Kye pivoted to face Hunter. "You realize that's the most honest thing you've ever said to me? In all the time I've known you?"

"I'm not big on talking," Hunter admitted.

Kye smirked. "Yeah. That's something I *do* know."

Dani felt slightly awkward being a bystander to their conversation, but she couldn't look away. The way these two men looked at one another … Hunter more than cared about Kye. And vice versa. Whatever they once had, it was deeper than mere longing or lust.

In fact, she'd go so far as to say it was definitely love.

She watched as Hunter lifted his hand, reaching for Kye. His fingers curled behind Kye's neck and he pulled him closer. It was a little strange to see. Kye appeared to be the more dominant one. Well, if looks had anything to do with it. He was so much bigger than Hunter, yet it was obvious Hunter held the reins when they were together.

The kiss that ensued practically incinerated the room. Dani got warm just watching them. Two rough, powerful men pawing at one another as their mouths ground together was definitely doing something for her.

But then they stopped.

Two sets of eyes turned toward her.

"Is that enough emotional shit for now?" Hunter asked.

Dani nodded, unable to find words.

"Good. Because I've got a helluva lot of time to make up for."

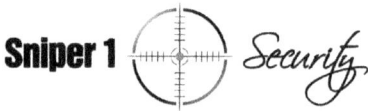

KYE DIDN'T BOTHER TO LET on that he'd heard the majority of their conversation. Especially the part where Hunter had admitted he had more feelings for him than he had for Josh. As for what that meant, he wasn't sure. Kye still didn't understand exactly what sort of relationship Hunter'd had with Josh.

Regardless, Hunter's admission had been unexpected but not unwelcome.

Still, Kye knew that this was going to be an uphill battle with Hunter all the way. If and when the man ever opened up, Kye would be shocked. But as much as he wanted to hold back to simply protect himself emotionally, he knew he couldn't. Mainly because he'd heard Dani's confession loud and clear.

Just like her, he didn't know what it was between them, but there were definitely feelings there. It required some exploration, there was no doubt about it.

And now that they'd cleared the air, he wanted to get his mouth on her again. Kissing that woman … he hadn't expected it. Well, that wasn't entirely true. The kiss he had expected, but how it made him feel, he hadn't. It was just as potent now as it had been the first time at the beach.

Perhaps his mother was right. She had always told him that when he met the person he was supposed to spend the rest of his life with, he would know it. There would be no questioning it, no trying to make it work. It would simply be. He honestly hadn't expected that he would ever find the *two* people, though.

Kye knew that Dani and Hunter were it for him. He belonged with them and they belonged with him. As for how things would turn out, that was anyone's guess, but Kye had never been the type to hold back due to fear.

"What're you waitin' for, Sterling?"

He peered down at the sassy woman who'd asked the question and smiled.

"You don't have to tell me twice." In two steps, he was in front of her. And in one quick motion, he had lifted her off the ground. "Put your legs around me, doll face, then put your mouth on mine."

Dani's smile was pure heaven. He loved to see her smile.

However, he loved to feel her kiss more, so when her lips fused to his, he spun around and carried her toward Hunter's bedroom. He could hear Hunter right behind them.

Unable to resist, Kye laid her out on the bed and crawled over her, all while his tongue danced alongside hers. The woman felt so damn good against him, all soft and warm. And she kissed him as though they'd been lovers for eternity.

"You have on too many clothes," she whispered when she pulled back.

Kye grinned down at her. "You're one to talk."

Obviously Dani was in a hurry because she was already pulling Kye's T-shirt up. He didn't stop her, allowing her to remove it.

"And you, too," she told Hunter.

Kye dropped to Dani's side, shifting so he could see Hunter. The man was standing at the end of the bed, seemingly content to watch them.

He didn't need to be told twice, either, because Hunter quickly shed his shirt, then reached for Dani's ankles, jerking her toward him. She giggled when he reached for the waistband of her shorts. Before he pulled them down, he met her gaze, his eyes heated yet serious.

"You sure this is what you want?"

She nodded. "It's the only thing I want."

Hunter relieved her of her shorts while Dani pulled her T-shirt over her head, tossing it at Kye. It landed in his face, making him laugh.

"You're a feisty one, aren't ya?"

"Oh, you have no idea," Hunter said gruffly.

When the three of them were finally naked, Hunter joined them on the bed. Kye had been in situations such as this one, but never had it felt quite so right. There was no awkwardness, no confusion. Hands began wandering. Dani's. Hunter's. His. The three of them touched and fondled, mouths shifting and moving together until the room had heated several degrees.

"You make me crazy, baby," Hunter whispered to Dani. "As much as I want to take my time … it's been too fucking long."

Kye was curious how long it had been for Hunter. The last time they'd been together was four months ago. That was the last time Kye had been with anyone until Dani a few short days ago.

Hunter's gaze lifted to his. "Not since you," he said softly, as though reading Kye's mind.

"Only Dani," Kye admitted.

Dani chuckled. "I'll do you both one better."

Both of them turned to look at her.

"Until Kye, I haven't been with anyone since you. And before you, I'd never been with anyone else."

Holy fuck. Until the other night, the woman hadn't been with anyone in … shit. Five years? Six? A long time. Damn. No wonder she was practically smoldering.

Granted, based on Hunter's wide eyes, Dani's admission meant something else entirely to him. She'd been a virgin when they met.

"Please tell me someone's got condoms," Dani stated, glancing between them.

Kye flew up off the bed and headed for the bathroom, where he'd left his bag. He retrieved the box they'd purchased yesterday before returning. He found Hunter lying on the bed, Dani straddling him as they kissed. Kye could've stood there all day and watched them. Naked, grinding. Hell, his cock was so fucking hard he could hardly stand it.

"How do you want this to go?" Hunter asked Dani.

She didn't hesitate with her answer. "I want you both to fuck me."

Kye's eyes went wide.

She giggled. "But not at the same time." Her head swiveled toward him. "Not yet, anyway."

Yeah. If the woman had only had sex a couple of times in the past five years, Kye knew there was no way she could handle double penetration. Not until they prepared her, anyway.

"I don't think any of us can hold out. Not this time," Hunter said, flipping Dani off of him before launching to his feet. He pointed toward the bed. "You. There. Now."

Curious as to where Hunter was going with this, Kye joined Dani on the bed. His hands immediately sought her smooth, warm skin as he relaxed onto his back.

"Put the condom on him," Hunter instructed. "And I want to watch."

The foreplay was minimal, but Kye didn't mind. They would have plenty of time later. Right now, he was so damn close to coming, it was a wonder he didn't shoot his load when Dani's soft hands glided over his shaft.

"Fuck," he hissed, watching as she rolled the rubber over his dick. "You're killin' me."

"We can't have that, now can we?" Dani straddled his hips, leaned down and pressed her lips to his.

Kye got lost in her kiss, moaning when she took him in hand and guided his cock to the slick, warm entrance to her body. He broke the kiss when she sank down on him, her body sheathing him tightly.

She was heaven.

"I'm not gonna last," he admitted, glancing over at Hunter. "I suggest you join us or you'll be left behind."

Hunter produced a bottle of lubricant from the nightstand, then crawled onto the bed between Kye's legs.

Ah, hell. Kye knew where this was headed.

"Lean forward, baby," Hunter whispered to Dani. "I want you right between us."

She shifted forward, keeping Kye's cock deeply lodged in her pussy. Dani was still moving, rocking back and forth on his dick, making his breaths race in and out of his lungs while her breasts crushed against his chest.

"You feel so good," Kye told her, cupping her face. "*So* damn good."

"I think Hunter's about to make you feel better."

When Hunter forced Kye's legs back, it shifted Dani again, but she remained where she was, impaled on his cock.

"Hold his legs, Dani," Hunter urged.

Dani moved again, wrapping her arms behind his knees and holding his legs back. He was practically folded in half and he didn't care because the sexiest woman on the planet was impaled on his dick.

Hunter's thighs brushed against his ass.

Kye knew what was coming and he was eager to feel Hunter inside him, filling his ass while Dani's sweet pussy caressed his cock.

"The next time he fucks you," Dani whispered, her face pressed into his shoulder, "I get to watch."

God, he liked her. In the bedroom, Dani was an entirely different woman. She seemed to shed her inhibitions, knowing exactly what she wanted and living only in that moment. It had been the same way at the condo and he found he missed being with her like this, even if it had only been a couple of days since.

"Ah, fuck," Kye groaned when Hunter's cock pushed in. The man didn't rush, but he certainly didn't take his time.

"Tight," Hunter growled. "So fucking tight."

"Somebody better start moving or I'm gonna come without you both," Dani teased.

"It'd be my pleasure," Hunter said, pushing Dani flat against Kye's chest as he began thrusting into Kye's ass.

Kye grunted, pleasure and pain assaulting him. He was overwhelmed by sensation. Hunter's movements effectively rocked Dani's body, the friction from her pussy on his dick making him sweat. He didn't want to come yet, but he knew it wouldn't take long.

Dani found Kye's hands and twined their fingers together as she pressed her lips to his neck. Her breath fanned his ear.

"Let us fuck you, Kye. I need to come."

There was nothing he could do. He was impaled on Hunter's cock and the fucking he was receiving threatened to blow his head off his shoulders.

At some point, the two of them found a rhythm, fucking Kye in every way imaginable. He held on, his fingers tightening around Dani's. When he looked up and met Hunter's gaze, he saw something he'd never seen before.

Gone was the anger, the rage, the need for revenge. Oh, Hunter still looked lethal, but there was something else.

"Oh, God," Dani cried out. "I'm coming."

Her pussy squeezed his dick while Hunter continued to ram deep inside his ass and Kye was lost. He tried to hold on but couldn't.

He grunted as he came, his eyes locking with Hunter's, his fingers still twined with Dani's.

"Fuck, yes," Hunter hissed. "Come for us, Kye."

Within seconds, Hunter's hips stopped moving, his cock pulsing as he came.

And for the first time in Kye's entire life, he felt as though he was exactly where he was supposed to be.

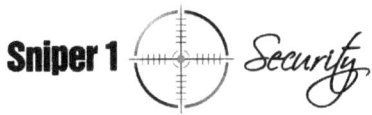

HE WALKED THROUGH THE SAFE house without touching anything. They weren't coming back, he knew it. He'd been so close, too. Just a few feet away when the army of men had descended on the place. It was a good thing he was a patient man, or he would've been a dead one. Thankfully, once Max showed up, no one seemed to give a shit that he was hiding in the small wooden shed about twenty yards from the house, waiting for the coast to be clear.

Unfortunately, he hadn't heard what had taken place inside the house. He would've given anything to be a fly on the wall while Dani gave Max all the sordid details of whatever crisis she was going through now.

The good thing was, he knew exactly where they were, thanks to the fact those men they'd hired liked to chat like old women. They fully believed Dennis Moroso was the threat to Dani. He liked that they had no clue what was really going on. In fact, he could probably shake Dennis's hand because the man was a good distraction. Dennis and his hired assassin.

It was working in his favor.

Of course, he was biding his time. He wanted to give them a chance to get comfortable back in Dallas, to stop looking over their shoulder. He had waited this long, what were a few more days? Even weeks? He had time.

Walking into the spare bedroom, he picked up the pillow Dani had slept on. Inhaling deeply, he smiled when the scent of tangerines filled his nostrils. That was her scent. He'd smelled it a million times. And one of these days, he was going to get up close and personal with Danielle Davidson, enough that he could do to her exactly what her father had done. He dreamed about it, fantasized even. He would strap her down, rip her clothes from her body, and watch as she sniveled and cried, begging for her freedom. Maybe for a day, possibly two. He wanted to see the fear in her eyes, the uncertainty.

He grabbed the pillow with both hands and ripped it at the seams.

He wanted Danielle to know the excruciating hell his sister had experienced at the hands of that madman.

Oh, Danielle would know what his intentions were. He would rape her again and again, taking exactly what she deserved until she was so battered and bloody she would welcome death.

Then he would do it again and again until she begged for mercy.

Once her pain filled the cold, dark hole in his soul, he would kill her.

Slowly.

Very, very slowly.

Then, he would make sure to send the pictures to her family so they could feel the same fucking pain his had.

Granted, he just might have to take out Dennis Moroso before that could happen. The man and his hired assassin were proving to be somewhat useful, but there would come a time when they would just be wasting too much fucking time.

FIFTEEN

Three days later

HUNTER WOKE BEFORE ANYONE ELSE. He peered over at the two people sleeping in his bed. Although they'd only been there for the past two nights, it had started to feel natural for Hunter. He wasn't sure he ever wanted to sleep alone again. He watched them, both looking so peaceful as Kye spooned Dani from behind.

Since that first night after the three of them had made love in his bed, for the first time in as long as he could remember, Hunter hadn't dreamed. With them there, he slept soundly, Dani cuddled up next to him, one arm and leg thrown over his body as though she couldn't get close enough.

He knew how she felt. These past couple of days had been incredible. And not merely the sex, although that was phenomenal as well.

But today was a new day and he had to get up. He had taken yesterday off—something he was not prone to do—and he knew the office would be bubbling with chatter about what was going on. Hunter needed to check in with Conner and RT, see if they'd found anything out. Before leaving the safe house on Saturday, Hunter had talked to Conner, asking him to do some digging into the Moroso brother. He wasn't sure who was after Dani, but if Max was convinced it was Moroso, there was probably a good bet that he was. But Hunter was tired of sitting on the sidelines waiting for Max to reveal whatever he was hiding.

Forcing himself out of bed, Hunter headed for the shower. He quickly washed up, eager for some coffee. Once he had downed some caffeine, he'd be ready to do a little digging of his own.

*

Twenty minutes later, Hunter sauntered into the kitchen. He found Dani sitting on the counter beside the coffeepot. He paused to watch her, the way her long hair hung down over her shoulders and all the way down her back. The woman was so beautiful, but she always had been. There was something about her now. Something a little darker than before. Or maybe it had always been there, and he hadn't seen it. Being that she was part of a family who used people as pawns, he had to admire the fact that she had a good heart. Oh, he hadn't seen it for years. Hadn't suspected she even had a heart when she disappeared on him, but now he understood.

Her eyes remained on the coffeemaker. It was gurgling and hissing, so he figured she was waiting for it.

Hunter shuffled into the kitchen and her eyes flew up to his face.

"Morning," she said hesitantly.

Without missing a beat, Hunter walked over to her, stepping between her legs and leaning in to kiss her.

When he pulled back, she smiled brightly. "Well, that's a nice way to be greeted in the morning. Want some coffee?"

Hunter retrieved two mugs from the cabinet. "Kye still asleep?"

"Yeah. I think we wore him out last night."

It was likely true. Hunter hadn't been able to keep his hands off either of them. He found he was insatiable, needing them both at all times of the day and night. And for the past three days, he had taken advantage of every opportunity.

"And what about you?" he asked, making his way back over to her. He found he couldn't stop touching her. It was as though he needed to assure himself that she was real, that this wasn't some fucked up dream that would have him waking up, the cold, stark reality of his life too much to bear.

"Oh, I'm definitely sated."

"Yeah?" He ran his hands down her thighs. She was wearing his T-shirt and he wondered what she had on beneath it.

When his fingers slipped below the hem of her shirt, Dani's eyes widened. She stared back at him, anticipation glittering her pretty eyes.

With his palms flat on her thighs, he inched them higher until his thumbs brushed her smooth mound. He smiled, loving that she had nothing on beneath his shirt.

"Are you sure about that?"

Her brow lowered, her words a breathless whisper. "Sure about what?"

"About being sated." When his thumbs shifted lower, separating her pussy lips, she hissed in a breath. "Or could you use another orgasm this morning?"

Dani was panting heavily as he teased her with his thumbs.

"Hunter…" Her hands reached for his arms, her nails sinking into his triceps. "I've missed your touch."

"I know, baby," he whispered, leaning in and kissing her again. He couldn't help himself. In fact, he wondered if he would ever get enough of her. "Put your feet on the counter."

Dani pulled her legs up, her knees pointed toward the ceiling as she put her heels on the edge of the counter.

"Spread your legs wide. I want to see your pretty pussy."

Without a word, she did as he instructed, her gaze never wavering from his. Hunter only looked away long enough to admire the smooth, slick flesh between her legs.

"You want my mouth on you, don't you?"

Dani moaned as she nodded.

He took one step back and leaned down so that his mouth hovered right over her pussy. He licked her gently, groaning. She tasted so good, so sweet. It had been so long. Too long. It would likely take months for him to make up for all the lost time.

Not that he minded one fucking bit.

Dani's fingers twined in his hair as he leisurely licked her, teasing her clit with the tip of his tongue.

"I want you to come for me, baby. Don't hold back."

She giggled. "I won't if you won't."

Taking her challenge, he dove in, licking, laving, suckling. He worked Dani into a frenzy as he fondled the swollen bundle of nerves at the top of her sex. Her hand tightened in his hair, but he didn't let up. He wanted to hear this woman scream for him. And once she did, he would be inside her. The first night, he'd taken Kye because he knew he couldn't be gentle with her. And last night, Hunter had let Dani ride him until she came, still worried he would be too rough with her. Fortunately, Kye could handle anything Hunter needed from him. It was one of the things he loved about the man.

Love.

It was hard to even think that, but he was tired of living in denial.

"Oh, God … Hunter…" Dani panted and moaned. "Please. *Please* make me come."

Suckling her clit between his lips, he flicked her with his tongue until she was rocking against him, holding his head as though he would stop. No way. He wasn't sure he could ever stop.

When Dani screamed his name over and over, Hunter reluctantly released her. He stood to his full height, shoved his jeans down his hips, then pulled her ass to the edge of the counter before pushing in deep.

Her arms came around his neck as she held on.

"God, baby," he moaned as he held her close. "I've dreamed about this. About feeling your pussy squeezing my cock. You feel so good."

Too good.

And he knew exactly why.

Hunter wasn't wearing a condom. Back when they'd been together, he hadn't worn them. But she'd been on birth control at the time. Now, he wasn't sure that was the case. Dani had been on the run for so long, and according to her, she hadn't been having sex, so it would make sense if she wasn't. Not that he gave a shit. If she wasn't, then they would deal with it. Having a baby with this woman…

His heart swelled in his chest. Hunter could practically see her, soft and round, pregnant with his child. He welcomed the mental image.

"Hunter … Harder. I need more." Her head tipped back as he slammed into her again and again.

He leaned in, latching on to the smooth skin of her neck. He wanted to mark her like a teenager, but he refrained.

"I'm…I'm…" Her arm tightened around him, but she didn't complete the sentence.

Not that he needed her to. Dani's pussy clamped down on his cock, milking him. Her orgasm nearly shredded him. Once she relaxed a bit, he continued to drive into her, slower this time.

"I need to come, Dani," he mumbled against her mouth. "But we both know I'm not wearing a condom."

He waited to see if she would say something.

She didn't.

"Tell me I can come inside you, baby."

Her hips rocked in rhythm with his. "I'm not on birth control, Hunter."

"I don't care." It was the truth. "In fact, I'm glad you're not."

Sure, it had only been a couple of days that she'd been back in his life, but he didn't give a shit. Too much time had passed. Too much wasted time. He wanted her with every ounce of his being and he knew that wasn't going to change. Six years hadn't done a damn thing to diminish his feelings for her, no matter how much he had tried to convince himself otherwise.

"Tell me, Dani," he ordered.

His hips were moving faster as he stood up straight, so he could look her in the eye.

"Yes," she whispered, her eyes glassy. "Come inside me, Hunter."

He did, and it might've been the best fucking orgasm of his entire life.

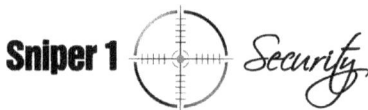

"WHERE'S THE COUSIN, DMITRI?" DENNIS demanded to know. "She should be dead by now."

"She's holed up at the Kogan compound," the man on the other end of the line stated.

"Well, fucking go in and get her!" Dennis was tired of playing this game already and it had only been four days since his man had missed her the first time at Devil's Playground. How the fucker could miss was beyond him, but Dennis was starting to think this little arrangement they'd made was a mistake.

The Russian's accent was thick when he said, "That would be suicide mission. I've staked it out for past twelve hours. They've got place armed to teeth."

Armed to the teeth? "Why the fuck would they do that? Max isn't protecting the others that way. Why her?"

"Maybe because of boyfriend?"

Dennis huffed as he stared out the window at the fucking corn. He hated this goddamn place. He was ready to be back in the city, back to getting his organization under control. He'd made plenty of headway during the past year, but taking over the Adorite territory was proving to be damn near impossible. At the moment, he couldn't get a single fucking gun shipment through the state. No one was willing to work with him on it, either.

"I seriously doubt that," Dennis said, thinking it over. "They aren't even together. She bolted on him on their wedding day. I'm sure he's as sick of seeing her as everyone else."

Dennis didn't know that to be true, but he had to wonder why all the fuss over a cousin.

"I will get her," the man stated firmly. "It might take time."

"I don't have time!" Dennis yelled. He could feel himself unraveling. This was worse than fucking prison. "Go get the fucking cousin and bring her to me. You've got until Friday. After that, you'll be moving into the top spot on my hit list."

Dennis stabbed the phone to end the call.

Seriously. Why all the fuss over Danielle Davidson? Something else had to be going on if Max had ordered her protection. Dennis knew the wife was connected to Sniper 1 Security. He even knew the old boyfriend was Courtney's brother. He simply didn't know why Danielle had become the main focus. It didn't make any damn sense.

He had to do something. As it was, Sabrina had refused to let him hide her, insisting that she was better off as far from him as possible. Didn't matter that he had threatened her and his nephew. His sister was a stubborn bitch when she wanted to be.

Maybe it was time to do something drastic. Something that would shake up the Adorites' world once and for all.

Since Sabrina wouldn't allow him to protect her, maybe she'd be willing to work with him. After all, the two of them together…

Yeah. It just might work.

SIXTEEN

Thursday morning

"I'M GOING TO LOSE MY mind," Dani announced when she walked into Hunter's living room. "I have got to get out of this house."

As it was, they'd been cooped up in Hunter's house for five days. At first, it hadn't been too bad because they'd spent plenty of time getting intimately acquainted with one another. It had been enough to keep her preoccupied, stop her mind from racing with all the questions as to who was after her, why they wanted to kill her. But now she was going out of her head with boredom.

It wasn't fair that Hunter and Kye got to leave but she had to stay there. Inside to boot. They were so overprotective she couldn't even go outside and sit on the porch.

"I'm sure it'll be over soon," Kye said, flipping through the channels on the television. He'd been doing that for the past two days, yet he never seemed to find anything interesting to watch.

Dani paced. "We're still no closer to finding this guy. I can't stay under lock and key forever. More importantly, I don't want to."

"I know, baby. Come here." Kye patted the couch cushion.

She pivoted, moving in the opposite direction. "No. I can't sit down, either. I'm wired." The six cups of coffee she'd downed already weren't helping. Probably all the sugar.

Dani wasn't used to sitting idle. Even when she'd been in hiding, she had always had something to do, someone to research, someone to hack for Max. Now, they wouldn't even let her on the computer for fear someone would track her down.

Honestly, she wasn't sure why it even mattered. She was locked up in a fortress. Between the security fences, the armed guards, *and* the numerous dogs roaming the property, she doubted anyone was coming for her here.

Nope. If Dani wanted to draw her attacker out, she was going to have to find a way to leave.

"Where's Hunter?" she asked on her next pass in front of the television.

"At the office." Kye hit the remote and the television went silent. "He's meeting with RT and Conner."

Dani stopped and faced him. "I want to go there."

Kye looked surprised. "I'm … not sure that's a good idea."

"Why not?" She knew they were keeping her here for her own safety, but Dani was tired of hiding. She was tired of everything. For six years, she'd been running from the demons that chased her, never getting any closer to figuring out who was responsible.

While everyone seemed to think it was Dennis Moroso, Dani couldn't see it. In the grand scheme of things, Dani was peanuts in the Adorite organization. Taking her out wouldn't do a damn thing to the business's infrastructure. So why would Dennis be targeting her? Unless it was personal, of course.

Kye didn't seem to have an answer for why it wasn't a good idea to go to the Sniper 1 offices. Maybe he feared someone there would take her out. Well, it probably wasn't farfetched, but she suspected Hunter's family would merely give her a piece of their mind, not any additional holes in her body.

"Call him," she demanded. "I need to get out of here."

Dani knew she sounded frazzled because she was. She'd never spent this much time locked indoors and she couldn't take any more.

"Please, Kye." Dani wasn't above begging.

"Let me call him." Kye pulled his phone from his pocket.

Dani headed toward the bedroom. She wanted to be ready to go as soon as he said it was okay.

Not that she believed Hunter was going to simply approve her request without an argument. Every time she'd tried to bring it up, he had shot her down.

"Yeah. I hear ya. We'll go straight there."

Dani paused for a moment, surprised by what she heard. That sure sounded as though Hunter had agreed to let her out of the house. Her belly quivered with anticipation. It wasn't that she looked forward to going to Sniper 1 Security and being surrounded by people who hated her for what she'd done to Hunter all those years ago, but at this point, she would face a firing squad if it meant she didn't have to look at these walls for at least a few hours.

"He wants you armed," Kye said when he joined her in the bedroom.

"Of course." Dani retrieved her gun from the nightstand drawer, checked the clip and the chamber, then ensured the safety was on. She turned to face Kye. "Ready."

He was watching her, but he didn't appear to be in any sort of hurry. In fact, the look on his face was hotter than hot and she got the feeling he was angling for something.

"You look so damn sexy when you're packing heat," he said with a smirk.

"Yeah?"

Kye took a step closer. "You look hot no matter what you're doing, though, so it's not surprising."

Dani glanced at the door, weighing her options. She could slip past him into the other room and out the front door. Force him to take her out of this place.

Or…

Well, her other option was to give in to what he wanted.

The truth was, she was looking forward to a little alone time with Kye. Specifically, naked alone time. What was thirty more minutes in the grand scheme of things?

When Kye moved another step closer and held out his hand, Dani knew exactly what he wanted. Without hesitating, she placed her gun flat in his palm. He set it on the dresser, never looking away from her.

"Now the shirt," he said, his voice an octave lower than normal.

"My shirt?" she asked, feigning innocence. "What are you planning to do with my shirt?"

"Hand it over and find out."

Slowly, Dani inched the cotton over her head, then passed it over.

Kye placed it with her gun.

"Now the bra."

She couldn't help giggling. This was the side of Kye she truly enjoyed. The sweet, teasing side. How the man could keep his sense of humor with all that was going on, she didn't know. She also didn't question it, because Kye had a way about him that helped to put her mind at ease.

"I'll need some help with it," she told him, slowly pivoting.

Kye moved closer until she could feel the warmth of his body at her back. Her bra was suddenly unfastened, and she allowed it to slide down her arms to the floor.

"Do you know how beautiful you are?" he asked as he pressed up against her bare back, his head lowering until his lips were gliding over her shoulder.

"No," she admitted.

"You're the most beautiful woman in the world, Danielle."

She knew that wasn't true, but it was hard to argue when his voice had turned to gravel and his hands were caressing her skin so gently.

"I could spend the rest of my life touching you, tasting you, sliding my cock deep inside you."

Her breath hitched. "What's stopping you now?"

His lips drifted down her spine and she could tell he was going to his knees behind her. Dani's breath quickened, and a delicious shiver danced down her spine. When he tugged her shorts down, her belly did a little flip. A few seconds later, she was standing naked in the middle of Hunter's bedroom with Kye still on his knees behind her.

Big hands cupped her ass and he kneaded the flesh.

"You have the sexiest ass," he said roughly before she felt his lips dropping kisses where his hands had been squeezing.

A soft moan escaped her. "I think you have too many clothes on," she said breathlessly.

"I want to take my time with you. Keeping my clothes on is the only way I know to do it."

"Yeah? Why's that?"

His lips grazed her right hip then moved to the base of her spine.

"If I'm naked, I'll want to be inside you."

"And there's something wrong with that?"

"Only if I want to make you come a few times first."

She liked the sound of that. "Do you?"

His lips moved up her spine until once again he was standing, his chest pressed to her back.

"I definitely do."

Kye's fingertips slid over her shoulders, then downward until he was cupping her breasts in his big hands. Dani relaxed against his big body, relishing the feel of his calloused skin against her flesh. She'd come to expect this from Kye and Hunter. They'd spent numerous hours worshipping her over the course of time they'd been trapped in this place. As much as Dani wanted to get out of here, she wasn't about to skip this part.

Spending time with Kye was important to her. They'd had the chance to talk at length during their time together, but there were a few things he was holding back. Not necessarily from her. More so from Hunter and she wanted to know why. They seemed to be dancing circles around one another.

Of course, sex wasn't an issue. They could go at it ten times a day if prompted. Hell, even if not prompted. They couldn't seem to get enough of each other. But Dani wanted Kye to feel comfortable opening up to both of them, sharing all his secrets and his dreams. It was the only way this would work. Getting Hunter to bleed emotion was impossible, but as long as they ganged up on Hunter in that regard, she knew the man would eventually break.

And every time they came together like this, she felt as though they were getting closer to that day, to the moment when Kye would drop the rest of the walls he kept so firmly in place and share his feelings.

Kye pinched her nipples, making her moan as she pressed back against him. She covered his hands with hers, holding him in place, wanting him to continue.

"You're so responsive," he said absently. "So fucking beautiful when you give yourself over to me."

It was because the man made her feel like she was irresistible. As though there was no one in the world he wanted more than her. The only other person she'd ever experienced that with was Hunter. Sometimes she wondered if this was real, if they were capable of spending the rest of their lives together. The three of them.

Back when she'd been with Hunter and Josh, it had always felt temporary. With Josh, that was.

And though she'd known that Hunter had feelings for Josh at the time, he was definitely different with Kye. Even if he hadn't admitted he loved him, Dani knew that he did. It was in the way they looked at one another.

"Stop thinking," Kye ordered, his mouth seeking her neck.

Dani tilted her head, giving him better access.

He bit her, and she sighed, her pussy clenching in eager anticipation.

"I need you inside me," she blurted, her body warming.

"We'll get there."

"No, now," she demanded, squirming under his hold, trying to get closer.

Kye stepped around her, causing Dani to look up into his eyes. The smirk he offered nearly scorched her insides.

"How about I take the reins for a little while," he offered, although Dani knew it was more a statement than an offer. "And you just enjoy."

Yeah. Well.

When he put it like that, how could she resist?

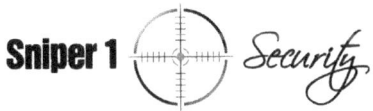

"SEE, THAT'S WHERE I'M CONFUSED," Conner mused.

Hunter was sitting in the conference room with RT, Conner, Trace, Decker, and Clay. He wasn't quite sure how it had turned into a party, but it seemed that people continued to gather, all trying to figure out who was after Dani. Initially, Hunter had sought out Conner and RT, but everyone else seemed to have an opinion. Since Hunter was at a loss, he damn sure didn't mind the brainstorming session.

"She said someone wrote it in blood on one of the safe houses' walls," Hunter clarified.

"Which safe house?" Clay asked.

"Does it matter?" Hunter didn't see how it did. "But Kye said he never saw it, so it wasn't the last house. He had cameras set up in there."

"It really doesn't matter." Clay looked up as Trace moved across the room. "The fact is he wrote it, which meant he was sending her a message."

"The child shall pay for the sins of the father," Trace stated as he wrote the words on the whiteboard before stepping back and staring at them.

"She believes that whoever it is knows that Samuel's her father and that's why he's coming after her."

"But that right there," Conner said, pointing at Hunter. "That's what doesn't make sense."

"Why not?"

"How many sisters does Max have?" Conner asked, although Conner already knew the answer to that.

"Two, not counting Dani. Madison and Ashlynn."

"Why not go after one of them instead?"

Good question. One Hunter had considered as well.

"Is Dani the youngest, maybe?" RT asked, glancing over at Hunter.

"No. Middle. Madison's twenty-four, Ashlynn's twenty-eight."

"So, why her? If this guy learned that Samuel was her father, why is he going after her? She's been in hiding while the other two have been right here in plain sight."

"I agree with Conner," RT said. "If this guy is after Dani for that reason, there would need to be something specific about her. Maybe she has something he wants?"

"Or maybe he's worried Max is watching the other two, so Dani was supposed to be the easy target," Trace added, obviously attempting to help them figure this out.

Yeah. Hunter could've told the guy Dani was anything but an easy target.

Conner sat on the edge of the conference table, his eyes pinned on Hunter. "Or maybe this has absolutely nothing to do with Samuel."

"If not Samuel…" Hunter held his brother's stare. "You think this has to do with Nick?"

"It makes sense, right?" RT said, leaning forward. "Those who know the family believe Nick is her father. And she's an only child, which would make her the perfect target if that's the case. The only target, in fact."

"I agree," Decker stated. "Maybe Dani only assumed this was about Samuel. Where is Nick?"

Hunter shook his head. "I don't know."

"I do," RT said, glancing down at his laptop. "Nick had a stroke several years ago, which left him partially paralyzed and suffering severe neurological damage. He never recovered from it. They've got him in a home with a full-time live-in nurse. Up until that time, Nick was the underboss of the Southern Boy Mafia. Max took over his position then."

"Which only makes it more confusing," Clay said. "If Nick is in such bad shape, how is going after Dani going to get back at him? The man probably doesn't even remember anything he's done."

Another good question. Another one of many that Hunter didn't have an answer for.

"When it comes to sociopaths, it only has to make sense to them. He would feel it's personal between him and Dani," another deep voice said from behind Hunter.

Hunter peered over his shoulder to see his father standing in the doorway. He was obviously engaged in the conversation.

"Did you know Nick Adorite?" Conner asked Casper.

"No," he replied as he stepped into the room. "But I didn't know Samuel, either."

"We do know that they were all sick and twisted," Trace said. "Patrick was a pedophile, Samuel was…well, he was deranged. And Nick…I think it's safe to say he wasn't innocent."

"It's a safe bet," Casper agreed. "Although, from the intel we've gathered over the years, when it comes to crimes against others, Samuel and Patrick are the two I'd be looking at to be responsible."

"Knowing the Adorites," RT added, "it's also safe to assume that the family covered up whatever heinous crime any of them were guilty of."

"Now the question is, if they're targeting Dani because of Nick," Hunter glanced at all the eyes staring back at him, "what is it that Nick Adorite did?"

"If he was anything like his older brothers," RT said, "I seriously doubt it was anything worth repeating."

Yeah. That was something they could all agree on. Sadly, though, it wasn't going to help them figure this out.

"Dani's on her way up here," he told the others. "Kye's bringing her. Maybe she'll have some answers."

If not, then they were right back where they started from.

At square one.

KYE ABSOLUTELY LOVED HOW FEISTY Dani was. She was always spouting off commands, especially when it came to their sexual encounters. Normally, he let her have her way. However, he wasn't interested in letting her have her way. Not this time. He would rather make her sit back and enjoy what he had in store for her.

Taking her hand, Kye led Dani toward the bed. With his free hand, he ripped the rumpled blankets off, tossing them onto the floor before guiding her to sit.

"Lie back," he ordered with a smile.

While she did as he instructed, Kye took those few seconds to admire her. The woman was spectacular in every way. And when she was naked ... Lord have mercy, he had a hard time focusing on anything except devouring her. Good thing that was in his current plan.

"Kye. Now I think you're just wasting time," Dani teased.

"I promise, there's nothing wasteful about this." Kye dropped to his knees at the edge of the bed, then grabbed her legs and pulled her closer. "You have a beautiful pussy."

He looked into her eyes as he said it, noticing the way the golden orbs glittered when he talked dirty to her. His girl liked it. A lot.

"And now, I'm going to eat your pussy." He grinned. "Until you ask me to stop."

Dani laughed. "Like that'll ever happen."

Knowing full well she couldn't resist his mouth on her, Kye leaned in and kissed her soft, smooth mound. He teased her for several seconds before feasting on her the way he dreamed about. He thought about last night, the way Hunter had held her down and licked her until she was begging and pleading for them to stop. At that point, Hunter had turned his attention on Kye, sucking him until he damn near lost his mind.

"Kye…oh, God…you're too good at that."

Yeah, he would take that compliment. He continued to lick and suck as she writhed and moaned, her hands reaching for his head. He stopped her, pinning her wrists to the mattress beside her hips while he tormented her.

"Kye! Oh, God! I'm…" Dani's hips bucked, grinding her luscious pussy against his mouth as she came.

"Such a beautiful sight," he told her as he quickly moved over her, brushing his lips against hers. "See how good you taste?"

She licked his lips before kissing him, her hands fumbling with his clothes. He didn't stop her. In fact, he helped her along, and when he finally sank into her, Kye's eyes were damn near crossing.

Okay, so maybe he didn't have all that much willpower when it came to her.

"Oh, fuck," he groaned, her pussy contracting around him. "Oh, fuck." Dani felt so good. Hot, wet…it was unlike anything he'd ever felt before.

And then he realized why.

"Shit! I'm so sorry." He pulled out, but Dani gripped his face.

"It's okay," she whispered, lifting her head and bringing their mouths together.

"I'm clean," he assured her.

"Me, too." Her eyes glittered.

"Are you on the pill?"

Dani shook her head. "No."

She didn't sound at all bothered by that fact, but if she wasn't on the pill, then he'd already put her at risk. If it was going to happen, it wouldn't take much for her to get pregnant. Surely she was thinking about that.

"Do you plan to have kids one day, Kye?"

Even the thought of having kids with this woman made strange things happen to his insides. He'd always wanted kids. A dozen of them.

"Yes," he admitted. "That's been in the plan."

He couldn't tell what she was thinking, but what she said next almost had him falling onto the floor.

"Well, I guess the next step is up to you then."

"What?"

"You can either fuck me like you were—without a condom—or you can be safe and get one."

"What if…?" He couldn't even get the words out.

Dani pulled his face closer. "I love you, Kye."

His heart slammed against his ribs as he stared at her with wide eyes.

Dani giggled. "And I'm not trying to scare you. Nor am I asking for anything in return. I just thought you should know."

With the arm that was holding his weight off her, Kye tucked his hand behind her head, realigned their bodies and slid deep inside her. He groaned again because the pleasure bordered on pain—it was that intense.

Reaching behind her leg, he lifted her knee to his hip as he pushed in deep and retreated, staring into her eyes as he made love to this woman. Never in his life had he expected to feel like this. It was quite possibly the greatest feeling in the entire world.

"I love you, Kye," she whispered again, still cupping his face.

"I love you, too, baby." He leaned in and kissed her, never increasing his pace. Kye took his time until they both came, wrapped in each other's arms.

*

"Yes, I know we're late," Kye told Hunter when they arrived at the Sniper 1 Security offices almost two hours after he'd talked to the man on the phone. "Something came up."

Hunter's eyes heated, but he quickly masked it before motioning for them to join him in the conference room.

Kye reminded himself that Hunter wasn't out to his family, that no one in this room would understand that Kye and Hunter were both with Dani. He had to be sure to keep that to himself, although he wanted to shout to the world that he was in love with the two of them and he didn't care who knew.

But he wouldn't.

"What's going on?" Dani asked as they stepped into the room where several others were sitting.

"Just the girl we were hoping to see," Trace said with a smile.

Kye glanced at every face, wondering if he needed to be on the defensive to protect this woman from them. Fortunately, based on the inquisitive looks, he didn't think that was the case.

"Good to see you again, Dani," Casper Kogan greeted kindly. "We were just brainstorming. Trying to see if we could figure out who's after you."

"So, you don't think it's Moroso?" Kye asked, pulling out a chair for Dani before taking the one on her left.

"Dani doesn't think so," RT said, nodding toward her. "And if she believes it's someone else, we're inclined to believe her."

Hunter took a seat across the table from Dani, next to his father.

"Plus," RT added with a heavy sigh, "as of nine thirty this morning, Dennis Moroso is out of commission."

Kye's eyes flew over to Hunter, seeking confirmation.

"It's true," Casper added. "I talked to Courtney and it looks as though Dennis is either dead or seriously injured."

"No way," Kye said firmly. "It's a trap."

RT was the next one to speak. "Actually, we don't think it is. Dennis's sister contacted the police a short time ago. She reported a crime scene, and based on their findings, there appeared to be signs of a struggle and blood—a rather large amount, in fact—in the living room of the house he was staying in."

Nope. Kye still didn't buy it.

"Whose blood was it?" Dani asked, her gaze darting between Hunter, Casper, and RT.

"Dennis's," Hunter confirmed. "Enough that they believe he likely died there."

"Where's the body?" Kye asked. Until they found a body, they couldn't consider the threat neutralized.

"No idea," Hunter replied.

"Do we know anything about the sister?" Kye asked. Something was wrong with this picture. "Has anyone talked to Max?"

"I'm actually on my way to his house when I leave here," Casper informed them. "I'll let you all know when I have more information."

"I'll go with you," Hunter said. It was more a demand than a request, Kye could tell.

Casper glanced at Hunter, then nodded. "As long as you promise to be civil."

"Always," Hunter agreed with a smirk. His eyes cut to Kye's briefly, then over to Dani.

It was evident Hunter had a plan. As for what it was, Kye had no clue.

Unfortunately, Kye knew they had no choice but to sit back and wait.

"HE'S DEAD," COURTNEY STATED WHEN Max joined her in his home office.

Max didn't need to ask who she was referring to, he already knew. However, he didn't believe it.

"I doubt it," he told her as he walked over to his desk. Nothing was ever that simple.

"Based on the amount of blood found at the scene, it's inevitable," she explained. "No way could he have faked his own death."

"It's a trap." Max wouldn't get his hopes up. He wouldn't.

"Actually…" Courtney moved closer to his desk when Leyton stepped into the room. "It's not a trap."

Max studied his wife. His beautiful, incredibly sexy wife. She seemed intent on making him believe what she was telling him. "What makes you think that?"

"This," Leyton told him, holding out his cell phone.

There on the screen was a picture of a very dead Dennis Moroso, his body slumped in the front seat of a car.

"It's legit, boss," Leyton confirmed. "I checked with my guy and he verified they have Dennis Moroso's body in the city morgue."

"Where did they find him?"

"In his car, just a few blocks from Devil's Playground."

"How?" Max leaned back in his chair.

"He was shot in the back of the head," Courtney relayed. "At close range. But definitely not in the car. His body was moved."

"I thought there were signs of a struggle at the house."

"There were," Leyton told him.

"It was staged."

Max peered around Leyton to see the owner of the voice.

Walking through the door was none other than his father-in-law, Casper Kogan, followed closely by Courtney's brother, Hunter.

Casper came to stand a few feet away. "I checked with DPD homicide and they verified it was staged. Dennis was murdered in his own house."

Of course, Casper appeared suspicious as he stared back at Max. He already knew what his in-laws thought about him. However, in this instance, they'd be wrong.

"So, he knew his killer?" Max questioned.

"I'd say so," Courtney surmised, sounding like a woman who knew far more than she was sharing.

Max frowned. "And that means what?"

Leyton was flipping through his phone when he said, "Sabrina shot him in the back of the head."

Max glanced between the two of them, still trying to wrap his head around it all.

That caught Casper's attention. "Sabrina?"

"Moroso," Courtney clarified. "Dennis's sister." Courtney sighed. "Unfortunately, she didn't do it because she felt threatened by him, either. Although that was my first thought. We all know she's good at playing the victim. But victim she is not."

"No?" Max knew Dennis was an even bigger asshole than Marco had been. It wouldn't surprise him if it had been a sibling quarrel that got out of hand. Then again, shooting him in the back of the head spoke of something much, much different. Personal, vindictive.

"No." Leyton held out his phone again. "This was taken an hour ago."

There on the screen was a picture of Sabrina Moroso, looking anything but remorseful that her brother had just been murdered. In fact, she looked as though she'd just…

Max looked between the four people staring back at him. "She's taken over as the head of the Moroso family."

His wife nodded. "And we thought Dennis was dangerous. It looks like there's a new bitch on the block."

Fuck.

Turning his attention to Casper, Max lifted an eyebrow. "So, what brings you over?"

Casper motioned toward Hunter. "We're trying to figure out who's after Dani. We've come up with a few theories, none of which included Dennis as the suspect. Thought maybe we'd get your take on it."

Max glanced at Hunter. "Is that why you're here?"

Hunter looked unfazed. "No, but we'll get to that."

"All right." Max turned to Casper. "So, what're your theories?"

"Based on some details we've recently uncovered, it appears this is personal against Dani. More accurately, against her father."

Max frowned. "Which one?"

"Good question," Hunter added. "Considering we believe he's seeking revenge against her father, we don't know specifically. He told her that the child shall pay for the sins of the father."

That piqued his curiosity. "Told her?"

"Technically, he wrote it on one of the walls in the safe house she was staying in."

"How would he know that Samuel's her father?"

Casper shrugged. "Dani seems to believe it's revenge on Samuel."

"I doubt that," Max said with a sigh. "My father might've killed a lot of people, but it was all business. Anything personal…well, he tended to seek revenge within his own ranks or within the family itself."

"We agree with you," Hunter noted. "Which means whatever his issue is revolves around Nick."

Max considered that for a minute. "My uncle detested the family business. He was in the ranks because of Samuel. He was a drunk, but I don't see him being responsible for something that would provoke this sort of reaction. Now, if you were talking about Patrick, that's an entirely different story."

"Patrick was a pedophile," Hunter stated.

"He was." Max held Hunter's stare. "And he's in hell, where he belongs."

"Was Nick ever involved in anything the other two did?" Casper asked.

Max glanced over at his wife. He wondered how much he should share with her family. While she knew the ins and outs of his life, including the deaths his family was responsible for, he wasn't sure he could trust all of the Kogans.

"I trust them," she said softly.

He nodded, then turned his attention back to Hunter and Casper. "There is one incident I'm aware of. As for the details, I don't have them."

"Incident?" Hunter probed.

Max leaned back in his chair. "I found some news clippings in my uncle's house. I was going through his things shortly after we put him in the home. I found an article about a little girl. It was from a few months before…Patrick died."

Hunter's eyes narrowed, and Max could see his obvious disgust.

"I don't think Nick had anything to do with it, honestly. However, I do believe Patrick did and Nick tried to stop it."

Max shifted his chair over and opened the file drawer on his desk. He pulled out a folder and passed it over to Casper. "Who knows if it's related or not, but it's certainly worth looking into."

"Thanks. We'll look into it."

Max glanced over at Hunter. "Now, why are you here?"

Hunter produced a sheet of paper from his pocket. "I actually came because I need a favor."

Max chuckled as he took the paper, unfolded it. There was a picture of a man. It was a mug shot. He looked up at Hunter again. "A favor? You're asking *me* for a favor?"

"I am."

"For?"

"I've been looking into a decade-old murder case," Hunter explained, his gaze never leaving Max's face. "And thanks to some impressive detective work, we've found the killer."

Christ. Was Hunter here to accuse him of murder? It wouldn't surprise Max one bit.

"Whose murder?" Max inquired.

"Toby Sterling," Hunter stated firmly. "Kye's younger brother."

Max didn't recognize the name, but he didn't think he was supposed to.

"And what do you want from me?"

Hunter lifted one eyebrow, his eerie eyes boring into Max. He didn't speak, but the silence was far louder than any words could've been.

Max's brother-in-law was asking Max to take care of a problem.

"Why was Kye's brother killed?" Courtney inquired, moving to stand beside Max.

"Because he was gay."

Max narrowed his eyes. "Someone killed him because he was gay?"

"Yes."

"And this is your suspect?" Max lifted the paper.

"No. He's the murderer."

"You have proof?" Courtney asked.

Hunter peered over at his sister. "I do."

"Why not bring him to justice?" she countered.

"It's too late for that," Hunter said simply.

Ah. So this was personal.

"I do request one thing, though," Hunter added.

Great. "What's that?"

"I want a written confession from him before…"

Max glanced at Casper. The older man gave a nearly imperceptible nod of his head.

Max looked back at Hunter and smiled. "It'd be my pleasure."

SEVENTEEN

Nine days later, Saturday

"IT'S BEEN A WEEK. NINE days, to be exact," Dani proclaimed when she stepped into Hunter's living room. "I think it's safe to assume that the threat was Dennis Moroso. Now that he's dead, I see no reason to keep hiding."

Hunter stared back at the woman as though she'd grown two heads. Was she serious? Did she honestly believe the bullshit she was trying to sell? No one believed Dennis had been the person who was stalking her. They'd determined that he had been responsible for the attack on Devil's Playground that had killed one of Max's bodyguards. Dennis was also responsible for the death of three others, including a doctor Max had on his payroll, but Hunter didn't think the man had ever gotten close enough to Dani to follow through with any of the threats he'd been making against Max's family.

"Come on, Hunter," she whined. "I can't stay in this house any longer. I'm going to lose my mind if I have to stare at these walls one minute longer." Dani threw up her hands. "I'm going shopping."

"Not a good idea," he told her, thrusting his hands in his pockets and regarding her carefully.

Ever since they had explained their theory that Dani's stalker was not after her because of Samuel but rather as payback to Nick, Dani had shrugged it all off. She'd given the excuse that Nick was in no way capable of even understanding a threat to his family, so how would it benefit anyone to follow through? She made a valid point, but Hunter knew that killers didn't generally work on the same thought process as rational people.

Kye, on the other hand, felt strongly that Dani was underestimating this ghost who was haunting her. Hunter was siding with Kye. Based on the information they'd received from Max, it was highly likely that the man was after Dani because of something Nick had done. Or rather, something he believed Nick had done.

Since they didn't have proof, Hunter hadn't relayed any of the information Max had given them. He was currently working with Claire to dig up information on the crime. Unfortunately, it appeared Samuel Adorite had worked his evil magic at the time and most of the evidence that would've proven Nick or Patrick had been responsible for the brutal rape and murder of an eleven-year-old girl had long ago disappeared.

And since Hunter hadn't shared that information, Dani was clinging to her belief that Dennis had been stalking her.

Regardless, Hunter knew he couldn't keep her locked up indefinitely. Two weeks had passed since they returned from the Oklahoma safe house. They had confirmation that Dennis Moroso was dead and no longer a threat to Max's family, so at least he was out of the picture. Granted, the Moroso sister was something else entirely, but Max insisted he was taking care of it on his side. The mob boss didn't believe that Dani was in immediate danger from the blowback of that. Not from the Morosos, anyway.

Still, Hunter knew there was still a threat out there. One they couldn't see. And in his experience, the threat was merely biding time, waiting for the right opportunity.

"Two hours," she stated firmly, as though this was a negotiation. "That's all I'm asking for. Give me two hours. I promise, I'll do my shopping and come right back here."

"Who's going with you?"

"No one. I need some...alone time."

Hunter shook his head. "No."

Dani glared at him and Hunter couldn't help but laugh. She was so damn cute when she wanted to get her way. And he did understand that she'd been cooped up longer than anyone should have to be. Didn't mean he was comfortable with her going shopping by herself.

"Where are you going?" Kye asked, rubbing a towel over his wet hair as he emerged from the bathroom.

Dani turned to face him. "The mall. It's a very public place and I seriously doubt anyone's going to hunt me down and kill me there."

It was Hunter's turn to glare. "Not funny."

Dani pivoted and moved closer to Hunter. "I'm sorry. You're right. I'm honestly not trying to make light of it. But I seriously think it's fine. I don't have that prickling at the back of my neck anymore."

He did, but Hunter wasn't going to tell her that. He knew for a fact that he was always going to be expecting something bad to happen. It was the world he lived in and he couldn't change who he was, even if Dani wanted him to.

"I'll go with you," Kye insisted.

"Nope," she replied quickly. "I don't want company." She held out her hand expectantly. "But I'll take your keys."

"Mine?" Kye frowned, wide eyes darting back and forth between Dani and Hunter. "Why mine?"

"Because my car is almost out of gas."

Kye peered over at Hunter as though seeking permission. Kye obviously wasn't on board with this and he was trying to make excuses.

Hunter cocked his head toward Dani, an affirmative sign to hand over the keys. He turned his attention to Dani. "Fine. You've got two hours. If you're not back here by three thirty, we're coming after you."

Her smile was so bright he could practically feel her happiness. "I promise, I'll be here. And if I'm not, I'll call you and let you know where I am."

Kye pulled his hand back, withholding his keys. "No. Absolutely not. You're back here by three thirty. No phone calls. This is serious, Dani. We don't know for a fact that the threat has been eliminated."

"It has," she said reassuringly, although Hunter knew she didn't believe what she was saying. Sure, Dani wanted it to be the truth, but she didn't quite believe it.

"All right," Hunter conceded. "Miss me while you're gone."

She giggled as she moved into his arms, kissing him sweetly before turning to Kye. "You boys better be good, too."

"Always," Kye said in that sexy, mischievous manner of his as he reluctantly passed over his keys.

Hunter watched as Dani walked out the front door. He moved to the window, keeping an eye on her as she backed Kye's truck out and headed for the main gate.

"You think she's really goin' shoppin'?" Kye asked, standing beside him.

"Yeah." He believed that much.

"You think she's really out of danger?"

"No."

Kye turned to face him, his disapproval evident. "Then why'd you let her go?"

"Because it's the only way I know to draw this bastard out."

Kye's eyes widened and he stepped back. For a brief moment, Hunter thought he was going to punch him.

"Why the fuck would you put her in danger?"

"Trust me, I'm not." He'd thought this through. He would never put Dani in danger. "I've got eight agents assigned to her. I guarantee he won't get anywhere close." He pulled his phone from his pocket and shot a text off to Conner.

Kye frowned. "I'm goin', too."

Hunter grinned, reaching for his wallet and his keys. "I knew you'd say that."

"Shit. She's got my truck."

Hunter tossed his keys at Kye, then nodded toward his helmet. "Take the bike."

"What'll you drive?"

"I'll catch a ride with Conner and Casper."

"How'd you know she'd insist on leaving?"

"Because she's Dani. That's what she does." Hunter smirked. "I just didn't know when."

"Am I as predictable as she is?"

"No."

Kye turned but Hunter stopped him by grabbing the front of his shirt and pulling him until they were nose to nose.

"I don't expect anything to go down, but if it does…" Hunter gripped the back of Kye's head. "Whatever happens, you be careful. You're comin' home to me tonight the same way she is. Understand?"

Kye chuckled. "So fucking bossy."

Hunter kissed him, squeezing his eyes shut and sending up a prayer. He needed them. Not only because he loved them but also because he didn't think he could live without them.

He'd been down that road once.

He couldn't do it again.

DANI HAD TO ADMIT, SHE was a little nervous leaving the safety of Hunter's house. This was the first time she'd been out on her own since she fled the beachfront condo. Although she was tempted, Dani was not going to turn back now. She was surprised Hunter hadn't tried to tie her up and lock her in the closet when she insisted she was leaving.

Oh, she didn't think for a second that he wouldn't follow her. Perhaps that was the reason she was being so stubborn about it. Honestly, she just wanted them to believe she needed a couple of hours to herself, to not think about all the shit that had transpired in recent weeks.

And yes, maybe she was doing this in an effort to get this madman to come after her. She had never believed that Dennis Moroso was after her, which meant someone else was. And it wasn't like he was making a move while she was locked up in the Kogan compound. If he never made a move, then that meant he would always be there waiting. And Dani would always be waiting, too.

She was tired of this nonsense. It was time to move on with her life. She had Hunter and Kye, and for the first time in her entire life, Dani felt as though she was moving forward. For heaven's sake, the three of them were having sex without condoms or birth control. If that didn't speak of a future, she didn't know what did.

As for the Moroso family…

"They are such assholes," she mumbled, glancing in the rearview mirror.

Dani knew more than she was letting on where that was concerned. She had been in contact with Max because she was far too curious to simply let Hunter and Kye handle everything. Her brother—it was still strange to think of him that way—was genuinely concerned about Sabrina Moroso and her intentions. He had told her that Sabrina had always played the victim card when it came to her family. Clearly, she wasn't a victim. She had murdered her own brother in cold blood. And now she was heading up the very family who had been targeting Dani's for years.

However, Max did not believe that Sabrina would go off half-cocked the way Marco and Dennis had. He had assured her that Sabrina would have a plan of attack before she bared her claws. From what Max had learned, she was currently aligning herself with a notorious Russian assassin. Hopefully, Max would be in a better position to defend himself against her. Once Dani could free herself of this crazy asshole who had targeted her for some reason, she would pitch in and help out her family. They could take Sabrina down, of that she had no doubt. Max had told her she had to stay out of it for now, and she was obliging him. Only because she was not willing to risk Hunter or Kye.

She loved them.

Her heart swelled just thinking about it.

A short time later, Dani pulled Kye's truck into the parking lot of the Galleria mall. She drove up and down a few aisles, paying attention to her surroundings. As far as she could tell, she wasn't tailed, which was a good thing. Perhaps the guy was merely taking a nap and he had no idea she'd ventured out of the house. It had to be rather boring lately trying to keep tabs on her when she never left the house except to go to the Sniper 1 offices. And in all fairness, that had only been one time.

Due to the size of Kye's truck, Dani ended up parking farther out than she would've liked, but there were several people in the parking lot, so she quickly exited the vehicle and headed into the giant four-story building. Her eyes scanned her surroundings, searching the shadows and corners where someone might be hiding. Of course, she didn't think it would be that easy. This guy was smart. Too smart.

Once inside, she breathed easier. There were people everywhere. Mostly teenagers laughing at one another as they walked around with their Starbucks cups and their cell phones. Dani had never really had those carefree days when she could spend the day at the mall with her friends. She envied the kids, wishing she'd had a normal childhood.

"Plan of attack," she said to herself. Although she didn't have anything specific to buy, she knew she would have to make a few purchases. Otherwise, Hunter and Kye would figure out she had another agenda. Since she might have to do this again in the near future, she knew she had to make it look good.

Not too hard.

She was at a mall, after all.

And shopping was in her blood.

"SOMEONE BETTER HAVE EYES ON her," Hunter stated, his voice sounding in Kye's hearing aid.

Since the others didn't know Kye was there, he opted to keep his mouth shut. This wasn't his assignment and he didn't want to interfere. He was only here to keep an eye on Dani because she was the woman he loved, and he wasn't about to leave her safety in anyone else's hands. Not even Hunter's.

Although, he would admit he trusted Hunter. He knew the man would not let anything happen to Dani if he could help it. Unfortunately, no one knew who they were dealing with or what he was capable of. He could easily grab her while she was in a dressing room and no one would be the wiser. Not until it was too late.

"I've got her," Conner confirmed. "We're on level one. She just went into the dressing room at Victoria's Secret."

For fuck's sake. That was probably more information than any of these agents needed.

"She buyin' somethin' for your eyes only, Hunter?" Trace asked.

"Fuck off," Hunter retorted. "Mind your own damn business."

"I'm just sayin'. If she's gettin' lingerie, I think it's safe to say you're gettin' lucky tonight, brother."

Kye grinned to himself. If they only knew.

"Then again, he does have another house guest," Decker noted. "Probably not getting a lot of action with Kye being the third wheel."

Okay, that earned a full-blown laugh, which caused a few people to glance his way. He smiled and kept walking, keeping his head down. He'd grabbed a ball cap at the first store he'd come to. Since Dani would likely recognize him if she saw him, he needed to do his best to keep that from happening.

"So, does that mean the two of you are back together?"

"Trace, if you don't shut the fuck up…" Hunter didn't finish his sentence, but they all knew what he was going to say.

Trace's laughter echoed in his ear.

Kye paused at the railing that overlooked the ice rink on the bottom level. He took up a casual position, leaning over, watching the area on the first level where Conner had confirmed they were. He caught sight of Conner almost immediately, but he didn't think Dani would've noticed him. He was pacing the floor with his phone to his ear, glasses on his face, and a John Deere hat on his head. The disguise was decent. Not foolproof but decent.

While Kye pretended to be texting on his phone, he scanned the area, both above and below him. He wasn't particularly fond of this mall—not when it came to surveillance—due to the sheer size. With three levels of shopping, plus the bottom-floor rink, there was far too much to observe.

So far, he didn't see anyone suspicious, unless a group of boys scoping out another group of girls counted. There were people everywhere. Groups of kids, some families, a few women carrying their haul, and of course, all the people down on the ice. All appeared normal. No crazy assholes lurking, waiting to grab Dani when she was least expecting it.

Didn't mean they weren't there.

But if they were, Kye fully intended to find them before they found Dani.

"Excuse me," a voice said from behind him.

Kye casually turned and cocked an eyebrow, noticing the man standing behind him. Thanks to his training, his brain instantly processed the stranger. Average height, average build. Brown hair, brown eyes. Small gap between his two front teeth. He looked harmless.

The man smiled. "I'm sorry to bother you." He motioned his head toward two little boys sitting on a bench. "We were looking for the play place that's supposed to be here. Do you happen to know where it is?"

Kye shook his head. "I'm sorry, I don't." He nodded down to the ice rink. "Maybe down there?"

"No, we already checked there. Damn it," he muttered softly, then offered an embarrassed smile. "It's just… Well, do you have kids?"

Kye instantly thought of Dani and a smile formed. "No, I don't." Not yet, anyway.

The man chuckled. "Well, one day when you do, I hope they don't beg and plead the way mine do. My wife's about to go out of her mind. She slipped away to the restroom just to get a break from them." He glanced around helplessly. "I promised I'd find it before she came back."

"Well, I'm sure it's around here somewhere," Kye said, feeling bad for the guy. The kids did appear a little rambunctious. He pointed toward the far wall. "There's a directory over there. Maybe that'll help."

The man peered over at the kids again, then frowned. "I hate to ask, but would you do me a favor? Could you possibly dart over there and find out where it's at? I don't want to leave them, and if I try to corral them over there, it probably won't be pretty. It took five minutes just to convince them to sit down."

Kye glanced down at the first level, noticing Conner was still in the same place, his eyes focused on the store Dani was in. For now, she was safe.

"Of course," he said, standing to his full height. "Give me two seconds."

"Thank you so much."

Kye hurried over to the sign, skimmed it briefly to find something that sounded like a play place. With four levels, he could see how the man couldn't find it. He had no idea what the name would be, but—

"Unless you want a bullet in your back right now, I suggest you turn and walk toward the exit. No grand gestures."

Kye straightened when he felt something hard pressing into his back. Instinct had him pushing the side of his watch to engage his mic, hoping the guy didn't notice.

"So, no play place today, huh?"

"Not for me, no," the man said, sounding pleased. "I'm not sure about those kids. If I had to guess, their parents are planning something fun. But it worked, didn't it?"

"Who are you?" Kye asked, dropping his hands as he moved in the direction the man said, toward the exit doors.

"I think you remember me," the man stated. "We had a little tussle at the condo on the beach."

Oh, yeah. Kye remembered him. Too bad he hadn't gotten a good look at his face that night. If he had, he wouldn't be in this position.

"What's your name?" he probed, wanting to keep the guy talking.

"It doesn't matter. Not to you, anyway. You won't be alive long enough to really get to know me." He chuckled. "But don't worry. I'll make sure to tell Ms. Davidson all the gory details of your death."

Son of a bitch.

"WHO'S ON OUR FREQUENCY?" CONNER asked, confusion ringing in his tone.

"Fuck," Hunter bit out as he ran toward the building. He'd been staking out the parking lot, keeping an eye on Kye's truck to ensure Dani didn't leave without them noticing. "It's Kye. Someone have eyes on him?"

"What the fuck is he doing here?" Conner blasted.

"Find him, Con! Anyone see him?"

A resounding *no* came back to him.

Shit.

"Interesting that you parked out this way," Kye said calmly, obviously talking to whomever he was with. "Everyone knows Macy's is nowhere near the play place."

Play place? What the hell was he talking about? Then it hit him. Kye was giving them clues.

"He's leaving through Macy's!" Hunter yelled. "I need someone on that side!"

His heart pounded in his chest as he ran through the mall, dodging shoppers and those damn kiosks. When Hunter hit the escalator, he bolted up the steps three at a time. As he reached the second level, he saw Trace running full out.

"Conner, you stay on Dani!" he shouted as his feet carried him toward the exit doors.

"Ten-four."

The second he stepped outside, the sun blinded him. It took several seconds for his eyes to adjust, seconds he didn't have. When everything came into focus, Hunter scanned the lot, seeking one man and one man only.

"Kye, where are you?" he asked, not knowing whether or not the man he loved would answer him or not.

"Keep walking, or I'll shoot you right here."

Fuck.

Hunter's eyes darted through the parking lot as he tried to find Kye.

"Dani, go back inside," Kye said, his voice eerily calm.

No. No, no, no.

The asshole had both of them.

Hunter frantically searched the lot. "Trace, eyes?"

"Negative," his brother said. "I don't see any of them."

"Get me more eyes out here!" Hunter yelled into his com.

"I'm coming around from the north," Decker informed them.

"I'm on the south," Jake noted.

"Casper, you're our eyes in the sky," Hunter said to his father. "See anything?"

"Negative. But I'm moving around to that side."

Hunter heard someone say something, but he couldn't make it out. He assumed it was Dani, but she was too far away from Kye for him to hear her.

"That piece-of-shit Ford is yours?" Kye said with a strained chuckle. "Granted, I do like the new-model Mustangs. Of course, white's not really my color. Dani, you need to walk away."

White Ford Mustang. Great. A needle in a haystack.

"I see them," Trace said, his voice low. "Third row to your left, Hunter. Far back of the lot. Kye's got a red ball cap on. Dani's armed. She's got him lined up in her sights."

How the fuck had Dani beat them out there? No way was she in that store as they'd thought.

Hunter jogged in the direction Trace advised and he saw them. The innocuous man was holding a gun to Kye's head while Dani stood a few feet away, gun pointed directly at the two of them.

"What are the chances you'll hit me and not him?" the man taunted. "Or does it even matter? You can take both of us out at the same time, right?"

Hunter was close enough to see them when Dani spoke.

"Trust me," she said, "I won't miss. And if you think I'm the only one with a gun aimed at you, you're mistaken."

"Oh, I know about Sniper 1 Security. I know about the other agents. The real question is whether anyone can get the shot off before I kill him. Your chances aren't looking good, Ms. Davidson. Or shall I call you Ms. Adorite?"

"Why are you doing this?" Dani asked, obviously trying to keep him talking.

The madman chuckled eerily. "Because your father killed my sister."

Son of a bitch. Hunter walked slowly as he spoke into the mic. "Claire, what do you have on the little girl's brother? Scott Butler. I'd bet money this is him."

"I'm pulling up the information now," she said. "I didn't think we were concerned with him since his current residence is in Hawaii."

Oh, they were interested.

Dani's words were steady when she addressed the gunman. "My father? Who? Samuel?"

That question seemed to surprise the man. "Nick Adorite."

"He's not my father," Dani stated firmly. "Samuel is."

God, Hunter knew she hated to admit that. Hell, he hated hearing it.

"What?" the gunman asked. "Never mind. It doesn't matter. You're an Adorite. All the more reason to kill you all."

"Okay, fine. You're right. It doesn't matter," she said calmly. "You said Nick killed your sister. Tell me about her," Dani probed.

The man's laugh was filled with rage. "The bastard raped her, then killed her and you want to know about *her*?"

From where he stood, Hunter noticed Dani frowning. She was realizing something didn't add up. It was the same conclusion Hunter had come to.

"Nick was a coward," she said defensively, "not a rapist. Or a killer."

"Shows what you know," Scott barked, his anger increasing. "My sister was eleven years old. Eleven fucking years old when that bastard got his hands on her."

Oh, hell.

"What was her name?" Dani asked. "Your sister?"

"Lisa. Lisa Butler. Does that name ring a bell?"

"No." Dani didn't falter, she held her gun up, aimed at the man holding Kye.

She was shifting and moving as the gunman did. He obviously knew not to hold his position, likely wanting to throw off anyone who had sights on him. No matter where he moved, he kept Kye in front of him, his gun aimed up at Kye's head. Due to the significant difference in their height, the man had to peer at Dani around Kye's shoulder.

"Not surprising," Scott snarled. "Lisa was nothing to you. Your father killed her."

"Trace, you got a shot?" Hunter asked.

"Negative. Dani's in my way."

"Casper?" Hunter asked.

"As soon as he stands still, I've got him," his father confirmed. "Say the word."

"Kye, turn your head to the left if you can hear me," Hunter instructed.

Kye slightly shifted his head to the left.

"I need you to drop when I give the signal. Got it?"

Kye glanced to the left once more.

"Casper, when you've got the shot, take it," Hunter stated, inching closer to the three people standing in the parking lot.

"Ten-four."

As though waiting for the shot to ring out, everything went quiet. No chatter, no birds. Nothing to disrupt the violent pounding of Hunter's heart as he counted down the seconds, waiting for that shot that would turn his world to rights.

Hunter watched as Scott Butler held the people he loved at gunpoint. It took everything in him to keep the beast at bay. He wanted to unload his clip, to watch the fucker as he fell to the ground and bled out before them.

"Hunter," Claire said, her voice feeding into his ear. "It appears Scott Butler has been MIA for a while now. I was able to track one of his credit cards. It places him in Dani's direct path for most of the past year."

"When did this happen?" Dani asked Scott. "When did your sister die?"

"Fifteen years ago."

Which would've made Dani twelve at the time. Almost the same age Scott's sister had been when she died.

"According to the information I found," Claire continued, "the police did find Nick's DNA at the scene, but it didn't match the DNA found on Lisa."

"I guarantee it wasn't him," Hunter stated.

"I agree. They also found someone else's DNA."

"Let me guess? Nick's brother Patrick. The pedophile?"

"Probably, but all the evidence went missing before they could get a match."

Well, that explained a lot.

Patrick got away with it because Samuel covered for him. The girl was eleven. The thought made Hunter's stomach churn. How could such evil walk amongst them?

It didn't surprise him that the police had reached a dead end. The Adorites had been able to cover up plenty. Luckily for everyone, Patrick no longer walked the earth. Max had sent him to hell years ago.

"They found your father's DNA," Scott told Dani. "It proves he was with her. That he raped her. And killed her."

Evidently Scott wasn't aware that the other evidence had disappeared. Which was the reason he was fixated on Nick.

"Killing Kye won't bring your sister back," Dani said calmly.

"No. It won't. But to see the look on your face when I do…that's all I need."

"Is it?" she asked. "Is it going to make you feel better? Will you be able to move on with your life? I somehow doubt it."

"Killing Nick certainly made me feel better."

Oh, shit.

"Claire, check in with the hospital where Nick is. See if he's telling the truth."

"On it, boss," she said quickly.

"I know you want to avenge your sister's death. And I don't blame you. But Kye didn't do anything," Dani continued. "If you want revenge, take me."

"Fuck, no," Kye growled. "Leave her out of it."

"That was my original plan," the man confirmed, speaking to Dani. "Taking you. I was going to tie you up and show you the horror of your father's ways."

"Nick is not my father," she repeated. "But it doesn't matter. You said he's dead. That should make you even."

"We'll never be even!" Scott yelled. "Never!"

Claire's voice was loud and clear once again. "It's confirmed. Nick Adorite died this morning. They're saying he had another massive stroke."

Fucking hell. Scott Butler wasn't merely making threats. He had followed through. Which meant he had nothing to lose.

The man continued to shift and move, keeping Kye in front of him at all times. The gun shifted out of sight, but Hunter knew he still had it directed at Kye.

"I'm sorry about your sister," Dani said.

"Shut up," Scott hissed. "You're just as evil as he was."

"There's a sniper on the roof," Kye blurted.

Scott's head jerked around suddenly, but he shifted Kye to the left, blocking Hunter's shot.

Fortunately, Casper wasn't on the roof of the building. He was on the fourth floor of the parking garage.

Hunter knew it was now or never. "Now, Kye! Drop!"

As Hunter watched, Kye jerked to the left seconds before a shot rang out. Another followed immediately after, and as if in slow motion, both Scott and Kye crumpled to the ground.

"No!" Dani screamed. "Oh, God, no!"

Hunter had never run so fast in his life. His heart lodged in his throat as fear threatened to strangle him. When he reached Kye, he found him lying in a puddle of blood, but he couldn't see where it was coming from.

Please don't be his. Please, God. Don't do this.

"Are you hit?" Hunter yelled at Kye.

His lover's eyes were wide, his face scrunched in pain. He wasn't moving.

"Fuck!" Hunter yelled. "We need an ambulance!"

He could hear Trace talking, felt Dani at his side, but the only thing Hunter could focus on was Kye. The way his eyes slowly closed, his breathing shallow.

No!

"Don't you dare," Hunter warned Kye. "Don't you dare fucking leave me. You understand? Kye? Kye!"

Dani was sobbing uncontrollably, and the only thing Hunter felt was…cold.

EIGHTEEN

DANI SAT IN THE WAITING room, her heart pounding so hard she thought for sure she would have a heart attack any second. Hunter was pacing in front of her while most of his family and a handful of Sniper 1 agents were spread throughout the room.

No one had any idea what was going on, just that the EMTs had appeared grim when they rushed Kye into the ambulance before bringing him to the hospital. Once here, they had rushed Kye to surgery, not giving anyone any updates. The only thing Dani knew for certain was that Kye had been shot in the back and by the time the ambulance arrived, he'd been alive but unconscious. That was four hours ago, and no one had told them anything yet.

Mr. and Mrs. Sterling had arrived, which was a godsend considering the only people the hospital staff would talk to was family. Since the rest of them didn't qualify, they were left in the dark. As of yet, they were still not certain what was going on.

Dani tried to consider that a good thing. If Kye was dead, they would've been told by now. They wouldn't be sitting here, they would be…

No. She wasn't even going to think it.

She sobbed as the memory hit her. Dani had heard one shot, then another. One of the bullets had landed between the madman's eyes, the other lodged somewhere in Kye. Right before her eyes, Kye had slid to the ground, his eyes wide, his face stark white before he even hit his knees. He'd been so still.

It should've been me.

It wasn't supposed to happen this way. Kye shouldn't have been there.

Her mind raced as she recalled everything that had happened from the second she saw Hunter racing past Victoria's Secret. She had known in that moment that they hadn't let her go to the mall by herself. They were there with her, and for Hunter to leave her unattended…something bad had happened.

Dani had spotted Conner immediately, taking advantage when she noticed he was watching Hunter. She'd slipped out of the store and headed in the same direction Hunter went, only she'd stopped at Macy's. When she'd looked back and seen him running toward the exit doors, she'd taken off through the department store and exited the same side.

It had taken her less than a minute to figure out what was happening, to find the man holding Kye at gunpoint.

It should've been me.

Dani couldn't stop the tears.

"Baby," Hunter whispered, his arm going around her shoulders as he took a seat to her left. "It's gonna be all right."

Her gaze cut to his face and she scowled, rage consuming her. She didn't want empty promises or lame platitudes. "He was shot in the back, Hunter. You don't know that."

"I do know that," he said softly, pulling her into him. "Kye's strong. He won't leave us. He's going to come back to us."

Although he was attempting to be strong, Dani felt the way his hands were shaking. He was pretending otherwise, but he was as terrified as she was.

Dani went into Hunter's arms without resistance, leaning against him, trying to absorb some of his strength. She wasn't sure how he was holding it together. She wanted to fall apart right there, to curl up in a ball and go to sleep forever.

And if something happened and Kye didn't pull through…

310

It should've been me.

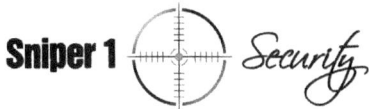

Sniper 1 — Security

HUNTER FELT AS THOUGH THERE was a balloon in his chest. It was taking up all the space, making it difficult to breathe. His heart continued to beat, but he wasn't sure how.

Even when the doctor came out and gave Mr. and Mrs. Sterling the news that Kye had pulled through the surgery and they were keeping him in ICU, the pain hadn't decreased. He wasn't sure it would until he could see Kye for himself, could know the man was going to open his eyes and smile at him one more time.

Last night, they hadn't allowed anyone back with Kye except for his parents, so the rest of them had remained in the waiting room. Hunter's parents, his brothers, even Courtney and Max had come for a while. RT and Z had set up in the waiting room as well. According to the doctor, it was now a waiting game.

"Son?"

Hunter peered up at his father. He hadn't realized the man was standing in front of him.

"Let's go down and get some coffee."

Hunter shook his head. He wasn't leaving. Not until he could see Kye.

His eyes swung over to Dani. She was curled up on a small sofa, her eyes closed. He had gotten her a blanket a short while ago, hating that she might be cold. He didn't think she was sleeping and if she was, it was only in spurts.

"Come on," Casper insisted. "We'll only be gone a few minutes."

Hunter stared blankly at his father but found himself rising to his feet. Casper stopped in front of RT and said something, but Hunter wasn't paying attention. The only thing he could think about was Kye, seeing him, touching him, feeling his heart beating under his hand.

He'd been so still, so...cold. No matter how hard he tried, Hunter couldn't get the image of Kye out of his head. Every time he thought about it, his chest ached. His heart physically hurt.

"Why don't you take Dani home for a little while," Casper prompted when they made it to the small coffee shop downstairs.

Hunter peered over at his father. "I'm not leaving Kye. Why would you think I would?"

Casper paid for two large black coffees. "I know this has to be hard for you, son. To see your partner take a bullet."

Hunter frowned, turning to face his father. "Kye's not just my partner, Dad."

Casper's eyes came to rest on his face, studying him momentarily.

"I love him," Hunter admitted. "He's so much more than my partner."

Casper's head cocked to the side. "And what about Dani? I thought..."

"I love her, too." Hunter wasn't sure he should be revealing so much, but he was past caring at this point. If Kye didn't pull through, Hunter wasn't sure what he was going to do. He knew he had to take care of Dani, but he couldn't picture his life without Kye in it.

"So, the three of you are...in a relationship?"

Hunter squared his shoulders and stared back at his father. "Yes. We are. Do you have a problem with that?"

"Should I?" The hard lines of Casper's face softened. "Of course I don't have a problem with it, Hunter. No one has a problem with it." A small smile formed. "It does explain a hell of a lot, though."

"Like what?" he asked as he followed Casper over to the stand that held the sugar and creamer.

Casper cast a sideways glance his way. "I'm going to assume that Kye isn't the first person you and Dani have been in a relationship with?"

Hunter looked at his feet. "No. He's not."

"Josh?"

"Yeah." He met his father's gaze. "But this is different."

Casper turned to face him fully, the coffee cups left on the counter. "It's forever."

It wasn't a question and Hunter was thankful his father understood.

"It is." That familiar pain shot through his heart and Hunter felt as though he would double over.

The next thing he knew, his father's arms came around him and he was jerked against the older man.

"Ah, hell, son. I know this is hard. Kye's strong. You know he is. And he's a fighter."

Hunter couldn't speak, emotion clogging his throat. He couldn't break down. Not here. He had a responsibility to Dani. He had to take care of her, had to make sure she made it through this whole. There was no time for his emotions to grab hold of him.

When Casper released him, Hunter straightened. "I need to check on Dani."

"Your mother and I will help look after her. We've always known she was important. And when she left..." Casper tilted his chin up. "You didn't take it well. We're glad she's back."

Hunter was happy to hear that. He hadn't talked to anyone about Dani being back in his life. His entire family had stood beside him when she ditched him at the altar and he knew they hadn't thought highly of her for the longest time. He was glad to know they could look past it because he loved her.

Casper picked up the two coffee cups. "If you need anything at all, let me know. Your mother and I are here for the duration. We aren't going anywhere until Kye opens his eyes."

Hunter nodded. "Thank you."

"For?"

"Understanding."

"Son, the only thing a parent wants in the world is for his children to be happy. That's all that matters. If I could take this pain from you, I certainly would. I would carry the burden, so you didn't have to. Because I love you."

His chest constricted, and he couldn't look his father in the eye. He'd dealt with the pain for so long it had become a part of him. Until he and Dani and Kye had finally accepted what this was. At that point, he'd been whole. For a little while.

He knew that he wouldn't be whole again until Kye opened his eyes.

NINETEEN

"YOU NEED TO GET SOME rest, baby," Hunter urged when he joined Dani in Kye's hospital room three days later. "Let me take you home for a little while."

Thankfully, Mrs. Sterling had taken pity on Dani and Hunter and the rest of the Sniper 1 crew, informing the hospital that they were to be allowed to see Kye whenever they wanted. Since the moment they said Dani could go back, she hadn't left his side.

"No," she said hollowly. "I'm not leaving until he wakes up."

Dani rested her forehead on her hands as she leaned toward Kye's bed. She'd been holding his hand, begging him to wake up, to come back to her. She'd napped off and on in the hard chair, waking every time the door opened and a nurse came to check his vitals, which was frequently.

According to the doctor, Kye had been lucky. The bullet hadn't done any irreversible damage. She said he must've shifted at the exact right time, because the bullet hadn't lodged in his spine, rather nicking one of his lungs and tearing through an artery. The surgery had been touch-and-go, but he'd come through without any issues.

Even with all the good news, Dani knew he wasn't out of the woods yet. Unfortunately, he hadn't woken up, and the concern that he never would was growing significantly with every passing day. They had no idea why he was still unconscious, but the doctor assured them he was doing well.

"All right," Hunter said. "I'm gonna step out for a bit, let Kye's mother come in and see him."

Dani nodded but didn't lift her head.

Hunter leaned down and kissed the back of her head. A few seconds later, the door opened, then closed. Only then did Dani look up.

"Kye," she whispered, "we need you to come back to us. Me and Hunter…we need you. We need you so much. Please, please, *please.*"

When Dani heard the door open again, she sat up straight, never letting go of Kye's hand. She offered a small smile over her shoulder when Mrs. Sterling stepped into the room.

The woman came over and put her hand on Dani's shoulder. For the past three days, Dani had spent quite a bit of time with Mrs. Sterling, sitting right here in the room with Kye, the two of them holding vigil over him, waiting for him to open his eyes.

"How're you holding up?" she asked, her voice soft, a hint of exhaustion in her tone.

"I'm not," Dani admitted. "It's…it's like I can't breathe."

The other woman squeezed her shoulder gently.

RT had been the one to contact Kye's parents before they even got Kye to the hospital. They'd been there ever since, along with all four of Kye's sisters, who continued to come and go, having families of their own to deal with. Dani hadn't spent much time with any of them because she refused to leave the room. She wanted to be there when Kye woke up. And he would wake up, she knew that much. She could feel it in her heart. He was resting, recuperating, but he was going to open those beautiful blue eyes.

"As long as you're here," Mrs. Sterling said, "he's going to fight his way back. So, don't give up, Danielle."

"Never," Dani assured her. "I will never give up."

Mrs. Sterling walked around to the other side of Kye's bed. She placed her hand on his arm and smiled down at him.

"Kye told me about you," Mrs. Sterling admitted. "We didn't talk all that much, but he texted me at least once a day. Quite a bit over the last few weeks." She looked at Dani. "He's been talking about you for so long now, I feel as though I know you."

Dani tried to force a smile, but it didn't come. Her eyes remained locked on Kye's face.

"He also told me about Hunter," Mrs. Sterling said, her tone careful.

Dani peered over at her, hoping she didn't give anything away. She had no idea how much Kye's parents knew about his relationship, and she certainly didn't want to say anything in the event he didn't want them to know.

"Kye said he was in love with you both."

Okay, well. It looked as though Kye didn't hide from his parents.

Mrs. Sterling smiled as she patted Kye's arm. "He's always been tough. His entire life. Even before Toby died. More so after. And he's a good man. The kind of man who goes after what he wants and never gives up."

A tear trickled down Dani's face. "He's the best man I know."

"You love him," she stated.

"I do. With every ounce of my being."

"He admitted to me that he was worried," Mrs. Sterling continued. "Worried that because you and Hunter had a history, he would be the third wheel in... Well, I'm not even sure how a relationship like that works, but Kye was happy, so I didn't question it. But his concern seemed to pass quickly. He was so happy." Her eyes met Dani's. "He texted me the day before he was shot. Told me he was ready to settle down and he was intending to do it with you and Hunter."

Dani sobbed. She'd been thinking the same thing. She was still thinking the same thing.

"Love goes a long way to healing someone, Danielle. Kye's going to fight for you and Hunter. I know it in my heart. But you have to remember, Hunter's hurting, too. More than anyone probably even realizes."

Dani frowned, wondering how Mrs. Sterling knew that.

"I was talking to Ryan," she admitted. "He was telling me about Hunter's former partner. Said he lost him."

"He did," Dani said, her voice a rough whisper. "Josh was killed while on assignment."

"Hunter's strong," Mrs. Sterling said. "But not nearly strong enough to make it through this alone."

Dani stared at Kye's mother as the words penetrated her brain.

The guilt suddenly shrouded her, covering her like a wet blanket. Dani's chest constricted. Here she'd been thinking only about Kye, worried about him, wanting to be there when he woke up. All the while, Hunter had been the strong one, taking care of her, making sure she had everything she needed.

No one was taking care of Hunter.

Dani stood for the first time in hours. Her legs were weak, but she managed to remain upright. "I need to go see Hunter."

Mrs. Sterling smiled. "I promise, I'll stay with him. And if he wakes up before you get back, you'll be the first person I notify."

Dani did manage a smile that time. She leaned over and kissed Kye's cheek, whispering softly into his ear. "I'll be back soon. You keep resting." She looked up at Kye's mother. "Thank you."

Mrs. Sterling looked sad as she glanced down at Kye. "Sometimes we overlook things when we're hurting. We let the pain consume us when there are other people who require our focus." Her eyes cut over to Dani. "Take care of Hunter. He needs you right now. We'll be right here when you come back."

With that, Dani took another long look at Kye, then went in search of Hunter.

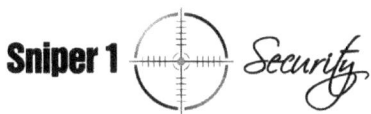

THE INSTANT DANI EMERGED THROUGH the ICU doors, Hunter was on his feet. His heart skipped a couple of beats, fear threatening to strangle him.

"Is everything okay?" he asked immediately as he moved in her direction.

More eyes shot over to them. Kye's father, Kye's oldest sister and her husband, Casper and Elizabeth, RT and Z. They were all there waiting for Kye to wake up.

"Yes, everything's fine." Based on her expression, she realized she had scared him. "Nothing has changed. He's still…asleep."

When Dani reached for his hand, Hunter clutched her cold fingers, pulling her close to him.

"Can you take me home for a little while?" she asked, peering up into his eyes. "I'd like to take a shower." Dani glanced back at the doors. "Kye's mother will stay with him until we get back."

"Of course. Let me tell RT."

Dani nodded, then allowed Hunter to lead her across the room to where RT sat with Z. The two of them had been at the hospital every day since Kye was admitted. They left occasionally to grab food and sleep, but they always came back. Everyone else at Sniper 1 had done the same, showing up randomly to check in, wanting to know if Kye had opened his eyes yet.

"I'm gonna run Dani home for a bit. Grab some food and a shower."

RT nodded. "We'll stay here until you get back. If we hear anything, we'll let you know."

"Thanks."

When Hunter turned toward the door, Dani shifted so that she was at his side. He tucked her in close and wrapped his arm around her shoulders, holding her against him. He had to be strong for her, for Kye. As much as he wanted to fall apart, Hunter knew it wouldn't do any good. No one needed to see him shatter into a million pieces, but that was how he felt. As though a strong wind would knock him over and he might never get back up again.

But for Dani, he could hold on.

*

Half an hour later, they were walking in Hunter's front door.

"You want me to make you something to eat while you take a shower?" he offered.

Dani shook her head. "I want you to shower with me."

"Of course." Figuring she needed support, Hunter wouldn't deny her anything.

He went to the bathroom and turned on the water, his eyes instantly falling to Kye's razor, which was sitting on the edge of the sink. Hunter planted his palms on the counter, feeling as though his legs would give out. He was shaking, still. Had been since he saw Kye lying there in a pool of blood.

His chest swelled but felt too tight, the ache intensifying until it was hard to breathe. He fisted his hands. He had to stay strong. The mere thought that Kye would never be there to shave or to leave his socks all over the house had Hunter's heart clenching painfully.

"Ah, God."

He couldn't… Hunter couldn't live without Kye.

A sob tore through him and his knees threatened to buckle. He kept his hands on the counter, forcing himself to remain upright as he fought to breathe. In, out. Again.

It hurt so fucking bad.

He couldn't live without Kye. No more than he could live without Dani.

Dani called out his name and he turned to see her standing behind him. She was crying, tears streaming down her face. She raced into his arms, her small body slamming against him and he grabbed on to her, squeezing her tightly as he let the tears fall.

"I can't…" he whispered. "Kye can't leave me."

"He won't," Dani said forcefully, pulling back and staring up into his eyes. "He won't leave you, Hunter."

"I can't live without him," he admitted. "He… God. Kye saved me at a time when I was ready to give up on everything. I don't want to live without him."

"I know," she said reassuringly. "He loves you, Hunter. He loves you so much."

"I never told him," he said, his throat constricting. "Never actually said the words."

Dani's arms squeezed him. "You didn't have to. Kye knows. He knows you love him."

"Do you know?" Hunter tightened his arms around her and buried his face in her neck. He couldn't hold back anymore, the pain he'd locked inside unbearable. "Do you know how much I love you?"

"I do." She was sobbing uncontrollably. "We both know, Hunter. Never doubt that."

"I have a hard time saying it," he admitted. "I…"

"You don't have to." Her hand curled around the back of his head as she held him. "Sometimes, words aren't necessary. Kye knows you love him. He does. And when he wakes up, you can tell him."

If.

He wanted to say it aloud, but he held back. Dani was clinging to hope that Kye would wake up. Hunter was, too, but even if he did, no one knew the extent of the damage the bullet had done. There was a possibility Kye could be paralyzed. Although they'd done some tests, the doctors said they wouldn't know for sure until he woke up.

Not that it would matter to Hunter or Dani. Kye would still be Kye, regardless. And they would love him unconditionally. But he had to wake up.

"He has to," he choked out. "I need him to wake up."

It hurt. The not knowing. Hunter needed Kye to open his eyes. He needed…

Unable to stand any longer, Hunter sank to the floor. He pulled Dani down with him, holding her as tightly as he could.

"I can't lose him," he whispered again, letting the tears fall as his body shook with the grief he fought to contain. "I can't."

Hunter had no idea how long they remained like that, but Dani was the one to finally pull away.

"Let's shower and eat," she said, cupping his face as she wiped a tear from his cheek. "Then we'll go back and sit with Kye so we're both there when he wakes up."

She was right. He needed to get ahold of himself. Falling apart wasn't helping anyone. He pushed to his feet and helped her up. A few minutes later, they were in the shower. The water was still warm, which meant they hadn't been huddled on the floor for too long.

After Hunter washed up, he turned to face the spray. Dani was standing there, staring back at him. Her hands came up to his chest, gliding higher until she was pulling his head down to hers. When their lips met, the kiss was both sweet and sad. Consoling. He could taste the salt from her tears, and it felt good to kiss Dani, to feel her arms around him, to know she was alive and breathing.

All thought fled momentarily. All the hurt, the fear, the anger. It disappeared, replaced by Dani's warmth, her kiss, her need. It would be back, he knew. But for now, he could lose himself in her.

"Love me, Hunter," she whispered, holding on to him.

"I will always love you," he assured her. "Always."

Within seconds, he had her backed against the tile wall, one hand behind her knee as he lifted her leg, opening her to him. He was hard, aching to feel her. He aligned their bodies and pushed inside, the heat of her pussy sending shockwaves through him. For a few blessed moments, he welcomed the distraction. Being able to hold her, make love to her, lose himself in her was what he needed in that moment.

Dani never stopped kissing him, her arms wreathing his neck, their bodies sliding together as he thrust his hips forward, impaling her on his cock. Hunter could admit he needed *this*. Dani. Needed her to hold him, take care of him. And she was. It was evident Dani was loving him because she knew he needed it.

And he did.

He needed her more than he needed air.

"Dani…" Hunter nibbled on her lower lip. "Ah, baby. Come for me, Dani. Let me feel you come."

She moaned, her head tipping back against the tile as he stared down at her, his hips gyrating forward and back, forward and back. She felt so good. Better than good.

"I love you, Hunter," she whispered, her eyes still closed. "I love you so much."

"I love you, too." He slammed into her several times. "Come for me, Dani… Oh, God." He wasn't going to last. It was too much. She felt like heaven, and hearing her tell him she loved him pushed him closer to the edge.

Reaching between them, Hunter rubbed her clit with his thumb, circling the bundle of nerves until she was crying out his name over and over, her pussy squeezing him until his release was inevitable. Hunter crushed his mouth to hers as he came, holding on to her for all he was worth.

*

When they arrived back at the hospital a couple of hours later, there had been no change. Mr. and Mrs. Sterling had left so they could go home and get some rest. They would be back soon, and Casper had promised to call if there were any changes.

Hunter's parents had been holding down the fort, sitting with Kye until they arrived. They slipped back out without a word, leaving Dani and Hunter alone with Kye.

"I need to call Max," Dani told him after they'd been sitting there quietly for a few minutes.

"Sure." He glanced down at Kye. "I'll be right here."

She offered a sad smile before slipping out the door.

Hunter knew Dani didn't need to call Max. She was giving Hunter a few minutes alone with Kye. He damn sure wasn't going to turn it down. He pulled a chair close to Kye's bedside, then dropped into it, reaching up and running his fingertips over the back of Kye's hand.

He glanced up at Kye's face. The man wasn't wearing his hearing aids, so he had no idea how much Kye could actually hear. His hearing loss was significant, but he had to believe that Kye could hear them, that he knew they were there.

"You know I'm not a patient man," he told Kye, staring at the spot his fingers traced over Kye's skin. "I never have been, doubt I ever will be." Hunter looked up at Kye's face again. "Which is why I need you to wake up. I'm reaching my breaking point, Kye." He leaned in closer, his voice raspy with emotion. "I can't take this anymore. I need you to open your eyes. I need…" He couldn't hold back the tears. "Kye, I need you to come back. I need you to wake up." He laughed, but it hurt. "Okay, fine. Maybe you're tired of taking orders from me. You've always said I was bossy. What if I asked nicely?"

Hunter twined his fingers with Kye's and held his hand up to his mouth.

"Please. Kye. Please come back to us. To Dani. To me. We need you." Hunter sucked in air. "It hurts to breathe without you here with me. It hurts so fucking much." Another tear fell, but he let it, holding Kye's hand against his face. "I haven't told you I love you yet. I get that much. I get to tell you that I love you. And I get to hear you say it back. You're not leaving me until then. No. Strike that. Not even after that. We'll be having babies and grandbabies, spending many, many years together. Me, you, and Dani."

He kissed Kye's hand, then laid his cheek against it.

"But you have to wake up soon because I fully intend to ask Dani to marry me and I know you're going to have an issue with that. You'll want to be the one to marry her. We'll have to fight about it. You'd make a much better husband to her than I would, anyway." Hunter choked on a sob as he crumbled, the tears falling unbidden down his cheeks. "Goddamn it, Kye! Come back to me. Please." He dropped his head, resting it on their joined hands. "Come back to me, Kye. Please, just come back."

TWENTY

ELEVEN DAYS.

Kye had been in a coma for eleven days and Dani's hopes were beginning to wane. Her heart physically hurt when she thought about Kye possibly never waking up. After all she'd been through, Dani wanted her happily ever after, and in order to have it, she had to have Kye.

Perhaps that made her selfish, but so what. She didn't give a shit. When it came to Kye and Hunter, she was selfish. She would *always* be selfish. They deserved that much. They deserved to be first in her life and that was exactly where she put them.

"Are you about ready to go to the hospital?" Hunter asked when he emerged from the bathroom after his shower.

She nodded, staring down at her hands.

Dani had plopped down on the couch, her body weak even though she'd slept for a solid eight hours last night. It had been a fight, but Hunter had finally convinced her to come home for one night. She didn't want to leave Kye for any length of time, but Hunter's parents had promised to stay with him, alternating with Kye's parents in the middle of the night.

The good news was that Kye was never left alone. That was the absolute last thing Dani wanted. To think that Kye might possibly wake up and no one would be there…it was a horrifying thought.

Hunter joined Dani on the couch. His big body dropped down right beside her, his arm going around her shoulder, his lips pressing against her head. Neither of them said anything. Then again, there was nothing to say. These days, it was all about prayers.

Several minutes passed before Hunter finally spoke.

"Courtney's going to go grocery shopping for us. Is there anything specific you want?"

Dani turned her head, her eyes seeking Hunter's. "I want Kye to wake up. I want him to come home." Her face fell, and she knew the tears were coming, but she had long ago stopped trying to hide them. "I want him to come home, Hunter."

"I know you do, baby. So do I."

"No!" she yelled, turning toward him as though by insisting, it would somehow make Kye open his eyes. "I want him to wake up. I *need* him to wake up." Her whole body shook with her sobs. "I can't take it anymore. I can't. I'm losing my mind. I need him here with us. I—"

"Shh." Hunter pulled her against his chest, his arms wrapping securely around her.

Dani gave in to the pain and the grief that continued to pull her under. She cried into his shirt, not caring that she was a snotty mess.

"I love him, Hunter. I want him home with us."

"I know, baby," he said softly. "I know."

It took a few minutes, but Dani managed to pull herself together. She was just about to tell Hunter what he could have Courtney get from the store when his cell phone rang.

"Yeah. Kogan."

Suddenly, Hunter jerked away from her, launching to his feet. For a moment, her breath lodged in her throat, her heart constricting. Every time his phone rang, she feared it was going to be a call that would shatter her entire world.

"We'll be right there, Con."

"What's wrong?" Dani asked, pushing to her feet. She studied Hunter's face, searching for answers before he even spoke.

"Kye's awake." He said the words as though he didn't really believe them.

"What?"

A smile slowly tugged at Hunter's mouth. "Kye's awake. And…fuck. We have to go. Grab whatever you need."

Dani snatched her cell phone from the bar and ran to the front door. Hunter beat her there, took her hand, then practically dragged her to Kye's truck.

Neither of them spoke during the short trek to the hospital. Dani wasn't sure what to say and she didn't want to say anything that might jinx this.

When they reached the hospital, Hunter pulled up to the main doors, then jumped out. She followed, wondering if the truck would get towed. Not that it mattered. Kye was awake. The hospital could have the truck for all she cared.

Of course, she shouldn't have been concerned, because a second later, Conner appeared holding out his hand for the keys. He had a huge grin on his face, the first one she'd seen in almost two weeks.

"Go!" Conner yelled, racing around and jumping in behind the wheel.

The elevator took its own sweet time. By the time they finally arrived on the ICU floor, she was vibrating.

Hunter's parents were there to greet them.

"Go on back," Casper instructed. "Kye's parents are back there now. They'll trade places with you."

It only took another couple of minutes to get to Kye's room, but Dani was already crying when Hunter put his hand on the door and slid it open. She held her breath as she stepped inside.

"Oh, my God." More tears poured down her face as her gaze settled on the most beautiful sight in the entire world. "Oh, my God."

Kye smiled. It was weak, but it was more than she'd seen in eleven days and she would take it.

"Hey, baby," he greeted, his voice raspy from not using it for so long.

Moving slowly, Dani finally reached the bed. She didn't pay attention to anyone or anything else, only Kye. When she touched his hand and he linked his fingers with hers, she felt how weak he was, but it didn't matter. He was awake.

Hunter was suddenly by her side, his hand covering both of theirs.

"What took you so long?" Kye teased. "I thought you'd never get here."

Dani choked on a sob/laugh, smiling until her face hurt.

"Are you… Can I…?" She wasn't even sure what she wanted to ask him.

"Can you hug me?" Kye suggested. "You bet your ass you can." He smiled as he squeezed her hand gently. "Come here, baby."

Dani draped herself over him, doing her best not to hurt him, but she couldn't help it. She needed to touch him, to feel him touching her. Kye's arm curled around her head and he held her face against his chest. She cried uncontrollably, so happy that he'd finally opened his eyes.

"Your mom told me the good news," Hunter said.

"That I'm going home tomorrow?" Kye joked.

"Yeah. Not that soon, but…"

Dani lifted her head, wondering what they were talking about.

"We'll see about that," Kye said. "And yes, good news. No paralysis. I'll be back to normal in no time." His words came out slowly, but there was that teasing tone that Kye was known for.

She leaned in and kissed his cheek, reaching behind her and gripping Hunter's hand.

Her world was finally right again.

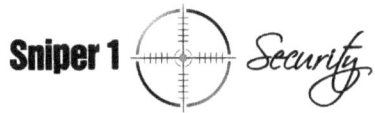

KYE HAD NEVER TAKEN A bullet before and he prayed like hell he never took another one for as long as he lived. The pain was excruciating. According to the doctor, he was extremely lucky that the bullet hadn't lodged in his spine or taken out some critical organs. How, they weren't quite sure.

Kye wasn't, either, but he wasn't going to question it. Whatever the reason, he was eternally grateful. He'd been told there would be extensive physical therapy, but eventually, he would be as good as new. Unfortunately, in the meantime, it wasn't as easy to breathe as it once had been, but he knew he could overcome that, too. With Hunter and Dani, Kye could overcome anything.

"Baby," he whispered to Dani, who was sitting at his side, her head resting on the edge of the bed. She'd been that way for several hours while he drifted in and out thanks to all the pain meds coursing through him.

She lifted her head. "Yeah?"

"Are you okay?"

Her smile was sweet. "I am now."

"Me, too." He brushed his hand through her hair, then glanced at the door. "Does everyone know?"

"That you're awake?" She smiled. "Of course they do."

"Not about that."

Her eyebrows drifted down. "About?"

"About me, you, and Hunter."

Although no one had said a word to him other than his mother, Kye was under the impression that everyone was up to speed on their relationship.

"Most of them, yes."

He figured it had been an accident that they'd found out. Probably due to Hunter and Dani spending so much time with him while he was in the coma.

"Is Hunter okay with it?"

Dani giggled softly. "Well, I hope so. Considering he's the one who mentioned it. He told his father first. Then his mother. After that, everyone seemed to know."

Kye's eyes widened. "Really?"

"Yeah, really."

A knock sounded and then the door opened. His ears must've been burning because Hunter appeared, carrying a cup of coffee.

Kye turned back to Dani. "Would you…uh…mind giving us a few minutes?"

"Sure. I could use a little exercise." Her smile was genuine. After standing, she leaned over and pressed her lips to his. "Take as much time as you'd like."

Before passing Hunter, Dani kissed him as well, then slipped out into the hall.

"Can you come over here?" Kye asked, motioning toward the chair beside his bed. He was still weak, but with every passing minute, he felt as though some of his strength was returning.

Hunter appeared slightly wary, but he moved around the bed. He placed his coffee cup on the table, then turned to face Kye.

"A little closer." Kye crooked his finger.

Hunter leaned over, their eyes locked together. Kye reached up and cupped his face. He stared at him for several seconds, trying to form the words. From the moment he woke up, he'd been overwhelmed by guilt and he had to get it out.

"I want you to know, I never would've left you intentionally."

Hunter's eyes turned glassy, but it was obvious he knew what Kye was referring to.

"I'm so sorry," Kye said. "I know it couldn't've been easy for you to see me…"

Hunter leaned in and pressed his lips to Kye's. "Don't you dare apologize. You came back to me. That's all that matters." When he pulled back, his eyes had cleared again. "I love you, Kye."

Kye smiled. "I know you do. But in all fairness, I loved you first."

Hunter laughed as he leaned in for another kiss. "I wouldn't bet on that."

"No?"

"No."

Kye smiled, but then sobered. "We've got a long road ahead of us. I'm gonna need your help getting my strength back."

"I'm not goin' anywhere," Hunter said, his voice gruff. "I'm right here. Whatever you need."

Another smile tugged at Kye's lips. "Although I'm a little fuzzy on specifics, I think I recall you wanting to talk about a wedding?"

Hunter's eyes widened.

Yeah, he'd been in a coma, but he had heard Hunter. He'd heard everything. Even unconscious and without hearing aids. Try as he might, he had fought his way back to them because this was where he belonged.

"You're right about one thing…" Kye reached for his hand. "I'm going to fight you for it."

"I wouldn't expect anything less."

"Granted, I'm gonna need a little time to recuperate before I'm up to my fighting weight."

"We've got time," Hunter told him.

And Kye realized they did.

They had the rest of their lives.

When Hunter pulled back, Kye's eyes shifted to the television. It reminded him of something he'd wanted to ask Hunter about.

"I was watching the news this morning," he admitted. "Something about a man taking his own life. The suicide note he left said he couldn't live with the crime he'd committed ten years ago."

Hunter frowned, glancing over at the television and back. "And that's relevant to us how?"

Kye lifted an eyebrow. "The man confessed to killing my brother."

Even as he said the words, his heart constricted. He still bore the loss of his brother, likely always would.

"That's good news," Hunter said, his eyes not giving anything away.

"It is. It gives my parents closure."

"And you," Hunter said.

"Yes. And me."

They stared at one another for a long moment.

"We never talked much about my brother," Kye finally said. "Yet you're not asking any questions."

"I knew enough."

Kye wasn't an idiot. He knew that Hunter was the reason they'd gotten the closure they so desperately needed. Not that Kye was happy the guy was dead. He wanted to be the one to steal his life the way he'd stolen Toby's. However, he didn't want Hunter to have to live the rest of his life with blood on his hands.

As though reading his mind, Hunter leaned in close again. "I only found him," Hunter whispered.

Ah. "And now you owe someone a favor?"

Hunter shook his head. "No. Now we're squared away."

"I love you," Kye whispered.

"I love you, too." Hunter stood up straight. "And now I suggest you figure out a way to get back to that fighting weight. I have no intention of putting off the wedding."

Kye chuckled. It only hurt a little to laugh.

But it was definitely worth it.

EPILOGUE

One year later

"YOU KNOW, I NEVER THOUGHT I'd fall in love with a man who rode a desk," Kye said when he stepped into Hunter's office.

As of three weeks ago, Hunter had officially stepped into the role alongside RT as the head of Sniper 1 Security. Oddly enough, the decision had been an easy one. Ever since their daughter was born, Hunter had accepted it was time to step out of the field and into something that would keep him at home with his family.

Even thinking about it made his heart swell. He had a family. Dani, Kye, and their sweet little girl. Hunter had learned that his priorities were entirely different now that he was whole once again.

Kye, on the other hand, hadn't been as optimistic.

"Close the door," Hunter instructed. "And lock it."

"Still just as bossy as ever." Hunter noticed Kye's smirk before he turned to do as he was told. When he pivoted back around, he was watching him intently. "You wanted to see me?"

"I did." Hunter motioned for the chair across from him. "Have a seat."

"Oh, no." Kye eased into the chair, his moves hesitant. "I thought for sure you were getting me alone so you could get me naked. I would've stalled if I'd known this was actually work."

Hunter laughed. "I have every intention of getting you naked," he assured him. "But first things first."

Kye relaxed in his chair, but his eyes remained wary.

"RT and I were talking, and we've decided to open a training facility for new agents."

"Yeah?"

"Yes. And we'd like for you and Z to run it."

"Sounds boring," Kye noted with a gleam in his eye.

"Does it now?"

"Yes. It's practically a desk job. And you know me and desks."

"I know that you look good bent over one," Hunter told him.

Kye winked. "I like where your head's at."

"And if you'd like to be bent over mine," he continued, "then I'll need an answer."

"You're not worried that we'll overwhelm the new recruits?"

Hunter knew what Kye was referring to. Both Kye and Z were six and a half feet tall. They were rather intimidating when they were together.

"Maybe that's part of my plan."

"Fine," Kye huffed. "I'll run your training facility with Z. But I have one condition."

"Which is?"

"You bring Dani on board. When she's ready, of course. I know she'd rather spend her time with Sadie right now, but when she's ready to go to work, I'd like her at the training center with me."

"What makes you think she'd be willing?"

"Because I asked her."

Hunter grinned as he leaned forward. "You asked her?"

"Yes."

"About the training facility?"

"Yes."

"And how'd you even know about it?"

Kye tapped his temple. "I'm smart like that."

"Are you now?"

"Of course."

"Well, come over here, smartass."

Kye got to his feet and walked around his desk. The man looked smug, but that wasn't unusual. It was one of the things he loved about Kye. One of many things he loved about him, in fact.

Hunter stood when Kye approached. In an effort to take him off guard, he grabbed Kye and jerked him forward, crushing their mouths together. He didn't get to see nearly enough of the man these days, which was why he'd agreed to RT's suggestion. Keeping Kye close to home was important to him. The fact that their wife and daughter wanted them both home every night helped to make his decision.

He remembered the wedding, the fact that Kye had refused to sit idly by while Hunter had the honors of marrying Dani. He had insisted the three of them would be married in the eyes of God and their friends and family. No, it wasn't legally binding, which was why Hunter had married Dani on paper. Only because Kye insisted that if something happened to them, he needed to know Dani and their children would be taken care of financially.

In turn, Dani had agreed to change her name, as had Kye. They were all Kogans now.

While their lips were fused together, Hunter worked Kye's cock free from his jeans, wrapping his fist around him and stroking roughly. It had been too long since Hunter'd had the chance to take Kye the way he liked. Roughly.

"Oh, fuck," Kye hissed as he thrust into Hunter's hand. "I want your mouth on me, Hunter. Fuck. Put your mouth on me. Please."

"I love it when you beg." Hunter jerked Kye's cock harder. "Beg me, Kye."

"Please…" His head fell back. "Oh, fuck, please. Suck me."

The man's words spurred him on and he went to his knees before sucking Kye into his mouth. He curled his fist around the base of Kye's shaft, working him with his hand and his mouth, enjoying the way the man moaned.

Thankfully, it was a Saturday and there were only a couple of people in the office, none of whom were in the back offices. Otherwise, Kye would've been broadcasting what they were doing for everyone to hear.

Not that Hunter gave a shit anymore. There had been absolutely no repercussions to coming out to his family. He'd spent his entire life convincing himself they wouldn't understand, when in reality, he'd merely been a chickenshit, trying to keep his emotions under wraps because he felt it made him weak.

He was anything but weak.

"Hunter…" Kye's hand landed on his head. "You keep that up and I'm gonna come in your mouth."

Hunter pulled his lips off Kye's cock and stood. "You can't come yet."

Kye was breathing roughly.

"Turn around and bend over the desk."

After pulling lube from his desk drawer, Hunter unfastened his jeans and shoved them down, sidestepping so he could move in behind Kye.

"Hold on," he told the man he loved when he pressed his lubed dick against Kye's asshole.

When Kye's fingers curled over the side of Hunter's desk, he pushed in deep, pausing when he was lodged to the hilt inside Kye's ass.

"This might be a condition, as well," Kye said on a grunt when Hunter retreated and slammed into him.

"What's that?"

"You bending me over your desk. Oh, fuck, yes…"

Hunter fucked him hard. "You like this?"

"So much." Kye groaned as he pushed back against him, taking every punishing thrust with a groan of pure pleasure.

Hunter didn't let up, driving them both closer to release as he smiled to himself. Never in his life had he expected to be this happy, this complete. With a husband, a wife, and a four-month-old daughter … it didn't get much better than this.

"Don't come yet, Kye," Hunter demanded several minutes later. "After I come in your ass, I want you to come in my mouth."

Kye growled, a fierce sound that made Hunter smile. The man was on the edge.

After slamming into him several more times, Hunter finally gave in, his hips stilling as he came.

Almost immediately, he dislodged himself from Kye's body, then turned the man around so he could get him off with his mouth. He dropped back to his knees, gripping Kye's cock and sucking him roughly. It didn't take long before Kye's fingers were threaded in his hair again, his cock pulsing against his tongue as he roared his release.

"Yeah, definitely should be a condition of employment," Kye said with a sigh as he caught his breath.

They took a few minutes to clean up and once they were, Kye went to the door, glancing over his shoulder.

"Seriously, though. I'm happy to take the position. Anything to keep me at home where I belong." His grin widened. "After all, Dani is going to need the help."

Hunter waited for the punchline.

Kye glanced at his watch. "Because in roughly seven and a half months, we're going to have our hands full." His thoughts instantly drifted to their sweet little blond-haired, blue-eyed daughter. "I wonder if little bit'll be getting a sister. Or maybe we'll have a little boy with light gray eyes."

With wide eyes, Hunter stared at Kye.

The information sank in and he grinned from ear to ear.

♥ ▫ ▫ ▫ ▫ ♥ ▫ ▫ ▫ ▫ ♥

I hope you enjoyed Hunter, Dani, and Kye. I have spent years thinking about Hunter's story and I'm so glad I finally sat down to finish it. It took some serious twists from what I originally thought it would be, but in the end, Hunter got the happy he deserved

Want to see some fun stuff related to the Sniper 1 Security series, you can find extras on my website. Or how about what's coming next? Find more at: www.NicoleEdwardsAuthor.com

If you're interested in keeping up to date on any of my series, as well as receiving updates on all that I'm working on, you can sign up for my monthly newsletter.

Want a simple, *fast* way to get updates on new releases? You can also sign up for text messaging. If you are in the U.S. simply text NICOLE to 64600 or sign up on my website. I promise not to spam your phone. This is just my way of letting you know what's happening because I know you're busy, but if you're anything like me, you always have your phone on you.

And last but certainly not least, if you want to see what's going on with me each week, sign up for my weekly Hot Sheet! It's a short, entertaining weekly update of things going on in my life and that of the team that supports me. We're a little crazy at times and this is a firsthand account of our antics.

ACKNOWLEDGMENTS

First and always, I have to thank my wonderfully patient husband who puts up with me every single day. If it wasn't for him and his belief that I could (and can) do this, I wouldn't be writing this today. He has been my backbone, my rock, the very reason I continue to believe in myself. I love you for that, babe.

Chancy Powley – I love getting your feedback, but more importantly, I love the hours we spend on the phone talking about everything else.

Allison Holzapfel – I am honored to call you friend and I thank you for being there when I need you.

Thank you to my proofreaders. Jenna Underwood, Annette Elens, Theresa Martin, and Sara Gross. Not only do you catch my blunders, you are my friends and it is an honor to call you that.

I also have to thank my street team – Naughty (and nice) Girls – Your unwavering support is something I will never take for granted.

I can't forget my copyeditor, Amy at Blue Otter Editing. Thank goodness I've got you to catch all my punctuation, grammar, and tense errors.

Nicole Nation 2.0 for the constant support and love. You've been there for me from almost the beginning. This group of ladies has kept me going for so long, I'm not sure I'd know what to do without them.

And, of course, YOU, the reader. Your emails, messages, posts, comments, tweets… they mean more to me than you can imagine. I thrive on hearing from you, knowing that my characters and my stories have touched you in some way keeps me going. I've been known to shed a tear or two when reading an email because you simply bring so much joy to my life with your support. I thank you for that.

About Nicole

New York Times and *USA Today* bestselling author Nicole Edwards lives in Austin, Texas with her husband, their three kids, and four rambunctious dogs. When she's not writing about sexy alpha males, Nicole can often be found with a book in hand or making an attempt to keep the dogs happy. You can find her hanging out on Facebook and interacting with her readers even when she's supposed to be writing.

By Nicole Edwards

The Alluring Indulgence Series
Kaleb
Zane
Travis
Holidays with the Walker Brothers
Ethan
Braydon
Sawyer
Brendon

The Austin Arrows Series
Rush
Kaufman

The Bad Boys of Sports Series
Bad Reputation
Bad Business

The Caine Cousins Series
Hard to Hold
Hard to Handle

The Club Destiny Series
Conviction
Temptation
Addicted
Seduction
Infatuation
Captivated
Devotion
Perception
Entrusted
Adored
Distraction

The Coyote Ridge Series
Curtis
Jared

The Dead Heat Ranch Series
Boots Optional
Betting on Grace
Overnight Love

By Nicole Edwards (cont.)

The Devil's Bend Series

Chasing Dreams
Vanishing Dreams

The Devil's Playground Series

Without Regret
Without Restraint

The Office Intrigue Series

Office Intrigue
Intrigued Out of the Office
Their Rebellious Submissive

The Pier 70 Series

Reckless
Fearless
Speechless
Harmless

The Sniper 1 Security Series

Wait for Morning
Never Say Never
Tomorrow's Too Late

The Southern Boy Mafia Series

Beautifully Brutal
Beautifully Loyal

Standalone Novels

A Million Tiny Pieces
Inked on Paper

Writing as Timberlyn Scott

Unhinged
Unraveling
Chaos

Naughty Holiday Editions

2015
2016

BECAUSE NAUGHTY CAN BE OH SO NICE®

NE LTD